𝒫rais...

GREETINGS FROM SOMEWHERE ELSE

"A cosy, lighthearted romp, highly recommended."
—*The Australian Women's Weekly*

"Her best yet . . . a funny and poignant story . . . a novel which fairly cracks along with a mix of humour, a touch of blarney and insight into the pressures and strains in contemporary relationships." —*Courier-Mail* (Australia)

"Fresh, funny and engaging . . . This is comfort reading—warm-buttered toast with Irish honey spread right to the crusts." —*Adelaide Advertiser*

"There's something about Monica's book that makes you want to escape into its world." —*Sunday Tribune* (Ireland)

"A highly entertaining tale of self-discovery, friendship and romance." —*Country Living* (Australia)

"A page-turner . . . McInerney has a great insight into human nature and relationships and a good line in humour."
—*Sunday World* (Ireland)

"A real page-turner to curl up with on the beach this summer." —*Modern Woman* (Ireland)

JUN 2010

ALSO BY MONICA MCINERNEY

GREETINGS FROM SOMEWHERE ELSE

GREETINGS FROM SOMEWHERE ELSE

a novel

MONICA McINERNEY

BALLANTINE BOOKS TRADE PAPERBACKS

New York

A Ballantine Books Trade Paperback Original

Copyright © 2003 by Monica McInerney
Reading group guide copyright © 2009 by Random House, Inc.

Published in the United States by Ballantine Books,
an imprint of The Random House Publishing Group,
a division of Random House, Inc., New York.

Originally published as *Spin the Bottle* by
Penguin Books Australia Ltd., 2003

BALLANTINE and colophon are registered trademarks
of Random House, Inc.
RANDOM HOUSE READER'S CIRCLE and colophon is a
trademark of Random House, Inc.

ISBN 978-0-345-50638-2

Printed in the United States of America

www.randomhousereaderscircle.com

9 8 7 6 5 4 3 2 1

Book design by Mary A. Wirth

for my three brothers
Paul, Stephen and Rob

GREETINGS FROM SOMEWHERE ELSE

S top the music please!" Lainey Byrne shouted, waving her arms as though she was fighting off a swarm of bees. The background music stopped with a screech. On the stage the ten dancers dressed in giant sausage costumes came to a wobbly halt.

Lainey quickly climbed the steps, looking for the lead dancer. It was hard to tell who was who when the entire troupe was dressed from head to toe in pink foam. "They look more like hot dogs than sausages," the sound technician had muttered unkindly that morning. Or something ruder, Lainey had thought privately. But it was too late to get new costumes and she could hardly scorch each of them with a cigarette lighter to get authentic grill marks. The fabric was far too flammable.

She spoke loudly, hoping they could all hear her clearly through the foam. "Can I just remind you again how it's supposed to go? You run on *after* the barbecue's been lowered, not before. Otherwise half of you will get squashed, which isn't exactly the look our client wants for his big event."

There were a few muffled laughs. Lainey turned and nodded at the sound man, and the opening notes of the Beaut Barbecues jingle filled the East Melbourne venue once more. As she moved off the stage and into the middle of the room, Lainey winced again at the lyrics.

> *Oh, believe me, mate,*
> *Sausages taste great*
> *On a beaut Beaut Barbecue-oo-oo.*

She'd tried to gently talk the managing director out of the jingle three months ago, when they'd first met to discuss the gala party celebrating his tenth year in the barbecue business. But it turned out his eight-year-old daughter had written the words and he wasn't budging. Lainey wondered now if his eight-year-old daughter had come up with the idea of the dancing sausages as well. Or perhaps it had been his four-year-old son. Or his dog. Lainey just hoped none of today's guests would think it had been Complete Event Management's idea. Still, it was her job to give her clients what they wanted, and if Mr. Barbecue wanted dancing sausages, he was going to get dancing sausages.

Lainey's mobile phone rang. She took a few steps back, keeping an eye on the stage. "Complete Event Management, Lainey Byrne speaking."

"Lainey, have I rung at a bad time?"

It was her mother. "Ma, of course not. Is everything okay? Is Dad all right?" As Lainey spoke, the dancers moved to the front of the stage to pick up the first of their props. Lainey held her breath as one of the fatter sausages teetered a little too close to the edge.

"He's grand. Well, no, not grand, no change there. This is a brand-new problem."

"What's happened?"

"It's to do with his sister's will."

"The will? I thought that had all been sorted out. Don't tell me she left the B&B to the cats' home after all?" The sausages were now making waltzing movements, each holding a giant plastic bottle marked Tomato Sauce. At the launch later that day the bottles would be filled with red glitter. For now the sausages were just puffing air at each other.

"No, she did leave the B&B to your father. But we've just heard from her solicitor in Ireland. There's a little bit of a hitch."

Hitches came in sizes? "What do you mean a little bit?"

"It's too complicated to talk about on the phone. I think it's better if we discuss it as a family. Can you call over tonight? If you and Adam don't have any plans, that is."

"No, he's working seven nights a week at the moment. Of course I'll come over."

"Thanks, love. I'm asking the boys to drop by as well."

The boys? Her younger brothers were hardly that. Brendan was nearly thirty, Declan twenty-five and Hugh nineteen. Lainey mentally ran through her appointments for the day. The barbecue party was from noon until three, then she had two meetings and a client briefing back at the office. "Around eight-ish then—sorry, Ma, can you hold on a sec?" She shouted over the music again as the sausages put down their sauce bottles and picked up giant barbecue tongs. "That's when the managing director comes in and you form a guard of honor with your tongs, okay? That's it, great. Sorry about that, Ma."

"I don't think I'll ask what you're up to."

Lainey laughed. "You wouldn't believe it if I told you. I'll see you tonight then. Love to Dad." She put her mobile away and turned her full attention back to the stage. The sausages were now brandishing the barbecue tongs as though they were samurai swords. It was hard to keep a straight face—she'd been picturing this event in her head for weeks now and it had looked *nothing* like the chaos in front of her. She stopped the music with another wave of her hands. "All right, from the top again please."

⋆ ⋆ ⋆

It was past seven by the time Lainey drove out of the office parking lot and through the Melbourne city center streets. Out of habit, she put on the language CD that she kept in the car. She listened to French language CDs while she jogged, and German CDs while she drove. Adam found it very funny. "You do realize you'll only ever be able to speak German when you're sitting in a car?" he'd remarked when he first noticed her system.

She listened for a few moments, repeating the words until the woman's breathy tones finally got to her. Stopping at the Flinders Street traffic lights, she put in a new CD, a bargain basement KC and the Sunshine Band greatest hits collection. She'd bought it for her brother Declan as a joke and then discovered she liked it too much herself. She wound down the window of the car, the tiny breeze it let in giving her little relief from the muggy late-January heat. The air-conditioning had broken down again and it was like driving around in a portable oven. A portable kettle barbecue, even. She certainly knew enough about barbecues now to understand how being in one would feel. "It was all fabulous, just how I imagined it," Mr. Beaut Barbecues had gushed as Lainey said goodbye that afternoon. "See you in ten years for our next big anniversary, sweetheart." Over my dead body, sweetheart, she'd thought as she nodded and smiled and tried to ignore his hand doing its best to grope at her behind. She'd had quite enough of Mr. and Mrs. Barbecue and all the little Barbecues for one lifetime.

She finished singing an enthusiastic, badly out-of-tune version of "Shake Your Booty" just as she came off the freeway. She was the first to admit she had an appalling singing voice. "No offense, Lain," Declan had said once, "but your singing sounds like a mating cat. Like a cat being slaughtered when it's mating, in fact." On the spur-of-the-moment, she made a detour to the local shopping center to pick up a few treats to save her mother having to cook. A proper daughter would bring homemade casseroles, she knew, but her cooking skills were basic and her cooking time nonexistent. She also knew her parents loved these ready-made meals in packs, even if the food inside never looked anything like the picture on the box—restaurant meal on the front, gray splodge on the inside, from what Lainey had seen.

The clock on the dashboard clicked over to 8:00 p.m. as she parked in front of the house. Mr. and Mrs. Byrne's red brick bungalow in Box Hill was the sixth house the family had lived in since they'd arrived from Ireland seventeen years ago. Of the four children, only her youngest brother Hugh had a bedroom in this house these days and even he was barely there, spending most nights at friends' houses. She took care not to stop under the jacaranda tree that had burst into bloom just before Christmas and was now showering blue flowers all over the street. There was no sign of her brothers' cars—she was first, as usual. She walked through the open front door, down the hallway to the kitchen and put the meals away in the fridge.

"Hello, Lainey. Oh, thanks a million, your father loves those. Shut the fridge door, would you? I don't want the flies getting in there." Mrs. Byrne specialized in greeting-and-command combinations. "I like your haircut, by the way. I wouldn't have thought hair that short would work with a biggish nose like yours, but it looks very well."

Lainey didn't blink at the mixture of compliment and insult—her mother had long specialized in them too. "Thanks, Ma." She gave her mother a quick kiss on the cheek. With the same tall, very slim build, the same dark-brown hair, they were sometimes mistaken for sisters. "Where's Dad?"

"Playing water polo. Where do you think he is? In bed, of course."

Lainey ignored the sharp tone. "Has he been up today at all?"

"No, for a few minutes yesterday. But the way he carried on about it you'd think he wanted me to hang banners and streamers around the house in celebration. He said he'd get up tonight to see you all, but there's been no movement yet."

"I'll go and say hello." She walked through the living room to her parents' bedroom. No, not her parents' bedroom, she corrected herself. Her father's bedroom. He had moved into one of the spare bedrooms several months previously, as a trial to see if he could sleep better without her mother beside him. The trial continued, still waiting on positive results, perhaps.

As she walked down the hall, she imagined what she'd like to see in her father's room.

She knocked softly on the door. "Hi, Dad."

"Lainey! How are you?" Her father was sitting up on his fully made bed, a book in his hands, newspapers spread all around him. She was delighted to see him taking such an interest in the outside world again.

He smiled at her. "How are you, pet? I love the haircut. Sit down now and tell me, what havoc have you been wreaking out in the world today?"

She knocked softly on the door. "Hi, Dad."

No answer.

"It's me, Lainey, your favorite daughter."

"My only daughter." His Irish accent was loud in the dark room.

She came in and sat on the edge of the bed, her eyes slowly adjusting to the dim light. The curtains were drawn. She could just make out his face, the bedcovers drawn up to his neck. "Just checking you remembered me. How are you?"

"In bits, still. Why, have you been praying for a miracle cure?"

"Burning candles for you every night, you know that." She kept up a jovial tone. "Can I bring you anything? A cup of tea? A cold drink?"

"A new life would be nice."

Her mother had been right, he was in very bad form.

She changed the subject. "Ma said there's a bit of a problem with May's will?"

"Of course there is. How long is it since anything ran smoothly in this family?"

Lainey tried to stay cheerful. "Nothing we can't sort out, I bet. What about I get you a cup of tea while we're waiting for the others to arrive?"

There was a long sigh. "Thanks, love, that'd be great. Tell Peg I'll be out as soon as I can."

Back in the kitchen, Lainey filled the kettle and tried to shake off her sudden gloom. "Honestly, the sooner he gets his own chat show the better, don't you think?"

Mrs. Byrne didn't smile. Lainey looked closer at her. "Are you all right? Have you been crying?"

"No, of course I haven't. It's hayfever."

"In the middle of the city? Imported hay, is it?"

"No, we've had a rough day, that's all. Here, look."

Lainey took the letter, immediately noting the insurance company logo. Since her father's accident on the building site there had been piles of correspondence bearing this logo. She scanned the latest.

RE: Gerald Patrick Byrne
In regard to your claim for compensation following your recent workplace accident, please be advised we require additional proof of your injuries and incapacitation. However, please note this evidence may or may not have any bearing on your claim, which is still under consideration . . .

Lainey gave up reading midway. She'd seen enough of these sorts of letters already. She felt like inviting one of the insurance people to come and look at the mark that slab of concrete had left on her father's back. "Ma, why won't you let me take over? I'd get in there and sort them out so quickly—"

"Because your father wants to handle it his way, for some reason. And you know what he's like with people in authority. He's never been able to stand up to them. I'll tell you who else wrote to us today—the physiotherapist. She says your father's been cancelling too many appointments at the last minute, she's going to have to start charging us soon. What am I supposed to do? I can't make him go. He's a grown man, isn't he? Though I don't know any more, half the time he's like a bold child, sulking and skulking in there . . ."

Quick, Lainey thought, don't let her get upset. Make her think of something else. "Is there something I can do in the meantime? Before the money comes through from the B&B sale? Handcuff myself to the railing in front of the insurance company, perhaps?"

That brought a faint smile. "No, it's far too hot at the moment. In the autumn perhaps."

"I could go on a hunger strike."

"You're skinny enough as it is."

"Seriously, there must be something I can do."

"Perhaps there is."

Lainey waited.

Mrs. Byrne shook her head. "Wait till the other three get here."

"You've collected the whole set? Well done."

"Well, Declan said yes. And Bren said yes. But Hugh . . ."

The back door opened to admit a tall, brown-haired man with a bag slung over his shoulder. "Saintly mother figure, greetings. Laineyovich, glorious being, ahoy to you too. Hideous haircut, by the way, you look like a boy. No offense, of course."

Lainey smiled serenely at her middle brother. "None taken, of course. How are you, Declanski? Still tunneling your way through the education system?"

"The work is hard, but yes, the rewards are endless. And how is your world of frivolous product launches and rampant commercialism? Shallow as ever?"

"I'll have you know I celebrated the birthday of a barbecue today that would make Lenin sit up and take notice, Declanski, let alone some baby-faced communist sympathizer like you."

Mrs. Byrne frowned. "Declan, you're not still a communist, are you? I thought you'd given up all that business when you left teachers' college. There's no future in it, you know that."

"No, Ma, Lainey is still living in the past. I'm actually between radical beliefs at the moment. I'm tossing up between the Fur Trappers Society and the Animal Rights Movement."

"Go for the middle ground, Dec," Lainey said. "Give up teaching and get a job inside one of those giant koalas that go begging for donations in the shopping center."

"I've been offered a job at the shopping center," their mother announced.

They both stared at her. "Doing what?" Lainey said.

"As a product demonstrator. In the supermarket there."

"Oh, brilliant," Declan said. "So now I'm *surrounded* by capitalists."

Mrs. Byrne was defiant. "We need the money. I'll be able to go out for a few hours in the evening during late-night shopping, while your father's friends call round. Any he's got left, that is."

"Good for you, Ma," Lainey said enthusiastically, trying to send an ESP message to Declan not to tease their mother about this. "What are you demonstrating?"

"New food products—anything and everything, apparently. I start next week. My friend Mrs. Douglas down the road suggested I do it. She's been doing it for years. Says it's great gas altogether, gets her out of the house as well. God knows I need to do something. If I'd known this was going to happen I would never have taken early retirement from the library. Oh yes, your father promised we'd finally get that caravan, go and see Australia, go home to Ireland once a year, but look what's happened instead. Stuck here while he lies in state feeling sorry for himself . . ."

Brendan arrived then, dressed in his suit, obviously straight from work. Lainey was relieved at the interruption. She knew their mother needed to talk about things, she just found it hard to listen sometimes. Declan tossed his older brother a beer from the fridge. "Golden boy himself. A little late, I'm sorry to see. We don't want a black mark on that perfect slate of yours now, do we?"

"Hi, Ma. Hi, Lain," he said, ignoring Declan and putting the beer back in the fridge. Lainey noticed Brendan had put on even more weight since she'd seen him last. Like herself and Declan, he was taller than average, and usually very slim. Ever since he'd moved into a managerial position at the recycling company he worked for, though, his edges had been getting flabby. She suspected he was in no mood for it to be pointed out. "How are the twins going, Bren? Eaten any more cat food lately?"

"It wasn't cat food, Lainey. It was a single dog biscuit between them."

Mrs. Byrne passed him a glass of milk. "Don't mind Lainey, Brendan. And it could have been worse—the daughter of a friend of mine came home to find her children had been working their way through her laxative chocolate. The babysitter hadn't even noticed, just thought they had a bit of a stomach upset."

"There's an idea, Bren," Lainey said brightly. "Laxative chocolate cakes for the twins' next birthday party. That'd give their parents a day to remember."

"I still can't believe anyone would voluntarily invite children into their homes. They're bad enough for six hours in a classroom each day," Declan said. "Tell me, Bren, are you planning on stopping this breeding program of yours soon, or do you intend to singlehandedly repopulate the eastern suburbs of Melbourne?"

"Leave Brendan alone," Mrs. Byrne said. "At least someone in this family has managed to get married and give me some grandchildren."

Brendan drank the milk in one swallow, then turned back to them, wearing a milk moustache. Neither Lainey nor Declan drew attention to it. "I have to go back into work tonight, so can we get started? Is Hugh coming?"

"Hugh knows," Declan said in a singsong voice.

"That really bugs me. I break my back to get here . . ." Brendan seemed to realize what he'd said and stopped short, embarrassed as he noticed his father out of the corner of his eye. "Dad, hi. I'm sorry about that. Just a figure of speech, you know."

"I know." Mr. Byrne was at the door, leaning heavily on his walker. On the wall behind him Lainey could see a large photo taken at the time of her parents' thirtieth wedding anniversary five years previously, Mrs. Byrne all elegance and beaming smiles, Mr. Byrne tanned, full of good humor and vitality. Lainey wished her mother would take the photo down. The man in front of her couldn't have been further from that image. He'd lost lots of weight, yet somehow he looked puffier, unhealthy around the face. He shuffled into the room. "How are things, Brendan? How are Rosie and the twins?"

"Going great guns," Brendan said in a fake cheery tone. "The twins are starting to run around so much, it's all we can do to keep up with them these days."

Mr. Byrne gave a mirthless laugh. "I wouldn't have a chance at all then, would I? Some grandfather I am. Can't even pick them up anymore."

Brendan's smile faltered. There wasn't anything he could say to that. It was the truth. The phone rang. Lainey picked it up, guessing correctly that it would be Hugh. She listened for a moment. "No, Hughie, of course I can't take notes for you. It's a family meeting, not a lecture. Okay, see you soon." She hung up. "He's running late. He had to do a double shift at the radio station."

"He's only a volunteer at that station, how can he get a double shift?" Declan asked, throwing his empty beer can into the bin and taking a new one from the fridge. He ignored a glare from Brendan who pointedly retrieved the can and put it in the recycling bin. "That's like nothing times nothing which equals nothing. Which sums up Hugh's contribution to society, really, doesn't it? The world hardly needs another media studies student. We need more teachers like me, don't you all think? Pushing back the boundaries of modern education, stretching young minds, exploring the frontiers of learning techniques. Or more like you, Brendan, our very own guardian of the environment, in there in your suit each day, pushing your pen and keeping Melbourne's recycling industry ticking over. As for you, Lainey, I'm afraid we still can't understand your role in society—"

"Declan, could you shut up?" Mrs. Byrne clearly wasn't in the mood for one of his rants. "Come into the living room, please. Your father and I need to discuss something with you all."

CHAPTER 2

Lainey helped her father get settled in his special high-seated chair, then sat on the sofa across from him. On the coffee table was a folder of paperwork. She picked it up. "Can I look?"

Mr. Byrne nodded. Since his sister May had died nearly four weeks before, there'd been a stream of correspondence between Ireland and Australia, trying to sort out the legalities. She had died suddenly, suffering a heart attack while out in her local shopping center collecting petitions against the construction of a new motorway in County Meath.

None of the family had attended her funeral, held in Dunshaughlin, the nearest town to her bed-and-breakfast. Mr. Byrne had wanted to go to Ireland to sort everything out, say goodbye in some way, but his doctor had been blunt. "Gerry, you're in enough pain lying in your own bed or sitting in your chair at home. That flight would kill you." Her funeral had been organized according to the strict instructions she'd left, the solicitor wrote in a subsequent letter. In further respect of her wishes, he'd advised, "her ashes were then scattered on the Hill of Tara."

On top of the file was a clipping from one of the local Meath newspapers. Lainey hadn't seen it before. It was a tribute to her aunt, headed with a large photo of her. There was no real resemblance between her father and May, Lainey thought, though that could have been the twelve-year age difference as much as anything. "*The Meath community this week mourned the loss of May Byrne, 72. Miss Byrne was well known in Meath and beyond through her involvement in the local tourist industry and for her love of Irish history and legends . . .*"

She wondered how her father had felt when he read the article. They had been estranged ever since the family had gone to Australia. May had been furious apparently, calling them traitors for abandoning Ireland. Her father had been too proud to try to heal the rift. He'd also insisted that she wasn't to be told about his accident, convinced she would tell him it served him right, that such a thing would never have happened in Ireland.

Lainey turned the clipping over. On the other side was an aerial photo of the Hill of Tara showing the distinctive circles marked in the green field. She skimmed the article. Work was starting on a new promotional film about the site, "*befitting the ancient capital of Ireland and one of our most significant tourist attractions,*" it said. Aunt May would have been pleased about that, Lainey thought. Or perhaps she wouldn't. Aunt May might not have approved of modern tourism promotions. But the exposure would surely help increase the value of May's B&B, just nearby.

Which would mean her father would get more money once the sale went through. All good news.

Mrs. Byrne came in with a fresh tray of tea and biscuits. "We'll have to start without Hugh, I think."

"Will you fill them in, Peg?" Mr. Byrne asked, shifting in his chair, still trying to get comfortable. "You're better at this business than me."

Mrs. Byrne nodded and picked up an envelope from the coffee table. "We've had a letter from May's solicitor in Ireland. It seems we started counting our chickens too soon when we asked him to sell her property."

"Chickens? What chickens?" Declan said. "I thought it was a B&B, not a chicken farm."

Mrs. Byrne ignored him. "It seems the will Mr. Fogarty sent to us just after May died, the one leaving her B&B and land to your father, wasn't in fact her final will."

"Oh, for God's sake!" Brendan crossed his arms. "Mr. Fogarty was her solicitor, wasn't he? Why didn't he have the most up-to-date will?"

"He thought he did. The one he had in his office had been signed and witnessed just three months before May died. But they've since found another more recent one, among her papers in the B&B, when they went in to start clearing her things away. She had a lot of paperwork, apparently."

"And this new one's valid, is it? Witnessed and everything?" Brendan snapped the questions.

Mrs. Byrne nodded. "It is, I'm afraid."

"And is it much different?" Lainey asked, looking from her mother to her father, trying to guess their mood. "Didn't she leave everything to you after all, Dad?"

"No, she did. It's just the conditions are a little more . . ." He paused. "Complicated."

"Complicated?" Declan said. "Did she owe money or something? She didn't own it after all?"

"No, it was definitely all hers." Mr. Byrne leaned forward, trying to straighten up in his chair. Lainey bent forward to help him. He continued. "There's no point beating around the bush. You know May was always raging at me for emigrating. Well, she has still left the B&B and the land to me, but only if a member of this family lives there for a year first."

There was a sudden and loud eruption of questions before Mrs. Byrne called for silence. "It's all in the letter. Let me read that section to you. 'In summary, May Byrne has placed a new condition that while the house, contents and land have still been left to you, Gerald Patrick Byrne, none of it may be sold until such time as a member (or members) of the Byrne family currently resident in Australia has lived in and operated the B&B for a year. Further instructions will be issued from our office upon arrival of the elected member of the Byrne family. Please be aware also that Miss Byrne has set aside a sum of money for the airfares from Australia to Ireland and return, as well as adequate living expenses for the twelve months' duration. Should this offer not be taken up within two months of Miss Byrne's death, she has directed that the property go to auction, with all proceeds to be divided among local history groups.'"

There was a heavy silence in the room.

Mrs. Byrne put the letter down. "We've phoned our own solicitor and it seems a will is a will. If she'd insisted we had to wear clown suits for a year before we could inherit the building and land, then that's what we'd have to have done."

"Well, it's ridiculous," Brendan said, picking up the letter and glancing through it. "Can't we challenge it? Prove she'd gone batty in the last years of her life?"

"She'd gone batty in the early years of her life," Mrs. Byrne said under her breath. An only child herself, her parents long passed away, she'd always enjoyed the luxury of insulting May without having to worry about any reciprocal insults to her family.

Mr. Byrne pretended not to hear. "We could. But that would take months or years. And we might lose. And the truth is I need that money as soon as I can get it. I can't wait for the insurance money to come through, if it ever does." No one questioned that. They were all too aware of the financial problems. Between legal bills, medical bills and the pay-outs to his former employees once he'd realized he wouldn't be able to work again, Mr. and Mrs. Byrne were already in debt. Lainey had wanted to help, but her father had refused.

Declan snorted. "Fantastic. So we're moving back to Ireland to run a bed-and-breakfast together. I can just see it."

"No, Declan, it doesn't specify all of us," Mrs. Byrne said. "It just needs to be one of us. If your father hadn't had his accident, he and I would have gone, of course. We would have enjoyed it, but it's impossible now, you know that. And the problem is we don't have the time to hope that your father makes a full recovery in the next few months. One of us has to be in residence in the house by the end of February or we lose the lot."

Lainey, Declan and Brendan went very still.

Mrs. Byrne broke the silence. "We could ask Hugh to go, I suppose."

Declan scoffed. "Come on, Ma. You wouldn't ask Hugh to mind a goldfish."

Mrs. Byrne looked solemnly at him. "You're probably right, Declan. There's always you, of course . . ." Declan stiffened. Mrs. Byrne continued. "But the timing's so bad, with you starting in that new school next month. It's taken you this long to get a full-time teaching position, who knows what would happen if you took a year off."

Declan beamed. "I'd go off the rails altogether, I'd expect. Never work again." He lay back on the sofa, arms behind his head.

Mrs. Byrne turned her gaze to her oldest son. "Or there's you, Brendan. You and Rosie have talked about going back, haven't you?" Rosie's family was Irish too and she had plenty of aunts, uncles and cousins still living in Ireland.

"Well, yes, but I'm so busy at work these days, and the twins are a handful here, let alone over there, but I don't know, perhaps . . ."

"No, Brendan, I know it's too much to ask." Mrs. Byrne turned her attention away from him. "Or there's you, Lainey . . ."

"Me?" Lainey looked from her mother to her father. She knew at that moment this meeting had been a setup. "You want me to do it?"

"It's a lot to ask, Lainey, I know," Mrs. Byrne said quickly, "but we really don't have any other option. We have to do what the will says or we lose the inheritance, and God knows you're well aware how badly we need it. And aren't you the best placed of all of us? Your boss thinks so highly of you, surely she'd give you a year off, leave without pay if it had to be that? And you're so capable, so quick, so organized, I'm sure you'd take to running a B&B like a duck to water."

"And you've been back to Ireland more recently than any of us," Declan said, not bothering to hide a big grin. Lainey had been in Dublin on a flying visit several months before to be a bridesmaid at her best friend Eva's wedding. "God, I can hardly remember the place myself. What on earth could I tell the tourists?"

"And Eva and her husband would be able to give you a hand, wouldn't they?" Mrs. Byrne added.

Lainey's mind raced. For a moment the only sound in the room was the hum of distant traffic through the open windows and the whir of the air conditioner from their father's room. Of course she couldn't go to Ireland for a year. She was up to her eyes at work, almost second in charge these days. She couldn't just drop everything and go away. Not when her boss Gelda had been hinting for the past month about a promotion. And she couldn't just leave her apartment like that. What about the rent? And what about Adam . . . ?

Then Lainey looked at her father. He was trying to twist into a more comfortable position, grimacing at the pain. All these months after his accident on the building site and he was worse, not better. The sight of him stopped her protesting thoughts mid-flow. If she didn't do it, who would? She glanced around. Not Brendan, far too busy at work. Not Declan, with his new job. And as much as she loved her youngest brother, Declan was right, you couldn't ask Hugh to do something like this.

Which left only her.

Her father's voice filled the room, his County Meath accent sounding stronger than ever. "Lainey, could you do it? For my sake?"

She opened her mouth, about to speak, when another voice beat her to it.

"Could Lainey do what?"

They all turned. It was Hugh, spiky scarlet hair, nose ring and all, standing in the doorway. "Sorry I'm late. Have I missed anything?"

CHAPTER 3

Lainey pulled away from her parents' house, honking the horn and waving at her mother on the front verandah. She was too distracted to play KC and the Sunshine Band again, much as she'd like to have screamed the words at the top of her lungs, to try and clear her head. She put on a relaxation CD for a few minutes, until the simulated water sounds got on her nerves. She settled for the radio instead.

At the freeway exit to Richmond, she made a sudden decision and turned left, heading to Camberwell. The road was free of trams for the moment. She slowed as she drove past Adam's restaurant, just up the road from the cinema complex, and peered in—nearly all of the ten tables were filled. No point going in to see him to tell him her big news. He'd be too busy cooking to talk.

Ten minutes later she was at her apartment building in Richmond. Walking up from the underground parking lot, she moved the potted plant in the front porch from the left to the right—her invitation to Adam to call up when he got home. There were times it was very convenient to live in the same apartment building as your boyfriend.

They'd known each other only as neighbors until a year before. On her way out for a run one morning, Lainey had tripped and fallen while chasing her cat Rex down the stairs. Adam had come out of his ground-floor apartment and found her, groaning from the pain of a broken ankle. He'd taken charge, driving her to hospital, looking after Rex, and later helping move her gear to her parents' house until she was mobile enough to come home and tackle the stairs again. She was surprised to learn he was a chef—she'd seen him coming and going at odd hours and always just assumed he had an active social life. He made a joke of overseeing her rehabilitation program, taking her to the swimming pool, going with her on walks along the river path. She slowly learned things about him—he was thirty-five, his father was Scottish, his mother Australian, he had worked as a pearl-diver, taxi-driver, carpenter and tour guide before he'd discovered a passion and natural talent for cooking. They became good friends, talked about lots of things, fought about lots of things, laughed a lot too.

And then one afternoon, when they came back to his flat after getting caught in a sudden shower, it changed from just a friendship between them. They were standing in his kitchen, both soaked to the skin. He fetched towels, then insisted they both have a whiskey to warm themselves. Watching him reach up for glasses, seeing the muscles move under his damp T-shirt, she felt like she was seeing him physically for the first time. She stared at the tall, lean body, the brown, muscular arms, the dark-blond hair ruffled from the wind and rain, and felt a jolt inside her. He turned from the sink and saw her looking at him, and his expression changed too. They gazed at each other for a long moment, then he moved across and took her into his arms. He kissed her softly at first, and she kissed him back just as softly. And then the kisses became hot and fast. She was overwhelmed at the sudden burst of passion, at how good he felt, what his kisses were doing to her. He lifted his head from her, and she saw his brown eyes had darkened, become almost black. He smiled. "I've wanted to do that since the first time I saw you," he'd said.

"So is it serious between the two of you?" her friend Eva had asked when Lainey was back in Dublin for the wedding. "Is he your Mr. Cholera at last?" Lainey had declared to Eva once that she was waiting for the real love of her life, Mr. Gorgeous, the man who made her weak at the knees, made her heart skip a beat and her stomach swirl. "You're not waiting for Mr. Gorgeous. You're waiting for Mr. Cholera," Eva had laughed.

Was it serious? Lainey had thought about it for a moment before answering. "I don't really know yet, to be honest. He's as busy as I am with work, especially now he's opened his own place, so to tell you the truth we don't get to see a lot of each other. But it suits me and it suits him, I think." That's what she'd been telling herself. And the truth was there was so much going on in her life with her family that there wasn't much room for matters of her own heart.

Rex was waiting to greet her as she opened the door to the third-floor apartment. He'd stopped making a dash for freedom every time she came in, instead winding himself around her legs as if he was trying to trip her up. She leaned down and scratched his black head. "Guess what, Rexie? I'm off to live in Ireland for a year. Isn't that funny?"

She kept walking, a little hampered by his figure-eight movements around her calves. She leaned down and picked him up, just as he yawned. She winced at the little puff of fish breath. What would she do with Rex while she was away? She couldn't take him with her, could she? Perhaps he could go to her parents' house again. He liked it there and he could sleep on the end of her father's bed all day, keep him company. She went into her bedroom, swapped her work clothes for a light summer dress, trying not to let herself be overwhelmed by the night's events.

"Lainey, are you absolutely sure about this?" her father had said just before she left her parents' house that evening.

She'd crouched down beside his chair, taking his hand in hers. "Of course, Dad. Honestly, it makes perfect sense that I do it. It'll be great to be back in Ireland again. And I only have to run the B&B for a year after all."

Only a year. But a year filled with bed-making, bacon-frying, sheet-washing, daily dusting and vacuuming . . . nothing but housework for a whole year. She fought back the dismay. Stop it, Lainey, she said firmly. Think of it as a work project. It has to be done and that's that. She just had to be practical about it, take her emotions out of the situation. In any case, it wasn't about her. She was doing it for her parents, who had emigrated from Ireland to Australia to give her and her brothers a better life. This was the least she could do in return, wasn't it? Exactly.

She decided to do what she always did when she was feeling overwhelmed. Make a list. She sat at the dining-room table and grabbed a notepad from the pile in the center. Top of the list? That was easy.

PANIC

She crossed it out. Focus your mind, Lainey. You don't have a choice so what *do* you have to do?

Tell everyone

Rex knew now, so that was the animal kingdom alerted. Adam was next, of course. She tried to picture his reaction. He'd listen to all she had to say, ask lots of questions, like he always did. He'd be practical about it, though, wouldn't he? It was hard to know for sure. In the year they'd been together, there had never really been a normal, ordinary time between them. They had been seeing each other for just a month or so when her father had his accident and her life changed so much. They had been planning to meet for dinner that night. She'd rung Adam from the hospital, not in hysterics, but in deep shock, she'd realized afterward. As always in the middle of a crisis, work or personal, she'd gone into super-efficient mode. "Adam, hello, it's Lainey," she'd said calmly. "I'm just ringing to say my father's had an accident and he may not live through the night. So unfortunately I won't be able to meet you tonight for dinner after all." Some months later, she'd actually been able to laugh when Adam had reminded her of her polite, matter-of-fact message. At the time, she'd turned down his offers to drive her or her mother to and from the hospital. But his offers had kept coming anyway. In the weeks after the accident, she'd come home from work or the hospital, exhausted, too tired to cook. There, waiting outside her door, she'd find a meal ready to be heated, or a bunch of flowers, a book, a note hoping she was okay. And then the opportunity had suddenly arisen for him to go out on his own and open his own restaurant. Since then, their relationship had existed on snatched nights together, notes and phone calls—no normal time at all. She rubbed her eyes, not caring about the mascara smudges. How could they handle a year apart when they'd hardly had that long together?

Her thoughts jumped from Adam to her boss Gelda's probable reaction. The word furious sprang to mind. She'd have to try and talk to Gelda first thing in the morning, before the presentation meeting. Lainey thought of all the events and launches she had already half planned for the year ahead. She wouldn't get to see them through now. She thought about her big plans for her birthday later in the year. She'd have to cancel those too. As her mind leaped from person to person, thinking of all the ramifications, the list started taking shape.

Book plane ticket
Sublet apartment
Pack

Would she have to buy some more winter clothes? What did a B&B operator wear anyway? Flowery dresses and an apron? Her clothes—mostly from young Melbourne designers—wouldn't really suit life in a country-side guesthouse, would they?

She rubbed her eyes again, willing herself to stay calm, be rational. It worked in her job, it would work here too. Think of all the tips in the management books, she told herself. "Think calm, be calm." "Make decisions with your head, not your heart." "Don't sweat the small stuff, and remember it's all small stuff." What did that last one actually mean? she wondered.

Distracted by Rex mewing beside her, she put down her pen, slung him over one shoulder and walked over to the kitchen. She caught a glimpse of herself in the glass of the oven door, the newly short dark hair, the mascara smudged in rings around her eyes. Rare white panda spotted in Melbourne. Her dress was quite baggy on her, she noticed as well. Her mother was right, she was look-ing a bit too skinny. It wasn't deliberate, there just hadn't been a lot of time to sit around enjoying food lately.

Shushing Rex who was now wailing as if he'd never been fed in his whole cat life, she chose a can at random from the cupboard—lobster-flavored, his current fa-vorite. As she spooned the stinky orange mess into the bowl, he slid off her shoulder and mewed again. "What was that, Rex? What will Eva say when she hears I'm com-ing over?" She punctuated her words with the clang of the empty can landing in the bin and the *ding* of the spoon landing in the sink, where she'd thrown it from the other side of the kitchen. "The very thing, Rexie boy. Let's call her now." She looked at her watch and calcu-lated the time in Ireland. Midmorning, just before the lunchtime rush at Ambrosia, the delicatessen and café her friend ran in Dublin.

Ten minutes later, Lainey was almost wishing she hadn't made the call. "Could you stop laughing for a moment, Evie, so we can have a normal conversation?"

"Oh, I'm sorry, Lainey," Eva said, laughter still bubbling under her voice. "And you know I'm really sorry that your dad can't sell the B&B straightaway. But I just keep getting this mental image of you making all those beds and breakfasts. You *hate* housework."

"I don't hate it. I only have a cleaner because I'm too busy for housework."

"You do so hate it. This is like some revenge on you, all the beds you never made, the floors you've never washed—they're going to come back and haunt you."

"Evie . . ."

"I'm sorry, I'm sorry. So do you really have to be here next month, as quickly as that?"

"Yes, or we forfeit the lot. It's like convict days in reverse, isn't it? The emigrant sails back. Except I'll be shackled to a stove and a linen cupboard, not a cell."

"Don't worry, Lainey, really. I'll help you as much as I can, come down every weekend if you need me to. Is there anything I can do now? Go down and get things sorted before you get here?"

"You're a darling but no thanks. The solicitor's been paying one of her neighbors to keep an eye on the house since May died. And anyway, I have to meet with him, sort out all the legal stuff before I get the key."

"It's a nice house, though, isn't it? And it's so beautiful around there, your aunt must have been turning people away. You'll be so busy the time will fly past. What did your work say about it all?"

"I'm telling them tomorrow. Well, asking rather than telling. I just have to hope my boss doesn't mind giving me a year off."

"And Adam? What will you two do?"

The million-dollar question. "I don't know. I haven't been able to tell him yet. Listen, I'd better let you get back to your olives and cheese. I just wanted to let you know the headline news. I can't wait to see you, and give my love to that beautiful husband of yours, won't you?"

"I will, of course. And you'll let me know when you want us to pick you up from the airport? We can bring you back here and teach you how to poach eggs and cure your own bacon. And Joe's really good at doing those hospital corners on the beds."

"If you're going to be so mean to me, I hope it's a six a.m. flight."

"You know where the taxi rank is then, don't you?"

Lainey was smiling as she hung up. What had happened to the good old days when Eva had done as she was told? They had been friends now for more than thirty years, growing up in the same street and going to the same school in Dunshaughlin, a country town not far from Dublin. Their friendship had survived the trials of Lainey and her family emigrating when Lainey was fifteen, kept afloat by letters and phone calls, and Lainey's two visits home to Ireland on holiday. Eva had come to Melbourne on a spur-of-the-moment holiday the previous year, and during that time met and fallen in love with Joseph Wheeler, a Londoner. Within a year, Eva and Joseph had been married. Another job well done, Lainey thought, looking back. She'd felt quite the matchmaker at their wedding in Dublin. "Eva really has you to thank, Lainey, hasn't she?" one of Eva's aunts had said. "She'd never have met Joseph if you hadn't been living in Melbourne."

"Well, it was mostly her own looks and charm that lured him in, of course," Lainey had said, looking at the pair of them on the dance floor, Joseph tall and dark-haired, Eva smiling up at him, her long black hair arranged in a beautiful style.

Who'd have thought at the wedding that she'd soon be back in Ireland, living less than an hour away from the pair of them? Lainey started a new list, headed "Good things about going to Ireland." "Eva and Joseph" was number one.

· · ·

By one a.m. there was still no sign of Adam. He must have had a late-night rush at the restaurant. Lainey went downstairs in her pajamas to move the potted plant back to its original position. She had an early start in the morning and needed to get some sleep. Her big news would have to wait.

CHAPTER 4

Lainey stepped out of the Complete Event Management lift just before eight o'clock the next morning. Her assistant Julie jumped in surprise, pushing aside a newspaper and nearly choking on what looked like half a banana.

Lainey bit back a smile. "Morning, Julie. Still trying to break that national fruit-eating record, are you?"

"It's my latest diet, actually," Julie said, swallowing awkwardly as she leaned down to throw the banana skin in the bin. "Fruit only. It's my last-ditch effort—if this one doesn't work, then I'm going for the knife."

"Oh, Julie, don't do that. You're too young for plastic surgery."

"Not that sort of knife. It's a new diet I read about last week. You cut everything you're planning to eat in two, eat one half of it and then give the rest away. That's why it's called the knife diet, because you have to carry a—"

"Knife with you everywhere. I get it. But why bother

with all that anyway? I think you look great just the way you are."

I think you look great just the way you are, Julie mimicked crossly, watching Lainey as she picked up her messages and walked into her office. It was all right for skinny old her. Lainey was obviously blessed with one of those metabolisms that burnt off food as soon as it entered her mouth. Julie herself couldn't even wear a chocolate-brown shirt without putting on weight. It just wasn't fair. Why did some people get all the advantages in life and others like her get left with the dregs? Life was too easy for carefee, confident, good-looking people like Lainey, Julie decided, sighing as she turned back to the computer.

*   *   *

Lainey took a deep breath to calm her nerves as she walked into the meeting. She'd given dozens of these presentations but her stomach still turned somersaults each time at the thought of standing up in front of her colleagues. Just pretend you're feeling confident and you'll fool yourself as well as everyone else, she'd read years ago in a public speaking handbook. It had become her life's mantra. She just wished she'd had the opportunity to meet her boss this morning—she wanted to break the news about her departure as soon as possible. "No time, Lainey. It will have to be after your presentation," Gelda had said when Lainey phoned her.

"But it's important."

"I'm sure it is, Lainey. But it will have to wait until afterward."

Lainey greeted her colleagues and started the presentation, outlining the details of the different events as they flashed up on the screen beside her. This year would have been one of her busiest ever, with seven product launches, the opening of a new hotel complex in St. Kilda, a gala birthday bash for the daughter of a local millionaire businessman, and a food and wine fair at a winery in the Yarra Valley. She detailed budgets, client information and special requirements, all the while knowing she wouldn't be there for any of the events. In some cases she didn't mind—the launch of the new outboard motor, for example. Boating journalists were notoriously hard to impress. But she had really been looking forward to organizing the food and wine fair. Which of her colleagues would get these jobs, she wondered, glancing around the table. Or would her boss take on someone new?

•   •   •

"So, Lainey, let me guess what this meeting is about," Gelda said two hours later, as she gestured toward the seat on the other side of her pale wood desk. The view of Melbourne behind her was partly hidden by a thin timber blind. The light in the room was filtered, the air peaceful, helped by the bubbling water fountain in the corner. "You're after a pay raise, is that right? Then I'll save you the effort of asking, because as it happens, I've just completed a staff review and I am pleased to be able to offer you not just a pay raise, but in fact a promotion. I want you to consider becoming my second-in-charge." She leaned back in her chair, groomed head against the leather headrest, and waited for Lainey's reaction.

Lainey had been anticipating this conversation for months. She knew it had been on the cards. Gelda had been dropping hints. But what a time to hear it. "Gelda, I'm thrilled. Really thrilled, actually. But I'm afraid I've got bad news in return."

"You're not resigning?" Gelda laughed as if that was the most hilarious idea she'd had in a long time.

"Not exactly . . ."

As Lainey explained, Gelda's wide smile narrowed and weakened and then finally disappeared. Lainey tried to lighten the mood, thrown by her boss's expression. "My friend in Dublin thinks it's funny, really. Me having to make beds for a year. I'm a famously bad housekeeper."

Gelda slowly shook her head. "I can't believe it. This is extraordinarily inconvenient, Lainey, you realize that." Her faint German accent seemed more obvious. Lainey knew from experience that it was a sign Gelda was upset.

"Of course I do. But I'm afraid I really don't have a choice."

"No one else in your family can do it?"

Lainey wished she'd made a short film about her brothers. "Here, look at this," she'd say. "What do you reckon?" "No, Gelda, they can't. I can resign, if you'd prefer. I'm sure I could find a job with another firm when I got back . . ."

Her bluff worked. "No, no, I don't want you to do that. We'll just have to juggle the workload around until you return." Gelda spoke into the intercom to her secretary. "Kath, could you please call Celia King up here. Urgently."

Lainey felt ill. Anyone but Celia. Celia who had been creeping and crawling around the company since she was headhunted eighteen months ago. Celia who had set her sights on Lainey's job within days of stepping into the smart foyer downstairs. Celia who had two business degrees, was studying for her master's and probably spent her weekends preparing food baskets for the poor. Celia, who was now getting Lainey's clients handed to her on a plate, garnish and all.

Celia knocked on the door what seemed like just seconds later. She must have traveled to Gelda's office on a skateboard, Lainey thought. In she came, Betty Boop herself. High-pitched voice. Tiny nose. A row of perfectly white, neat teeth, gleaming like a lighthouse around the room.

"Yes, Gelda?" A 200-watt smile. "Oh, hello, Lainey." A 60-watt smile.

Gelda gestured toward the spare chair. "Sit down, Celia, and let me explain the situation here." She quickly summarized it. "It's extremely short notice, I know, but do you think you would be able to take on Lainey's clients while she's in Ireland?"

Lainey watched as Celia seemed to swell with self-importance. "Of course I can, Gelda. If I have to work seven days a week to make sure they're happy."

"Well, I don't think you'll have to go that far. But you could manage?"

"Oh, yes, definitely."

Lainey's heart sank. She knew right then she'd never get those clients back.

* * *

It wasn't until three o'clock that afternoon that she had a chance to ring Adam at work. As they spoke she could hear a radio playing in the background. "Four days since we've seen each other, Miss Byrne," Adam was saying.

"This is a scandalous situation. I may have to write a letter to the editor, get a petition started. What's your boss's number again? I'm demanding you get the day off right now and we go straight into the pantry here and make up for some lost time."

She laughed. "Oh, she'd agree immediately, let me tell you. So how are things tonight? Can you spare me an hour, for a quick drink?"

"I'm really sorry, but I don't think I can. We've got a table of twenty due in early, a birthday, I think it is. Are you okay, Lainey? Something's wrong?"

It threw her when he guessed how she was feeling before she was ready to reveal it. "I'm fine."

"But it's something important?"

"A bit." Was she being mistress of the understatement? Did leaving for a year in Ireland in less than a month's time count as (a) a bit important, (b) very important, or (c) incredibly important?

"Is it about your dad?"

"No. Well, not exactly."

"Tell me."

She was tempted for a moment. "No, it's probably better face-to-face. I'll try and nip down after I finish work." The other line on her phone was flashing. "Ad, I better run. See you tonight."

•   •   •

It was closer to nine by the time she got to the restaurant. Her client meeting had run over and then she'd taken the woman for a quick meal on Brunswick Street to seal the deal. As they enjoyed spicy Indonesian noodles and a glass of full-bodied shiraz each, Lainey had explained how Complete Event Management's expert team would organize a launch of the new bin refreshers that no one would ever forget. All the while, her mind had been far away.

Adam's restaurant manager looked up from behind the cash register as she came in past the full tables. "Lainey, hi, how are you?"

"Great, Dave. You too, by the looks of things. Has it been this busy all night?"

"Since six o'clock. We were flat-out with the late film showing last night too. That French film is playing, the one with all the banquets in it, and people are starving when they come in here afterward. Your timing was spot-on."

Lainey had organized a dinner–film ticket deal between Adam's restaurant and the cinema down the road. She was glad to see it had been such a success. "That's good to hear. Is he available for visitors?"

"Well, I will have to see your pass. Only joking, in you go."

The small kitchen was bustling, six plates spread on one of the stainless steel counters, the large industrial stove covered in pans at various stages of boil or bubble, the pop song on the radio adding another layer of sound. There was an enticing mix of cooking smells—sizzling garlic, fresh herbs, something rich and spicy. Adam was behind the main counter, dressed casually in black jeans and a long-sleeved T-shirt, the sleeves pushed up over his brown forearms. The closest he came to formal chef's clothing was the black apron tied around his waist, a dishcloth tucked into it. He was talking to the young waitress. "Zoe, I can't read your handwriting at all on this order.

Are you thinking about becoming a doctor rather than a waitress?"

The young woman grinned, glancing at the order form he was holding. "Sorry, Adam, I was in a rush out there. It should say one paella and one fish . . . oh, hi, Lainey."

Adam looked over, his lean face creasing into a smile. "Lainey, hi, take a seat. I'll be right with you."

She sat down in the corner, watching while Adam started plating an order, narrowly missing bumping his head on the overhead shelves as he moved around. He'd told her the first thing he would do when he made some money was turn his kitchen into the right size for his height. Six-foot-two, lanky chefs were obviously unusual in the restaurant world. She looked down at tonight's menu. The dishes were very familiar—Adam had tried most of them out on her first. If she was eating here tonight, what would she have chosen? She loved his seafood paella, made with yabbies and prawns. The middle-eastern-style dish, lamb shank tajine with prunes and almonds over saffron couscous, was fantastic too.

"So how are you, gorgeous?" Adam called over his shoulder as he expertly turned something in a pan on the stove behind him.

She put down the menu. "I'm fine, gorgeous, how are you? I love the new hat."

"It is something special, isn't it?" Adam said with a grin, turning slowly to show his Richmond football hat to its full advantage. As a self-taught chef, he'd told Lainey he felt he couldn't wear the proper chef's hat. He improvised instead with an ever-changing range of headwear, from scarves tied pirate-style to baseball caps to tonight's black and yellow woolen hand-knit one.

"It's certainly something, anyway. That's a great crowd. Well done."

"That crowd's all thanks to your marketing brain, Miss Byrne, not my cooking yet," he said, as he glanced at the order again. "Where have you been, looking so smart? Not over at your parents'?"

"Not tonight. I was there last night though. A crisis meeting."

She had his full attention. "Is your dad bad again?"

"No, it wasn't his health. It was about my aunt's will. That's what I wanted to talk to you about."

"He can't work out what to spend all that B&B money on?" Adam deftly added garnishes, wiped the edge of each plate clean with a tissue dipped in ice-cold water, then rang the silver bell on the shelf in front of him, talking all the while. "Tell him I have a few ideas if he needs them—a new fridge, a new extractor fan . . . actually, Lainey, let's invite him to step in as my silent partner. He and your mother could eat here free for the rest of their lives, guests of honor."

Lainey waited until Zoe had collected the plates and she and Adam were alone in the kitchen before she responded. There was no point dillydallying with news like this, she knew. She'd have to come right out with it. "There's actually been a catch with the will. I have to go and live in Ireland for a year and run the B&B before we can sell it."

Adam stopped, pan in hand. "You have to do what?"

She repeated it.

"When?"

"I have to be there within the month."

"Oh, I see. Great. Well, have a lovely time, won't you?"
He looked at her closely. "You're not joking, are you?"

"No."

As she explained the whole story, Adam listened and
worked, asking questions, moving pans and cooking all
the while. "And there's really no alternative? Your family
can't challenge the will?"

She shook her head.

He was watching her carefully. "So how do you feel
about it? Are you pleased at the chance to be back in Ireland for a while?"

"I am. It's just what I have to do when I get there that
worries me. All that cleaning."

"All that cooking, you mean." His eyes were warm with
amusement. "You're not going to try and get away with
stir-fries for breakfast, are you?"

She knew he found it very funny that her cooking skills
extended to just a small selection of simple Asian dishes.
"Well, Ireland is multicultural these days. It might be just
what people want. Stir-fried bacon and eggs. I might start
a trend." She quaked a little inside at the thought of
the cooking. She'd been so focused on the leaving-
Melbourne side of things that she hadn't thought much
about the what-happened-when-she-got-to-Ireland part.
Bed and breakfast would involve the full Irish breakfast,
which she only ate when she had a hangover or there was
someone else around to cook it for her. Maybe her aunt
had left instructions.

"Well, you can always just give them plain toast and tell

them it's a health retreat. Don't poke your tongue out like that, Elaine, it's not ladylike." He finished plating several meals, then rang the bell again. "And what about your work? This is really going to mess up your plans to take over the event management world, isn't it?"

"A little. But I've no choice, really. It has to be done."

Zoe came back in to collect the next order. After she'd gone, Adam left the stove and came over to where Lainey was sitting, his face very serious now. He gently tucked a piece of her hair behind her ear. "And us, Lainey? Ireland's a lot farther than two floors away."

She tried to ignore the effect his touch was having on her body. The same question had been going round and round her head for the past two days. "You'll be so busy here, making a huge success of this, setting up franchises and counting your mountains of money that you won't even notice I'm gone."

"Oh, I think I will."

"Seriously, Adam. I know how important this place is to you. Now you'll be able to work every hour of every week, not worry about me at all. Put all your energies into this place."

"What if I like worrying about you?"

Zoe came back in again. "Order for the table of ten, Adam."

"Thanks, Zoe." He turned back to Lainey. "We need to talk about this a lot more. Can you wait here, have a drink and tell me all about it when this rush is over?"

"No, I'm sorry. I've had to bring some work home. We've got a big client presentation tomorrow. What about later on? Will you be home early, do you think?"

"I can't tonight. The stockroom has to be emptied before the rewiring is done in the morning. What about tomorrow afternoon?"

She shook her head. "I've got meetings all day. Oh, and the little matter of handing over all my clients to my archenemy."

"Celia got your clients?"

"Celia got my clients."

Zoe came in again with yet another page of orders. Lainey stood up, feeling very in the way. "I'd better leave you to it."

"Come here, Lain," he said softly. He leaned down and kissed her quickly, his lips warm against hers. "Your parents are lucky to have you. So am I. We'll talk about it all soon, okay?"

She nodded. "Thanks, Ad."

At the door she turned to wave goodbye but he was already distracted by the new order and the sudden boiling of a saucepan on the stove behind him.

CHAPTER 5

E va's voice went up a pitch. "You're going to break up with Adam? For God's sake, why?"

Sitting at her desk, Lainey moved the phone to her other ear and rubbed at her temples. Behind her the Melbourne city lights were flickering on, the late-summer sky fading away to night. It was past eight o'clock. "Because it makes sense, Evie. I've given it a lot of thought and I've realized it's the fairest thing to do. The most practical thing to do. I can't ask him to put his own life on hold while I go away for a year. He's up to his eyes as it is. This is the last thing he needs."

She had been thinking it over, rationally, methodically, every day since she'd known she was leaving. Their workloads hadn't eased at all over the past few weeks. She'd unexpectedly had to go to Sydney for four days to oversee a big product launch and then to Brisbane for a weekend trade fair. He was flat-out as usual, working seven days a week. They'd had just two nights together in that time. On the plane one evening, tired, immersed in work matters, she'd found herself thinking about their relationship in work terms. If Adam had been one of her clients and this year in Ireland the project under discussion, what options would she have suggested? Surviving on email and phone contact for a whole year? A difficult situation, she would have advised. Long-distance relationships were hard work for little immediate reward, that was well known. He certainly couldn't come over to see her, financially or time-management-wise. She had made a long list in her mind of the pros and cons of staying together. The more dispassionately she viewed the situation, the more the right solution had presented itself.

They would have to break up. That way he would be free to concentrate on the restaurant without worrying about emails and phone calls and feeling guilty if he hadn't had time to be in touch with her. She could concentrate on running the B&B, getting everything organized to sell it in a year's time. And then, when she got back, they could reassess the situation. But in the meantime, there it was—the easiest, simplest, most practical solution.

"Forget what's fair or what's practical," Eva said, not sounding at all convinced with Lainey's measured arguments. "Do your feelings come into this at any stage? Or his feelings?"

"Evie, I leave in just over a week, I *have* to be practical about things."

"But you're in a relationship with him, Lainey, not a business partnership. Who's ever practical about relationships?"

"I've told you before, there hasn't been time for it to become serious between us."

"It's certainly sounded serious to me."

"What's sounded serious? I've hardly talked about him."

"That's what I mean. It's when you have to talk about things all the time, analyze his behavior and your behavior, that you know things aren't going to work. From what you've said, you and Adam just get on really, really well."

"Eva, you're on the other side of the world, how can you tell from there?"

"From the bare bits you feed me. Like that time you came home and he'd cooked all those meals for you and put them in the freezer. And when he did the same for your parents after your dad came out of hospital."

"He was trying out dishes for his restaurant."

"It sounded to me like he was spoiling you. And what about all those notes you told me he leaves you?"

"He has to leave me notes. We never get to see each other."

"Lainey, when exactly did you build this moat around yourself? Can't you just admit he's a lovely man or you wouldn't have been going out with him for a year?"

Eva's words momentarily pierced Lainey's resolve. Yes, he was indeed a lovely man or she wouldn't have been going out with him for a year. Then she snapped out of it. This was no time to be emotional, no time to be thinking of herself, what she wanted to happen. She'd looked at the whole situation matter-of-factly and this was the best thing to do. "I think it's the only option, Evie. It's not fair on him otherwise."

"And will he have any say in what is or isn't fair on him?"

"Of course he will. And I bet you anything he agrees

completely. It'll leave him free to get on with the restaurant and me able to concentrate fully on the B&B."

"This isn't anything to do with that Mr. Cholera, is it? You're not still waiting for some make-believe hero to show up?"

"Of course not. Mr. Cholera was just a joke. This is about Adam, what is best for him. It just makes sense, can't you see?"

Eva suddenly sounded distracted. "Yes, I'll be right there," she said to someone in the deli near her. "Lainey, I'm sorry, I have to go. But please don't do anything rash about Adam. And don't worry about what it will be like over here, either, I'll do all I can to help you. It'll all just unfold, you wait and see."

Unfold? Lainey had a horrible mental image of herself in the B&B folding and unfolding hundreds of sheets. As she said goodbye and hung up, she fought off the panic that seemed to be permanently simmering away inside her these days. It took all her energy to keep it from boiling over. She tried to banish the ghosts of doubt that Eva had put in her mind about breaking up with Adam. She'd made her decision, given it careful thought and knew it was the right way for her to go. Adam would see it that way too, she was sure of it. She'd pictured the conversation in her mind many times, what she would say, how he would respond. He'd be a little surprised, but relieved too, she suspected.

Feeling she was back on steady ground again, she reached for her To Do list. Her assistant Julie called her the Queen of Lists. It was lists that made the world go round, she'd answered. This latest one was more of a volume of lists than a list list, though. But where would you be without lists? Listless, she thought. Mooching about with nothing to do—she hadn't known that feeling in a long time.

"We're really very lucky to have you, Lainey," her mother had said at a family dinner the evening before. "So in control, so organized. I don't think any of us could have done this as well as you're doing." Behind her mother's back, Declan had been making vomiting-mimes, rolling his eyes at the praise. Brendan had just looked cross, as usual. Hugh was running late and hadn't arrived yet, also as usual. Lainey had been surprised to hear her mother say those things, but she knew without any false modesty that it was true. She liked the feeling, too, liked it when people said, "Leave it to Lainey. She'll be able to sort it out. She'll get things under control." And usually she had. Except with her father. She hadn't been able to make him better, had she? Not yet, anyway. But perhaps once the B&B was sold, once the financial worries had gone, things would change. She fought off another twinge of anxiety.

Adam had seen through her calm exterior. It had thrown her and touched her in equal amounts when the week before, lying together on her big sofa on a rare night together, he had kissed her and told her everything would be all right.

She'd pulled away from him. "What do you mean everything?"

"In Ireland. It'll be a bit odd at first, but you'll be great."

"I'm not worried."

His dark-brown eyes had been warm, amused. "You're not? You weren't lying there thinking about it, getting anxious that you'll be able to keep the B&B running so you can sell it and your dad can get the money he needs?"

That was word for word what she'd been worrying about. She denied it though. "No, I was actually thinking about the mayhem Celia's going to cause with my clients."

"Were you? Okay, let's pretend you were worrying about that."

"I was."

"Were not."

"Was."

"Were not."

Then she'd hit him with a cushion and he'd hit her with a cushion and then they'd kissed again and kissed for longer and then both of them had stopped talking about Ireland or B&Bs or Celia or anything much at all.

•   •   •

The next night, she let herself in through the back door of her parents' house and was surprised to find her father sitting at the kitchen table. The promise of money in a year's time had lifted his spirits a little. He was watching a current affairs program on television. Lainey kissed the top of his head in greeting and watched the program with him for a few moments. It was a piece about the Australian actress Hilly Robson, in Sydney for the premiere of her latest film, fighting the unwelcome attention of the paparazzi every moment of her stay.

Mr. Byrne shook his head with a sigh and turned it off

with the remote control. "Investigative journalism at its finest, wouldn't you say, Lainey? Insurance companies persecuting thousands of us every day and programs like this are more worried about pretty blonde actresses being chased by photographers."

Lainey was too embarrassed to admit she was quite interested in Hilly Robson's media trials. She resisted the temptation to turn the TV back on. "Ma's not here?"

"No, she's out at that food demonstrating job in the supermarket."

"She's started already? How's it going?"

"She said it's a breeze after bringing you four up. At least the customers don't throw the food back at her like you used to."

"Dad, I did not. I used to drop it under the table." As a child she'd taken a strong dislike to vegetables—peas and carrots especially—surreptitiously spooning them under the table, imagining it as some kind of black hole. Her mother had thought they'd fallen by accident until Brendan had told her the truth. Lainey had been put on solo dishwashing duties for a month as punishment.

Her father laughed at the expression on her face. Lainey realized it had been a long time since she'd heard him laugh like that. She had a rush of how much she missed her father. Her real father. Not the bad-tempered one who had come back from the hospital. She wondered sometimes if they'd brought home the wrong person. Perhaps there had been another Irishman in the emergency ward that day.

"And how are you, love? Nearly organized?"

She sat down opposite him. "Just about. The flight's

booked. The apartment's sublet to one of the secretaries from work. I'll bring Rex over here next week to get him settled before I leave. And my bags are already packed." She'd been packed for more than a week. She *loved* packing. "Just have to get on that plane now." She gave a cheery smile, hoping it would fool her father.

It didn't. "You know how grateful I am, don't you? I know all the others think you're just taking it in your stride, but of course it's a shock. And a big change. And not what you would have planned for yourself, I know that."

For a moment it was like having her old dad back. The one she used to sit and chat over the table with, the one who laughed at her need for order, her planning, her finely tuned organizational skills. "If you ever leave event management, Elaine, there's a job in the army for you for sure. You'd have them terrified and sorted out in no time." The father who spoke like that, joked around like that, had nearly disappeared though. Except for occasional flashes.

She was surprised to feel her eyes well up. She blinked quickly. "Well, they say a change is as good as a holiday," she said lightly. "It'll be fun, I bet. And I'll get to see lots of Eva, too." Eva and Joe were going to meet her at Dublin airport on Sunday morning. She'd stay the night with them, then make the forty-minute trip to Dunshaughlin from their house the next day to meet the solicitor.

"You know, it was a lovely house once, though too big for us even back then. I'm amazed May stayed in it on her own all these years. I suppose that's why she started the B&B, to fill up the rooms again. We used to have great fun there when we were kids, roaming around Tara as though it was our own backyard."

"I can't imagine it."

"Me roaming around Tara or May and I having fun?"

She smiled, caught out. "Both, I suppose. She was fun as a child, was she?"

"She was. She wanted her own way, of course, and would kick up if she didn't get it. Quite like someone else in this room as a little girl, actually."

"Dad! I was an angel as a child, I thought we'd agreed that. Why was May so cranky with us, do you think?"

"Cranky?"

"You know, so mad at you for emigrating. I remember when we all went back to Ireland for that first holiday, she was furious with us the whole time. Don't you remember? What had she expected, that we'd pick up and move back to Ireland just when things started going well for us here in Melbourne?"

Her father shifted into a more comfortable position in his seat. "She had a hot temper on her, all right."

"Perhaps it was harder for her to understand why we'd left, not having been married, not having any kids."

"You're probably right, Lainey."

"Anyway, I'm glad we came here. Imagine if we'd stayed there. I probably would have been running the B&B with her by now." She pulled a face. "God, it's all just come full circle, hasn't it? I'm doing it after all."

There was a knock at the door. It was Ken, one of her father's friends, carrying a six-pack of beer and a video. "Got some soccer here for your dad, Lainey."

"Come in, Ken." She decided to leave them to it. She'd go down to the shopping center instead.

• • •

It didn't take long to find her mother. Mrs. Byrne was in aisle six of the brightly lit supermarket, standing behind a cardboard stall crammed between the baked beans and the spaghetti sauces. She was wearing a bright-yellow apron and a cardboard saucepan hat.

"Lainey, how are you? Pass me that cloth over there, would you? Are you here to try some Pronto Pot? From can to table in just five minutes. All you have to do is add water and one beef stock cube. Your family will be amazed and impressed."

Lainey tried not to laugh. "I don't have a family, unless you count Rex and he's far too fussy." She gingerly took the little sample pot from her mother and tasted the gloopy contents.

"Horrible, isn't it?" Her mother leaned forward conspiratorially. "It's made by the same people who make the pet food and I think they've mixed up the cans."

Lainey stood back as two genuine customers came up for a taste. She marveled as her mother switched into full professional selling mode. The two shoppers were quickly convinced by Mrs. Byrne's spiel and headed off to the counter clutching several cans each of Pronto Pot.

"Well done, Ma. You're a natural at this."

"I spent years convincing all of you to eat my disgusting food. This is simple. Did you call in home before you came here?" her mother asked, scraping more blobs of muck into the white cups. "How did you think your father was?"

"Not too bad, actually. Ken had just arrived with a soccer video."

Mrs. Byrne's mouth tightened. "That Ken, turning up as soon as he knows I'm out the door. Do you know he—" She was interrupted by a couple and their five children wanting a Pronto Pot tasting session. Lainey stood back as they emptied all the tasting cups and asked for more. They finished off all the samples, then walked off without any cans of the product.

"Saves me washing up, anyway," Mrs. Byrne whispered, stacking the empty cups. She looked at her watch and removed her saucepan hat. "Let's get out of here. I'd kill for a coffee."

Sitting at a café table near the supermarket, they had just taken a sip of their cappuccinos when Mrs. Byrne leaned over and whispered to Lainey. "See that woman there? I used to work in the library with her husband, till she upped and left him, with the three kids and all. That's her new fellow, that one with the beard at the counter, see? Turned out she'd been having an affair for months and the husband had no idea."

Lainey looked at the couple. The woman seemed like an ordinary suburban mum, the man beside her slightly built, with a beard. "That's terrible. How could she do it?"

"Kiss a man with a beard? God knows, they're horrible, aren't they? Thank heavens your father never grew one."

"I don't mean the beard. I mean have an affair and just leave the kids like that."

"Well, she wouldn't be the first woman who wished she could up and leave her kids behind. She told a friend of mine she just fell in love with the other man and couldn't help herself."

"Of course she could help herself. I hate it when people use excuses like that, that they were all overcome with emotion, that it had nothing to do with them. Surely you get a choice about things like that."

Mrs. Byrne put down her cup and gave Lainey a long look. "Good Lord, Lainey, you've obviously never fallen head over heels in lust. It happens, you know."

"Oh, I see," Lainey spoke in a joking tone. "This is your way of gently telling me you were off having affairs while we were at school, isn't it? Do you know, I always suspected something like that about you. Who was it? The postman? No, not that fellow that came to do the roof? The one with the long ginger moustache? Or perhaps it wasn't here. It was in Ireland, was it? Let me think, not Mr. Doherty in the shop. Oh, Ma, you didn't, did you?"

Mrs. Byrne lifted her chin. "Elaine, a mother must have some secrets from her daughter."

Lainey felt a prickle of unease. "Ma, stop it. You're joking, aren't you? You didn't have an affair with that roof man, did you?"

Mrs. Byrne finally laughed. "Him? Of course I didn't. I have some taste." She took a sip of coffee. "So what do you think you'd do if you found out Adam was having an affair?"

Lainey blinked. Where on earth had Peg learned to be a mother? Watching *Oprah*? "When would Adam have an affair? He's hardly had time to have a relationship with me let alone anyone else."

"Would you have one yourself?"

"Of course not!"

"Why 'of course not'?"

"Because I just wouldn't. It wouldn't be right."

Mrs. Byrne laughed at the serious expression on Lainey's face. "You're a great one for everything in its place, everything under control, Lainey, aren't you? Where did I go wrong raising you?"

"I'm not like that," she said, stung yet again by this new, particularly plain-speaking version of her mother. She had always been one to speak her mind, but since her father's accident Peg seemed to be using a megaphone. "I can be very flexible, actually."

"When it suits you, yes, you can be. But you do like your own way, always have, ever since you were a young one. Still, I'd rather you were like that than some spineless, wishy-washy thing, jumping to everyone else's tune or whatever that saying is." To Lainey's relief the subject was changed. "Now, are you absolutely sure you don't want your father and me to take you to the airport? He would make the effort for that, for once."

"I'm sure, really." She knew how difficult it was for her father to maneuver himself into a car seat. "Adam and I will drop by on the way, to say a final goodbye."

"And everything's fine with Adam, is it? He really is okay about you going away?"

"Things are perfect." She'd decided that was all her family needed to know.

"Good. And you're still coming for your farewell dinner next week? All the boys will be there. Rosie and the twins too."

"You're sure you're up to cooking for all of us? You look tired. This job won't be too much for you, will it?"

"Too much? The job will be a relief. At least it's a break from sitting at home, coping with your father's moods, trying to coax him to do this exercise, try this new vitamin, visit his physio."

"But he was up tonight. He seemed quite bright."

"Because Ken was coming over. Oh yes, he'll make an effort for his friends. But not for me. Not for his family. We've just become his whipping boys. His nursing staff. Or his slaves, more like it."

"He can't help it, you know that. You think he wants to be in pain all the time? That he's glad that accident happened?"

Mrs. Byrne looked steadily at Lainey. "Will I tell you something? When your father first had that accident, when they rang me at work and said there'd been an accident with the crane, that he'd been badly hurt and was being rushed to hospital, I remember driving from the library and praying, please God, let him live. I'll look after him. It doesn't matter how bad he is, just don't let him die." She paused for a long moment. "And my prayers came true, Lainey. He did live. And I am looking after him. And the worst of it is, sometimes I wish I wasn't. Sometimes I wish my prayers hadn't come true." She sat back and looked at Lainey, her expression a mixture of defiance and misery.

"You don't mean that, do you?"

"I do, Lainey. I don't know this man. He's not the one I married. Miserable most of the time, depressed, no energy, he won't try and do anything for himself. It's as if his life force was crushed that day, not those discs in his back. And I'm sick of it. Sick of his self-pity, sick of him moaning on about how terrible his lot is. Well, what about my lot? Doesn't he think it's hard for me? Does he think I wanted to spend my retirement nursing him, lying in bed day after day like a big, miserable baby?" Her eyes filled with tears.

Her mother didn't mean this, surely. She couldn't. She was just tired. That was it, of course. "Maybe you just need some time away. It's hard on him. He doesn't like it either."

"Then why doesn't he bloody well do something about it, then?" Mrs. Byrne's voice was too loud. She colored, embarrassed, and then lowered her voice again. "I've half a mind to leave him. Some days I've just wanted to open that front door and walk out and never come back."

Lainey didn't want to hear this. Her parents were a united front. She didn't want to hear they were having problems. Young people had problems, not old people. And not parents. Her parents, especially. She tried to make a joke of it. "Well, just as well we live in Australia now, you can get divorced here. Though you can get divorced in Ireland these days, can't you? You could go back, make a special trip of it."

"I've thought about it, believe me. I've thought about lots of things these past months. Is this it, Lainey? Is this what's become of my life? I had a life once, you know, once upon a time. I was actually a person, before all of this, all of you took me over." She waved her hands as if to encompass not just her husband, Lainey and her brothers, but the whole shopping center scene around them. "What happened to that person, Lainey? Where am I in all of this?"

Lainey didn't want to hear any of this either. It didn't feel like it was any of her business. It was far too private. And it definitely didn't feel like something a daughter wanted to hear her mother say. "Ma, come on. It's just a rough patch. And you'll have money in a year, even sooner if the insurance comes through. Dad will be able to get all the proper treatment, you'll be able to pay off all the bills, take that trip around Australia. It will be fine, you wait and see." She felt like she was a mother speaking to a child, cajoling, pleading, not the other way around.

Mrs. Byrne looked exhausted. "I don't know if I want to wait around anymore, that's the problem, Lainey. I don't know if I can wait."

CHAPTER 6

At her own suggestion, Lainey's three farewell parties took place on the same night. She'd decided it was the most efficient way of doing it. Her work one was first, held in the Complete Event Management boardroom. She moved around the room, glass of champagne in hand, laughing off teasing remarks about making beds for the next year, answering all their questions. "Yes, it's out in the country, that's right, about an hour from Dublin . . . No, not isolated at all. It's about halfway between two towns, Dunshaughlin and Navan. Yes, they have shopping centers and all . . . About four guest rooms, I think. No, people usually only stay a night or two . . . Full Irish breakfast? Well, the works—bacon, eggs, sausages, tomato, toast, black pudding. No, black pudding's not a dessert and, believe me, you really wouldn't want to know what it is."

Gelda made a charming speech, which Lainey would have enjoyed more if Celia hadn't been standing in the corner looking so smug. And if Gelda had restricted her comments to how much she was going to miss Lainey, rather than including a smiling reference to Celia, who she was sure would fill Lainey's shoes very capably.

"Absolutely, Gelda," Celia called out. "I'll be there for you twenty-four-seven."

Lainey hated that expression. It was clearly nonsense. When was Celia going to sleep? And would she really be her bright, perky self if a client called at three a.m. on Sunday morning to discuss the launch of his new range of sliced peaches?

"Good luck, Celia," she said through the biggest smile she could muster. "And Gelda has my contact details in Ireland if you need them."

"Oh, I won't, Lainey, but thanks anyway."

*   *   *

As she drove to her parents' house for the family farewell dinner, she had to play KC and the Sunshine Band at maximum volume just to get Celia's voice out of her mind and her temper down to manageable levels. Brendan and Rosie and the twins were there when she arrived. She leaned into the double stroller to say hello to her niece and nephew. As usual, Liam was crying, Sinéad smiling. Lainey glanced over at her brother. "Did you ever think of calling them Sweet and Sour?"

"Yes, Lainey, absolutely hilarious, as usual," Brendan said in a bored voice. "Your cat's name is bad enough, God knows what you'd call your children."

"I'm thinking about Lucifer for a boy and Scurvy for a girl, actually, if I ever get around to having any."

"Well, you really would want to start thinking about it," Rosie said earnestly. "It's supposed to get much harder the older you get. And you're nearly thirty-three, aren't you? A friend of mine . . ."

Declan arrived just in the nick of time. "I've come to pay homage to the champion of our family," he announced in a theatrical voice, waving two bottles of wine. "Keep that noble thought in mind during those long, dark, damp Irish days, will you, Lainey? While you're over there cooking up a fry, trying to dry dozens of sheets, I will be back here doing my bit as the King of the Classroom, molding the next generation, slowly but surely brainwashing them to my way of thinking . . ."

Brendan stood up suddenly. "Put a sock in it, Declan, would you? I've got a headache."

"I'm just joking, Brendan," Declan said, unabashed. "Remember jokes? Those things people say with something called humor in it? That you laugh at the end of? Remember laughing?" Brendan just grunted and went back into the kitchen, nearly tripping over Rex as he walked by. Lainey was glad to see her cat was settling in so well.

"What's up with Bren tonight?" she said in a low voice to Declan.

"He's always like that these days, haven't you noticed?" Declan answered at normal volume. "Wouldn't you be, if you were married to the Queen of Rabbitsville?"

"Dec, don't be mean." Lainey glanced at Rosie on the other side of the room. Sitting primly on the sofa, nibbling at a biscuit with her unfortunately prominent front teeth, Rosie did have a certain rabbitty air about her. As they watched, she leaned across and settled Mr. Byrne more comfortably, smiling patiently at him. Lainey and Declan felt guilty just watching her.

Mrs. Byrne came into the room carrying a tray of glasses. "Lainey, Hugh's just rung to say sorry but he won't be able to make it tonight after all. He's finishing some video editing or something. To be honest, I couldn't really work out what he was talking about."

"Who's his victim this week?" Lainey asked. Hugh had been studying video production as part of his media studies course, and in the past year the whole family had been involved in his mini documentaries as subjects, voluntarily and involuntarily. Lainey had only learned about it when she'd gone out jogging one morning, getting the fright of her life when Hugh leaped out at her with his camera. He'd been exploring paparazzi techniques, he'd tried to explain, while she tried to beat him around the head with her raincoat.

"Some poor soul, I suppose, but as long as it's not your father or me anymore, I don't care really. I hate seeing myself on the TV, it's scarier than a mirror. He said to tell you he's going to try and see you before you leave on Sunday. He's got something for you."

"What would that be, do you think, Lainey?" Declan asked. "A business proposition perhaps? A bit of dope smuggling? Whatever he gives you, just run it through an X-ray before you go to the airport, won't you?"

Mrs. Byrne sighed. "Declan Byrne, could you minimize the chin music for one minute? I swear there is no one in the world who talks as much nonsense as you. Now, come on, all of you, and sit down before your dinner goes cold."

"It's already cold," Declan said. "It's seafood and salad. Do you mean, sit down before it gets hot?"

"Shut *up*, Declan."

• • •

By eleven o'clock that night Lainey was with Adam and a group of friends in the lounge bar around the corner from her apartment in Richmond. Adam had taken half a night off and met her in the bar, where her friends had taken over the whole back section, furnished with old sofas, orange lamps and other seventies decorative touches. The background music was from the same era. Her friend Christine beckoned her over, patting the seat beside her. "Come here, you. My friend Lainey the house-maid. You of all people swapping your stellar career for a sea change life in rural Ireland."

"I'm Irish, remember—it's a homecoming, not a sea change."

"You're not Irish, not anymore. You're one of us now. I still can't picture it, Lainey, the idea of you lazing about in a guesthouse. Not Action Girl herself. The shock will kill you."

"You're just jealous. You'll be juggling memos and fighting with IT people while I'm wafting about with a teapot, classical music playing in the background, smiling sweetly at all my guests . . ."

"You'll have to send us video evidence of it. What's the B&B like anyway? An old castle or one of those suburban houses where you get to sleep in the kids' room, the sheets still warm from them?"

"Oh, no, far more charming. Two story, with a rambly garden around it. It's down the end of a lane a few hundred meters from the Hill of Tara itself."

"Is that named after that film, what is it, *Gone with the Wind*? That Tara?"

Lainey tried not to smile. "Other way round, actually. It's the ancient capital of Ireland, the home of the High Kings of Ireland. A very important historic site, I'll have you know."

"Like Stonehenge? Brilliant. So you'll have all these old hippies and new-agers coming to stay with you, getting upset about you serving bacon and sausages and insisting on hand-blended muesli."

"I hope I do get vegetarians. A few less things to cook."

"I'd hate to be one of your guests," Christine laughed. "You'd have them up out of bed by eight a.m. 'Go on, get out there and go for a run before breakfast. What do you mean you want bacon and eggs? Far too unhealthy. Here, have some whole-grain toast instead. Now, go on, out the door with you. Here's your sightseeing itinerary. Come on, hop to it.'"

"I'm not that bad, am I?" Lainey said.

"You're worse."

Another woman, Kim, joined their table then. A friend of Lainey's since college—though they rarely saw each other these days—Kim had also studied event management before going on to set up her own wine-marketing company. Small, dark-haired and pretty, Kim also specialized in wearing very low-cut tops. Tonight was no exception, Lainey noticed. Her brothers had always been keen supporters of Kim's visits to the Byrne house.

Christine stood up as Kim sat down. "Another drink, Lain?"

Lainey held up her half-full glass of champagne. "Thanks, Chris, but no, I'm fine."

As Christine walked away, Kim lifted her glass up to

Lainey in a toast. They clinked glasses. "To you and your big year, Lain. You're all set to go, I guess?"

"Practically. All I need to do is appoint someone to organize a minute's silence in my memory once a week, so none of you forget me. Can I interest you in the job?"

Kim just smiled. "So when do you actually fly out?"

"Tomorrow afternoon. That's why I'm lashing back the champagne. This is my last night of freedom."

"And everything's okay with Adam? He's all right about you going?"

Lainey looked over at her boyfriend. He was talking to a friend of hers, a plumpish blond-haired man called Greg Gilroy who owned several cafés and bars around Melbourne. "He'll be fine," she said shortly, the conversation they still had to have looming nearer every minute.

"Will you miss him?"

Yes, very much, she thought, surprising herself. She batted the question away, laughing casually. "Of course, why wouldn't I miss him?"

Kim shifted in her chair. "I don't know, I've never been too sure how serious you are about him. You seem to talk about your work as much as him." She gave an odd giggle.

Lainey knew from experience that giggle meant Kim was either drunk or nervous about something. "Well, work's important to both of us."

Kim glanced over at Adam again, then back at Lainey. "But you still have to be careful you don't take people for granted, don't you think? Let them know you appreciate them."

What exactly was Kim getting at here? "I know that. And I have appreciated Adam. It's just the two of us are so busy." Lainey realized she was sounding very defensive. Perhaps Kim was joking? No, she looked deadly serious. "Have you been saving this up especially for my farewell party? It's not very nice timing."

Kim had two spots of color high on her cheeks. "Please don't get cross. I suppose I'm just saying that there might be other people more interested in Adam than you seem to be. People prepared to put him first, not work."

"People? You? Is that what you mean? Kim Deakin, if I didn't know better I'd think you were interested in him yourself." Lainey spoke in a mock-stern voice, trying to lighten the conversation.

"I'm just speaking hypothetically." But Kim wouldn't meet her eyes again. She stood up. "My turn to go to the bar. Can I get you anything?"

Speechless for once, Lainey just shook her head and watched as her friend walked away.

. . .

It was after one o'clock as she walked up the street arm in arm with Adam, a little unsteady from all the champagne she'd drunk and still thrown by her conversation with Kim. Moments after Kim had walked away, Christine had called for everyone to be quiet. She'd made a funny speech, then handed Lainey a large box marked THE B&B SURVIVAL PACK, filled with presents from them all. She'd unwrapped their gifts one by one—an apron embroidered with her name, a copy of *Mrs. Beeton's Book of Household Management,* binoculars to spy on suspicious guests. The final gift had been a Polaroid photo of all of them taken that night, minutes before she had arrived. They were holding up letters that spelled out Hurry Home. All of them except Kim, Lainey had noticed. Perhaps she'd been at the bar.

Was Kim right? Lainey wondered as they walked. Had she taken Adam for granted? A series of memories flashed into her mind. Adam ringing to invite her somewhere, her having to say no because she had a client dinner or other work to do. Or waking up beside him on weekend mornings and having to turn down his suggestion they stay in bed all day, because she had to go over to her parents' and give her mother a break . . .

Through the sudden clarity gained by drinking champagne all night, she realized Kim was right. She had taken Adam for granted. She'd never put him first. The revelation made it even more clear that she couldn't expect him to wait around for her while she was away for a year. Her stomach lurched at the idea, but she knew it had to be done. She had to break up with him this evening. This couldn't wait any longer. But how to start a conversation like that?

She squeezed his arm. "Ad, can you sit here with me for a minute?" She pulled him down onto a low wall beside them. "I know we've talked about this, but how do you really feel about me going away?"

He smiled at her. "The same way I felt when you first asked me. And when you asked me a week ago. And yesterday. I'm going to miss you very much but I know it's something you have to do. We don't have a choice."

Yes, we do, she thought, wondering where her clear-minded decision-making had gone all of a sudden. She tried another tack. "What if you meet someone else while I'm away?"

"But I won't."

"But you might. Seriously, think about it. If you met someone else while I was away and you thought she was lovely and you were interested in her and she was interested in you, what would you do?"

"What if you meet someone in Ireland?"

"I'm talking about you, not me. If someone said, oh, poor Adam, all on his own, that nasty Lainey out of the way, I'll give him a ring and see if he wants some company, what would you do?"

"Well, I'll mostly be throwing myself into work, of course, trying to distract my pining heart. But I might go out on one of my rare nights off. I know you wouldn't want me to mope for twelve months, howling like a dog."

"And if you did meet someone and they wanted to see you again? What then?"

"I promise to call you the moment I meet her, to keep you up-to-date. I'm sure she won't mind if I just nip out to a phone box, as long as I explain what I'm doing."

Why wasn't he listening to what she was saying? Was he actually laughing at her? She cursed the champagne she'd drunk. Her head was all muddled. "Adam, I'm serious."

"Can you stop organizing things for a single moment, do you think?" he said, laughing. He took her face between his hands and looked at her, then gently kissed her lips. "There's a difference between thinking and planning ahead and getting absolutely paranoid." As he looked at her his expression changed, became serious. "But while we're sitting here, there is something I'd like to talk to you about as well. I'd thought tomorrow would be the best time, but perhaps now is just as good."

There was something in his tone of voice that set all her antennae quivering. This was an Important Moment in their relationship, she knew it in her heart. And she wasn't ready for it. She turned panicked eyes on him. "Ad, I think it's too late."

"Too late for what?"

"Whatever it is you're about to say."

"What am I about to say?"

"Something mushy, I think."

He smiled at the childish term. "It's the night before you go away and abandon me for a year, of course I've got something mushy to say. Something more than mushy. Bigger than mushy."

Lainey had to fight a strong temptation to put her fingers in her ears. She hadn't expected this, not for a minute. She thought she'd get to say her piece, explain rationally why it was best they called it off. She thought that he would agree, perhaps a little sadly, but without fuss, and then they would part as friends. She hadn't thought he'd laugh at her, and she definitely hadn't thought he would turn the tables like this. "Ad, can this please wait till tomorrow? I think I'm too drunk at the moment." She cast her mind around for something to prove it. Could she sing a sea shanty in a loud voice? She stood up and walked a few meters, weaving across the footpath. "See, I can hardly walk a straight line."

He laughed. "All right, champagne girl. I give in. I'll leave it until tomorrow. Let's go home and go to bed instead. It's our last night together for a while, after all."

She sat down again, feeling an odd sense of relief that the moment for splitting up had passed. She really was too drunk to do it tonight. And why ruin their last night together? "I'm sorry, Ad. I'm just not in the mood for anything serious tonight. And I'm sorry for other things too. I do take you for granted, don't I? I'm too bossy, too judgmental, too organized, too pushy." What else had Kim and her friends said tonight?

"That's absolutely right, and too sweet, too generous and too drunk. Now, come on, let's go home. Which would you prefer, my bed or yours?"

She thought for a moment, then sadly shook her head. "I'm sorry, I'm too drunk to decide that either."

"The stairs it is, then," he said firmly.

CHAPTER 7

Lainey woke before the alarm the next morning to the glorious sensation of a pair of lips slowly kissing their way from her face to her neck to her breasts. She opened her eyes slowly, watching in the muted light of his bedroom as Adam moved slowly, surely down the length of her body.

"Adam?"

"Mmm?"

"We need to talk."

"Shh, I'm busy."

"Adam, wait . . ."

"Lainey, please, I'm really busy. Can't you see?"

She couldn't see it but she could feel it. As his lips and tongue found just the right spot, she shut her eyes again and turned her brain off as well. He was right, he was far too busy to talk.

• • •

An hour later, Lainey came down the front steps of her apartment building, squinting at the sunshine, her head throbbing slightly from the hangover. Her anxiety levels were hovering in the high to very high range now, as the time to leave came closer. She still hadn't had The Conversation with Adam. It had been too nice to be in bed with him, making love, feeling the length of his body on top of her, feeling his kisses, laughing at the outrageous compliments he liked to murmur while he made love to her.

There'd been the last-minute packing to do afterward. The last-minute checking to see her flat was ready for the new tenants to move into the next day. The last-minute ticket, passport and luggage check. Now Adam had gone to the underground parking lot and she was realizing they'd have to talk about it in the car. No, she decided, that wouldn't be any good either, not just before they called in to say goodbye to her parents and Rex. It would have to be in the car on the way to the airport. Or at the airport itself.

She heard her name being called and turned. It was her brother Hugh, running along the street toward her. Shorter and much stockier than Lainey and her other two brothers, he was panting by the time he reached her. "Shit! I knew I was cutting it fine. Are you on your way to the airport?"

"Just seconds away, Hughie. I thought you were going to be over at Ma and Dad's this morning. We're calling in there on the way."

"I know, but I stayed at a mate's house last night and my car's acting up this morning and I couldn't get out there. So I caught a tram here instead. I've got something for you. I made it myself." He passed over a present wrapped in what looked like handmade paper. "Have you got time to open it now? I'd really like to see what you think of it."

"Of course I have." She waved across at Adam as he drove out of the parking lot in Lainey's red hatchback. Adam was gazing at Hugh, trying to recognize this creature with the blue hair. Hugh had been blond when she and Adam first started going out, then bright scarlet for the past few months. "I like the new hair, by the way."

He tousled his blue locks. "Yeah, I needed a change. It's very calming, isn't it?"

"Right up there with dolphin sounds. I see it matches your shoes, too."

He wriggled his sky-blue Doc Marten boots. "Matching accessories are the key to style, Lainey, you should know that. Come on then, open the present."

She carefully removed the sticky tape and the paper. Inside was a flat cardboard square, covered in hand-painted drawings of beds and eggcups. "Oh, I get it, my life for the next year. Thanks, I'll hang it in the kitchen over there to remind me what I'm supposed to be doing each morning."

"No, it's not just a painting. Look closer."

She looked and this time noticed that there were per-forations around each bed and eggcup.

"It's a little reward-calendar for you, like an Advent cal-endar," he explained. "See, there are drawings of six beds and six eggcups, painted on little doors. At the end of each month you can open one up and there's a surprise for you behind them. I thought it might make the year go past more quickly. Or help you mark each month. Or something . . ." He trailed off, embarrassed.

She turned the drawing over and noticed cardboard pockets here and there on the back. She shook it gently and heard rattles. "This is fantastic, Hughie, thanks. What's in them?"

"Well, I did think about ecstasy tablets. To cheer you up when it gets too boring."

"Are you joking? I'll be arrested."

"Yeah, that's what I thought. No, they're just choco-lates. Nice stuff though. Swiss, full-cream milk. They cost me a fortune."

She was really touched. Hugh always had been the sweetest of her brothers. Brendan and Declan wouldn't have done something like this in a million years. "Hughie, thanks very much, you're a darling."

He shrugged, a little awkwardly. "I just wanted you to know I was glad you were doing it. You know, going to Ire-land for Dad. I know I couldn't do it."

"No, I don't think you could," Lainey said with a grin. "No offense."

"None taken. But if I can do anything to help from here, I will, I promise."

She ruffled his blue hair. "A soft heart beats under that wild exterior of yours, doesn't it? If I think of anything for you to do, I'll let you know, I promise."

Adam got out of the car, his mobile phone at his ear. As he walked closer, lifting a hand in hello to Hugh, they could overhear the conversation. "No way, Greg. No, sorry, you'll have to talk to her yourself."

"Is that Greg? Greg Gilroy?" Lainey mouthed the name of their café-owner friend. Adam nodded as he passed over the phone to her. Lainey put on a very cross voice. "Greg Gilroy, what are you doing calling me at a moment like this?"

"Lainey, I'm so desperately sorry to have to ask you this." Greg didn't sound in the least bit apologetic. "I've had an emergency and I need to borrow your boyfriend. Right now."

"But we're on our way to the airport. Can't it wait?" Out of the corner of her eye, she saw Hugh and Adam laughing. They'd always got on well together.

Greg had put on his best wheedling tone. "If it was up to me alone, sure. But I've got fifty guests about to arrive at my café for a special lunch and my first and second chefs are ill and I need your talented boyfriend right here and now."

"But Greg—"

"It's a birthday lunch for a very old lady, Lainey. Her hundredth, I think. Possibly even her hundred and tenth. Imagine her disappointment if I had to tell her, sorry, no food, I couldn't get a chef. A frail old lady like that."

"We're about to leave for the airport."

"Well, can't you have your tearful farewell there at the house as easily as at the airport? Fewer people around, far more private . . . I'll even organize your taxi to the airport, if you like. I took the liberty of ordering one to pick up Adam, seeing as his car's in the garage at the moment, but you can have that one and he can take your car. I'll cover the cost, of course."

"That's a lie and you know it. You still owe me for a taxi from six months ago. Hold on, Greg, let me do some sorting here." She turned to her brother, deep in conversation with Adam. "Excuse me, Hughie. Have you still got your license or have you been busted again for drunk driving?"

"It wasn't drunk driving. I was busted for driving without a license."

"But you're legal now?"

"After a fashion."

Lainey decided she didn't want to know what after a fashion might mean. "Would you have time to take me to the airport and then bring the car back here?" She noticed Adam didn't look happy at the idea.

Hugh did, though. "You're going to let me drive your car?"

"If you promise to bring it back here afterward."

"Can I go via my house? For a month or two, you know, take the long way? Till I can afford to fix my car up?"

She should have thought of offering it to him earlier. His car was always breaking down. "Of course you can."

"Cool, thanks."

Lainey spoke into the phone to Greg again. "All right, Greg, but you seriously owe me now." She hung up.

Adam wasn't pleased at all. "Lainey, I said no to him, it's our last morning together—"

She interrupted. "I had to agree, Ad. Greg's in dire straits and work is work, we both know that." She was oddly grateful to Greg. His call had placed it all in the right perspective. There was a time for emotions and there was a time for clear-headed, rational business thinking and it was that time right now. She'd have to say all she had to say to Adam here, it was as simple as that. "But I really need to talk to you before you go."

"I really need to talk to you, too. Have we time to go back inside, just you and I?"

That feeling of dread was back, as though she was in a dentist's waiting room. She tried to lighten the mood. "Good God, Adam, you're insatiable."

He didn't laugh. "Just for a moment?"

There was a particular look in his eyes. The look that made her feel good and warm and safe. The look that also unsettled her and made her anxious. She wasn't just in the dentist's waiting room anymore, she was now sitting in the chair with her mouth open, the drill coming closer and closer . . . She tried to ward it off a moment longer. "Ad, I really don't think we have got time, not if we're going to call in to see Ma and Dad on the way. And Hugh's driving is so appalling, I need to factor in near-accident time and all of that, too."

Hugh was listening to every word. "Lainey, that's rubbish, my driving's good these days."

"She's joking, Hughie," Adam said, before turning back to Lainey. He lowered his voice. "You see, I want to give you something. I had it all planned for the airport, in the club lounge, with a glass of champagne and a flowery speech . . ."

"Oh, this is just as nice," she said, looking around at the warehouse buildings, the road busy with traffic.

"It's not very romantic," Hugh said, edging even closer.

"Hugh, go away." Lainey and Adam spoke in unison.

He frowned. "Oh, come on. How am I going to learn about relationships if I don't observe those happening around me?"

"And how are you going to walk again if I break your legs?" Lainey said, glaring at him. After Hugh had made a show of sidling dejectedly toward her car, she turned back to Adam. Her stomach lurched again. "Ad, I need to say something to you, too, and I think I need to say it first."

He smiled. "I'm all ears."

She'd thought it over, rationally and for some days. She'd made her decision. There was now nothing to do but say it. "I think we should break up."

"I beg your pardon?"

"I think we should break up. Now, before I go to Ireland."

"Do you know, I think it's that subtle approach of yours that first drew me to you, Lainey. This is a joke, right?"

She shook her head. "No, Adam, it's not."

"You're telling me this is it, it's all over between us? You've just had this thought now? Minutes before you leave for the airport?" There was the rehearsal of a smile wavering over his face, as if he still wasn't sure if she was serious.

"No, not just now. I've been thinking about it since I found out I had to go."

His near-smile disappeared, giving way to something closer to shock, disbelief. He took the smallest of steps back from her as she kept talking.

"I don't think it's fair to ask you to wait for me. We really hardly know each other, you're up to your eyes with the restaurant. I just think it makes much more sense if we call it quits now, so we're both free to do whatever we need to do while I'm gone. What's the point of keeping it going when we're on opposite sides of the world? It's cleaner this way, don't you think?"

His voice was now as cold as his eyes. "Did you say what's the point? We really hardly know each other?"

She felt stuck for words, standing there, mouth open, shocked at his reaction. She grasped for something to say, searching for some justification for what she'd suggested. "We don't, Adam. You're so busy, I'm so busy, it hasn't been that serious, has it? For either of us? Don't you think it makes good sense to break up now?" It was coming out all wrong but she couldn't work out how to put it properly, how to tell him what she really meant. Not when he was looking at her like that.

"You've never heard of telephones? Keeping in touch by email? Letters? You're going to Ireland, not Mars, Lainey."

"It's too much to ask. You're so busy here, I'll be caught up with the B&B, I just think it's better this way." She knew her voice sounded firm, even though she was feeling shaky inside.

"And did you ever think that I might like a say in this? That I might have an opinion on what might or might not make sense? What was fair or unfair? Serious or not serious?"

His coldness helped strengthen her belief that she was right. "Of course I thought about you. I thought about both of us. I weighed all the pros and cons—"

"You weighed the pros and cons?" He narrowed his eyes, as if he couldn't quite believe what he was hearing. "And did you run through a complete cost analysis and profit and loss statement as well? We're not talking about a business here, for God's sake."

"Adam, please don't make this harder than it already is."

He slowly shook his head, his face stony. "Lainey, this can't get any harder than you've already made it. Or any worse." For a long moment he just stared at her as if he was seeing her for the first time. "I can't believe that this is how you've felt about me all this time."

She blundered in. "Please don't get me wrong, I've really enjoyed it, but—"

"But it wasn't serious for you. It was just two busy people having a bit of fun together in their spare time, nothing more than that. Is that what you mean?"

She stared at him, unable to answer. None of this was happening the way she'd pictured. He wasn't supposed to get upset, go cold. He was supposed to have agreed with her sensible decision, given her a nice affectionate hug and wished her well in Ireland. Not reacted like this. She desperately searched for something to say and grabbed the first thing that came to mind. "You said you wanted to say something to me as well?" Please let it be that you wanted to break up too. Please don't let it just be me that has made a stupid decision today.

He gave that laugh again, the awful one that wasn't in response to anything in the least bit funny. "Oh, yes, this is the perfect time to say what I had to say. I wanted to give you a present, actually. But hell, why not give it to you anyway? What else can I do with it?" He took a package out of his pocket and passed it without grace or ceremony to her. "I had it made especially for you."

Even his voice didn't sound like him anymore. She just looked at the parcel, not knowing what to do next.

"You may as well open it."

With shaking hands, she tore back the paper, opened the box. Inside was a silver bracelet, stunning, simple. Engraved on it was a sentence. *Come live with me and be my love.*

"Is it Shakespeare?" she said, sick to her stomach, but needing to say something.

His voice was flat. "No, it was Christopher Marlowe and then John Donne. I'd always loved that, the fact that two poets used the same line."

She hadn't known he read poetry. Her voice was soft. "It's a beautiful bracelet."

"Except you don't want it. Or you don't want the invitation. You don't want me."

She reacted against the sudden bitterness in his voice. "It's not that. I don't want to hurt you. But can't you see this is the best thing? What we have to do?"

"No, Lainey, I can't see. I thought things were terrific with us." He gave a mocking laugh. "Funny how wrong you can be, isn't it? You see, when I thought about you going away, I realized I hated the idea. And the more I thought about it the more I realized I didn't like us living in separate apartments, let alone separate countries, with some potted plant controlling when I see you or when I don't. I wanted to ask you to live with me when you got back from Ireland, Lainey. Marry me, if that was what you wanted. Have a tribe of children with me. Retire young and drive around Australia in a caravan with me." He paused. "Just as well I didn't, isn't it? Or I would have made an even bigger fool of myself than it seems I have already."

She felt as though she couldn't breathe. For one moment she wanted to give in completely. To just relax into it, fall into his arms, say you're right, to hell with going to Ireland, this is where I want to be. But then the moment passed and everything else came tumbling into her head. She was leaving for a year, she had so many other, bigger things than her own life to worry about—her father, her mother, her parents' marriage, the money they needed. There wasn't room for anyone else at the moment. Not even Adam . . . "I'm sorry, Adam." The words burst out of her.

"That's it? You're sorry?"

She couldn't change her mind now. Head, not heart, she repeated to herself. The look in his eyes nearly broke her resolve. They both looked down at the bracelet, still in her hands. She moved to pass it back to him.

He shook his head. "Take it. Have it anyway. Think of it as a farewell present. I'm sure a jeweler over there can get rid of the inscription."

His words stung. If this was the right thing to have done, why was she feeling as though the ground was crumbling beneath her? Had she misjudged it all? He wasn't supposed to have been upset. He wasn't supposed to have had this bracelet ready. And now it was too late to change anything. She blinked away tears, steeling herself, willing herself not to cry. "I'm sorry, Adam," she said again.

This wasn't the Adam she knew, this cold, angry one. "So am I, Lainey."

There was a loud honk of a car horn behind them. It was Hugh, leaning from the driver's seat of Lainey's car, pointing at his watch.

They both turned to him, then back to one another. There was an awkward moment when they moved as if to hug, moved their faces as if to kiss. Less than two hours ago they had been naked, entwined in each other's bodies. Now they could barely touch.

Finally, she brushed her lips against his. He wouldn't look at her, she could think of nothing more to say to him. He stepped back first.

Hugh enthusiastically honked the horn as they drove away, waving back at Adam who was standing by the foot-path. Then he glanced over at Lainey and gave a cheeky smile. "Lainey and Adam sitting in a tree, K-I-S-S-I-N-G."

"Shut up, Hugh."

"He just proposed to you, didn't he?"

"I said shut up, Hugh."

"He did. I saw him take a ring out of his pocket. Jeez, what style, in the middle of a road, with your brother watching. That's really romantic. Where are you going to get married, on the South-Eastern Freeway?"

She felt a searing rush of anger, at Hugh, at herself, at the whole stupid, messy, horrible bloody situation that she had just utterly mishandled. The feeling kept the tears away, leaving just a cold hard tightness. "Hugh, shut up. And you didn't see anything, all right? You don't say a word to Ma or Dad or anybody. Especially Declan."

"But I did see it."

"And I saw you moving those dope plants from the back of Ma's tomato garden last year and I never ever mentioned it. But I still can."

"Touché," he said with a wide grin, as he crunched the gears and pulled out onto the main road.

CHAPTER 8

Lainey stretched, hitting her arm against the wall and giving a surprised yelp. She wriggled, feeling a weight on the bed beside her. It felt cold, not the warm bundle Rex usually was. She slowly opened her eyes. This wasn't her bed, this wasn't her bedroom. The cold Rex was, in fact, her coat.

She was in Dublin, in Eva and Joseph's flat above the Ambrosia delicatessen and café. She must have been cold during the night and pulled the coat on top of her. She lay back, stretching again, stiff from the long flight, and listened to the sounds around her—the traffic two floors down on Camden Street, the faint noise of a siren, a car radio. She knelt up on the bed and peered out the window. She was definitely in a different hemisphere. The sky outside was Irish February gray, not the blue, blazing February sun she had left behind in Melbourne a day and a half before. She opened the window and leaned out into the cold air, shivering, dragging the warm quilt up around her shoulders. The travel agent opposite was advertising cheap fares to European capitals. Down the road two men were unloading shiny silver kegs from a brewery truck, passing them down into a hole in the footpath in front of a shuttered pub. Directly below her window was a double-decker bus, its roof damp with rain.

Draping the warm quilt over her pajamas, Lainey came out into the living room. It was a lovely room, the walls covered in sketches and paintings, the sofa a deep green, shelves piled high with books. There were framed photographs displayed on the walls and shelves. Lainey glanced at a few of them—many of them were of her and Eva, as children and during their Dunshaughlin schooldays. They hadn't changed drastically over the years—she was still at least a head taller than Eva, and Eva still had that gorgeous long dark hair and big beautiful smile. There were several photos from the wedding, fun, informal ones that exactly captured the mood of the day. There was a lovely one of Eva, tall, dark-eyed Joseph and herself, the three of them dressed to the nines, laughing at something. Joseph's hair probably—despite their best efforts, his black hair had stuck up in tufts all day long. Not that Eva had minded, Lainey remembered. Her friend had just beamed with happiness all day long. She put the photo down and looked around the room again, admiring it. Eva's uncle Ambrose, who owned the delicatessen and the building, had given them complete freedom to do what they wanted, Eva had told Lainey. "He's traveling all the time these days, said he only needs the small flat upstairs to come home and recover for a week or so before he heads off again. We've the run of the place really."

There was no sign of either of them. Lainey guessed that Eva was downstairs in the delicatessen and Joseph had mentioned the evening before that he had an early start at art college. After working for many years as an industrial designer in London, he was now studying jewelry design. Lainey had a quick shower, changed into a warm jumper, a long woolen skirt and boots. On her bedside table was Adam's silver bracelet. During the flight she had taken it from her bag, put it on, taken it off again, then finally left it on. She looked at it for a moment now, then put it on again, pushing it under her sleeve out of sight.

She came down the front stairs that led directly into the Ambrosia delicatessen and café. Eva was behind the counter, wearing a white apron over a bright-red shirt, her long dark hair pulled back in a braid. She looked up and gave Lainey a big smile. "Well, good morning. It's Sleeping Beauty herself."

Lainey pulled a face. "Sleeping Troll, more like it. I feel like I flew Gnome Airlines." She gazed around the delicatessen and café and breathed deeply. "You lucky, lucky girl, Eva Mary. Imagine coming into this for work every morning. It's like Aladdin's cave, isn't it? All the smells and the colors. I'd live down here if I were you."

"I practically do sometimes. How are you feeling? Did you manage to sleep?"

"Sleep or coma, one of the two. I didn't even hear you get up." Lainey yawned. "Oh, I'm sorry, I've left my manners on the plane. Joe's gone to college, I guess?"

"He has, but he said to say good morning to you."

"When did he say that? After he'd brought you breakfast in bed after rising at dawn to skip down to the park and hand-pick a bunch of rare blooms for you?"

"Cup of tea in bed, yes. But no flowers. Not today. That's just at weekends. Now, what do you want for breakfast?"

"Another ten hours' sleep and a full-body massage."

"Can't help you there, I'm afraid. But I can make you a huge pot of coffee. And I can pull a few strings and get you the best table in the house and even make your breakfast myself."

Lainey looked blearily at her friend. "Evie, are you the cook here now as well? Oh God, did you tell me that last night and I forgot? I'm so sorry, I must be hungover as well as jetlagged."

"No, I only cook on special occasions. Like when my cook hasn't arrived for the day's work yet because it's only eight a.m. and we don't open until nine. And when my best friend has arrived from Australia and I want to spoil her. So what would you like? Bacon and eggs? Pancakes? Toast and a hundred different jams? An omelet made with fresh herbs? I've started up a little herb garden out the back. That would perk you up."

"You can't cook for me. You'll just put me to shame for the year to come, when I see what you can serve up compared to the muck my guests will be eating. Come on, grab your coat and let's go somewhere else. My treat."

Eva left a quick note for her assistant manager, who was due to arrive any moment. Then they walked out into the cold, crisp air, down Camden Street, past the tailor, the pottery shop, the charity shops, all still closed. Lainey breathed deeply. Dublin didn't just look different to Melbourne, it smelled different. The air was a mixture of winter smells, fresh rain on pavements, a hint of smoke from open fires burning in nearby houses, beer and Guinness aromas from the pubs along the street. They hurried into the warmth of a small diner on the corner, more smells adding to the mix—warm toast, sizzling bacon, hot tea. Lainey found a table at the back, while Eva stood at the counter and ordered a full breakfast for each of them. The windows were covered with condensation. Lainey used her sleeve to rub a little porthole to look out at the crowded pavements, the double-decker buses, the newsagent opposite selling copies of the *Irish Times* and the *Irish Independent*. "I'm hallucinating, Evie, aren't I?" she said as Eva took the seat opposite, balancing two cups and a very large pot of steaming tea. "I'm not really sitting in a café in Dublin having breakfast with you a few hours before I take possession of a bed-and-breakfast for a year?"

"I'm afraid you are. Are you feeling a bit weird after the flight? I'm not surprised, that journey really took it out of me as well."

Lainey was feeling not just weird, but heavyhearted, and she knew the flight wasn't completely to blame. She produced a smile from somewhere. "Oh, I think it's more astonishment than jet lag, to be honest. Do you know what I should have been doing today? I should have been at the new museum in Melbourne, overseeing the launch of a new exhibition, mingling with guests, checking that there was enough champagne, thinking I might go down to the beach for a late swim. That's my real life, not this, surely?"

"Actually, you did say something along those lines last night." Eva grinned. "In fact, you were outspoken about quite a few things last night."

Lainey winced. "Oh no, was I? I was so wired after all the delays with the flights, I bet I wasn't making any sense at all."

"No, you were very clear actually," Eva said nonchalantly as she poured their tea. "A little outraged about the cold. Appalled at the traffic, why didn't we get trams like Melbourne, so much more efficient. Then you cursed your aunt a fair bit, double-cursed the insurance company for refusing to pay up, told Joe he treated me far too well and I'd turn into a spoiled brat if he wasn't careful. Then you rang your parents, drank most of a bottle of wine, sort of collapsed on the couch and we put you to bed."

Lainey put her head in her hands then looked up, laughing. "Well, they do say the secret to a long life is to speak your mind, not let anything build up."

"Then you'll live to be one hundred years old at least. Actually, Lainey, you talked about lots of things last night except Adam. You very obviously didn't talk about Adam."

A long pause. "Is that right?"

"Did you do it, then?" Eva asked gently. "Break up with him?"

Lainey nodded.

"And was he okay about it?"

Lainey dug her nails into her palms to keep the tears from welling. "Um, no, he wasn't exactly okay." She dug the nails in harder. "Evie, do you mind if I don't talk about this just yet? I still think it was the right thing to do, it's just I was a bit surprised—"

"How much he didn't want it?"

Head, not heart. She *had* made the right decision. She surreptitiously pushed the silver bracelet further up her sleeve and spoke firmly. "He'll realize it was the right thing too, once he's back at work, flat-out busy again."

"And *you're* still sure it was the right thing to do?"

Lainey wasn't sure of anything in her life anymore, but she needed to be. She longed to be. She sat up straight. "I'm sure."

Eva looked at her for a moment, then seemed to decide this wasn't the time to ask any more. She held up her teacup in a toast. "In that case then, here's to your big adventure."

"Adventure?" Lainey laughed, relieved at the change of subject. "What's adventurous about making beds?"

"All right, here's to your big challenge."

"Oh yes. Will I or will I not be able to cook six dozen eggs a week?"

Eva was laughing now too. "Here's to your extended holiday?"

"It's not a holiday either, Evie, not really. It's not like when I was here for your wedding, that was like being trapped in some wonderful golden bubble. This is real life now." Her tone changed. "And it's not really my country anymore. It's all different, isn't it? Prosperous, booming, go-ahead."

"Lainey, that's all just surface stuff. Nothing's changed really, I don't think. And you've come back to run a B&B, remember, not be the president. You'll fit in again straightaway. It'll be like falling off a bike."

"Muddy and painful? I hope not."

"Anyway, you'll be so busy chasing away guests you'll hardly notice where you are. The time will fly, you wait and see."

* ' * *

Lainey was in her rental car on the road out of Dublin just after lunchtime, in plenty of time to make her late-afternoon appointment with her aunt's solicitor in Dunshaughlin.

As she drove, she was struck by an overwhelming feeling of being home, being within a familiar landscape. She loved the feel of Dublin, the crammed streets, the River Liffey winding through the center, the shops packed tightly beside one another. On the surface, it was any city—people hurrying back to work, others out shopping, the footpaths crowded with a lively mixture of people, their umbrellas and bright winter scarves adding splashes of color to the moving picture. The streets were crammed with modern cars, crowded buses, some packed with tourists, others with commuters, jostling with taxis and cyclists, just as they would be at home in Melbourne. But in Melbourne she wouldn't be driving past Trinity College, or the curved Bank of Ireland building, or over the river down O'Connell Street, past familiar shops like Eason's bookshop, Clerys department store, the GPO, a gaggle of tourists outside probably being told of its role during the 1916 Easter Rising. And her car radio in Melbourne wouldn't have been playing the RTÉ jingles and the announcers wouldn't have Irish accents or be having a phone-in on the latest clashes between Fianna Fáil and Fine Gael, the two main political parties. "I'm in Ireland," she said aloud. "This is Ireland. I'm home." Saying it aloud helped make it real.

As she left the city center she passed suburban streets

lined with rows of identical terrace houses, many with little porches out the front as protection against the wind and rain. She drove past little pockets of shops and pubs, the signage on many of them new but the lettering raised and ornate, in the old-fashioned style. A new highway took her past the sprawling outer suburbs, past large shopping centers and new housing estates. Soon there were fields, each a different shade of green, stretching out either side of the road, their colors softened by the mist, the trees bare but beautiful in the gentle light. Everything was vivid to her, the green road signs, showing their destinations in Irish and English. The cars on the road boasted their Irishness too, their number plates advertising which county of Ireland the drivers were from, D for Dublin, C for Cork, G for Galway. She tried running through the thirty-two counties of Ireland in her head and was embarrassed to find she got stuck about three-quarters of the way through. A scandalous state of affairs, she thought. She'd have to fix that as soon as she could. Buy an "Ireland for Beginners and Returned Emigrants" guidebook perhaps.

She'd been driving for less than thirty minutes when she saw the sign up ahead. DÚN SEACHLAINN. DUNSHAUGHLIN." Her old hometown. She hadn't had time to visit the previous year, too busy with Eva and Joseph's wedding. The last time she'd been here was ten years before, when she'd come home for two months' holiday.

She pulled over just as she reached the start of the main street. It was like a different town. There were new shops, new pubs, new street lighting and the footpaths were as crowded with people as Dublin had been. She'd always told people she'd grown up in a small country town just outside Dublin. She couldn't say that anymore. She started the car again and drove until she reached her family's old house, a bungalow on what used to be the edge of town. It was now surrounded by new housing estates. Eva and her parents and sister Cathy had lived just a few doors up. She slowed, debating whether to get out and knock on the door, ask the new owners if they minded if she had a quick look inside. They'd probably think she'd come to rob the place, she decided. There was no rush, in any case, she was here for a year. She could ease herself back in slowly.

Her mobile phone rang as she drove away, the tone loud in the small car. She pulled over again.

"Miss Elaine Byrne?"

"That's right."

"This is Deirdre from Fogarty and Gleeson solicitors. I'm afraid Mr. Fogarty has been delayed in court and won't be able to meet with you this afternoon after all. He's sorry for any inconvenience."

Damn, Lainey thought. She'd been expecting to pick up the keys to the B&B from him so she could stay in the house that night. "Can I still get the keys this afternoon, though? We could run through the legal side of things tomorrow."

"Oh, I'm afraid not. There are quite a few documents to sign before Mr. Fogarty can legally give you the keys. And he does of course want to fill you in on the whole situation."

"The whole situation? Is there something we haven't been told yet?"

The voice became prim. "I'm afraid it's up to Mr. Fogarty, not me, to advise you of those particular details."

"I see." Lainey checked her watch. It would be dark soon, the roads already wet and too slippery for her liking, especially driving an unfamiliar car. She could turn around and go back to Dublin, stay another night with Eva and Joe. But she decided to keep going. "Never mind. I'll call in to you in the morning instead, then? About ten? Eleven? That's grand. Thank you." That's grand? Here less than one day and she was back using Irish phrases. She pulled back out onto the main road, deciding she'd just book into a B&B for the night. Then she changed her mind. She'd book into a hotel in Navan, the next big town. She'd be staying in a B&B for the next 365 nights. The 366th night could just tip her over the edge.

She'd driven past the first turn-off to the Hill of Tara when she decided she couldn't wait until the morning to see the B&B. It wouldn't matter if she had a look at it from the outside, surely. She took the second turn-off a few miles further on, surprised at how familiar the road seemed. It had been years since she'd been here, but they had visited often when she was a child, either to see May or for family picnics on the Hill itself.

The road was as narrow as ever, the trees on either side bare, the hedges dripping from the rain. She passed two other cars, pulling in close to the side of the road to avoid them and then even closer when a tourist bus appeared around one bend. "Bloody hell," she said aloud, as she felt her wheels slip. She looked over her shoulder. The bus driver was oblivious, heading back toward the main road. Hill of Tara, tick, Lainey thought. What next for the tour group? The nearby Trim Castle probably. They'd want to hurry if that was the case. It'd be dark before too long. She rounded a corner, turned left down a bumpy lane for a few hundred yards and there it was in front of her. Her home for the next twelve months.

It looked awful.

There was no other word for it. It had been just over seven weeks since Aunt May had died, but the house looked like it hadn't been lived in for years. It was two-story, built of a dark stone that was smothered in parts by thick ivy. A small porch was attached to the front, in urgent need of a coat of paint, the bricks mottled and unappealing. There were two big windows on either side of the porch and another two on the first floor. The B&B sign was stuck on the front of the house, half covered in ivy. Lainey looked over her shoulder to see if there was another sign on the front wall. There wasn't. You'd have to know what you were looking for to find this place.

She got out of the car, hugged her jumper close around her and pushed the gate. It swung open easily. The path leading to the house was overgrown. She walked closer, half expecting to see a flash of lightning, bats flapping around the chimneys, the silhouette of an old woman in a rocking chair in one of the top windows. The dark afternoon didn't help, the mist adding to the air of gloom.

There was a faded sign by the front door. GREEN GABLES, Lainey read. She didn't remember it being called by that name. She looked up. The gables were actually red. She tried the front porch door and the back door. Both were secure. She peered through the windows, but the lace curtains were fully across and the heavy drapes half drawn, blocking any view she might have had. That pleasure would have to wait until tomorrow. A drizzle of rain started, carried in a gust of cold wind. She shivered and ran back down the path.

From the warmth of the car, she studied the house again. All right, it looked grim but what had she expected? A house crammed with smiling guests, waving through the windows? A bright blue sky, swaying palm trees, brightly colored flowers in the garden? After all, it wasn't the house's fault she'd arrived on a bleak midwinter February afternoon. And once she did a bit of weeding, got the fire going, had a comforting stream of smoke pouring from the chimney, fixed up that sign, it would be warm and welcoming.

As she started the car, she remembered something else she needed to do before she went on to her hotel. Her aunt's ashes had been scattered on the Hill of Tara. If there had been a grave site she would have visited it, paid her respects on behalf of the family. Even though it was cold and darkening quickly, she decided to visit Tara right then. Her father would have wanted her to, surely.

The parking lot beside the café and gift shop at the foot of the hill was half full. Things had changed here, too, she realized as she looked around. When she used to come here as a child, there was nothing formal like a nice coffee shop. She remembered her father remarking on it with some pleasure. He'd loved its wildness and windswept fields, the fact that the site of the ancient capital of Ireland was so undeveloped and accessible.

She parked her car and got out, gasping as a cold wind tugged at her jumper. She was out of the shelter of the

valley now, the wind fierce across the fields. She opened
the backdoor and rummaged in her overnight bag until
she pulled out her big sheepskin jacket. Buttoning it up
tight and pulling the hood over her head, she faced the
wind again.

She'd heard there had been lots of improvements to
the site over the years but the same entrance was still
there, with the curved bars and unusual swinging gate,
designed to stop the sheep that grazed on the hill from
escaping. Inside the gate was a new sign spelling out the
history of the site.

The path had been improved, gravel laid down in a
curve, heading toward the old church, which was surrounded by a clump of trees and gravestones. She didn't
follow it all the way, wanting to go up onto the Hill itself
first. To her left was a tall, white statue of St. Patrick on a
stone plinth, enclosed by an iron fence. He'd moved
since she'd been here last, from the top of the Hill to this
new position—was he the latest in Ireland's miraculous
moving statue phenomena? she wondered. The ground
was springy beneath her feet, the air damp with mist. Her
shoes were getting wet from the long grass. She reached
the first ditch and leaped over it, remembering the first
time she had seen aerial photos of Tara. What they had
thought of as ordinary ditches had been revealed as foun-
dations of ancient buildings and burial mounds, curving
in rings across the green fields. She remembered describing all of this to Adam, how interested he'd been, all the
questions he'd asked. Then that memory sparked other
memories and she had to stop herself thinking about
him anymore.

She kept walking, heading up onto the top of the Hill itself. The county of Meath lay all around her, the mist obscuring much of the view but adding to the quiet. There were no buildings up here, just green fields stretching on either side, rising and falling into grass-covered ditches and mounds of earth, one marking the site of a prehistoric passage-tomb, another the site of a sacred well. Black-faced sheep grazed among them. Far off to the left of the Hill she saw a clump of people. A guided tour, she guessed. That was a shame, she'd have liked to have the place to herself.

She stopped near the Lia Fáil standing stone, the Stone of Destiny said to have been brought to Tara by the magical Tuatha de Danann people. She touched it, recalling the legend that it was supposed to roar when touched by a true king of Tara. There wasn't a sound out of it. It seemed she was still a mere mortal. Off to her right was the Celtic Cross, protected by an iron barrier. It was a good time of day to be here, the winter sun weak and watery, the light soft around her. She remembered standing here on a clear summer's day as a child with her father and brothers, Mr. Byrne pointing out all the other historic sites around them. "The most important county of all Ireland, this one is. See, all roads lead to Tara." He pointed out the Mountains of Mourne far off in the distance, the Hill of Slane, the Hill of Skryne. "And over there, those white stones in the distance, can you see them? That's Newgrange, more than five thousand years old, that tomb is. Legend has it the kings of Tara were all buried there."

"Hello, Aunt May," Lainey said quietly. This was a fine place to end up, part of the landscape, part of history.

She wondered if May had loved this place for its beauty or for its history alone. Perhaps she'd find out over the next year. Talk to her friends, learn more about her. She muttered a quick prayer for the repose of her soul, feeling self-conscious.

She stood for a moment longer, looking around, trying to imagine it in her mind's eye as it would have been centuries before, with kings, poets and heroes, horses and chariots leading parades, sacred rites and rituals taking place . . . Then a sheep bleated, and once again it became just an ordinary green hill with a good view.

The wind swirled around her and she shivered, turning back and heading through the other gateway that led into the churchyard. The light was failing but she wanted to have a quick look around, find the old stone with the carving that she and Eva had always thought was so rude. She remembered Eva, at ten or eleven years of age, being shocked by it. "Is it really a nudie lady showing her, you know, *bits*?" "It's not rude, Evie. It's a futility symbol," Lainey remembered answering. Behind her, her aunt May had overheard. "Fertility, actually, Elaine." Lainey had thought she'd detected a smile in her aunt's voice, but when she'd turned around her aunt's face had been serious as usual.

The carved stone was still there. It surprised her that something all those thousands of years old was lying out in the open, not under glass in some museum or covered up for being so rude. She pulled her jacket in around her and crouched down to look more closely at the stone, tracing the carvings with her finger.

"Leave that alone!"

She spun around. A bearded man was striding toward her, dressed in a tunic, cloak and heavy boots, a gold amulet on his chest. She blinked. Was she seeing things? He came closer. In a few seconds, she registered curly dark hair and angry eyes. "I've told you already, this isn't a theme park and these aren't souvenirs to be pawed over and damaged."

She stood up straight, stung at his words. "I wasn't pawing over it. And this is the first time you've asked me."

"No, it's not. I recognize your clothes."

Lainey looked down at her sheepskin jacket. "This old thing?" she joked. He didn't smile. She tried again, pushing the hood back off her head. "I think you've mistaken me for someone else. I really was just looking. And I just got here."

"You're not with that tour bus?"

"No."

His eyes stopped flashing at her. "I'm very sorry. There was a whole group of them, crawling all over the stones. I caught one of them trying to break off a bit as a souvenir and I thought you were her, back for a second attempt."

"Well, no, I have a bit more respect for my Irish heritage than that."

"You're Irish? You sound Australian."

"I'm back from Australia but I was born near here."

He nodded slowly. "And you're back home on holiday? Seeing the sights?"

He was a tour guide, she guessed. Which would explain the clothes as well. "No, I'm back to live for a year actually. Just down the road."

He smiled then. A big, sudden smile. "Lainey? It is you,

isn't it? Lainey Byrne? May Byrne's niece, come home to run the B&B?"

How did he know about that? "You know May? I mean, you knew May?"

"Everyone around here knew May. But you and I know each other too."

"We do?" She looked more closely. There was something familiar about him, though it was hard to tell with so much of his face covered with beard. Was it the eyes, now looking at her with amusement, waiting for her to remember him? Or that dark hair, a mass of curls in the wind?

A voice called out behind him. "Rohan, we need you right now. The light's perfect." It was a young woman carrying a clipboard and a walkie-talkie, looking curiously at Lainey.

"In a moment, Beth."

"Did she say Rohan?" Lainey said. "Not Rohan Hartigan?"

He grinned. "Right first time."

"Rohan Hartigan! I don't believe it. I haven't seen you in years." They shook hands.

"It must be seventeen years at least. How are you, Lainey?"

"I'm fine, just fine. And you?"

"Grand, thanks."

Looking at his smiling face, seeing the landmarks of Tara all around them, she suddenly remembered the circumstances of their last meeting. She was surprised at the rush of guilt she felt. "And your arm? That's grand too?"

He touched his elbow and then flexed it. "Oh, fully

recovered. I never did thank you for that card you sent to the hospital, did I?"

"I was so sorry about that accident, you know," she said quickly. "About what happened here that night—"

He gave a casual shrug. "We were just kids. And it's long forgiven and forgotten, Lainey, don't worry yourself."

Relieved to hear it, she hurried to change the subject. "So what are you doing here? I'd heard you left Ireland years ago."

"I did, but I'm back for a while. Just like you, it seems."

"Different circumstances, I hope?"

That hint of a smile again. "Oh, we're both servicing the tourists in our own way, I think."

Beth came closer. "Rohan, sorry to interrupt, but we really do have to get moving before we lose the good light. I'll tell them you're on your way, will I?"

"The good light?" Lainey asked the woman. "Good for what? Don't tell me I've stumbled on a clan of druids? You're about to sacrifice a goat or something?"

"Not exactly," Beth said with a grin. "We're filming the opening scene of a documentary about Tara. Our presenter fell ill today, and Rohan kindly offered to stand in for the silhouette scenes. Which we're about to lose for another day if we don't get a move on." She looked pointedly at Rohan.

Lainey turned too, taking in his outfit again. He appeared to be wearing thick tights under the tunic, presumably as protection against the freezing wind. "So this wouldn't be your everyday wear these days, Rohan?"

"Not everyday, Lainey, no," he said solemnly.

The walkie-talkie crackled. Beth spoke into it. "Yes, I know, we're coming. Rohan, sorry to boss, but . . ."

"I'll be right there." He turned to Lainey. "See you again soon, Lainey. And welcome home." As he started walking up the hill, Lainey saw his outfit in all its magnificence again.

"Rohan?"

He stopped and looked back.

"Nice tights, by the way."

She saw just a flash of a smile before he walked away.

CHAPTER 9

At eleven the next morning Lainey was sitting in a badly decorated room opposite Mr. Fogarty, the solicitor. As he moved around his office, taking folders from various piles here and there, she decided he was like a mouse changed into a man by a not wholly successful spell. She felt like a giant beside him. He was small, in height and build, and wore a neat little suit. She imagined his tail tucked safely away into a back pocket. His house would be small scale too, with tiny cupboards and a neat bed. Did he have a wife and children? They'd be tiny too, she supposed. With a tiny mouse-sized cat as a pet . . .

He found the folder he was looking for and settled into the chair on the other side of the desk. Lainey had to fight a temptation to see if his legs touched the ground or dangled over the edge of the chair.

"I do apologize for the inconvenience regarding my unavailability for yesterday afternoon's appointment, Miss Byrne. I trust your hotel accommodation was satisfactory last night?"

Why was he talking as though he had a bit part in a Charles Dickens BBC adaptation? "I did indeed, my good sire," she wanted to say. "Yes, thanks, it was fine," she said aloud. "And would I be able to get the key this morning? I'm anxious to have a look around the house, start getting things organized."

"Of course you are, and indeed you can have the key, once we have dealt with the necessary legalities, obtained your signature on several documents . . ."

Taken our snuff, ordered the coal, chased away some street urchins and enjoyed a fine glass of mead, Lainey thought. "Splendid," she said, smiling innocently.

An hour later she was wishing she did have a glass of mead. She'd never heard such a complicated will in her life, or signed her name so many times. She discovered May had also left various amounts of money to a number of local organizations, from the Meath Birdwatching Association to a local ceili band, all with detailed provisos, such as naming a new bird species after her, having an annual dance in honor of her. There was even a car for Lainey, an old but well-serviced Toyota Starlet, Mr. Fogarty told her, currently in the local garage being serviced, as directed in May's will. Lainey could collect it when she returned the rental car he assumed she had been driving. She was quite surprised to hear him say "driving," expecting "motoring" or "perambulating." Mr. Fogarty wanted her to be aware of every detail.

"Why did she go to all these lengths?" Lainey asked, blinking hard, battling either a sudden rush of jet lag or information overload.

Mr. Fogarty peered over his glasses. "Did you know your aunt well, Miss Byrne?"

"I'm afraid not. The last time I saw her I was a teenager, when we were back here on holiday, and when you're that age . . ." She left it there. When you're that age you don't care about crabby aunts in drafty B&Bs. They hadn't even stayed with her that time. Her father had thought it wiser for them to rent a house for a month, rather than be in May's pocket. And in May's debt, more to the point.

"To put it bluntly, Miss Byrne could be a very contrary woman."

Lainey waited for more. And waited. But it seemed that was all the solicitor was going to say. "I see," she said, even though she didn't. "And am I allowed to change things at all? Or has she left strict instructions on what sheets go on which bed and on which side of the plate I should put the bacon?" She knew she was being childish but the strangeness of it all was starting to catch up with her.

The solicitor scanned the document. "No, there is no wording to that effect. In fact, she has specified a sum to be used for 'living expenses and necessary refurbishments,' as she put it. It's a little premature to be making such plans, of course, as you haven't actually viewed the interior of the premises, but it seems she has made provisions for any such decision regarding interior decoration that you may make."

Lainey tried to make sense of his words. "There's some money for new paint and curtains if I want it, you mean?"

"Yes," he said, looking hurt that he needed to explain it further.

"And can you give me any idea what sort of occupancy rate she had? Being so close to the Hill of Tara, I presume she was full most nights?"

Mr. Fogarty gave a small cough. "I find it is best never to make too many presumptions, Miss Byrne."

"She wasn't full most nights, then?"

"No, not most nights."

"Some nights?"

"As I said, Miss Byrne could be a very contrary woman. Guests sometimes found her, how shall I put it, a little difficult to take. And I believe some of the other local tourism operators may have had difficulties as well."

This conversation was like doing a cryptic crossword. "Do you mean she rubbed people the wrong way?"

"Some people may say that."

"Would you?"

"I wasn't paid by your aunt to offer opinions of that sort, Miss Byrne."

She tried another tack. "Would you be able to find a causal link then between the fact that my aunt was a woman of strong and presumably frequently expressed opinions, and the fact that in recent years fewer and fewer people were staying in her bed-and-breakfast lodge?" She wished she carried a horsehair wig in her handbag. She would have slipped it on.

Mr. Fogarty squirmed in his seat. "Perhaps," he conceded after a moment.

"So I have a little bridge building to do in the local area, would you say?"

"That could be one way of looking at it."

"With who exactly? The tourist association? The other B&B operators?"

"They would probably be good places to start."

"To start? There are other bridges to build as well?" She'd come all this way to be a civil engineer?

"I understand she had several differences of opinion with the national tourism body."

"But wouldn't they be the people who would recommend her B&B?"

"Under normal circumstances, yes, they would."

But not under these circumstances, it seemed. "But she advertised the B&B in tourist guides and booklets, I presume?"

"I believe she used to, yes."

"She used to?"

"Until she had something of a falling-out with some of the publishers."

"What do you mean by something of a falling-out?"

Mr. Fogarty looked uncomfortable. "I understand there was a disagreement about the placement of one of her ads several years ago and a lawsuit ensued."

"She sued about the placement of a B&B ad?"

"I think she was unhappy with the way the photo of the house looked, too."

"And did she win this lawsuit?"

"Oh no, of course not. But unfortunately the publisher was the leading tourism publisher in the area, and I understand they refused to take any more ads from her."

Lainey frowned. "So if she didn't get recommendations from other B&Bs, if she didn't advertise, if she wasn't part of any tourism association, how did she get any business? Just from a sign on the side of the road?"

"Unfortunately there was a small problem with that sign."

"What, she broke it in two over someone's head?"

"No, I believe there was a disagreement with the local council regarding the permitted size of signs and placement on the roadway."

"All right, Mr. Fogarty, I give up. How did my aunt attract customers to her B&B?"

A long silence. "The fact of the matter is she didn't in recent years."

"She didn't?"

"Not really."

"No one stayed in her B&B, is that what you're saying?"

"I don't think it's strictly true to say no one. It's probably more accurate to say her B&B didn't enjoy the highest occupancy rates of guesthouses in the area."

"Hardly anyone stayed with her, you mean?"

"That's another way of putting it, yes."

"Mr. Fogarty, can I get this straight in my head? A condition of the will is that we are unable to sell the B&B until we have been running it for a year?"

He nodded.

"Even though my aunt's B&B seems to have been less popular as a guesthouse than the Amityville House of Horror?"

Another nod.

Her idea of stepping straight into a working B&B, greeting guests and prancing about with a teapot was dissolving before her eyes. "I'm sorry if I seem a bit dim, but what am I supposed to do for a year if I don't actually get any guests? Go out on the main road and club some tourists as they drive past? Drag them home?"

His little lips twitched into an almost-smile. "It could be worse. Looking on the bright side, she did have new plumbing put in last year. That will help when you want to sell it in twelve months' time."

When they sold it in twelve months' time. A glance in a property shop in Dunshaughlin that morning had given her a rough guide to the sort of price she could get. House and land prices in Ireland had skyrocketed in recent years. The Hill of Tara was less than an hour from Dublin. Lainey knew that the proceeds from the sale would keep her father in top-class medical treatment for more years than he would probably need.

Mr. Fogarty looked at his watch. "I'm afraid I have another appointment, Miss Byrne. If you have any other questions, perhaps we could arrange to meet again later in the week."

"Thank you, Mr. Fogarty. But in the meantime, may I now have the keys?" Prithee and forsooth. She'd become as eighteenth-century polite as him.

He flicked through the pages, checking he had all the signatures he needed. "Yes, it all appears to be in order now." He reached into the desk and handed her a large bunch of keys. "Mrs. Gillespie, your aunt's neighbor, has been keeping an eye on the place these past weeks, feeding the chickens and suchlike."

"The chickens?"

"It's a B&B," he said mildly. "You need eggs. It's been a while since you were in the house, I suppose?"

"I drove past it yesterday, but yes, it's been some years since I was inside. Well, thank you, Mr. Fogarty. I'll be in touch again soon, I'm sure. When I have more of an idea about how things stand."

"I'll look forward to seeing you, Lainey." She was surprised at his sudden drop in formality. He gave her a warm smile, sweet in his little mouse face.

As instructed, Lainey swapped her rental car for her aunt May's car at the garage, then drove back toward Tara. This time she parked right in front of the B&B and stood looking at it again before she went inside. No, it hadn't got any cheerier since the previous day. But it was hers now, and she felt her fingers itching to get stuck into it.

The key opened the front door easily. Lainey was surprised, expecting it to stick or to open slowly with a loud creak, revealing a hall with a suit of armor and portraits with real eyes following her around. She stepped into the hall, conscious that she was holding her breath. There was a staircase going up ahead of her, rooms off either side. She tried a switch—good, at least the lights were working. And it looked clean, at first glance, anyway. No cobwebs hanging in thick gray curtains in the hallway. It was many years since she had been in this house. Had the decorations changed since then? Lainey doubted it.

It was a big house. There were four rooms downstairs: a living room, a dining room with a long wooden table, a drawing room, then at the back of the house, a large kitchen—with a wood-fired stove, an Aga, in the corner. She was surprised at how pleased she was to see it. It wasn't lit yet, but she'd do it soon, if she could remember how to light a fire. It was years since she'd had to do anything but flick a switch to get heating.

She walked up the stairs. The landing had a small table and a dusty vase filled with artificial flowers. They'd be the first to go, she decided, tempted to throw them out right then. She stopped herself. She'd better look at everything first, in case they turned out to be the nicest thing in the house. Beside them was a pile of brochures promoting the nearby tourist attractions.

There were four good-sized guest bedrooms, two with double beds, two with two single beds each. All the rooms had handbasins in the corner, with gleaming new taps. The shared bathroom was at the back, also displaying new plumbing. Behind that was an extension with three smaller bedrooms. Her aunt's rooms? One had a bed, a large wardrobe filled with clothes, and a small table. The other two had just a cupboard and a single bed each, bare as nuns' cells. She opened one cupboard drawer. It was filled with blank paper, piles and piles of it. She opened another drawer. Envelopes, all different shapes and sizes. She tried one of the tall cupboards. More paper. It was like a stationery storeroom.

She returned to the guest bedrooms. They were all clean, but strangely uninviting. The carpet was ancient, the colors faded. Several smaller rugs had been thrown on top but the effect was still drab. She did a quick scan of the walls. The wallpaper and paint looked old, but at least there were no damp patches.

The house was very cold, though. She'd have to go and chop some more wood for the Aga and keep it burning twenty-four hours a day to get the chill out. Twenty-four-seven, even, she thought, remembering Celia and trying to ignore the sudden sick feeling the thought gave her. Then what she had to do was give the whole house a thorough spring-clean, from top to bottom, from corner to corner. Get to know it all, inch by inch, before she decided how to tackle it from a business point of view. She went downstairs again, ignoring the feeling of jet lag that

was trying to overwhelm her. This was no time for sleep—
she had work to do. She sat at the kitchen table, pulled
out her notebook and started writing a nice long list,
hoping that would make her feel normal.

Clean bedrooms
Clean kitchen and tidy pantry
Clean bathroom
Polish woodwork, furniture and floorboards
Wash windows and curtains
Sort linen cupboards
Sort May's clothes

It was like an Olympic event—the cleaning decathlon—
and that was just the inside of the house. The garden would
have to wait, she thought, looking out the window. The
trees in the garden were bare, the shrubs bedraggled, the
flowerbeds empty. There was a ragged-looking vegetable
patch beside what she presumed was the chicken run, a
small wooden hut surrounded by wire. The grass was a very
bright green, completely overgrown, spreading out in a
lush carpet toward the wall at the back of the garden. She
felt her spirits sink. Not so much a garden as a massively
overgrown higgledy-piggledy mess of green leafy stuff.

She made one more entry to her list.

Hire gardener

Then she looked outside again and added one more
word.

Tomorrow

F our days later Lainey looked around the kitchen and made a high-pitched sound of exasperation. Had she just imagined—dreamed, even, in her jet-lagged state—that she had been trying to clean it? She'd been at it since she arrived and it didn't look a scrap tidier. Every cupboard in the kitchen and all the shelves in the walk-in pantry had been crammed with cans, bags of flour, rice, bottles of oil, vinegar—most of them not even opened. It was as if her aunt had been given some insider tip that there was about to be a nuclear war and gone into a frenzy of food stockpiling. Lainey was discovering items that she hadn't seen since her childhood—malt, prunes, kippers, some of them in jars so old their seals had broken, the contents now seeping onto the shelves.

She'd needed to drive into Dunshaughlin twice to buy more cleaning products, having used up all of May's supplies by the end of the first day. She'd bought all earth-friendly biodegradable products to begin with, including a huge packet of bicarbonate of soda. She'd read in a book somewhere that it was the perfect cleaning product, could be used anywhere. Not in this house, though. Well, perhaps if she had ordered a truckload of the stuff, poured it through the windows, then hired a crane to shift and shake the house up until it went effervescent. She'd driven back to the supermarket and loaded up with chemicals instead. Sorry, environment, sorry, waterways, she thought, as she poured more fierce-smelling cleaning agents into the sink, hoping that would get rid of some of the stains. Her brother Brendan would kill her if he knew. Ever since he'd got the job with the recycling company nearly ten years before he'd been hounding them all to think of the environment and the water supply.

She jumped as a sudden shower of rain pelted drops against the kitchen window. No problems with the water supply here, at least. The KC and the Sunshine Band CD was playing loudly from the living room. She should have bought a Handel's *Water Music* CD instead. She looked out into the garden. At least it was looking a little more under control, even if the house was still a mess. Mr. Fogarty had recommended a local man, in his sixties at least, who had appeared the day before, grunted at her once or twice and then set to work with a mower and a spade for several hours. Lainey had wandered outside hoping for some conversation but been quickly disappointed. She was going to have to look further afield for friendship, it seemed.

Hearing a noise outside, she dropped the cleaning cloth and practically ran to the front door. She poked her head out just in time to see a tractor heading across into the field opposite the house. She waved to the farmer but he didn't see her. Damn. Still no chance of human contact. If it hadn't been for her regular phone calls with Eva she'd be starting to seriously worry for her sanity. She'd quickly learned a personality like hers was not suited to this kind of solitary confinement . . .

"Can you talk?" Eva had said in a theatrical whisper when she phoned on Lainey's first morning. "I left it until now so you'd have time to serve your guests' breakfasts."

"Guests? The only living creatures wanting breakfast around here are four chickens." She filled Eva in on her meeting with Mr. Fogarty. "Not quite what I expected, really. I'm hoping there's an entry for 'least popular B&B in Ireland' in this year's tourism awards. I'll be a shoo-in." Lainey was midway through describing the house when she remembered something much more interesting than old wallpaper and dusty cupboards. "Evie, forget the B&B for a minute. You'll never guess who I ran into on Tara the other night—Rohan Hartigan!"

"From school? I haven't seen him in years! What's he look like these days? Is he still gorgeous?"

"I couldn't tell, to be honest. He's grown this kind of bushy beard."

"A beard, oh, how awful. What are men thinking when they grow those things? They may as well glue a burlap bag to their chins. Why is he back in Meath? I'm sure my mother told me he'd left Ireland years ago."

"I've no idea. He was all dressed up filming a documentary or something about Tara. Perhaps he's an actor."

"How old would he be? Thirty-four, thirty-five? And is he married? Has he got kids?"

Lainey laughed at Eva's interest. "I don't know, I really only saw him for a minute."

"And has he forgiven you for the accident, do you think?"

"Forgiven and forgotten, he told me. I've been absolved of all guilt."

"Oh, good on him. He always was a lovely fellow." Eva's tone of voice changed then. "And are you feeling okay, Lainey? Not about Rohan and the B&B, but about Adam and everything?"

Please don't ask me, don't make me think about it any more than I already am. Thoughts of him had been constantly going through Lainey's head, what he might be doing, how he might be feeling . . . "I'm fine, really," she said in a bright voice.

"Really?"

"Really. Now enough about me, tell me about life in Dublin, Evie. Describe everything you can see, the cheeses, the olives, the bread. Have you had a lot of customers so far today? Did Joe get off to college on time this morning?"

"That is the most blatant attempt at a change in subject I have ever heard, Lainey Byrne."

It had worked, though. She'd managed to successfully steer the topic away from Adam during their other conversations too. They'd talked every day, sometimes twice a day since then. Eva had been keen to come down, but Lainey had begged a week or so's grace. "Let me make it as habitable as I can, then you can both come down and I'll spoil you to bits."

Making it "habitable" might have been wishful thinking, Lainey thought now, as she stood, hands on hips, looking around the kitchen. Perhaps she'd start with making the house "bearable" and work her way up to "habitable." She decided to abandon the kitchen for the time being and went upstairs to see if things were any better up there.

They weren't. She was momentarily depressed by the sight of her aunt's clothes piled on the beds in the back rooms. She'd emptied the wardrobes the day before, with hopes of finding classic Chanel dresses, Yves Saint Laurent jackets, pure Irish linen shirts, gorgeous vintage clothing that she could share with Eva. Sadly, her aunt had veered more toward the sensible tweed and trousers approach to clothing. She had also been at least six inches shorter and ten inches wider than Lainey. Off to charity shop heaven for all of them, she'd decided.

She shut the bedroom doors and turned instead to the job of sorting all the sheets she'd taken out of the linen cupboards. Her aunt might have been short on guests, but there was certainly no shortage of bed linen. Lainey had never seen so many sheets in her life. Perhaps her aunt had planned to open a fancy-dress shop for ghosts. There were enough white sheets to costume a truckload of Caspers. The worst of it was every one of them needed bleaching and washing. They had been lying unused in the cupboards for so long there were crease marks along the folds and a faint musty smell hanging around them.

They were good quality at least, Lainey guessed, standing in the landing surrounded by a billowing white pile. She had unfolded each of them, shaken them out and now felt like she was standing in the middle of a big white cloud. She made herself fall forward and landed with a big soft bump in the middle of them, laughing. Then the laugh died as she got a nose full of mustiness and dust.

* * *

She rang her parents that evening, determined to be upbeat, to put a positive spin on everything. Apart from ringing home the night she arrived in Dublin, she'd put off calling them again. She'd also only managed to send Christine and her other friends in Australia a very brief group email from her laptop computer, holding off until she could package the B&B story in a bright way.

Her mother was delighted to hear from her. "Lainey, love, how are you? We've been dying to hear all the news, but of course you've probably hardly had time to call, have you, looking after all those guests? How does everything look? We've been trying to picture you there."

Think of a feral version of *Better Homes and Gardens* and you'll be close. "Oh, it's a bit run-down, but Aunt May left some money in the will for some renovations, so I'm thinking about those already."

"You'll enjoy doing that, won't you? That's right up your alley, getting things organized. So how many people have you had staying so far?"

Lainey tried to buy some time. "So far?"

"Yes, since you've been there."

"Um, none, actually."

"None at all? What's wrong with the place?" Her mother was as blunt on the phone as she was in real life.

"I think it's a really quiet time for tourists," Lainey said, ignoring the memory of the B&B down the road that she'd passed that day, the one with the full parking lot.

"It's perfect really, gives me the chance to get the inside all spick-and-span before the peak season." Business tip number fifty in a continuing series: Always sound optimistic. Never let the client know you're worried. Be like a duck, serene on top, paddling like hell underneath. And change the subject as quickly as you can. "So, how are you all? How's Rex, more importantly?"

"Rex?" Mrs. Byrne made a derisive sound. "You've spoiled that cat so much he's convinced he's a small furry human, I'm sure of it. He gave me such a look last night when I tried to put him outside after dinner. If he'd been able to talk he would have been swearing, no question about it."

"You put him outside? Ma, Rex is an indoor cat. He hates being outside."

"So I discovered. He's got very sharp claws, hasn't he? Hold on, Lainey, I'm just walking into your father's room." She lowered her voice. "You're in luck, he's awake for once."

The phone was passed across. "How are you, Lainey?"

"I'm great, Dad. I've visited Tara, said farewell to May from all of us."

"Thank you, love. And everything's all right, is it? The weather's not too bad?"

Her father had never been great on the phone. Once he got on to the weather you knew he was trying to finish the call as quickly as he could. What could she expect, though? A cozy heart-to-heart about how he was really feeling, his worries for the future, how the accident had not only taken his health but somehow sapped his life spirit? She'd probably get such a shock she'd throw down the phone in surprise. No, she'd stick with the weather herself for the time being. "Not too bad, Dad. A little grayer than I'd like, but they're promising some good weather next week. And it means I don't have to worry about watering the garden, at least." She was surprised to hear herself give a hearty laugh. "And what about you? How are you?"

A few minutes later Lainey was wishing she hadn't asked. Her father hadn't had a good few days, it seemed, with an old pain getting worse and a new pain developing and no good sleep at all. She tried to be patient, stopping herself from saying aloud, "I'll get the money for you as soon as I can, I promise, but it is going to take a year." She interrupted. "No news from the insurance company since you sent them that last letter, I suppose?"

"Not a word. But they're only in a rush when they want something from me, not when I want something from them. I tell you, Lainey . . ." She was almost glad when her mother took the phone back and said goodbye.

"No change here, love, you might have guessed," Mrs. Byrne said in a whisper. "I'm in the kitchen now, out of his hearing."

"He's been bad?"

"Oh, no, it's been the House of Fun here. He's driving me up the walls, since you ask."

Lainey got the feeling of panic again. The same one she'd got in the coffee shop at the shopping center that night. "Ma, you're not going to leave him though, are you? I know a year seems a long time, but think of how much easier it'll be when we're able to sell this place and get the money for him. Honestly, it won't be long, I'll be back before you know it." Who was she trying to convince, herself or her mother? "So tell me some more news? How are the boys? Any big news from them?"

"You have only been gone a few days. No, they're all fine, I think."

Of course they were fine. Life in Melbourne went on as normal, while she was trapped in the Castle of Housework. "Well, I'd better go, in case someone is trying to ring and make a booking." She was surprised her nose didn't suddenly grow six inches, Pinocchio-style.

"Goodbye for now, then, love. And thanks again."

"It's my pleasure, honestly. I'm really enjoying it." She could almost hear a stretching noise as her nose grew even longer.

· · ·

That night she woke suddenly to find the room dark around her. Her first thought was fear, finding herself in a strange bedroom, unfamiliar furniture around her, the door and windows not where she expected them to be. Half awake, she instinctively felt for Adam's warm body beside her, wanting to fold her own body up against his, tuck herself into his shape, slide her hand around his waist. It took her a moment to realize she was in bed alone, in a strange house, out in the countryside on the other side of the world from Adam. She forced herself not to think of him. It was jet lag, that was all. She was still on Melbourne time. It always took her a week or so to adjust properly.

As she thought about her call home that night, she started worrying about her parents, her mother threatening to leave, her father spending day after day in bed. She squeezed her eyes tightly shut, like a child, but it didn't work. Like a horror film unfolding in her mind, she started thinking about the day of her father's accident. For months after it happened, the memory had been lying in wait for her each morning when she woke, was there each night as she tried to sleep, like some film on a pause button. It started again now, step by step, beginning with the phone call from her mother, the panicked sound in her voice, as she told Lainey to hurry to the hospital, to come as quickly as she could. A few key words kept appearing in Lainey's mind, as though they were engraved in big letters on her memory. Accident at work. Spinal damage. Loss of blood. Life-threatening.

She remembered the rushed trip to the hospital from her office, driving through the city streets, running through the hospital doors, feeling as though everyone else around her was moving in slow motion. Her father had been in the operating theater when she arrived, her mother and Brendan sitting hand in hand in the waiting room outside. Declan had arrived just minutes after her. Their father had been moved to the intensive-care ward by the time they were able to contact Hugh. Lainey remembered thinking how young Hugh had looked when he finally arrived, his hair spiky, bleached blond at that time. He'd looked like a round-faced chick, she'd thought. She'd pulled him to her in a big hug and he hadn't stopped her.

A knot of them had gathered outside the intensive-care ward, her mother, Declan, Brendan and two of their father's workmates. The two men were still in deep shock. One of the men kept describing the accident, how their father had been standing in the middle of the site, signaling for the crane to lower a concrete slab. How it had suddenly begun to slip from its chains, started to fall, as though it was in slow motion, though of course it had been just seconds. Over and over he had said that Gerry hadn't had a chance to get out of the way, that they thought he was dead, even as they somehow dragged the slab off him. Lainey had listened intently to the story each time, her eyes fixed on the man. As he had spoken, she had been aware of so many other things at the same time—the smell of the hospital, the voices of nurses and doctors, the ringing of telephones, the sitting in the ward corridor, the waiting . . .

"Stop it," she said aloud now, forcing herself not to go any further down that thought path. She made herself concentrate on the good things. He had pulled through. He had eventually come home from hospital. And he would walk again, without that horrible frame, just as soon as all the insurance money came through and all the proper treatment could start. Their family would get through this. It could have been so much worse, after all.

It worked, the positive thoughts calming her as usual. They reminded her too why she was here in this B&B, and stopped her from feeling sorry for herself. It was all going to work out perfectly well, wasn't it? She just had to get moving on it.

She sat up and looked out the window. Dawn was breaking, the dim light of the winter sun revealing a low, morning mist. The warm bedclothes tempted her again and she slid back under the covers so that only her nose and eyes were peeping out. She lay there, listening to the noises around her. There was a low, rumbling sort of sound, the water in the pipes leading to the central heating radiators. A quiet patter of rain against the window. Lainey took a hand out from under the bedclothes and tested the air temperature. Cold but not freezing. She huffed, and was pleased to see she couldn't see her own breath. In Melbourne she'd be hearing muted traffic noises, the occasional rumble of the trams on Bridge Road, early morning shouts from the rowing instructor on the Yarra River flowing beside her apartment building, urging his charges on. Adam had said once he was tempted to find out where that man lived and wake him up one morning with shouts from his front lawn, see how he liked it.

The memory made her smile.

* * *

By nine o'clock she was in full housekeeper mode again, carrying loads of wood into the kitchen, her hands protected from splinters by bright-orange oven mitts. No wonder her aunt hadn't needed Chanel dresses, she'd realized. There wasn't time to dress up with all this housework to be done. Lainey's usual wardrobe of designer skirts and dresses hadn't seen the light of day since she'd arrived, having been swapped for jeans and warm jumpers. The most makeup she'd worn was lip gloss. She hadn't bothered with hair mousse or blow-drying either, just running her fingers through her short dark hair after her shower each morning and leaving it at that. Businesswoman Barbie had turned into Rural Barbie.

She was glad she was so busy, relieved to be able to distract herself with all this physical work. All morning her head had kept filling with images of Adam, especially the look in his eyes the morning she'd broken up with him.

But not just the painful memories. She kept being surprised by thoughts of him, telling her a story, making her laugh. The notes he would leave her, written in flowery language one day, worthy of Shakespeare, or comically businesslike the next, set out in memo style.

It felt odd, unsettling, to even have the time to think about him like this. Her life was usually so crammed, every minute filled with activity, she didn't often have the luxury to think things over. She set herself goals, she reached them, then it was on to the next project. Occasionally at work there was a brief period of review, looking over what she'd done, picking any faults, making decisions about how to do things better, more efficiently, next time. She applied the same principles to her personal life. But now, with no work to do, no projects to think about and no clients to meet, there were vacancies in her thinking schedule and thoughts of Adam were filling them all.

She pictured his slightly crooked smile. His dark-brown eyes. His hats. She thought about the soft skin at the back of his neck, where she had liked to kiss him. He always smelled beautiful, clean and fresh, from either the soap or aftershave he used. She recalled little things about him—the way he was ticklish on his left side, but not his right. His habit of wearing odd-colored socks. The feel of his skin, even the little raised scars here and there on his hands, caused from burns and cuts in the kitchen. His enthusiasm for food, for music, everything from pop songs to classical symphonies . . .

It was no good. She had to stop herself from thinking about him. She had made her decision. There was no going back. Kim's words about taking him for granted suddenly came into her mind. But she hadn't, had she? She'd just taken him as he was, as he had taken her, in the only way they could have fitted into each other's life. *Come live with me and be my love.* She touched the bracelet on her arm. She'd hesitated that morning, then slipped it on again, without thinking too much why. She felt a tightness in her chest, the one that used to signify an imminent asthma attack and just as often these days meant she was feeling panicked. That things weren't under her control anymore. It was a horrible feeling.

* * *

She had just finished washing the kitchen windows the next day when she noticed the calendar stuck to the side of the fridge. It took her a moment to realize it was still turned to the date May died. On the square for January 22 May had written "protest/shopping center." What would she have done that morning? Lainey wondered. Fed the chickens, perhaps, then got dressed, got into her car, driven toward the shopping center, maybe even helped set up the table for the petitions against the new road, with no inkling that she was about to die, that any mess she had left behind would be found by someone else, any dishes she hadn't washed would have to be washed by someone else. That her will stating that a member of the Byrne family had to come and live here for a year before they could sell the place was about to be activated. What if she hadn't really meant that will to be her final one? God knows she had written dozens of other variations. It had been too late to change her mind, though. According to Mr. Fogarty, one minute May had been alive, urging someone to sign the petition, and the next minute her heart stopped, no chance of revival, even if there had been a doctor nearby.

"I'm sorry, May," Lainey whispered now. She'd been having the occasional one-sided conversation with her aunt, mostly in exasperation at the filthy cupboards and lack of guests. But seeing the calendar had softened her heart again, reminded her that May had been on her own here. Perhaps it was as well she'd died at the shopping center. If the heart attack had happened at home, it could have been days before she was found. That would have been far sadder.

Lainey decided to keep using May's calendar, feeling guilty enough about everything else she had thrown out. Life did go on. May had used the calendar until she died. There had been a short period of mourning, a few weeks when the calendar was unturned, and now Lainey was in residence and it was back in operation.

Except it wasn't in operation yet, was it? Not without any guests. It was a major worry. Not just for her own sanity, but also for the future value of the property. The family would be able to sell it for a much higher price if it was demonstrably a successful business, with existing clients, everything in place. But who would she attract the way things were at the moment? Gardening enthusiasts? Compulsive cleaners? Hermits?

"Stop that worrying," she said out loud, cross with herself. Once everything was spruced up a bit, of course she'd be able to get guests. There were plenty of ways of attracting them, after all. Advertisements for a start, of course, in local and national tourism publications, or even a web site, perhaps. And promotional flyers, too. Yes, she could produce some flyers as well. With a nice picture of the B&B on the front, a bit of information about the place, maybe a photo of one or two of the bedrooms. Once that hideous wallpaper was gone. And the carpets replaced. And the curtains taken down . . .

Slow down, Lainey, she told herself. Take it in steps. This is just another challenge. Break it down and tackle it bit by bit, day by day. Keep busy. Make lists . . . and above all, don't go crazy.

CHAPTER 11

I'm going crazy, Evie," Lainey said passionately into the phone several days later. "I've done so much housework I'm actually dreaming about mop buckets and scouring pads. And I'm stomping around the place, you should see me. Like a bad-tempered child." She had hung Hugh's B&B reward-calendar on the wall and it had taunted her so much she'd had to turn it face in. "I just can't understand it. My aunt didn't have any guests and she clearly didn't do any cleaning—what did she do with herself all day?"

"Redraft her will and go shopping for food products, by the sound of things," Eva said.

"Very funny." It was nice to be able to laugh about it. She'd been getting very worried. Each night she had lain in bed, fiercely concentrating on her mental pictures, distracting herself, imagining exactly what she wanted to happen . . .

The doorbell rang. She opened the front door and beamed a

*welcome at the busload of tourists waiting on the doorstep.
"Come in, all of you. Make yourselves at home."*

*She showed them to their rooms, happily accepting their com-
pliments about the wonderful smell of bread baking, the beautiful decor, the spectacular views of Tara from the sparkling clean
windows.*

*"Just wait till you try my bacon and eggs in the morning," she
said. "People tell me they are simply out of this world."*

She used the technique when a client was describing
the sort of event they wanted—she'd ask dozens of questions about it until she had a vision of it clear in her head
too, could run through it like an imaginary mind-film.
Positive visualization, she supposed it was. Imagining
something so strongly that you almost willed it to happen.

Except it didn't seem to be working here yet. "Evie, is
there anything I can do for you or Joe while I'm down
here? Have you any bread that needs kneading? You
could send it down on the morning bus, I could spend
the day kneading it and then send it back at teatime."

Eva laughed. "Could you ever just relax? You've been
going at full tilt for years. Maybe this is all happening for
a reason, to slow you down . . ."

"If you say anything about me taking up a hobby or
stopping to smell the roses, I swear I will . . . oh, I don't
know, drive up and bulldoze your café down."

"Well, have you thought about that? Gardening, I
mean. Couldn't you spend the days in the garden? Bring
the phone outside so you don't miss any calls? It would
paint a lovely rural picture if any potential guests drove
past."

"The only way potential guests will drive past is if I reroute the main road."

"Okay. Well, put the gardening in your diary for spring. Come on, you're the ideas person here. If our positions were reversed, what would you be telling me to do?"

"Fly straight back to Australia and tell your dad to start buying lottery tickets."

"No, you wouldn't."

"All right, let me think—am I allowed to suggest powerful medication?"

"No."

"Excess alcohol?"

"No."

"Hypnosis?"

"Lainey . . ."

"I know. Don't worry, I'm sure this is just culture shock. Stopping-full-time-work shock. Doing-too-much-housework shock. You're right—what I'll do is use this quiet time to really hone my washing and clothes-pegging skills. Do you know poor old May didn't even have a clothes dryer? If I ever actually get any guests, I'm going to have to take their sheets into the laundromat in town."

"How on earth did May manage on her own through the years?"

How did any B&B operator manage? Lainey wondered. It was like being in charge of a two-story brick baby. "Maybe she never washed them, just did that old trick of turning them around the other way."

"Oh, Lainey. She wouldn't have done that, would she? Imagine that, sleeping in someone else's sheets."

"I bet that's the real reason she didn't get any guests.

Word got round about the recycled bed linen." Lainey laughed at her own gloomy tone. "Eva, thanks a million, you've cheered me up again. You are the best friend a girl could have and when this is over I am going to take you and Joseph for the biggest, most expensive meal of your lives. Fly you to Monte Carlo for the weekend. Buy you matching his and hers sports cars. Hire Moby for a personal gig for you both. Send you on a world cruise or a—" She stopped as she heard the beep of another call coming in on Eva's line. "Sounds like you're in demand. I'd better let you go."

"That's a shame, I was enjoying your list of thank-yous. It'll be Joe ringing to say he's finished at college. We're heading out to meet some people tonight. And Lainey, I love that you're here. Do you know that? Even if you hate it."

"Hate it? I'm having the time of my life, really. And I love being near you, too. Have a great night and give Joe my love."

Lucky Evie, out with Joe and some other living human beings, Lainey thought as she hung up. She seemed to be existing only on phone conversations at the moment, unless she counted the grunting gardener and the three words she'd exchanged with the boy in the supermarket. In a normal day in Melbourne she'd talk to scores of people, from her colleagues, to her friends and family, to clients, to venue managers, caterers, sound technicians, costume hirers, lighting specialists, singers, actors and other entertainers, waitresses . . .

That was it, of course. She wasn't feeling this way because of Adam, she was just lonely—simple, run-of-the-mill lonely. Perhaps Eva was right, she should use this time to expand her life, develop a new interest. It must have been years since she'd had a hobby—unless running to keep fit counted, though that was more personal maintenance than hobbying. There wasn't time for anything else anymore. Any spare time she had—or any of her friends had, in fact—was spent exercising or catching up on sleep, not collecting porcelain figurines or birdwatching or watching *Star Wars* movies or spending the weekend dressed as medieval princesses and jousting with hay bales made up to look like horses. Rex was her interest, her little cat-love, but she could hardly classify him as her hobby, could she? He'd be appalled at the idea.

·   ·   ·

The phone rang the next morning just as she was on her way outside to tell the chickens there was still no rush with the eggs. It was Mr. Fogarty's secretary Deirdre. "Miss Byrne, we wanted to arrange a time for you to collect your aunt's papers."

"What papers?" Surely there couldn't be more. She'd left the office that first day with a wheelbarrow full as it was, between the will and the various codicils and explanatory booklets and circulars. She'd put them all straight into the kitchen drawer when she got home, glad to see the back of them for the time being.

"The ones we collected when we began clearing out her house after she died."

"Oh, I see. No problem. I'll come in right now." Good, she thought. Not only would she get to speak to some more human beings—she could put off cleaning the oven for another day.

. . .

There were five large folders waiting for her by the reception desk and no sign of the secretary. She heard a little rustle and turned around. "Oh, Mr. Fogarty. How are you?"

"Lainey, hello. You've come to collect your aunt's papers, I see. That's good. They've been taking up rather a lot of room these past few weeks."

They both looked over at the pile of folders. "There seems to be rather a lot of them," Lainey said.

Mr. Fogarty nodded solemnly. "Yes, she was a prodigious letter writer."

"Prodigious? Is that another word for bad?"

"No, plentiful. Letter writing was quite a hobby of hers, I believe."

"Did she leave any instructions about who should read them, whether they should go to anyone in particular?"

"No, nothing at all. Perhaps she had plans for them at a later date, but her death took her by surprise as much as it took the rest of us."

For some reason Lainey found that funny. "Yes, I suppose it did." She pinched the back of her hand to stop herself from laughing. "Did she have any close friends, Mr. Fogarty, who might prefer to look through them? I feel I'm prying slightly."

"Close friends? No, I don't suppose we would be able to stretch a point as far as that."

"So it's up to me what I want to do with them?"

"It is, I'm afraid. Your father might like to see them, perhaps. Or there is a paper recycling collection bin at the shopping center, if you decide that's the best option. From the brief glance I had, they seemed to be a mixture of the personal and the not very important."

"So you've seen them all yourself?"

"Oh, I've even received a few of them in my day. Good afternoon, Lainey."

There was a van parked outside the B&B when she arrived back. A young man was standing on the doorstep holding an enormous bunch of flowers. He glanced down at a clipboard in his hand as she walked toward him. "Lainey Byrne?"

"That's right."

"These are for you. Sign here, please."

They were from Adam. She read the note. *Thinking of you and your bed-and-breakfasts and missing you in my bed. Love, Adam*

"That's your boyfriend, is it? He rang a month ago and ordered these, said they had to be delivered to you sometime this week. You've got a romantic one there, love."

She'd barely shut the door behind her before she burst into tears.

. . .

She was still lying on the couch in the living room, the cushion damp under her cheek, when the phone rang. It was nearly dark outside. She sat up, tried to pull herself together and reached for the phone. "Green Gables B&B, Lainey speaking. Can I help you?"

"Lainey? You sound all choked up. Have you got that asthma back? You're going to have to go back to the doctor if that's the case."

It was her mother. She sat more upright, blinked hard

several times, determined not to start with the tears again, not to sound upset. "I'm fine, Ma. It must be the line." She cleared her throat. "How are things with you all?"

"Oh, no change here. How are things there, more to the point? We're dying to find out if you've had Hilly Robson and Noah Geddes staying with you yet."

An easy subject. Lainey leaped at it. "Ma, that's very hip of you. How do you even know about them?" The Australian actress had apparently started an affair with Noah the bad-boy English singer. The Irish Sunday papers had been full of the gossip that the two were apparently on holiday together somewhere in Europe. The racier paper had set up a hotline for readers to call if they spotted the pair anywhere in Ireland.

"Oh, they're all over the papers here too. Scandalous, isn't it? Why don't they leave the poor things alone? I was reading about them in all the magazines as well."

Lainey was pleased at the excuse to laugh. "That's why they don't leave them alone, Ma, because people like you enjoy reading about them in the magazines so you keep buying the magazines so the magazines keep running stories about them."

"Oh, stop that. You're sounding like Hugh. I can't make a comment about a newspaper or a TV show without him lecturing me about the sociological impact of modern media on today's society. Really, why couldn't he have decided to study plumbing or dentistry or something useful?"

"He's a fine one to talk, mister paparazzi-in-training himself. And how are the others going?"

"Oh, fine. Declan's happy at the school, Brendan's working all the hours God sends, as usual."

"And Rosie? Worn out watching daytime TV, I suppose?"

"Elaine, don't be catty. Just because she hasn't taken the career path you have doesn't mean she's not as busy. It's no picnic looking after two young babies, you know. The four of you had me up the walls half the time. Many's the time I would cheerfully have sold you to the gypsies."

"I'm sorry. I know she's busy. I'm just in a mean mood. And Dad?"

Mrs. Byrne's voice lowered. "Up and down. He's spent the last few days in bed, hardly come out at all, with your cat snoring away beside him, if you don't mind. We had a bit of a talk about things last night, as it happens."

Oh, her poor father, Lainey thought. Her mother's "bit of a talk" was usually more like "a bit of a lecture."

"I've asked him to get out of the house and—"

"Ma, you can't do that. Where's he going to go?"

"Lainey, don't interrupt me please, or of course you'll jump to conclusions. I've asked him to at least try and get out of the house once a week, even if it's just for a short trip in the car. I'm worried he's spending too much time in that room. I looked it up on the Internet, and all the medical sites say it's not good for him, lying there thinking about his own problems all the time. The thing to do is try and get him interested in the outside world a bit more, encourage him."

Lainey was relieved. Her mother didn't sound as though she was about to abandon her father, not if she was doing things like Web-surfing for solutions. "So where are you going to take him?"

"We haven't agreed on that yet. And it's only short trips, anyway. He can't cope sitting up for long. But it might take his mind off waiting to hear from the creatures from the black lagoon."

"The who?"

"The creatures from the black lagoon. That's what Hugh's started calling the insurance people. Apt, don't you think? So tell me, you and Adam are burning the phone lines between you, I suppose? Oh, here's your father now. Gerry, it's Lainey. Will you have a word?"

Her father came on the line. After giving him a thorough rundown on the meteorological conditions over Ireland the previous week, including mention of isobars, cloud formations and weather pressure systems, she remembered the folders of May's letters she'd collected from Mr. Fogarty. She switched from weather girl mode and told her father about them. "So would you like me to ship them back to you in Melbourne?"

"Ship them to me? Why? What would I want with any of them, Lainey?"

"She was your sister. Aren't you interested in her life, in what she was up to?"

"Not to that extent. She wouldn't like me to have known too much about her, I don't think. No, keep them there, by all means."

"Would it be all right if I looked at them?" She was dying of curiosity. Even if the letters only turned out to be rants against various tourism associations, she'd learn something about her aunt. And it was something to do other than housework . . .

"Of course you can."

She'd save them up, she decided. Keep them as a treat, a reward for when she'd passed the one month point.

As she said goodbye and hung up soon after, she had a

sudden urge to call Adam, to tell him the latest, have him make her laugh like he usually did. She blamed the flowers for putting the idea into her head, the tears for wearing away at her resolve, for making her doubt her own mind. She couldn't ring him, could she? She had finished it between them. And today's tears were just an accumulation of things. Her life had changed so much in the past few weeks, of course she had to let off a bit of steam, relieve some emotional pressure.

She stopped her fingers from dialing his number, but her thoughts went through with it. She pictured his phone ringing, on the cupboard by the kitchen, by the open-plan living room which led onto the balcony overlooking the river and the trees. She pictured him lying on the couch, the lean, lanky body in faded jeans and an old T-shirt, flicking through recipe books or travel books on France and Italy, picking up ideas for his cooking . . .

Then she blinked and the image disappeared. She insisted on it.

. . .

It wasn't until the middle of the night, as she lay in bed unable to sleep, that something occurred to her. Why hadn't Adam canceled the flower delivery?

CHAPTER 12

Three days later, the wind was howling, the rain spitting, the rose bushes and the small shrubs in the garden tossing and bending against the storm. Inside, Lainey put down the phone and gave an excited shriek. Guests! Company! Two of them—walking, talking, paying customers.

When she'd picked up the phone and was asked if she had any vacancies, she'd thought at first it was Eva speaking in a funny accent. Then she'd realized the call was authentic. At last. A reason to make the beds. A reason to set up the breakfast room and to light all the open fires. A reason to live. They'd booked for just the one night, but after she'd bombarded them with all she knew about the area, filled them up with delicious authentic Irish breakfast food, why, they were bound to want to stay a few more nights. A week even. She couldn't wait.

● ● ●

Her guests had barely driven away the next morning before she was on the phone to Eva.

"They hated it."

"Hated it? Hated what?"

"Where do I start? According to them, the rooms were musty and too hot. Too hot? I felt like saying this is an Irish winter—your room can't be too hot. They said there was a funny smell. The only smell in the house was all the cleaning products I've been hurling around the past week or so, so they must have had very sensitive noses. The woman even made a mean remark about the *wallpaper*."

"They must have liked something. What about your breakfast?"

"They especially hated my breakfast. He said the eggs were hard. She said the bacon was raw. She managed to eat the cornflakes but I heard the man say my muesli looked like something chickens eat."

"You didn't actually serve them chicken food, did you?"

"Of course I didn't. It was a special hippy brand I found in Dunshaughlin, all whole grains or something."

"How did they hear about you, anyway?"

"Coincidence. Their house in the north of England is called Green Gables, so it was a sentimental thing. Is that going to be my market, do you think—only people who live in houses called Green Gables around the world? Evil, fussy people?"

"Lainey, this isn't like you to be so upset. Are you okay?"

No, she wasn't okay, she was scared witless that she was going to make a bags of this. But she didn't want to admit it—not to Evie, not to anybody. "Oh, just annoyed, I guess. Don't mind me. They were unpleasant people. Probably as well to get the bad ones early, don't you think? Of course everything's going to be fine." She nearly convinced herself.

.   .   .

Two hours later she was outside hanging up the sheets that Mr. and Mrs. Crabhead had slept in, feeling much cheerier. She had recited every statement of positive reinforcement she could remember. She'd applied her brightest lipstick, styled her hair with gel and mousse and dressed in the brightest jumper she owned to cheer herself up. She'd put on her favorite mix CD at full volume while she continued her cleaning. She'd sung along as loudly as she wanted, too, safe in the knowledge no one could hear her screeches.

As she pegged the sheets, doing her best to ignore the gray clouds covering half the sky, she clung tightly to her upbeat mood, batting away each doubt and worry as it came into view in her mind. She *had* made the right decision about Adam. This year *was* going to be fine. And she *wouldn't* let a single pair of complainers defeat her, of course she wouldn't. She *would* make a success of the B&B. She just had to see it as a challenge, the B&B as another venue needing a complete transformation. She'd organized hundreds of events in her life, after all. She'd turned ordinary venues into rooms of mystery and beauty, filled with people and music and wonderful food. This was just a small—all right, a biggish—house. Of course she could make it work. She could almost hear her brain click into gear and slowly start to turn for the first time in many days. So, then. What had been the first step in any major project she'd undertaken? An easy question. Some informal market research, generally starting with the people she knew and trusted best—colleagues, family, friends . . . Her fingers started to tingle as an idea came into her head. She left the washing where it was, ran straight inside to the phone and dialed the Dublin number she already knew off by heart.

"Ambrosia Delicatessen and Café, good morning."

"Evie, my darling, gorgeous friend, it's me again . . ."

"Yes, Lainey," Eva said warily.

"Did you tell me you and Joe go off around the country on romantic weekends all the time and stay in lots of B&Bs?"

"We've been away a few times, over to Galway and that, sure."

"Were there ones that stood out for any reason? The most romantic? The coziest? The most welcoming?"

"Well, they're always different to one another, but yes, there have been some lovely ones."

"Can I beg a big favor? Beg, borrow or steal a favor? Would you and Joe come down and stay a night here as soon as you can?"

"I thought you'd banned us?"

"I hereby lift that ban. Could you come soon? This weekend, if you haven't got any singing gigs?"

Eva sang in cover bands around Dublin now and again. "No, we're free this weekend."

"Would you come, then? Pretend you are normal tourists who have happened to see this wonderful-looking B&B so close to the Hill of Tara that you simply have to stay a night?"

"What, arrive out of the blue? Surprise you, do you mean?"

"Well, I have invited you and I probably will recognize you both when you arrive, so it won't be a huge surprise. But could you both just go through the whole place as if you were here as guests and then tell me at the end what was good and what was really bad? In a proper way, not in that mean-spirited, cruel and heartless way that other couple did it?"

"You just want another chance to cook those bacon and eggs, don't you? I know what you're up to. We're your guinea pigs."

"I wouldn't put it quite like that." Well, perhaps she would, actually.

"Hold on, Lainey." Lainey overheard Eva have a quick conversation with Joseph. She came back on the line. "How about this Saturday night? Would you be ready for us by then?"

"I'll be climbing the walls in anticipation. Thanks a million, Evie."

Excellent, Lainey thought as she hung up. She was off and running.

· · ·

Back in the kitchen, she made a big pot of coffee and took out her notebook, ready for a mini brainstorming session.

Right, then, she thought, pen in hand. Who stayed in B&Bs? Mostly tourists. Why were tourists in Ireland? To experience Irish culture. Did they want real Ireland? No, not usually. They wanted film and TV Ireland. Something local to County Meath, preferably, she thought. Of course! Pierce Brosnan was born in County Meath, James Bond himself. She could fill the place with James Bond memorabilia, hire Bond girl lookalikes to make the beds and cook the breakfasts. Then she dismissed that idea, too. There'd be licensing difficulties, surely.

Forget films. Think of popular Irish books. *Angela's Ashes*? Oh yes, that would be a fantastic B&B experience. No, I'm sorry, sir and madam, there are no blankets on the bed, we're too poor. Sorry, no breakfast either, we're too poor. What about Roddy Doyle's *The Commitments*? She could picture it, loud soul music playing in every room and young Dubliners looking after her guests—"Do you feckin' well want bacon and eggs, or not?"

Perhaps not. Could she work with what she had, and create attractions out of the livestock? Pretend the chickens were special, highly trained Australian imports, capable of laying super eggs and doing tricks? Or could she make the food her main selling point? Go for the gourmet approach to B&B stays? Eva could come down from the delicatessen and give her a course in cheese and breads and olives. But would her guests want that? People stayed in Irish B&Bs wanting the full Irish breakfast, didn't they? There was no point meddling with that formula, though she could take the organic approach—only free-range eggs and home-cured bacon. That was worth investigating. She scribbled a note. But it wasn't enough. Think harder, Lainey, she told herself. You're near the Hill of Tara, the ancient capital of Ireland. That's your main selling point.

That was it. She'd have to base it on the Hill of Tara, on Irish myths and legends.

* * *

She was up at the Hill of Tara coffee shop within an hour. The notices and other bits of paper stuck to the notice-board in the porch at the entrance flapped in the wind as she opened the door. When she had everything a bit more organized, she'd ask if she could stick up a flyer for Green Gables. Maybe even invite the people from the café down to have a look. Word of mouth could be as good as advertisements, she knew that from experience. The little shop was busy. There were German tourists try-ing on Aran jumpers and flowing capes, a trio of French or possibly Spanish teenagers peering into the glass cabi-net of Celtic jewelry. The café was nearly full too, most of the tables taken by small groups of tourists, the air fra-grant with brewed coffee and the spicy warmth of fruit scones and cake. Lainey had a sudden longing to be a tourist for the day too.

To hell with it, she would do just that. She was the boss, after all. She formally gave herself the day off. She'd ex-plore the Hill of Tara as if she had never seen it before, take it all in bit by bit. As she made her decision she no-ticed several of the people check their watches and stand up, gathering their coats and scarves. A guided tour was about to begin. Lainey joined in as the group filed along the gravel path to the old Protestant church that was now the visitors' center. Lainey could remember being at Tara as a child on the occasional Sunday when it was still in use, hearing the bell ringing. It still looked like a church in-side, with just a few rows of narrow pews, a large video screen above the altar. The group shuffled in, wriggling along the seats and making room for one another.

The young guide introduced herself as Siobhan. "We've a short film for you, then we'll go out onto Tara itself. You'll see we've arranged for authentic Irish weather for you today." There were a few laughs. "That grass doesn't stay green by magic, let me assure you."

The film began, a twenty-minute documentary about the history of Tara, the various excavations over the years and the story of the Lia Fáil. Lainey caught herself keeping a special eye out for Rohan Hartigan in the silhouette scenes at the end, before realizing they wouldn't have been edited yet. This was probably still the old film.

She walked behind the tour a little way, trying to hear Siobhan's commentary over the heads of the other tourists. The wind was swirling around them, sending clouds buffeting, changing the light from clear winter gray to dramatic purple in moments. It was the perfect backdrop to some of the stories she could hear Siobhan telling, even if the wind did keep breaking her paragraphs into short snatches of words. Lainey strained to hear. ". . . once the most powerful place in Ireland . . . thousands of years old . . . seat of more than one hundred and forty High Kings of Ireland . . . Celtic heroes such as Finn McCool, King Cormac Mac Airt . . . it was on Tara that St. Patrick was said to have used the shamrock to explain the mystery of the Holy Trinity . . . in the 1840s more than one million people heard Daniel O'Connell, the great Irish leader, speak here . . ."

Lainey stayed with the group a few more minutes before realizing she was going to need more specific facts and figures about Tara than a tour like this could offer. She'd come back on a less windy day, she decided. In the meantime, there were other places to find information.

• • •

She was in the local library by ten o'clock the next morning. As she waited to be served she flicked through a copy of the local paper lying on the counter. There were stories on local sporting clubs, a ruckus in the council, increasing traffic problems in the area. As she turned toward the back she noticed a familiar name above a column on Irish myths and legends. Rohan Hartigan. So he was a writer these days, not an actor. The piece was a retelling of the legend of the Children of Lir, the sister and her two brothers turned into swans and banished for nine hundred years by their evil stepmother. It was really well written, she noticed. None of the old wisha-wisha folky Irish that had turned her off as a child.

The young woman behind the counter was very friendly. "Were you after anything in particular, Lainey?" she asked after Lainey had supplied all her details.

"I'm looking for books about Tara, actually. On Irish myths and legends."

"Oh, we've plenty of books on Tara. The trouble is, do we file myths and legends under fiction or nonfiction?"

"Nonfiction, of course, Ciara."

They both turned around. A good-looking blue-eyed man with dark curly hair was standing there, smiling at them. "Hello again, Lainey."

It took a moment before she recognized him. "Rohan? You've shaved your beard off?"

"That one was fake, I'm afraid," he said, briefly rubbing his chin. "They were trying to match me up with the actor I was replacing, so I got to try one for a day."

Now Lainey could see his face. The last time she'd seen it properly, he was fifteen, still boyish. Now he was a man, the jaw firm, the eyes more knowing.

"I think I'd like you with a beard, Rohan," Ciara said with a flirty smile.

"He looks even better in tights," Lainey said before she could stop herself.

"Tights? Really? I'm sure he did. He's a lovely pair of legs on him, haven't you, Rohan?" Ciara was smiling as she moved to serve some other customers.

Rohan turned back to Lainey. "Thank you for that. It'll do my reputation in this town the world of good."

"Don't worry. I'll tell her I saw you out dancing."

"Oh, that's fine, then. I'm well known around town for my ballet skills."

For a moment they looked at each other. He was wearing normal clothing today, dark jeans, heavy boots, a blue jumper. His curly hair was damp with rain. He must have come in right behind her. "So, Lainey, how are you settling in?"

She felt oddly self-conscious in her faded jeans and the warm jacket. "I'm grand, thank you. The weather's taking a bit of getting used to again."

"You've been living in Melbourne, is that right? That's got its own unique brand of weather too. Four seasons in one day, isn't that it?"

"How did you know that?"

"I was there for work several years ago."

"Touring with the ballet?"

His lip twitched. "No, that's just a hobby. I was there for a history and tourism conference. That's what I do these days. I'm a tourism consultant."

"Specializing in Irish historical sites?"

"I've worked all over Europe, really. You're looking for books on myths and legends of Tara, did you say?"

She didn't say it was for research for the new-look Green Gables. "I am. I thought I should know as much as I can about the area, when guests ask me questions."

He gave her a big smile. "I'd be happy to help you if you need any information on the area. I'm actually working on an oral history project about the Hill of Tara at the moment." He took out a pen and notebook and scribbled his name and number. "Perhaps you could ring me when you're more settled. I'll do what I can to help."

She looked at it. "Thanks, Rohan. If it's no trouble."

"No, it would be my pleasure. It'd be good to catch up properly, hear all your news."

Just then he pushed back the sleeve of his jumper and glanced at his watch.

As he did so she looked at his arm and saw a long scar. "Good God, Rohan, is that from the accident on Tara that night? After that . . ."

"Spin the Bottle game we played? Yes it is."

"I thought you'd just broken your arm. I didn't realize you'd done that as well."

"I did break it. But that fence post gave me a fairly spectacular gash before it got to the bone."

She winced. "Can I see?"

Rohan rolled his sleeve up further. The white of the scar was very obvious, running from just below his wrist, over his elbow and further up. "It shouldn't have left such a scar, but the doctor on duty that night wasn't the best, I'm afraid, and he made a bit of a mess of things."

She touched it without thinking. Then it felt like too

intimate a thing to have done and she moved back. "But there was no lasting damage, was there? I mean, it still works and everything?"

He flexed it. "Almost like new. It just looks like that."

"Rohan, I'm so sorry. I never realized it was that bad."

"It was a tragedy. All those ambitions I had of being a male model destroyed in one moment."

"We're ready for you, Rohan." A voice behind them. It was the librarian. In the corner of the library a group of schoolchildren was waiting.

He turned to her. "I'm giving a talk about Newgrange. You're welcome to stay, get a refresher course on local history if you like."

For a moment she was tempted, needing all the distraction she could get at the moment. Then she decided she had enough to think about now before she started learning about life five thousand years ago. "Thanks anyway, Rohan. Another time perhaps."

•　•　•

The man was haunting her, she decided as she got into the car. Appearing out of the darkness that first night on Tara, now here in the library. As she drove out of the parking lot and headed back toward the B&B, she remembered the first time she'd met him, nearly eighteen years back, when he'd first moved back to Ireland from England with his family. He'd been paraded in front of the class, all of the kids looking curiously at him as the teacher introduced him. Mrs. Byrne had known the whole story, sharing it with the family over dinner one night. Rohan's mother was originally from Dunshaughlin, had married an English fellow, gone to Birmingham, had a daughter, Caroline, and then Rohan some years later. But then her husband had died and she'd decided to come back to her home place.

"Where's the sister, then?" Lainey had asked.

"She stayed over there apparently. Studying in London or something. Hard on Rohan, wouldn't you say? Be nice to him, Lainey, won't you? You too, Brendan and Declan." Hugh had been in his pram then, too young to be nice to anyone yet.

"Yes, Ma," they'd chorused.

It had been easy to be nice to Rohan, Lainey recalled. He had been friendly, easy-natured, gangly but good-looking even back then, with his dark curly hair and blue eyes. He had fallen easily into her group of friends, joining in as they hung around the schoolyard together in the daytime, and then in the back lanes and fields around Dunshaughlin in the weekends and holidays, arguing, flirting with each other, playing games, messing around. She cast her mind back, trying to recall all the details of the night when their games had gone a little too far. There had been about eight of them, fifteen and sixteen years old, three boys, five girls, gathered in her living room, taking advantage of the fact her parents and brothers were in Dublin for the day. It had been her idea that they play Spin the Bottle, starting with the innocent version of the game, trading in dares rather than kisses. Lainey remembered hoping it would move on to the kissing version. She'd had her eye on Niall Hogan for a while. And perhaps even Rohan as well? she thought now. The first few spins had been very ordinary. "I dare you to run into the kitchen and drink all the milk in the refrigerator." "I dare you to stand up and sing the national anthem right now."

Lainey remembered being impatient. "Come on, let's make them much more exciting." Her spin of the bottle had pointed straight at Rohan and she'd said the first thing that came into her head, influenced by a class trip they'd had earlier that week. "I dare you, Rohan Hartigan, to ride across the Hill of Tara on a motorcycle." She remembered everyone's shocked reaction.

Eva had been especially appalled. "Lainey, he can't! What if he damages something?"

Lainey had stood her ground. "A dare's a dare, isn't it, Rohan?"

Rohan had hesitated, looked around the room at all the others watching him, then after a long pause, accepted the dare.

Two nights later, a gang of them had gathered at Tara, whooping as Rohan turned up on a motorbike "borrowed" from a neighbor. Lainey could remember the feeling of excitement, the knowledge that she had made this happen, that it was her dare that had brought all of them up there. It had been a powerful feeling. But that feeling had quickly faded away.

Rohan had done one loop of the outside of the Hill when it happened. They'd heard the rev of the engine and judged him to be near one of the big mounds of earth when the engine sound abruptly cut out. His back wheel had slipped in the muddy ground, throwing the bike off balance, sending Rohan flying from the seat into the remains of a fence post.

They had all run toward him, Lainey with her heart thudding, excitement turned into fear and guilt. Eva had been in tears beside her. "Oh, Jesus Mary and Joseph, he's not dead, is he? Oh, Lainey, what if you killed him?"

Lainey had wanted to slap her for saying out loud what she herself had been thinking. "Of course he's not dead," she said, running as fast as she could toward the figure just visible in the grass ahead of them. "He's got a helmet on. He'll be fine."

He had been dazed, moaning in pain but alive. The worst sight had been his arm, bent into an ugly shape, the denim of his jacket torn all around it. Lainey had felt a sudden rush of nausea, a cold then hot sensation. "We need an ambulance," she'd said. "Evie, run to the shop, quickly. If they're not there, then keep going. Go to Aunt May's house. Just hurry."

Lainey and three others had stayed with Rohan. He was breathing still. One of them went to take off his helmet. "Leave it," Lainey had ordered. "Don't touch him. In case."

"In case what?"

In case his back is broken and we make it worse, she thought. "Just in case."

Twenty minutes later the ambulance had come. They had all stood and watched, Eva and Lainey tightly holding each other's hands, as Rohan was picked up and put on the stretcher. Lainey was still the spokesperson. The others looked for her to ask the ambulance people the question. "Is he all right?"

"Don't know yet. What in God's name were you kids doing? Have you all gone mad, or something?"

"It was a game, a dare," Lainey had said in a small voice.

"He could have been killed. A stupid dare if you ask me."

She'd called his mother first thing the next day, her

own mother standing behind her, still angry and as worried as Lainey herself was. "What in God's name were you all doing there?" Mrs. Hartigan had asked. "What was this ridiculous business about a dare?"

"Rohan told you about that? He's talking?"

"He's talking but he hasn't said a word about what happened. The ambulance man told me. Good God, Lainey. What were you all thinking?"

"It was my fault, Mrs. Hartigan. I dared Rohan to do it."

"Then, young lady, you very nearly killed my son. I've grieved for a husband already and I do not want to grieve for a son. You stupid, silly girl."

"I'm sorry," she'd said again, nearly in tears. "Can I come and see him, say sorry?"

"No, you can't. You keep away from him."

"I just want to apolo—"

"No, Lainey."

She'd tried later in the week to get in to see him, but Mrs. Hartigan had told the nurses not to let anyone in. One of the nurses, the big sister of one of her friends, had taken pity on her. "So it was your fault. Well, no wonder she won't let you in. I can't either, Lainey. She'd kill us if she found out. Can I give him a message for you?"

"Tell him . . ." She stopped. "No, I'll write him a card." She'd gone to the shop in the hospital and bought the first card she picked out, a hideous one with a photo of a kitten nestled in a basket of flowers. She wouldn't have given it to her grandmother if she had one, let alone Rohan, but this was no time to be choosy.

Rohan, I'm so sorry this happened, she'd scrawled. *I'm thinking of you and hope we can still be friends.*

Still be friends? Was that right? She'd hardly known him, really. But it was too late, she'd written it. How to finish it, though? Love, Lainey? Best wishes, Lainey? She'd settled on *Yours sincerely, Lainey*.

That night at home, her father had announced to the family they were emigrating to Australia. She hadn't seen Rohan again before they left. And she'd certainly never known about that scar.

CHAPTER 13

Okay. Now, can you go back to your car, drive back a bit and then come in and start from scratch?"

"Lainey, we just got out of the car," Eva protested. "And it's freezing out there." She and Joseph were standing on the porch, raindrops in their hair, damp coats over their arms, and bags on the floor beside them.

"I know it's cold, but we have to do it properly. I wouldn't normally greet my guests with a big hug, so we've got off to a false start. I really need you to come to the door and pretend you're casual guests this time, so I can get the whole thing sorted out in my mind."

"And I suppose you'll make us do it again if we don't knock properly, will you? Well, you'd better think again because it's lashing rain out there and the sooner we get shown to our room and get a drink by the fire, the better."

Beside her, Joseph was laughing openly. Lainey turned to him for sympathy. "Joe, you understand what I'm doing, don't you? You're an artist, you know how important it is to visualize something before you do it properly."

"I know how important it is to let you get your own way."

She swatted him with the tea towel she was holding as Eva pulled on her thick coat again, flicking back her black braid. "All right, Lainey, we'll do it. But can we do the entrance just the once? At least until the rain's stopped?"

"We'll see. Okay, lights, camera, action—go."

Eva and Joseph went out and got back into their car. Lainey went back to the kitchen and fussed around the Aga, checking the temperatures. It was working very well, keeping the whole house nice and warm. And she had been right—the plume of smoke from the chimney did make the house seem more welcoming. She waited for the sound of their knock.

Five minutes later she was still waiting. She'd heard the car start up and had assumed they were moving it closer to the house. She looked out of the window—there was no sign of them. Good God, was there some sort of black hole on these roads? Perhaps that was where all her guests had disappeared to. The Bermuda Triangle of Ireland.

By the time they pulled up twenty minutes later she was out by the gate in her raincoat, an umbrella held up above her head. Eva wound down the window. "I don't think that's quite the right look, Lainey. It's a bit desperate."

"Where were you? I thought you were just going to turn the car and come back up."

"You told us to pretend that we were proper tourists," Joseph said as he got out of the driver's seat.

"So we did as we were told," Eva said. "We stopped at a shop back on the main road and said we were on a trip around the country, felt like staying in the area and could she recommend anywhere?"

"And?" Lainey asked, as they quickly walked up the path together, the three of them crammed under one umbrella.

"And she recommended every place in a ten-mile radius," Eva said.

"Except mine."

"Except yours," Joseph said.

"So we said what about that Green Gables one, down the road from the Hill of Tara. That looked nice," Eva continued.

Lainey opened the porch door and let them both in before her. "And what did she say about it?"

Eva looked at Joseph. "She sort of shuddered, didn't she?"

"Shuddered?" Lainey said.

"Maybe shuddered is a bit strong," Joseph said. "Trembled, perhaps."

"You two, come on. What did she actually say?"

"She said she hadn't heard good reports about that place. We said, what do you mean? And she said the old woman who used to run it was a bit of a battle-axe, prone to lecturing people a bit. And the rooms used to be cold."

Joseph took up the story. "So we told her we understood it was under new ownership. And she said that could only be good and that she wished the new owner luck."

"Well, it's bad news but brilliant market research. Well done."

"So can we come in now?"

Lainey slowly shook her head. "Sorry, no. You really do have to do it properly. Back out to the car, come on."

"Lainey . . ."

"Please? For me? It'll be fun, really."

Once again, Eva and Joseph went out to their car.

· · ·

Two hours later, just as night had fallen, they were finally allowed to drop the tourist personas and be themselves.

They were both now stretched out on the sofas in the sitting room, cups of tea in hand. Lainey came in with another log of wood and threw it into the fireplace. She'd had the fire going since early that morning and it had warmed up the room nicely. She picked up the teapot and topped up their cups. "So what do you think? Do you need a moment to compare notes or do you want to just hit me with the bad news?"

Eva looked at Joseph. "Will I go first?" At his nod, she pulled out her own notebook. "The first problem is where you're situated."

"Oh, no worries then. I'll get the house moved."

"Lainey, you asked us down to tell you what we thought."

"Sorry, go on."

Joseph spoke up. "From what Eva had said, I thought it was on the main road to Tara but you're actually tucked away down this lane. You're not going to get much passing traffic, are you?"

"Not unless tourists are keen to see the cows in the field across from me, no."

"That's a shame. And the sign on the front of the house is hard to see, which doesn't help. You're nearly past the house before you notice it and these roads are hard to turn around in. If I was a tourist and happened to be on this lane, I'd probably keep driving until I found another B&B up the road."

Eva was looking at her notes too. "There's still lots of ivy over your sign, Lainey, which makes it even harder to see. You'll have to cut it all off or pull it down or something."

Lainey made a note.

"The driveway is good," Joseph offered. "The gate is wide and there's plenty of room for parking."

"Fabulous. I can open a parking lot if nothing else."

"And the fact that it's an old house is in your favor, from a tourist point of view. Lots of B&Bs are in suburban houses, so this one has a bit of character at least."

"Oh yes, it's a real character."

Eva ignored that. "Your greeting, that final one, was a little sudden. But that was probably because you were lying in wait behind the door waiting for us to ring the bell."

Lainey nodded sheepishly. "It did seem a bit desperate, I suppose. Under normal circumstances, I'd probably be in the kitchen."

"Good. That might lessen the shock value. Just try and give people more than one second after they ring the bell before you open the door. You nearly gave us a heart attack."

Lainey poked out her tongue.

Eva consulted her notes again. "Now, moving on to the accommodation aspects. The first two rooms are okay— nothing special, just okay. But a bit dank. The front two are fine, lovely even, but too old-fashioned. But there's a funny smell in one of those small back rooms, a kind of mousy smell."

"Mousy? As in a smell left by mice? Are you telling me I've got mice here?"

"You might have," Eva said matter-of-factly. "It's a house in the country, it's been empty for a while. You might want to set a few traps, just in case."

Lainey made a note.

Set LOTS of traps

She didn't like mice.

Eva went on. "Now, this room is gorgeous, especially with the fire going. The tea you brought us was lovely, but it would have been nice to get a biscuit after our long drive from Cork."

"Cork? You drove from Dublin."

"We were method acting by that stage," Joseph said.

"The breakfast room looks nice," Eva continued. "The classical music playing is good, and the flowers on the table are a nice touch. I like your idea of having the fire burning and the morning papers there too, though it means you're going to have to be up very early."

"I'll be up for my run, in any case. But there's something else wrong with the breakfast room, isn't there? I can tell by that look on your face."

Eva was trying not to smile. "I think you've gone

overboard with the choice of cereals. Either muesli or cornflakes would probably do. You don't really need the other six varieties. It's like a supermarket shelf in there. Besides, you're giving them the full Irish breakfast as well, aren't you?"

"The whole glorious mess." Lainey counted the items off on her fingers. "Eggs—fried, scrambled or poached, or more likely just burnt. Bacon—probably underdone or burnt. Tomato—cut up or whole, rolling around the plate. Sausage—small and pink or burnt. Black pudding—delivered to their table by me either gagging or wearing a surgical mask."

"It's actually delicious, you know."

"Delicious? A sausage made out of congealed blood? If you're a vampire, maybe. So are you hungry at the moment? I could cook you bacon and eggs now for dinner, if you like, get into practice. It'd save me time in the morning, actually, if we got it over and done with now."

Joseph stood up. "No way. I want to visit that pub with the thatched roof we passed on the way here."

"Okay, a drink first and then dinner's on me. Or on Aunt May, if the truth be told. Come on, you two. Let's go celebrate."

"What are we celebrating?"

"The start of my renovations. You've both confirmed everything I thought myself. Aunt May left me a nice big renovation fund and I'm going to ring Mr. Fogarty first thing on Monday and get the whole thing started."

"Renovation?" Eva said, trying to keep up with Lainey's bionic thought processes. "You're going to paint the whole place, you mean? Redecorate it? All on your own?"

Lainey gave her friend a warm, friendly smile. "On my own? Oh no, not necessarily."

Eva went still.

Lainey turned the smile up a notch. "What do you think, Evie? How do you feel about a nice break in the country? A chance to get out of that Dublin smog? A chance to give your assistant manager a taste of responsibility? Not to mention all the exercise you would get. Did you know that painting is apparently the equivalent of a complete body workout in a gym? So it wouldn't be renovating so much as a lovely stay in a health farm, with me as company, your oldest friend. Think of all that catching up we could do. We could reminisce about the past, share our hopes and dreams for the future . . ."

Eva put her hands over her ears, shut her eyes and groaned.

· · ·

Lainey called Mr. Fogarty's office early Monday morning. He listened patiently as she explained the situation, then kept her waiting for a few moments as he padded across the floor on his little feet to get a copy of the will.

"Yes, Lainey, your aunt has earmarked a sizeable sum, presumably with the intention that you might like to use it in an aggregate way but certainly there is no codicil disallowing you from spending it all in one hit, as it were. And you may as well spend it. Any money left over from that fund at the end of the twelve months is to be divided between her other beneficiaries."

"And how much is it, Mr. Fogarty?"

In a low voice, he named a high figure.

Lainey whistled. "I could do a fair bit with that, couldn't I?"

"You could go for your life, as you Aussies say."

"Mr. Fogarty, how do you know an Australian phrase like that?"

"Lainey, I must confess I watch Australian soap operas on cable TV every single day."

CHAPTER 14

Three days later Eva arrived after breakfast, dressed in the strangest pair of overalls Lainey had ever seen. They were a faded green, patchworked in dozens of scraps of material, tied at the back with a piece of rope. She'd even tied a green ribbon in her long braid.

"You drove down in that?" Lainey said, pretending to be horrified. "What if you'd got a flat tire and someone had seen you?"

Eva was very proud of her overalls, cast-offs from her uncle Ambrose. "You're just jealous, glamour puss. Remember Joe and I spent months last year renovating our flat. I know how to strip wallpaper and paint walls in my sleep, and let me tell you your glamorous clothes won't last ten minutes."

Lainey looked down at her low-slung jeans and cashmere jumper. "Glamorous? These?"

"Yes. It seems you can take the girl out of Melbourne but—"

"You can't keep her sane. Okay, okay, hold on, I'll go

and change." Minutes later she was back wearing her pajamas, with a bright scarf tied jauntily around her short dark hair. "They're the oldest things I've got. Don't laugh. Better I ruin these than my other clothes."

Eva eyed them. They looked like they were made from silk, beautifully cut, like an elegant pantsuit except for the fact they were a bright, gaudy pink. "They're designer label, aren't they?"

"Well, everything in the world is designed in some way, isn't it? Sorry about the color. They were samples from a client and for some reason no one else wanted this pair."

"I can't imagine why."

. . .

They tackled the front bedroom first, steaming off the first layer of wallpaper, only to find several other layers underneath.

"This must go back decades," Lainey said as she dug away at the damp paper, pulling off a big wet wad. "My father probably used to look at this stuff."

They scraped away as music from the radio filled the room. Eva leaned down and turned it off. "I've realized I have you trapped now, so you have to answer my questions. Will you tell me about Adam, Lainey? All about him?"

Lainey paused mid-scrape, a long strand of orange wallpaper dangling near her face. "There's nothing to tell. Not anymore."

"But I'd still like to hear about him, what he was like, so I can understand how you're feeling. I never got to meet him while I was in Melbourne. I feel like I need to get a picture of him in some way."

"Didn't I send you photos?" An image leaped into Lainey's mind of the photos she had sent Eva—she and Adam on a trip to the Great Ocean Road, arms around each other at the Twelve Apostles. A smiley Japanese man had taken the photo, she remembered. Afterward, they'd driven back to Apollo Bay and had lunch in a pub there, then decided on the spur of the moment that they'd stay the night. They'd imagined a big, airy room overlooking the water, a queen-sized bed, French windows open to the air, muslin curtains drifting and swaying in the air currents. "This is all we've got left," the hotel manager had said, pushing a key across to them. It hadn't been a room so much as a converted broom cupboard. Harry Potter would have felt at home. There was a narrow single bed, a battered-looking trundle bed pushed underneath it, a small cupboard and that was all. Not even a TV. "Well, we shall have to make do," Adam had announced in a fake British accent. He had lain down, a third of his legs dangling over the end, as he must have known they would. Lainey had laughed at the sight, taking Adam's outstretched hand, falling forward as he wanted, lying stretched on top of him. He had traced her cheek with a long finger, then cupped the side of her face in his hand.

"I've often read in books about enchanting young women throwing their heads back in laughter. You do exactly that. It's lovely." She remembered thinking what an oddly formal speech that had been and remarking on it. "I find it best to be polite," he'd said then, speaking in the British accent once more. "Miss Byrne, may I have permission to remove your outer garments, to first kiss your shapely body through your exceedingly sexy undergarments and then remove them swiftly so that I may—"

She'd been laughing and saying yes all at the same time as he did that and a bit more. She blinked and erased the image.

"Lainey, are you listening? I did see the photos but what was he like as a person?"

Kind, funny, sexy. Lainey blinked again. It wouldn't get her anywhere thinking of those things. "He's hardworking. Really motivated."

"That sounds more like a job reference. What's he actually like?"

"Friendly. Good-mannered."

"Now he sounds like a labrador."

Lainey wasn't finding this easy or funny. "Eva, no offense, but do you really need to know? I mean, it's over between Adam and me, why do you need to find out what he was like?"

"I suppose I'm trying to work out why you were so sure that it had to be over. Please don't get defensive. I just want you to be happy, you know that."

Lainey started scraping again. "Why is it that as soon as anyone gets married they immediately assume all their single friends want to be wed as well? I've been single for years before this, you know, and I didn't curl up in a dried-up old ball of dust and die."

"I'm not saying there's anything wrong with being single or anything about you getting married. I've just been doing a lot of thinking about you being here and I'm wondering if there's a reason for it."

"We're currently standing in the reason, remember? This B&B? And the money my father needs to get better?" To her embarrassment, her voice faltered.

Eva stopped working and went over to her immediately. "Oh, Lainey, I'm so sorry. There's me interrogating you about Adam. Your dad will be fine again, you wait and see."

Lainey put down the scraper. "I'm sorry, too, for being snappy, especially when you've been so fantastic about coming down to help me, I'm so grateful to you. It just gets at me sometimes. Ever since he had that accident, it's like I'm on edge, waiting for something else bad to happen in my family."

Eva hugged her. "That's not surprising. It was an awful few weeks for you all, wasn't it, when you didn't know if he was going to pull through or not."

"It's been an awful year. It's like it had a ripple effect. Everything else is shaky since that happened."

"Everything? Like what?"

"Ma said she'd been thinking about leaving him."

"But she's been saying that for years, hasn't she? She left him once before and came back, remember?"

Lainey remembered it very well. It had happened the year before they left for Australia. Hugh had been a baby, Lainey about thirteen, fourteen. She'd known for weeks that something was wrong, coming in and finding her mother crying, hearing voices raised long after she'd gone to bed, her mother lying in bed all day, unhappy, while Hugh wailed in his cot in the nursery. Then one day Lainey had come home from school and her mother wasn't there. Her father and a neighbor had been at the kitchen table. "Your ma's gone away for a little while. With Hugh." The mother of one of Lainey's school friends had died and she had been told her mammy had gone away to God. "Is Ma dead, is that what you mean?" she'd asked matter-of-factly. Her father had actually smiled. "No, she's not dead. She needed to go away." "Where?" "She's gone to England." "Why?" "No more questions, Lainey. Off to bed now. You're going to have to be good now and help look after Brendan and Declan, all right?" "When's she coming back?" There'd been an exchange of glances between her father and the neighbor. Lainey had clearly seen it. "I don't know for sure," her father had said.

One afternoon, two months later, she'd come home from school and her mother had been sitting at the kitchen table, Hugh on her lap, as though she'd never been away. "You're back," she'd run into her arms. "I'm back, Lainey." And that had been that—no further explanation, then or later. Less than a year later the family had moved to Australia.

"Yes, I remember," Lainey said now.

"So they got through that hiccup, whatever it was about. Besides, haven't they always had a fiery sort of relationship?"

"This is different. She used to enjoy their fights, I know she did. They both did. This is different, as though she's really fed up with him."

"But it must be hard for her, looking after him all day."

"But she married him for better or worse. She has to stick with him."

"Has to? Lainey, I don't remember you being this conservative."

"What's conservative about wanting your parents to stay married? Are your parents happy together, Evie?"

"I suppose they are. I mean, they go away together and they talk a lot, so I suppose they are."

"Did they ever fight in front of you?"

Eva frowned as she tried to remember. "Fight? Um, I don't know really."

"Then they didn't, or you'd be able to remember straightaway. I thought it was only when you're a kid that you're supposed to hate hearing your parents fight, but I think it's worse as an adult."

"Lainey, please, can't you try and relax a bit? Things will work out."

"I guess I'm just worried what will happen if I'm not there to help if Ma gets worn out."

"Your brothers are going to have to step in, then. They're not babies anymore, Lainey. Ring up and ask them to help. Maybe they haven't even noticed how hard it's been for your ma."

"Of course they haven't noticed. Brendan's too wrapped up in his work and the kids, Declan looks after Declan, and Hugh . . . well, you know what Hughie's like."

"Then you can't do anything more about it, except what you're doing now, living here for a year so they can get more money. And that will ease all the tensions, won't it, once your da can sort out all the bills?"

"I suppose so," Lainey said, hoping it was true.

CHAPTER 15

By the next afternoon two rooms were completely scraped back to bare walls. The old wallpaper was piling up in a damp heap in the middle of the hallway, beside the large tins of paint waiting to be applied. In the paint shop the day before, armed with a fat check from May's estate, Lainey had made a decision about the colors. No pale walls, no more dull cream paint anywhere—with that gray sky outside, she needed some color in her life and paint was the closest thing to hand. The living room would be a bright apricot, the hall a warm red, each of the bedrooms a different color, shades in some way reflecting Tara, Eva had suggested. They'd settled on different autumn shades of green, orange, red and even a purple. It wasn't exactly traditional, but it was certainly welcoming. They had worked right through until midnight the night before, stopping to eat fish and chips fetched by Lainey in Dunshaughlin, then falling into bed, exhausted.

They finished scraping the other two guest bedrooms

and the downstairs living room by the end of the day. While Eva washed and changed, Lainey set up her computer and collected her emails for the first time in some days. She watched with pleasure as six messages poured into her inbox.

There were three from work, including the weekly circular updating all the employees on the week's events. Lainey had asked to be kept in touch. She skim-read it, fighting a flicker of jealousy as she read Celia's report. Talk about gush-o-rama, she thought. Everything had been wonderful, top-drawer, smooth and slick, seamlessly organized. Surely something had gone wrong? The microphone squealing feedback in the middle of a speech? The backdrop falling off the wall right at the crucial moment? All the guests contracting food poisoning caused by Celia booking a dodgy caterer?

There were two jokes from Hugh, neither of them funny. Best of all, there was a long, newsy one from her friend Christine, berating her for not writing properly yet: "you call that one-line email keeping in touch??? I want more news than weather reports and scenery descriptions, madam!" There were several paragraphs of work gossip: "That witch of a boss of mine said no to a pay raise, so I now have my nose severely out of joint and will jump ship at a moment's notice." There was also a scathing review of a film Christine had seen: "Not that you'll get to see it. I don't suppose you have films in rural Ireland, darling, do you?" As Lainey read to the bottom her heart gave an odd flip. "P.S. A gang of us went to Adam's restaurant for Kim's birthday last Saturday, wanted to make sure he isn't pining to death without you. The place was packed so we only got to wave at him in the kitchen. He was wearing this great hat, rriit reel (that was the sound of a wolf-whistle). You must have been MAD to leave him behind!!! His manager was telling us he's started opening lunchtimes as well as seven nights a week now, obviously trying to fill those long empty hours in his life without you . . ."

Lainey read the final paragraph three times. He was opening lunchtimes now? He wouldn't have a minute to himself if he was doing that, between all the shopping and the preparation he'd need to do, let alone the cooking. "Obviously trying to fill those long empty hours in his life without you . . ." She wanted to ring him suddenly, ask him if he was all right, whether he should really be working those long hours. Then she remembered the last time they'd seen each other, and the cold look he'd had in his eyes. She didn't think he'd particularly want to hear from her, somehow.

She started a reply message to Christine, fingers over the keyboard, trying to find the words to tell her she and Adam had broken up. Then she realized she didn't want to tell Christine yet and she wasn't exactly sure why not. At that same moment she also realized that she didn't like the idea of them going to the restaurant for Kim's birthday. As she re-read Christine's email, there was a quick battle in her head:

Mature Lainey: "Of course it was all right for Kim to go to Adam's restaurant. She can go to any restaurant in Melbourne that she likes."

Immature Lainey: "How dare Kim go to Adam's restaurant! I'm barely out of the country before she's moving in on him."

Mature Lainey: "That is great that my friends are supporting Adam's restaurant like that. I'll have to email them back and tell them. And I should probably tell them that Adam and I have broken up, in case there are any awkward moments in the future."

Immature Lainey: "No way am I letting Kim know that Adam is free. The last thing I want is to come back home and find he and Kim are a couple."

She stared at the screen, thinking hard. Was that the last thing she wanted? And why was that the last thing she wanted? Because she wanted Adam for herself still?

She couldn't stop herself. Her fingers seemed to find the keys of their own volition, not replying to Christine, but opening a new message, keying in the email address she knew off by heart. The blank white square invited her to pour out her thoughts, to say sorry, to admit she'd made a terrible mistake.

TO: adamblake@ozmail.com.au
RE: US
Dear Adam
It's been over two weeks since I said those things to you and I keep expecting to feel that I was right, that I have made the right decision. But I don't feel good. I feel like I might have made the biggest mistake in my life. I was listening to reason, thinking of us as though what we had was some kind of business dealing, an issue to be looked at with a cold eye, to be analyzed from an efficiency point of view.
I think I was . . .

"Lainey?"

wronggggggggggggggggggggggggggggggg

Lainey jumped at the sound of Eva's voice right behind her. She quickly deleted the email as Eva came out of the kitchen, a towel wrapped around her wet hair. "Lainey, I've just looked in your fridge. What on earth have you been eating since you got here? You haven't been going to that chipper every night, have you?"

She swiftly closed down the computer. "No, of course not. Well, once or twice maybe. I haven't really been thinking about food, to be honest."

"How can you not think about food? I think about it all day long."

"You run a deli and a café, of course you do." It had been the same with Adam, always asking her to try this new taste, that new cheese, a new sauce he'd invented. Another memory she had to try and erase. "I mean, I really like food, but as fuel, I guess, not for pleasure."

"Then you need to slow down and start enjoying it more. Look how skinny you are. Maybe it's as well you've been press-ganged into coming here. It's the break you need."

"What, so I can learn to cook as well as make beds? I'm already an old hand at bacon and eggs. Would you like some for your dinner?"

"No, thanks all the same. Come and show me what else you've got in your pantry and I'll cook for us tonight."

Lainey followed her back into the kitchen. Out of habit she looked around and checked the five mouse-traps she had set in the pantry, at Eva's suggestion. They were all still empty. She didn't know whether to be pleased or disappointed. There still hadn't been a con-firmed rodent sighting, just an occasional rustling noise. Lainey had almost convinced herself it was the wind mov-ing the ivy outside.

She opened the fridge for Eva now. There was only milk, butter, cheese, bacon and eggs inside. "That's it, really. Everything else May had here was prehistoric. Powdered moose horns, that kind of thing."

Eva took out the eggs and cheese. "Okay, I'll make us some cheese omelets for tonight. You need some variety, at least."

"I haven't just been eating the bacon and eggs. I've been eating a lot of the cereal as well."

"You don't have to take the B&B diet to heart that much. What if a guest asked you to cook their evening meal?"

"They wouldn't."

"They might. Some B&Bs supply evening meals. It's a good way to earn more money."

"It wouldn't lift my occupancy rate, though, would it?"

"It might, if word got round that you served fantastic authentic Irish dinners as well as breakfasts."

"I don't know any authentic Irish food. My mother hates cooking, you know that, and all I know how to cook is a few Asian dishes."

"Cooking is easy, Lainey. Like anything, it's all in the preparation. You should think about learning. My cousin Meg teaches at a great cooking school in County Clare. Maybe you could do a course with her. Or I could teach you a few things, if you like."

"Thank you, Eva, I'll think about learning," Lainey answered in a flat, monotonous tone of voice.

"Lainey, I'm serious. Look me in the eye and tell me you really will think about it."

"Ever since you got married and started managing that café you've got very lippy, young lady."

"You're just raging because you know it's a good idea and you wish you'd thought of it first."

Lainey laughed. "All right, I promise I'll think about it."

•   •   •

The next day they had just started painting the front room a warm fuchsia color when Lainey turned down the radio. "How did you know for sure how you felt about Joe, Evie?"

Eva didn't seem surprised at Lainey's sudden question. "That I wanted to be with him, or that I wanted to marry him?"

"Both. Either."

"I just did. I just thought he was great. I still do."

"But aren't you nervous that you might have made the wrong decision?"

Eva looked closely at her friend. She wasn't being flippant. She wasn't being confident. She looked genuinely, painfully worried. "Lainey, this isn't about me. This is about you and Adam, isn't it? What's the matter? Do you think you made the wrong decision about breaking up with him? Are you having doubts?"

Yes, I am, she thought. "No, I'm not really," she said. "I was just thinking about it, wondering how you know for sure if the person you're with is the right one. Adam, for example. If he really was my one true love, if there is such a thing, then shouldn't I have heard a clanging of bells the very first moment we met?"

"If he was a bell ringer, yes, you would have."

"I'm serious, Evie. Look at you and Joe, meeting on the other side of the world. If there was such a thing as fated falling in love out of the blue, if Adam and I were truly soul mates, then wouldn't it have been a bit more dramatic than it was? We're neighbors. We met when he helped me after I hurt my ankle. Hardly the stuff of romantic films and songs, is it?"

"Lainey, just because Joe and I met under those sort of circumstances doesn't mean the rest of our lives have been lived in some kind of rosy hue. Life got normal. We fight."

Lainey covered her ears. "Eva, don't you ever tell me those kind of untruths again. You'll destroy me."

"But we do fight, of course we do."

"What about? Whether the poem he's written for you this week scans properly?"

"He doesn't write me poems all the time. Where on earth did you get that idea from?"

"Oh, you know you two. You seem so smoochy all the time."

"It's just we're well mannered. We keep our fights to ourselves."

"So what do you fight about?"

"Normal things. I want my own way, he wants his own way. Neither of us wants to compromise."

"Oh, yuck. Who wants something as boring as compromise in a relationship?"

"That's what a relationship is, Lainey. And it is boring sometimes. Of course I'd much rather I spent every day being swooped off to romantic dinners or being sent love letters, but the cold hard truth is the rubbish has to be put out, we have to shop for toilet paper and toothpaste and mouthwash . . ."

"Now you're telling me Joe needs mouthwash? Oh God, all my illusions are cracking around me."

"Lainey, we're human beings, not some characters in a TV soap. And Adam is real too. Why are you expecting him to be like some romantic hero?"

"Isn't that what everyone expects? Someone to come charging up, sweep us off our feet, take all choice out of it?"

"Arranged marriages, you mean? Lainey, I'm shocked at you."

"It'd make life easier in some ways, though, wouldn't it? Don't you get sick sometimes of having to make decisions, weighing up the pros and cons? It'd just be a relief sometimes if it all just happened."

Eva laughed. "As if you'd settle for that. You'd only like it if it happened exactly as you pictured it, you mean."

"What do you mean by that?"

"You know what you're like, Lainey. You get this idea in your head of how things should be, and that's that."

"I'm not that bad."

"Yes, you are."

"I blame Joe for this, you know. You used to be terrified of me. I think I prefer the old days."

The doorbell rang, making them both jump.

"I'll get it," Lainey said, relieved at the interruption.

"Don't think we've dropped the subject, by the way," Eva called after her.

"Want to bet?" Lainey called back as she threw aside the scraper and tore down the stairs.

She was back up just moments later. "Don't you think the whole B&B idea has to be the most ridiculous accommodation concept in the entire world?"

"That wasn't a guest then, I gather?"

"No, someone looking for directions. Seriously, don't you

think it's strange? It's so inefficient. No bookings system, no check-in time, no real codes of behavior. It's just some weird kind of free-for-all, isn't it?"

"It's not inefficient, it's just the way it is. People drive around, decide on the spur of the moment where they want to stay, see a B&B, knock on the door and there they are."

"That's what I mean. Spur of the moment. I mean, really, how am I supposed to plan my day, work out how much food to get in?"

"You could always just relax and see what happens, if that isn't too foreign a concept to you."

"You can't relax in the middle of this sort of chaos. If this happened with work in Melbourne, we'd be bank-rupt in days. Can you imagine it? 'Well, we're organizing a banquet for Saturday night, or maybe Sunday night, and there will be five hundred people or maybe there won't. It depends if they turn up or not. There might only be twenty and even then they might decide to go to the hall next door rather than ours.' Honestly, how do these other people cope? I'm a bag of nerves just sitting around waiting for someone to turn up."

Eva laughed at her friend's mock outrage. "I suppose they have other interests."

"What, macrame? Knitting? The way I'm going I'll have a four-hundred-foot scarf done before spring ar-rives."

"They have people in to help them, too. Maybe you'll have to think about that, to have someone here when you're not, so you can get away occasionally."

"That's a good idea. Just what I need. A nice weekend in a B&B somewhere."

• • •

They moved into the second bedroom, dragging the ladders and dust sheets and pots of paint in with them. They worked in silence for a while and then Eva spoke up.

"Lainey?"

"Mmm?"

"I've been thinking about this. Perhaps there is another reason why you were unsure about Adam, you know. Why you felt you had to break up with him. A simple reason."

"Like what?"

Eva stopped painting. "Perhaps he really wasn't the right one for you. Maybe all your instincts were just trying to tell you the truth. It's hard for me to know for sure because I never met him, but perhaps he's not right for you. And perhaps that's why you're here, out of the blue like this, to discover that for sure and maybe meet the person you're fated to be with. Your Mr. Cholera."

"Are the paint fumes getting to you?"

"No, Lainey, think about it. Maybe this is all meant to happen. Here you are, beside the Hill of Tara, one of the most mystical places in Ireland. Everyone knows special things are supposed to happen here, call it fate or mysticism or ancient Celtic gods at work or . . ."

"Evie, things happen as a result of your actions, by putting your mind to it, not through fate or some preordained life plan."

"But don't you ever think things happen for a reason?" Eva said earnestly. "Like me going to Australia unexpectedly to visit you. If that hadn't happened, I would never have met Joe, would I?"

"But if you were destined to be together, then surely you would have met in some other way? Maybe he would have come to Dublin on holiday, called into the deli, ordered a kilo of mortadella from you and fallen instantly in love on the spot."

"Well, that would have been simpler. Saved a lot of air travel anyway. But maybe it's your turn and *that's* what this year is all about for you. You've been snatched out of your usual work, dropped here in Ireland for a year, forced to slow down so there'll be some space in your life for something great to happen to you, too."

"I'm going to be pronounced the long lost Queen of Tara, you mean?"

"Talking to you is like playing table tennis sometimes, you know that? Do you have to hit everything back?" Eva moved the paint pot one step higher up the ladder so it was level with her shoulder. "Couldn't I be on to something? That this is the fates intervening, showing you the person you're supposed to be with?"

"Do you know, I thought that boy in the paint shop was winking at me. I mean, he's only about twelve, but that's okay. Perhaps he likes mature women."

"Not him. Maybe it's, oh I don't know, Rohan Hartigan. Perhaps he's the man for you."

"Rohan. God, I think you're right. Will you call and tell him or shall I?"

Eva didn't laugh. "Lainey, stop the joking. Can't you just give in to the world a bit for once?"

Lainey sighed theatrically. "All right, Evie, I will try and calm down, just a tiny bit and be as open as I can to great mother universe and all her mysteries."

"Don't mock. That's not being open or calm."

"All right, all right. But tell me, can I still step in and change things if I see a real problem?"

"Like what?"

"Like the fact your braid is in the paint tin."

"Oh *shite*."

CHAPTER 16

It took them six days of solid work, but the rooms finally looked better, brighter. Under all the layers of wallpaper, the walls had been in good condition, easy to paint. They'd arranged for new carpets to be laid in four of the rooms, deciding that the old colored mats would be good for another year in the back bedrooms.

They stood in the hallway, all the doors and windows open around them to clear the house of paint and new carpet smells. Lainey gave her friend a hug. "I can't thank you enough, Evie, you're a marvel. I couldn't have done even one room without you." She put her hands on her hips and looked around. "Now all I need to do is lure people here."

Eva grinned. "Perhaps you could hire a psychic to give free sessions. That'd attract the new-agers, wouldn't it?"

"Well, at least a psychic would be able to tell me when I could expect guests. No, what I should do is have some sort of drinks party, I think. Invite all the other B&B

operators over, and the tourism people, so they can all see what we've done to the place."

"They're certainly curious," Eva said. Both of them had noticed several cars driving past in recent days and they hadn't all been tourists. "A party's a great idea. Launch the place with a bang. What will you have? Jugglers and fire-eaters greeting people at the door?"

"Well, I thought more about hula dancers."

"A Hawaiian-themed Irish B&B, that's novel."

"I could change the name from Green Gables to Green Pineapple, couldn't I?"

"No, what about something more Irish, so tourists feel like they're getting the authentic Tara experience?"

"And then get greeted by a true-blue Aussie at the door? They'll have me up for false advertising. No, what I really need are a couple of celebrity guests to turn up and give me the vote of approval. Where are Hilly Robson and Noah Geddes when I need them? If they're driving around Ireland like the papers say they are, surely they're going to turn up on my doorstep at any moment?"

"All those paint fumes are going to *your* head, Lainey."

Lainey ran her fingers through her hair. "No, the right idea will come to me, I know. I've still got a bit of money left in what my darling Mr. Fogarty calls my Refurbishment and Other Miscellaneous Expenses account as apart from my General Living Expenses and other Associated Day to Day Requirements account. I just have to give it some thought."

The phone rang as they were folding the last of the dust sheets in the now crimson-walled dining room. It was Joseph, wanting to know how much cheese to order from the supplier who was in the shop at that moment.

Lainey guessed from Eva's answers what it was about and interrupted. She took the phone. "Joe, this wonderful woman is all yours again. I've worn her out, worked her fingers to the bone, showered her with thanks, so you can have her back now, overalls and all, poor, pale shell of a thing that she is."

• • •

After Eva had gone, Lainey moved the old stereo into the main room and started flicking through the CDs she'd brought from Melbourne, trying to find one that matched her mood. It was difficult—she didn't feel particularly jazzy, bluesy, poppy or funky at the moment. She spotted the KC and the Sunshine Band CD. Perfect. Their music had helped rid her mind of ideas left over from different launches she'd organized, so maybe the reverse would work just as well—it could blast ideas into her currently empty brain.

She turned it up to full volume and sang along at the top of her voice as she turned on the TV, sound down, and flicked channels. She stopped at an exhibition of Irish dancing. It looked funny playing to a soundtrack of KC and the Sunshine Band. Every now and then the movement on the television matched the disco beat. Perhaps that was the idea she was looking for—she could run dancing classes, ship in busloads of tourists and teach them all disco dancing one night, Irish dancing the next. Or even better, Irish dancing to a disco tune.

The idea made her laugh. She stood in the middle of the lounge room, trying to remember the basic Irish dance steps she'd learned under sufferance as a child. It wasn't exactly *Riverdance*, but if she wriggled her legs really quickly she could keep up with the music. She finished an energetic movement, threw up her arms with a flourish and turned around.

Rohan Hartigan was standing in the doorway.

"I was dancing," she said, for lack of anything better to say and through sheer and absolute embarrassment. She turned the music down, grabbed at a nearby jumper and pulled it over her paint-splattered pajamas.

"You certainly were." He was making a very bad job of trying not to laugh.

Lainey decided attack was the best defense. "How did you get in, if you don't mind me asking?"

"The front door was open. I did knock, but unfortunately you were otherwise occupied and didn't hear me." He was still trying not to smile. "I'm sorry to have interrupted your, um, exercise class like that, but I just came to bring you these. Some of the oral histories I've collected about the Hill of Tara legends."

Lainey glanced at the folder in his hand, still feeling mortified. "Oh, great, thanks. And, um, can I offer you a cup of tea?"

"If you're sure I'm not interrupting . . ."

"Of course not. Come into the kitchen." She let him go first, noticing he knew his way around. Of course he did, if he had visited May here in recent months. Walking beside him, she saw again how the years had changed him. As a teenager, Rohan had been thin. Now he was tall, quite broad too, she noticed. Attractive. Without bidding, Eva's words came into her mind. That she was here to meet Mr. Cholera. And that perhaps he was Rohan Hartigan.

Putting on the kettle, she looked over her shoulder. "How do you have it, Rohan?"

"*I don't want tea, I want you,*" *he said huskily. He cupped her face in his hand, staring deep into her eyes* . . .

Lainey blinked, sure the color was rising in her face. Where in God's name had that thought come from?

"White with one thanks, Lainey." He looked around the room. "You've been busy."

"It needed the work, really. It was fairly run-down."

Rohan nodded. "Your aunt lost interest in it as the years went by. It was hard for an old woman to manage on her own, I think."

Lainey felt a spark of guilt. "Because we weren't around—is that what you mean? Rohan, if we'd stayed in Ireland we wouldn't necessarily have all lived in Meath, dropped in to see her every morning to help her make the beds." She was stung by the suggestion that her father and her family had abandoned May.

"I didn't mean that at all, actually," he said mildly. "I meant she was in her seventies. The stairs were getting a bit much for her, so she was hardly going to start climbing ladders and wallpapering."

"Oh, I see what you mean." She'd obviously taken an overdose of her paranoia pills today.

"She was lonely, though, Lainey. She missed you all, I know that. She often mentioned you."

"Did she?" Lainey was surprised to hear that.

He nodded. "She had some great stories to tell about Tara, too. She had some great stories about all sorts of things."

"She didn't happen to tell you why she named the

B&B Green Gables, did she? The gables being red and all?"

He laughed. "I wondered if you'd notice that. She'd actually planned to call it after one of Tara's earlier names, *Druim Cain*. You know, the Irish for Beautiful Hill."

Lainey nodded as if to say of course she'd known that.

"She ordered it from the sign-makers in town, with some very specific instructions about the design and the lettering and the size, from what I could gather. But she got very impatient with them, kept ringing them to hurry them along. And you know human nature, the more you push someone, the more they resist. So apparently she had enough one day, stormed in there, said she wasn't waiting for her sign any longer and just grabbed the first sign on the counter."

"Don't tell me, which happened to say—"

He grinned. "Exactly. Green Gables. You have to laugh, don't you? I think she thought it was quite funny herself, once she calmed down. Even funnier, once she'd actually hung up the sign."

Lainey didn't remember her father saying that May had possessed a good sense of humor. She passed Rohan his tea, and offered him a chair at the kitchen table. She was about to ask him what he had been up to for the past fifteen years when he got in first with a question.

"So have you big plans for this place? Beyond the redecorating, I mean."

She sat down opposite him. "Well, the first thing is to let people know I'm back in business. I'm going to join every tourist association in Ireland I can, take out all the ads I can, walk the streets of Dublin shouting the name of the B&B if necessary." She realized it felt good to be having a conversation with someone other than Eva for a change. She really had been suffering from spoken word shortage.

"You can't just rely on passing traffic like May did?"

Lainey decided not to go into that at the moment. "I guess I don't want to leave it to chance."

He shook his head. "The world can't live without advertising anymore, can it? It gets you from the moment you wake up until the moment you sleep. Buy this, do this, stay here, eat this, wear this. Don't you ever get sick of other people telling you what to do?"

"They don't try very often," she said with a quick grin.

"But they do it all the time without you realizing, Lainey. In subtle ways."

"Well, I can't complain about that. I do those types of things in my real job." In my real life.

"You work in advertising?"

He made it sound as though she worked in an anthrax laboratory. "Well, no, not advertising specifically. But I do event management and product launches. You know, a different sort of advertising, getting attention for things in other ways."

"Don't you get tired of it? Spending every day trying to influence people, brainwash them?"

She kept her voice low and calm. After Declan's attacks over the years she was well used to defending her job. "No, I don't think it's brainwashing actually. It's all free choice at the end of the day. And you have to eat and wear clothes. You may as well be well-informed about your choices." He still looked skeptical. She smiled. "What are you longing for, Rohan? Days back on the Hill of Tara when you men just grew your beards, didn't have to worry about what brand of shaver you used? Just got up in the morning, popped on your cloak and you were dressed? Bit the head off a deer and that was breakfast done?"

He smiled then. She was pleased to see his sense of humor had survived adolescence. "No, I don't want to go back that far. But I remember thinking it was really good when I first went to Germany and I didn't know the language. There was something peaceful about it, being able to walk around and not understand the billboards and the radio ads and newspaper ads. I made the choices I wanted to make, without any outside influences."

"You lived in Germany?" It was the first piece of personal information she'd had from him.

He nodded. "I still do. I've been there ten years. I'm just back here temporarily."

"So you're a fluent German speaker now?"

"I am, yes."

"And are you married to a lovely German Frau? Haben Sie Kinder?"

"You speak German too?"

"No, don't be impressed. Mine is basic, language-tape German."

"Mine was for years, too. But no, I'm not married, to my mother's shame. But I have a . . . what's the word? I'm too old to say girlfriend and the word partner's just as bad . . ."

"A special friend, you mean? Eine spezielle Freundin?"

He smiled at her terrible German. "A special friend, yes. I have a special friend. Her name's Sabine."

Lainey had a million other questions. Why is Sabine

there and you're here? She had to pinch the back of her hand to stop herself. He got in first again anyway.

"And are you married, Lainey? Have you left a tribe of children and a shearer back in Australia?"

"No children, no. And no shearer." And that was enough personal information from her for the time being, she decided.

The KC and the Sunshine Band CD clicked as it reached the end, making her jump. She leaped at the change in mood, picking up the folder of papers on the table. "Well, thanks for dropping these off, Rohan. Much appreciated."

"No problem at all. Just call if you need any more information. We could meet for a pint or something. It'd be good to catch up properly."

"Yes, it would."

With the music playing loudly again once he'd gone, she went back to her cleaning, thinking of him as she worked, cringing again that he'd caught her flipping her legs about like some demented whirling dervish.

Funny that he should turn up like that the day after she and Eva had been talking about him as a possible love candidate, Lainey thought. Mind you, if the love fates had been at work her Mr. Cholera would hardly have caught her making a fool of herself, wearing her paint-splattered pajamas, would he? He would have rung the doorbell for a start, and she would have been much more prepared. As she cleaned, she pictured the scene clearly in her mind . . .

The doorbell rang. She checked her appearance in the hall mirror, smoothing her long red dress, before she opened the door. She couldn't explain why, but something that morning had made her dress up far more than she normally did around the house. She'd carefully applied her makeup as well, knowing her eyes looked smoky and alluring, her lips full and welcoming. She opened the door.

Standing there was Rohan Hartigan, wearing a full dinner suit.

"Rohan, hello." Her voice came out huskier than normal.

"Hello, Lainey."

She noticed his dark eyes, the windswept curls. She had a sudden longing to run her fingers through them . . .

She stopped there, laughing out loud at her own thoughts. Why wasn't real life ever like that? It really would be so much simpler.

She finished scrubbing the final cupboard and stood up with a groan, clutching her lower back. A body obviously had housework muscles that were quite distinct from living-a-normal-life muscles. Passing the phone, she debated whether to call Eva, fill her in on the latest about Rohan. Then she decided against it. Eva would probably decide that his sudden arrival was meant to be, that the scar on his arm was some kind of mystical brand linking Lainey and Rohan through the years. No, she wouldn't tell her after all.

CHAPTER 17

Her youngest brother answered the phone the next time she rang home. "Hugh? What are you doing there?"

"Call me old-fashioned, but don't most people start a phone call with hello?"

"Sorry, Hughie. Hello, hello, hello. Now I'm in credit for next time. But what *are* you doing there?"

"I live here."

"When it suits you."

"Well, it suits me at the moment. How are things over there, Lainey? That reward-calendar is up on the wall, I hope?"

She softened at the thought of it. "It sure is, Hughie, thanks. How are things there? You all up and about already?"

"We've been up for hours. Ma's gone out for the day with Mrs. Douglas. She said she needed a break or she was going to crack up. Dad's in bed, you'll be surprised to hear." He lowered his voice. "He's been bad lately, hardly out of his room."

"Is it physical or mental?"

"Mental. Completely mental. The insurance company are at it again. They've delayed it, said the person in charge of Dad's case is on sick leave."

"Sick leave? What, a headache? A sore toe? God, Hugh, if I was there I would—"

"Want to do what we all want to do. You're not the only one upset about all this, Lainey."

"Well, can't we do something? Report them to the ombudsman, or the insurance council or something?"

"Dad's solicitor checked it all out. They would just argue that it is going through due process, or whatever the term is, and we have to be patient. A friend of Dad's called around the other night, said he knew of two other people who'd had exactly the same trouble with this insurance company, had been through months and months of delays like this. And every time they queried it, there'd be another delay."

"You really are up-to-date with this, aren't you?"

"Why wouldn't I be? I worry about Dad as much as you do. I just don't go on about it as much."

"Sorry, I know you do. I'm just raging because I'm so far away and I can't do anything."

"Then maybe one of us will have to step in. Can't have you taking all the credit all the time."

"What's that supposed to mean?"

"Don't worry about it, Lainey."

There was an awkward pause. "So, any other news?"

"I had a drink with Adam the other night."

"You *what?*"

"I ran into him on my way to the cinema up the road from his place and he invited me for a beer after he finished work that night. So we met up, had a bit of a chat, man-to-man. He had lots of questions about you, actually. To be honest, I was a bit surprised he didn't know anything until he explained that you'd dumped him the morning you left."

"I didn't *dump* him."

"Well, that's what it sounded like. Are you mad, Lainey? He's a great bloke and now you've really hurt him."

"What do you mean? What did he say?"

"It wasn't what he said, it was the way he was. He just seemed really low. You know that's really bad karma, don't you, to hurt another human being like that? You'll come back in your next life as a slug or something now and you won't last a day. You'll be out in the garden and before you know it someone will be pouring salt on your back and you'll die a slow, agonizing death."

"Hugh, stop that. I will not turn into a slug."

"You might. So why did you dump him, then?"

"For the second time, I didn't dump him. And it's all very complicated and more to the point it really isn't—"

"Any of my business. Why is nothing ever my business? Next time I'm coming back as the oldest kid in a family and I am going to tell my younger brothers and sisters everything, whether they want to hear it or not."

Lainey swallowed her pride temporarily. "And how is he, Hugh?"

"Who?"

"You know who I mean."

"Apart from being obviously heartbroken?"

"Hugh, *please.*"

"Well, he's tall, funny, very decent to me, unlike my older brothers or any of your past boyfriends . . ."

"But how is he?"

"He was asking me the same question about you, actually. For two people who have split up you seem very curious about one another. That's odd, isn't it? I mean, not that I know much about relationships, being the youngest and all . . ."

"Hughie . . ."

He gave in, too kindhearted to torment her anymore. "He's okay. Really busy, he said, opening more hours or something. Distracting himself with work, if you ask me. So, do you want me to give him a message from you?"

She wavered. No. What was the point? It didn't change anything. They were still going to be apart for a year. "I'll need to think about it."

"You're like Ma. You always say that when you really mean no. Okay, I'll tell him no, you didn't have a message for him."

"But wait, can you tell him . . ." Tell him what?

Hugh was waiting. "Yes?"

"No, don't worry, Hugh. No message."

"Okay, on your head be it. By the way, that friend of yours was at the restaurant, too. You know, Kim, the one who wears the low-cut tops. The one you always tell me not to stare at."

"Kim? Kim was at Adam's? Are you sure?"

"Sure I'm sure. I never forget a cleavage like that. Declan and I used to love it when she'd come and visit you. All our sex education lessons packed into one body."

"Don't be vulgar. What was she doing there?"

"I didn't ask her, but she was sitting at a table with a knife and fork in front of her and it is a restaurant, so my hunch is she was having dinner."

"In a big group?"

"No, with two women. Why, has she been banned from going out on her own?"

"But why was she there again? Why doesn't she go somewhere else? Was Adam talking to her?"

"Lainey, listen to you. What do you care? You dumped him, didn't you? He can run off with all the Kims in Melbourne if he wants to."

No, he can't. Lainey was shocked at her reaction to the news. "Did anything happen between them?"

"I think she ate the food he cooked. I can't tell you what happened after dinner but I'm assuming it went down the usual digestive path."

"That's it. Next time Declan and Brendan start bullying you, I'm going to join in. My days of rescuing you are over."

"I didn't see anything, I promise," he said, laughing. "I just called in for a beer like I said. Do you need to know exactly where we went and what he was wearing? Or if any other women walked past his line of sight?"

"You've become very cruel since I've left, Hugh. I'm disappointed in you."

"I'm sorry, Lainey. I promise I've told you all I noticed. And I promise to keep a very close eye on him from now on."

"Don't you say a word to him about this. I was just curious, that's all."

"Of course that's all it was. And you'd better go or you'll eat up all our inheritance with phone bills."

She said goodbye and hung up, then stood looking at the phone, unsettled. She was tempted to pick it up again and call Adam, then and there. Tempted to hear his voice. Very tempted to hear exactly what had happened with Kim. Tempted just to talk to him about anything, in fact.

Before she left Melbourne, she'd have sworn that she and Adam hardly had time to talk to each other. But since she'd been away from him, she'd realized that they did actually talk a lot—little snatched phone calls throughout the day, a quick call from the restaurant in between sittings, messages left on each other's voicemail. She'd occasionally been out with clients or at some formal dinner and had received a text message on her mobile from him—a quick remark, a joke, once or twice an outrageously sexy message knowing she was among clients and would have to keep a straight face. She'd talked to him about her father a lot. And her mother, and her brothers. And Celia. And she knew about his family too, about his plans for the restaurant, his staffing hassles, the difficulties with his suppliers, the menus he wanted to try . . .

She twisted the bracelet round and round, feeling jealous, lonely and very far from home.

* * *

As Lainey vacuumed the rooms several days later, collecting nonexistent dust left by her nonexistent guests, she made a decision about the B&B. The idea had come to her during the night, while she'd lain there unable to sleep. She'd forced herself to think of work, keeping her mind away from unsettling thoughts about Adam. Instead, she'd run through campaigns she'd worked on at Complete Event Management, sifting through them, trying to find ideas that she could use for the B&B. One in particular had come to her, a promotional campaign she'd worked on for a new brand of chocolate milk. Sales had been terrible until the manufacturer had changed its name—not the packaging, not the milk inside, only the name, after which sales had taken off. Maybe the same approach would work on something bigger than milk . . .

She turned off the vacuum cleaner and ran downstairs to the phone, grabbing the will from the folder in the kitchen drawer as she went past.

"Mr. Fogarty, it's Lainey Byrne."

"Lainey, how are you?" There was a long pause, with just the occasional sigh audible, then a rustle.

Probably putting down his cheese sandwich, Lainey thought. "I'm just grand, thank you. Mr. Fogarty, can I check something with you? You know I think that Green Gables didn't enjoy the greatest reputation around Meath."

"No, Lainey. I think it would be fair to say that."

"Can I change the name? Is there anything in May's will that says I have to keep calling it Green Gables?"

"Just one moment, Lainey. Let me check for you." She sat there, imagining his little feet padding across the carpet.

He was back moments later. "No, Lainey, there don't seem to be any subclauses regarding illegality of any name change, so my feeling would be I can grant you permission to use any name as desired. In fact, I think that's a marvelous idea."

Flicking through her copy of the will, she saw something she hadn't taken notice of before—the name and address of one of the witnesses, R. Hartigan. Dunshaughlin, Co. Meath. "This witness, Mr. Fogarty. R. Hartigan? Is that as in Rohan Hartigan? The tourism consultant? Curly dark hair?"

"I believe it's the same young man."

"Did he know my aunt that well?"

"I can't say how well, Lainey, but certainly they were acquainted with one another. Mr. Hartigan is involved in an important project regarding the Hill of Tara and he and your aunt shared a great love of Irish mythology, history, legends, you know the sort of thing. They were working on an oral history project together before your aunt's sudden death. I presume Mr. Hartigan was there the day she decided to revise her will. It was all legal, I assure you. All of her wills were."

Lainey felt a sudden rush of frustration about her father's situation, against May, who could have just left her house and land to him. Against Rohan, for being a witness to the will. "Mr. Fogarty, does it go against all your legal training to answer a few simple yes or no questions?"

There was a pause. "Possibly."

In her mind's eye Lainey was now in a gripping courtroom scene in *Law & Order*. "In your opinion, do you think Mr. Hartigan may have had something to do with this change of mind? With this new element of her will?"

"Well, I know that they both felt strongly about the importance of young Irish people being aware of their heritage. Mr. Hartigan is a staunch supporter of that issue.

An enthusiast, even. I believe Miss Byrne was very taken with his ideas and energy."

"What sort of ideas?"

"I believe he is concerned that the history is being diluted, that people, those of Irish ancestry in particular, come back to Ireland looking for picture-postcard Ireland—"

"Picture-postcard? And he doesn't like that? What, he's planning on changing the scenery for them?"

"Perhaps picture-postcard is the wrong term. I believe he feels the tourist-brochure image of Ireland of leprechauns and little thatched cottages does the country a great disservice. That it makes a laugh of us, if you like."

"So he and my aunt were planning a revolution together, were they? What were they going to do, storm the tourist offices?"

"You'll have to ask Mr. Hartigan that yourself, Miss Byrne. All I know is that your aunt was greatly taken with the idea of Irish people abroad being made fully aware of their heritage and history, in particular through spending time here learning about the real Ireland."

Irish people abroad. Like Lainey and her family. Would May have been so taken by the idea she changed her will to make them come back for a year? "Thank you, Mr. Fogarty. You've been very helpful."

And was it thank you for nothing, Rohan Hartigan? Why would he have done it, though? As part of his master plan to re-educate the people of Ireland, to banish the paddywhackery approach to tourism? To get her back for the dare-gone-wrong all those years ago? Or just pure and simple mischief? She was going to find out. She pulled out the piece of paper with his phone number on and rang it. He answered on the first ring.

"Rohan, hello. It's Lainey Byrne."

"Lainey, how are you? Settling in?"

Her voice was brisk. "Perfectly, thanks. You mentioned that you might be able to spare a minute, to answer any questions I might have and to give me a crash course in Tara legends. Did you mean it?"

"Of course. When would suit you?"

"Is that arm of yours able to hold up a pint?"

He laughed. "Oh, it is indeed."

"Then what about Friday night? In that pub with the thatched roof?"

"Perfect. At nine?"

"Yes, see you then." She hung up, pleased. She could have asked him on the phone but she had a feeling it was better to have that sort of discussion face to face, where she could see his reaction. Besides, it would be nice to be out and about. Her life was being lived over the phone too much at the moment in any case.

Back to the kitchen table—her office, she liked to think. She pulled out a copy of the Meath B&B guide. All the obvious names, the best names, would be long gone, she knew. She pulled out the Hill of Tara guide book next. Could she call it after any of the features? She frowned as she read down the map. No, perhaps not. Who would want to stay at a B&B called Mound of the Hostages? Or The Sloping Trenches? The Banquet Hall, maybe, but she'd hardly call her breakfast a banquet.

She'd have to think laterally. Tara, the ancient capital of Ireland. Home of the Kings? No, it sounded more like a casino or a sporting ground. Something more noble, perhaps. Other B&Bs called themselves things like The Priory or The Grange, which sounded very alluring. She could call it The Temple. The Castle. The corny names? Dunroamin? Neverome? No point running a B&B, then. A friend of hers in Sydney had called her house High Dudgeon. No, not right for a B&B either. High Fidelity? High Hopes? High Moral Tone? No, no, no.

She stopped herself. She'd clearly lost her mind. She shut the notebook. It was time she went into Dunshaughlin and saw some other human beings.

She drove past her family's old house again, stopping outside and checking to see if she had any sentimental attachment to it at all. She didn't, she realized. Perhaps there wasn't a sentimental bone in her body. She drove past Eva's old family house. Her parents had moved too, and were now in a newer housing estate on the other side of town. No sentimental yearnings to be had there, either. She drove past the school and parked in the main street, narrow and clogged with traffic, deciding to do some shopping while she was in town.

She was in the wine shop choosing a bottle of red when through the window she saw Rohan Hartigan walking down the opposite footpath. He had a young woman with him, eighteen, nineteen years old perhaps. She was too young to be his girlfriend, surely? Was it his daughter? Lainey felt like a spy, looking out at them. Rohan was doing all the talking, the young woman shaking her head occasionally. They walked into the coffee shop on the corner of the main street. She considered for a moment whether to go in and say hello, then decided against it, in case it was his girlfriend. Her German wasn't feeling up to scratch today. She'd be seeing Rohan soon enough in any case.

An idea for the name came to her as she was driving home. She parked the car and stood in front of the house gazing at it. What was another name for a bed-and-breakfast or guesthouse? A lodge. Where was she? Just near Tara. Of course. It was the perfect name. She could picture the new nameplate already. *Tara Lodge*.

CHAPTER 18

A date with Rohan? Lainey, well done. That was quick work!"

Lainey laughed into the phone. "It's not a date, Evie. I invited him for a drink because I think he had something to do with May's will and I want to find out what."

"That's all, really? You're not attracted to him at all?"

"Of course I'm not. Oh, I see, this is your meeting of the fates idea again, isn't it?"

"Well, don't you think it's weird? You're only here because of that will and Rohan is the one who witnessed it. So maybe you are meant to meet him for some reason. Lainey, maybe he really *is* your Mr. Cholera."

"Are you on some sort of commission from the marriage license board?"

"Don't tease. You know I just want you to be happy. And I'm just saying that maybe you should stay open to anything that might happen."

· · ·

That night Lainey dreamed about Adam. She woke in the morning expecting to find him in bed beside her, convinced for a moment that she could feel his silky skin, the hard muscles of his back, the brown arms wrapped around her. Those kinds of dreams weren't doing her any good at all, she thought crossly, thumping the pillow and turning over in the bed. She had to try harder to put him out of her mind.

· · ·

There was a traffic jam in Dunshaughlin when Lainey drove in to meet Rohan the next night. Sitting in the car, the radio playing, her mind started drifting toward an Adam memory. No, Lainey, stop it, she told herself. She mustn't go there. She had to think of other things. Eva's phone call about tonight's drink with Rohan came to mind. She tried to picture what would happen if Eva had her way . . .

The pub was small, cozy, intimate. There was a fire burning in the grate at one side, music playing softly in the background. Not Irish folk, but a low, sexy, jazz-type song.

She saw Rohan instantly. He was sitting in a corner, dressed in a dark woolen jumper, his hair ruffled, reading a book of poetry. He seemed to sense her eyes on him and looked up. For a moment his face was still, then he slowly smiled as she walked toward him.

"Lainey, hello. Can I take your coat for you?"

She nodded, shrugging out of the dark woolen garment, glad she'd taken the extra time with her hair and makeup, knowing that the dress she'd chosen accentuated her curves, clung to her body. She knew he noticed, could feel his eyes on her.

"Can I get you a drink?"

"Martini, please."

"Don't tell me—a dry, is it?"

"You guessed."

"I did." His look was long, hot . . .

The loud blast of a horn behind her jolted her to reality. As the traffic started moving again, she turned left and found a parking place across the road from the pub. After quickly checking her lipstick in her rearview mirror, she hurried across the road, hugging her coat tightly in around her body.

She had to blink to make the scene from her imagination disappear. The noise helped—the pub was rowdy with the combination of jukebox and sports results blaring from a TV in the corner. It took a moment to find Rohan. He was sitting at a table to the left, with a nearly empty pint of Guinness in front of him, reading the sports pages of the local paper. She had sat down in front of him before he noticed her. He had an earplug in his ear.

"Lainey, good to see you. Sorry about this." He pulled the earplug out and smiled apologetically. "Bayern Munich are playing tonight. I'm just getting the results."

"No problem at all. Can I get you a pint?"

He made to stand up. "No, let me. What will you have?"

He'd always had nice manners, even as a schoolboy, she remembered. "I'm happy to go to the bar, Rohan, really. A pint?" He nodded. "Grand, I'll be right back." She was trying to be as businesslike as she could be, knowing this wasn't a social drink, that finding out about the will was the real reason she was here tonight.

"Two pints was it, love?" The barman had half an eye on her, half on the television behind the bar.

"Pint and a glass, thanks." She wanted to keep her wits about her.

As Lainey waited for the Guinness to settle she looked around the bar. It was getting hard to tell what was authentic old-style Irish pub decoration and what was new replica Irish-style decoration. This pub had the usual collection of old Guinness and tourism posters on the wall, glass-fronted cupboards filled with old books and newspapers and pottery dishes, but she couldn't tell if they had been there for decades or been bought as a job lot from a refitting company.

She returned to Rohan's table with the two drinks. He really had turned into a good-looking man, she thought again, though his face still had a certain boyish quality, probably helped by the dark curls. As she came up he took out the earplug again and gave another apologetic smile. "They're through. It's brilliant. It's been a real roller-coaster year, you see. Their key defender got injured early in the season and there's been trouble with the striker as well, so we——" He stopped, laughing. "Do you know, I've never noticed anyone's eyes glaze over quite so quickly. Football's not a great interest of yours, I gather?"

"It was that obvious?"

"It was that obvious. Pick your audience. Isn't that the first rule of public speaking?" he said cheerfully. "Sláinte, Lainey. Thanks for the pint." They clinked glasses. "So how are you? How are things coming along at the B&B?"

"Fine, just fine. I've had a few more ideas."

"Don't tell me, you're going to open up an advertising and marketing company there, to exploit us simple country folk?"

He was teasing, she realized, but she wasn't in the mood for it tonight. She'd just opened her mouth to defend her choice of career yet again, when over his shoulder she saw an old Bord Fáilte poster aimed at the American market, all thatched cottages and bonny-faced colleens. It was time for some teasing of her own. She gave him a winning smile. "Oh, nothing like that. Actually, one of these pubs gave me the idea. I'm going to turn it into a theme B&B."

He stopped mid-sip. "A what?"

"I've been doing my research and I've realized that's exactly what the tourists want. Irish history delivered in nice, comfortable chunks. So that's what I'm going to do. Turn it into the Hill of Tara theme B&B."

He looked appalled. "What, redecorate it, dress up in costumes, that kind of way?"

She had no intention of doing any such thing. "You've got it exactly. I'm even thinking of getting a donkey for the back field. And old-style beds, with a bit of straw thrown around the rooms. And I'll be serving authentic Irish breakfasts, of course."

He relaxed slightly. "Authentic? You've done some research into it, then?"

"Oh, no. I'm not going to go as far as *cooking* authentic old meals. I just thought I'd rename some of them." Lainey noticed with some delight that Rohan's eyes were narrowing into slits, just like her cat Rex's did when he got cross. "I'm going to call porridge gruel of course, and bacon and eggs will be, I don't know, ye olde Irish breakfast, something nice and simple like that. And I thought I'd get some old newspapers made up, with events from the old days. You know, 'Finn McCool wins another battle,' or 'Great bargains on Tara brooches at the Mound of the Hostages jewelry store this week.'"

"What?" He was making no pretense about being polite anymore. "That's Hollywood-ism, exploiting the past."

"Exploiting it? I'm trying to understand it, give myself a crash course. And I'm sure the people who come to Ireland and stay in my B&B will appreciate the chance to learn about Irish history too."

"That's not history. Like hamburgers aren't real food. This is fast history you're talking about."

She was starting to believe her own arguments now. "Rohan, history is history, surely, no matter how it's communicated. You're not being a snob about this, are you? Saying history is just for the elite? That you can only learn about it in a lecture hall or in a hardback book covered in dust?"

"There's something called the truth, though, and what you're doing isn't the truth. It's peddling fantasy, like opening a theme park. I've spent the past ten years of my life fighting exactly that sort of madness."

"Have you really? Then surely you've discovered that what I'm suggesting is what most tourists really want. They arrive here, they want history in bite-size pieces, three counties in ten minutes. And what I've always said is give your customers what they want."

"There's fake history and there's authentic history. And you're peddling something fake if you go ahead with this, Lainey."

She was enjoying herself. "I should go the whole way, you mean? Really reenact Tara life? Have beds completely made of straw? Tell the guests, 'Sorry, no breakfast this morning, the servant girl was killed by a tribe from the south who then ransacked our scullery and took all the food. Oh, and there's no hot water either because hot water services still haven't been invented.' Is that what you mean?"

He was trying not to smile, she just knew it. There was a glint of something there for a moment. Like a flash of light against a dark night sky. Then it was gone. She kept talking. "It's called tourism, Rohan. Nothing to get upset about."

"It's called lies, Lainey. You should know better than that."

"Well, it seems we'll just have to agree to disagree," she said, laughing inside at her prim remark.

"It seems that way." They sat there silent for a moment, before he spoke. "So, another drink, then?"

She thought he sounded reluctant about it. "Great, thanks." She passed him her not-quite-empty glass with a friendly smile. Not exactly off to a flying start with the match made in heaven, Lainey thought, recalling Eva's words again. As she watched him move up to the now crowded bar, her imagination fired up again . . .

"Here you are, Lainey. Another martini."

He sat down beside her, a little closer than he had been before. "So tell me, are you finding it difficult being home?" His eyes searched hers, as though he really wanted to know.

"It's fine. Grand, really."

"Tell me the truth, Lainey."

She turned until she was facing him full on. "I'm a little lonely."

"So, Lainey, are you finding it difficult to be home?"

She jumped as he appeared back with her new drink. "No, I'm not lonely at all," she said, far too quickly.

He gave her a puzzled look. "Oh, good. And your family, how are they all going back in Australia?"

Did he know about her father's accident? May hadn't known, so he wouldn't have either, she realized. She didn't want to talk about it tonight. She wanted to sort out something else first. "They're all fine, thank you." She took a breath. "Speaking of my family, I understand you were the witness to my aunt's will, which is why you knew about me coming over."

He didn't react as she expected—guilty or defensive. He nodded calmly. "I didn't know it was going to be you, just that it would be one of your family. And I didn't expect it to happen so soon. I really thought she'd go on for years. It was a big shock when she died."

He looked genuinely sad, she thought. "And what did you think of her idea about one of us coming back here?"

"I thought it was great."

"And was it you who put this idea in her head?"

"I wish I had." His smile disarmed her.

"You *wish* you had. What does that mean?"

"I'm all for it, bringing emigrants back to get to know their country again. There are probably other ways of doing it, though, not as extreme as your aunt's approach."

Her hackles were half-lying, half-standing, awaiting further instructions from her brain. "So you didn't talk her into it?"

"Talk May into something?" He laughed. "Lainey, there's nobody in this country who could have talked

May Byrne into doing something she didn't want to do. I wasn't even sure it should have been me who witnessed the will. I'd got to know her a bit over the few months I'd been collecting the oral histories, but witnessing a will seemed too formal for such a short friendship. But she insisted."

"You liked her, didn't you?"

"I did. She was bad-tempered, of course, but sparky with it."

The hackles retreated back under her skin. Lainey realized she'd have to confess to him that she wasn't planning on opening the Hill of Tara theme B&B. She'd just opened her mouth to tell him when they were interrupted.

"Rohan, hello there. Mind if I join you?"

They both turned around. It was a middle-aged, ginger-haired man with a moustache. Rohan smiled up at him. "Bill, good to see you. Sure, have a seat. Lainey, you don't mind, do you? Bill, this is Lainey Byrne from the B&B near Tara. Lainey, this is Bill O'Hara from Oldcastle. I was out talking to his grandfather last month for the oral history project I'm doing." Rohan turned back to Bill. "So how's your grandfather going?"

"I don't know what you said to him, but the old fellow hasn't stopped drawing maps of rocks and vaults and standing stones since. Now he's got some idea of digging up the back field, convinced he might find old gold or ancient artifacts."

Rohan grinned. "And so he might. Think of the money, Bill. He'd get a finder's fee, remember."

After a little while, Lainey started feeling in the way.

Rohan was doing his best to include her, but she had the feeling the pair of them were just dying to get into a discussion about the football match. She was tired, in any case. "If you'll excuse me, I'll be off I think. I've a busy day tomorrow." Wishful thinking, if ever she'd heard it.

"You sure you won't stay for another?" Rohan asked.

"No, really. Thanks all the same."

"Well, good to catch up, Lainey. See you again soon."

They both gave her a friendly wave and went back to their pints.

An hour later, she was in her pajamas and about to climb into bed when the phone rang. It was Eva.

"I've been thinking about you all night. I just had to ring. How did it go? Did you find him attractive? Sexy?"

"Eva!"

"Did you?"

"Yes, he is good-looking," she admitted. "In a kind of old-fashioned, wild-haired way."

"And was there plenty of conversation?"

"Well, yes. But we went to school together, Evie. It's not like it was a blind date."

"But no awkward silences? Lots to talk about? Excellent." Eva made it sound as though she was ticking off boxes in a questionnaire. "So what happened exactly, from the moment you arrived?"

"It was just a simple drink, really. We had a pint, a bit of a disagreement about history versus tourism, he told me he liked May and that the condition about us running the B&B wasn't his idea and then I left."

"You had a disagreement and then you left? Just like

that? You stormed out, you mean? That's supposed to be good, isn't it? Getting off to a dramatic start?"

"I didn't storm out. I left when a friend of his turned up and I felt in the way."

"But you had a disagreement? That could mean there's a fiery kind of attraction between you."

"Or it could just mean we disagree about something. Eva, please stop it, you're reading things where nothing exists. And you also seem to be forgetting the fact he has a girlfriend-slash-partner in Munich."

"But what's she doing in Germany if they're supposed to be a couple? Lainey, please, be positive. Maybe he is attracted to you, and that's why he gave up a night to meet you. There was even some big football match on, wasn't there? I know I couldn't get any sense out of Joe until it was over."

Lainey didn't mention Rohan's earplugs and mini transistor. "Tell me, Madame Eva, is that your crystal ball I can hear you polishing?"

Eva laughed. "No, I'm cooking actually. And I'd better finish it and let you go to bed and dream sweet dreams about Rohan. Keep me up-to-date with what happens, Lainey, won't you? I really have got a feeling about all this."

And I've got a feeling my friend's turned into a new-age fantasist, Lainey thought as she hung up.

• • •

She woke up in the middle of the night, still enveloped in the dream she'd had. It had been sexy, sensuous, passionate, fast. Sudden attraction, hot kisses, naked bodies.

Lying there remembering it, slowly stretching, still feeling the pleasant aftereffects, she frowned. It wasn't the dream itself that worried her. She'd thoroughly enjoyed it, in fact.

The weird thing was it had starred Rohan, not Adam.

CHAPTER 19

The first opening of one of the squares on Hugh's reward-calendar took place on a clear, crisp day. She'd woken to a blue sky, the first in days, a different, softer blue to the one she was used to in Melbourne. She knelt up on her bed and looked out the window. The trees were still bare, the rose bushes without flowers. One blue sky did not a spring make. But the fresh light lifted her spirits. Even though it was cold outside, she went around the house, opening all the windows, letting in the fresh air, her "Songs to Play When in a Mellow Mood" CD sending tracks by Moby and Massive Attack drifting through the rooms.

She put off opening the cardboard square until after breakfast, making the pleasure last. The actual moment of discovering the little Swiss chocolate was anticlimactic, in fact, even if the chocolate itself was delicious. What had she expected? Sirens to sound and streamers to come flying out from behind the cardboard square? But it was a good day. One month down, eleven to go.

She had just hung the calendar back on the wall when the doorbell rang. She went out in time to see the postman driving off after leaving a small parcel on the doorstep. It had been sent express mail. She read the label—it was Hugh's handwriting. She shook it. It felt like a videotape.

She fought her curiosity until she had made a coffee, then came into the living room, put the video in the machine and pressed play. There was a crackle, a few seconds of black and white fuzzy light, and then there on the screen was a close-up of her cat Rex, a handwritten sign above him reading A HUGH BYRNE PRODUCTION. Rex meowed in slow motion and the scene became a pastiche of the MGM lion. Lainey laughed, leaning forward, hugging her knees, as another handwritten sign came up, taking over the whole screen.

The Byrne Family Update
Presented by Hugh Byrne

The next shot showed Hugh standing in an office, wearing an appalling ginger wig and glasses, with a whiteboard behind him. He started speaking in a slow, deep voice, staring straight into the camera.

"Welcome to the program. Tonight, I'm asking some important questions. How does an ordinary, Irish-Australian family cope when the linchpin ups and leaves for Ireland to run a B&B? Who will organize them? Who will keep track of everyone's movements? Will they be able to manage? In the first of a major seventy-five-part series, we're going to investigate the cause and effects of The Disappearance of Lainey, the Family Control Freak."

Next on the screen was her mother, tugging at her dress, wriggling on one of the living-room chairs, looking a mixture of amused and embarrassed. "Well, at least this is better than having you leap out from behind the car. You nearly gave me a heart attack last week. Oh, it's on, is it? Lainey, love, hello. It's your mother here."

"She can see you, Ma." Hugh's voice from behind the camera.

"Oh, of course. Well, how are you, pet? I know we've talked on the phone but we just wanted to say hello, say we're getting on fine. Look, we've had the living room painted. What do you think?" The camera panned away for a moment, showing some fresh cream walls, then came back to Mrs. Byrne. She leaned forward and started whispering. "Your father's okay. No change."

"A little louder please, Ma."

Mrs. Byrne looked behind her and then said in a loud voice, "No change with your father." A pause. "Unfortunately."

Another pause.

"Keep going, Ma."

"What do I tell her, though? It's only been a few weeks since she was here and saw us all for herself."

"You could tell her how your job at the supermarket is going."

"Oh, yes." Mrs. Byrne beamed at the camera. "My job at the supermarket is going just great, Lainey. There are some marvelous new products out, which I know you'll love. They're called Vegie-Voomers, and they're just terrific, freeze-dried, ready-chopped vegetables. All you have to do is add water and one beef stock cube and you've an instant, nutritious meal—"

"That tastes like baby sick," Hugh interrupted.

"It does not taste like baby sick," Mrs. Byrne said indignantly.

"Worse than baby sick. Dog sick. Pig sick."

"Don't mind him, Lainey. Your father's had it for dinner the past three nights and he hasn't complained at all."

There was a flash of static and then Brendan and Rosie and the twins appeared, sitting on their own sofa at home. Brendan was clearly unhappy about being dragged away from his recycling for something as frivolous as a video message and Rosie just looked uncomfortable. They looked like a before ad for marriage counseling, Lainey thought, trying not to laugh. On their laps, one twin was grizzling, the other smiling obligingly.

"You can't just sit there," Hugh's voice floated in. "Can you send Lainey a message, say something?"

Brendan looked crossly in Hugh's direction. "Well, you haven't said Action or whatever the hell it is you're supposed to say, have you?" Rosie glanced at Brendan, then in the vague direction of the camera. "Hi, Lainey, hope it's going well."

"Yeah, hi, Lain." Brendan halfheartedly made one twin wave, while Rosie tried to soothe the other, who was now wailing like a banshee.

Another flash of static, then Declan appeared on screen, filmed outside his school, coming out of the gate with an attractive young woman—another teacher, Lainey guessed. He spotted Hugh and came over toward the camera. "Hugh? What are you doing here?" There was a mumbled conversation, Lainey heard Hugh mention her name and then the camera went into a close-up of Declan's face.

"Send her a message? Oh, my pleasure." He dropped his voice to a low and mournful tone. "Lainey, oh, Laineyovich, things just aren't the same without you here. Wide shot please, Hugh." The picture went wide. "See these empty plains around me. These empty schoolyards? That's how my heart feels without you close by me. It's an aching nothingness. A gaping wasteland."

Hugh's voice spoke off camera. "A sandy desert."

"A sandy desert. Yes, I like that too. Hurry home, sister dear, and bring that money, won't you?" He twirled an invisible moustache. "And now back to where I was before I was so rudely interrupted." With that he walked back to the female teacher and put his arm around her, turning to wink salaciously at the camera.

There was an unsteady edit, then her father came into view, lying in bed, the light dim around him.

"Dad, any message?"

"Feck off, Hugh, and leave me alone."

"You really want to tell Lainey that?"

There was a silence, then her father's voice. "I can see that red light. Are you using that bloody camera thing again?"

"Any message for Lainey?"

"To hurry home so we can send you off in her place."

Then it was back to Hugh in front of the whiteboard, beaming at her. "That's it for now. Don't forget about the reward-calendar and we'll see you next month."

There was a crackle, then a sudden storm of white fuzz

and then a weather map appeared, fronted by a perky young man in a suit. Lainey thought it was Hugh again before she realized he'd taped over a TV program. She kept watching as there was another crackle, a flash of pictures and then the tape went black again. Lainey leaned back into the sofa, feeling better than she had for the whole month. She wasn't on her own doing this. She was part of a family, doing all this for them. She picked up the phone to ring and thank Hugh right there and then. He was still her little darling after all.

CHAPTER 20

There definitely was a mouse. It had kept her awake the night before, scampering about. She'd eventually given up on sleep, deciding instead to hunt it down. But her quarry had given up for the night, heading back to its lair or mouse hole or wherever the hell it lived. It had left behind a charming calling card, though, she discovered—several neat little lines of poo. She decided to leave them there till morning and went back to bed, before realizing a half-awake state was the best time to deal with it. With a sigh she climbed out of bed again, swept them up and threw them outside.

The next day she was paying for her broken sleep, feeling lethargic. She had things to buy at the shopping center, but she didn't have the energy to drive in there. She should be racking her brain for ideas to get the B&B moving, but that part of her brain had shut down for the day too. All she felt like doing was sitting by the fire and reading.

Then she realized she could do exactly that. In fact,

she could go back to bed for the day if she wanted. Lie on the kitchen floor all day and eat toast. Put a bag on her head and run up and down the stairs all day singing "Waltzing Matilda" if she wanted to. Who would see her? What else did she have to do?

She took the least weird option, fearing a little for her sanity. She had just settled in front of the fire with one of the Tara books from the library when she remembered she had something much more interesting to read—May's folders of letters. She'd promised herself she could read them after the first month was up and now it was. Where on earth had she put them, though? She racked her brain. She'd picked them up from Mr. Fogarty's office, then just shoved them away into a cupboard when she and Eva started on the painting.

She found them in the smallest of the spare rooms, in one of the wardrobes. She flicked through the papers on top, a mixture of bills, circulars and newspaper clippings. Good, she could sort them, pretend to be Sally Secretary for the day. She was certainly sick to death of pretending to be Harriet Housekeeper.

With the radio on in the background, the comforting murmur of voices on the local radio station, she started emptying the folders. The files inside them were all in a mess, like a paper version of the chaos Lainey had found in the kitchen cupboards. May had obviously had some secretarial training in her life, had kept copies of all the letters she had written, attached any reply to them with a paper clip. But that was as far as her filing had gone. She'd clearly just flung them all into files after that. There were letters of complaint to politicians, filled with ideas about how the country could be run more efficiently. There were letters about improving the state of the roads, several of them written in cross capital letters. Overhanging trees were the bane of her life too, it seemed. Drains were a problem. Noisy cars. The lack of road signs. Too many road signs. Lainey wouldn't like to have been at the receiving end of any of her aunt's letters—May hadn't taken no for an answer and in some cases the correspondence had shot back and forth between the two parties for some months, before her aunt had seized on a new issue. But at this distance it was great entertainment. Lainey made herself another pot of coffee, put her feet up on the warmth of the fireguard and kept reading.

As she read letter after letter, she started to form a real picture of her aunt. She was not only fierce, but funny at times too. Not only judgmental but lively minded, curious at least. This was no old woman taking a backseat, content to let the world pass by. May was in there in the thick of things, passing remarks on any issue, big or small, firing letters off in all directions. It was just as well she hadn't had any guests. There wouldn't have been time to look after them, with all these letters to write and trips to the post office to make.

Her father's words came back to her. That Lainey reminded him of May sometimes. The awful thing was she was starting to recognize some of the traits in herself. Certainly she liked to have as many things on the go at once. But was she as hot-tempered? No, she didn't think so. As stubborn? She felt an uncomfortable shimmer of recognition. Then again, who did like admitting they were wrong about something?

She picked up the final file, packed with newspaper clippings, snippets cut from magazines, handwritten scraps of paper. The subjects ranged from recipes to handy household hints, herbal cures to health tips. Lainey read a couple. "Don't despair if you run out of dental floss, the string of a tea bag makes a handy substitute." "A cut onion in a freshly painted room will quickly banish those fumes!" If only she and Eva had known that all those days ago. Tucked in the back of the file she found an unopened envelope, addressed to her father in the Melbourne suburb of Broadmeadows. Scrawled across it in block letters was the message: *Return to sender. No longer at this address.* Lainey could only just remember the Broadmeadows house. They'd rented it for only a few months, leaving in a hurry when a gang of bikies had moved in next door. It had been the third or perhaps the fourth house they had lived in during their first few years in Melbourne. So could she open this one? She thought for a moment of checking with her father, but then she had his permission to read May's letters already, didn't she? She opened it. It was short, to the point. Just the one line, in fact, written in an angry scrawl.

Don't you dare blame Peg. This is YOUR fault.

That was it. Lainey turned it over, but there was no explanation. What had been his fault? What had he blamed her mother for? Feeling as though she'd peeked through a curtain and seen something she shouldn't have, she hurriedly poked the page back into the envelope. She gathered all of the folders and stowed them back in the cupboard upstairs.

• • •

For the next week, she worked on her ideas for the revamp of the B&B. She'd devised dozens of marketing plans in her working life, knew all the steps. Define your product, then your market, then work out a way of letting the market know about your product. So what was her product?

She had a nice old house. Good views. It was peaceful. Beside an historic site, already on lots of tourists' itineraries. But also less than an hour from Dublin, just the right distance for stressed city people wanting a weekend getaway.

The hair at the back of her neck prickled in the way it always did when she knew she was onto a good idea. She had actually been joking when she'd spoken to Rohan about opening a theme B&B, but perhaps that was exactly what she could do. Run theme weekends. Theme luxury weekends, with great food and wine, maybe even a guest speaker. People would book to come, so she wouldn't have to rely on passing trade. She'd know exactly who was coming, how many, what time to expect them, how long they'd be staying.

She grabbed one of the tourist board booklets. Why did people come to Ireland? Music. Scenery. History. Family roots. She turned away from the keyboard of the computer, the ideas flowing so fast she wanted to feel them through a pen, not watch them appear on a screen.

* * *

Ten days later she was with Eva and Joseph in their flat above the Ambrosia deli and café. She had handed each of them an information sheet and was standing beside her laptop computer, the screen of which displayed the title: "A Feast of Ireland."

"Right, then, are you ready?"

"Lainey, you really could just tell us about it," Eva said, fighting a smile. "You don't have to go through with this presentation, you know. We're your friends, remember?"

Lainey looked slightly shamefaced. "I know it's ridiculous, but it's just habit. Can you indulge me? If I run through it like this, it'll make it all clear in my head." They weren't just ideas, either, she explained. She'd done all the research to back them up. She'd decided to forget all about competing with the other B&Bs in the area. Instead, she was launching a series of gourmet weekends, under the title of A Feast of Ireland.

"Sorry, Lainey, I don't quite understand it yet," Eva interrupted. "It's more like a mini country house hotel thing than a B&B, do you mean? With just the four rooms?"

Lainey nodded. "It's the intimate experience people want these days. That combined with the theme weekends. You know, people will come and stay on Friday and Saturday nights and I'll really lay it on for them, drinks on arrival, two dinners, two nights' accommodation, and a guest speaker, all following a particular theme."

"Oh, right, I see," Joseph said. "I read about a hotel that did weekends based on the Seven Deadly Sins. I wanted to go on the sloth one, just lie around all weekend doing nothing. Or the gluttony one, and just eat all weekend."

"Why don't you try that idea, Lainey?" Eva said. "Start with the lust theme, and organize a wife-swapping party on the Saturday night."

"Then the next weekend could be a Ten Commandments theme to get everyone back on the straight and narrow," Joseph suggested.

"Have you two finished?" Lainey said, arms folded. At their nods, she continued, flicking through the slides on the screen. The first four weekends would each be based on a different topic—Irish art, music, language and literature. All the guests had to do was lap up the luxury, sit by the fire or out in the garden if the weather was good, enjoy wine and fine food and take part as much or as little as they wanted.

And her secret weapon? Fantastic food cooked by Meg, Eva's cousin, who would travel across each weekend from the Ardmahon House cooking school, where she was a lecturer.

"I hope you didn't mind me contacting her, Evie, but she jumped at it," Lainey said. "It'll be the best of Irish produce cooked in a modern style, simple but really top class. Meg will look after the two dinners and I'll do the breakfasts. I've just about got them sorted out now."

Eva and Joseph diplomatically didn't mention the burnt breakfast she'd served them the weekend they first stayed.

She passed them a copy of the suggested menu that Meg had emailed to her. She'd chosen an interesting mix of dishes combining Irish produce with modern food trends. The starter the first night would be Galway oysters served as fresh as they could be, with homemade brown bread—"Mrs. Gillespie down the road's agreed to make all my bread for me," Lainey explained—and even a glass of Guinness for those who wanted it. The next night she'd serve crab claws from the Ring of Kerry in a simple garlicky fresh tomato sauce. For the main courses Meg had suggested oven-roasted Connemara lamb or fillets of wild Irish salmon. For dessert there'd be a choice of golden syrup dumplings with Tipperary cream, a spicy fig and walnut pudding, or perhaps even a rich chocolate pudding.

"And plenty of Irish farmhouse cheeses to follow, we thought. Meg said you are queen of the cheeses, Evie, and that I had to take your advice as gospel. And I'd love to be able to buy everything from you at Ambrosia, if that's all right. And I don't want you to think of any discounts or anything, just see it as a nice, big, fat windfall."

"Lainey, are you mad? Your food bills will be big, you know."

"I can't think of anyone better to get all of May's money than you, then. I thought you might even like to put up a little display in the B&B—some of your favorite goods, and of course I'll advertise everywhere that the Ambrosia delicatessen is my official supplier."

Lainey forgot all about the computer presentation then, just sat in front of Eva and Joseph, getting passionate as she explained the rest of the program. Her guest speakers were tentatively booked, each of them flattered at the thought of being feted for a weekend and happy with the fee she was offering too. All they had to do was deliver an hour-long talk on their subject of interest, or play music for an hour, or show paintings and then be available to answer questions and talk with guests. She'd tracked down a young music lecturer who could play the violin and the uilleann pipes and specialized in the history of Irish folk music. The literary editor of one of the new lifestyle magazines had agreed to come and talk about modern Irish literature. He'd hinted that he might be able to coax a friend of his, the latest voice of Irish writing, to come along and read from her new book. An Irish language expert was coming over from Galway, delighted with the thought of a weekend near Tara. Lainey had also contacted the National Gallery and invited one of their curators to come and talk about the work of Jack B. Yeats and Roderic O'Conor. She'd also decided to ask Rohan Hartigan if she could hire him to take her groups on personally guided tours of the Hill of Tara at some stage over each weekend.

As a first step, she was going to throw a launch party, inviting everyone she could think of from the local tourism industry, the other B&B operators in the area and local journalists. She was going to place just a few select advertisements, but mostly try and operate on a word-of-mouth basis. Far more exclusive. She'd done a similar thing with a party in Melbourne once, not sent out invitations, just had a word with a few key blabbers around town. It had worked beautifully. People had started ringing her, casually mentioning that they'd heard there might be a party happening and how did one manage to get on the guest list? The party had been a huge success.

"So, what do you think?" she said, finally coming to the end of her spiel.

Eva and Joseph raised their glasses. "It's brilliant."

· · ·

As she let herself back into Tara Lodge a little later that night, she heard a faint rustle, a scuttle of feet across the floors above. Her friend, Mister Mouse. He—and his friends?—seemed to come and go, treating this place like a boardinghouse, thumbing their noses at her traps and baits. She'd have to do something about them before she opened for business. That would hardly excite her high-paying guests, the sight of mangy rodents tearing across the bedroom floor. Unless she convinced them they were the ghosts of the famous Tara mice, known far and wide as surely the wisest, canniest mice ever to set foot on Ireland's shores . . .

No, perhaps not. She took her notebook out of her bag and made one last entry for the day.

Buy more traps/poison

CHAPTER 21

She rang Rohan the next morning. First she confessed that she'd been exaggerating slightly—well,
hugely, in fact—about her theme B&B ideas. He sounded
relieved. Then she explained her real plans and asked
whether he would be interested in running personally
guided tours of the Hill of Tara.

He didn't hesitate. "I'd be happy to, Lainey. Thanks
for asking. Perhaps we could meet for a drink and you
could tell me exactly what you imagined me doing?"

She blinked. What I imagined you doing? Rohan,
you'd blush if I told you. "Great idea," she said, a little too
brightly.

"Mind you, all my research papers and books are a bit
awkward to carry around. Why don't you come over to my
house instead?"

"Um, sure, yes, that makes more sense," Lainey said.

They arranged the time and confirmed his address.
Hanging up, she had a sudden mental image of Eva

beaming at her, giving her the thumbs-up, waving a banner with the words IT'S A DATE! written on it.

"Oh stop that," she said aloud.

• • •

She was hardly out of the driveway the next night on her way to Rohan's house, windscreen wipers working double time against the heavy rain, when the mind-film started playing . . .

His living room was warm, welcoming, the open fire flickering, sending light around the room. There was a small table set beside the sofa, a bottle of wine and two glasses on it. He made sure she was comfortable, had everything she needed, and then sat down beside her. "Your ideas for the B&B sound really fascinating, Lainey. Tell me everything about them."

In a soft voice, very conscious of his closeness, she told him, hardly aware of the words, thinking instead of their hands brushing against each other as they reached for their wine, his arm carefully resting against the back of the sofa, against the back of her head.

He nodded thoughtfully as she spoke, smiling a little sometimes as she said something witty, giving her his full attention. She took a sip of her wine, then placed the glass back on the table. He did the same.

He looked at her with those dark-blue eyes. "And tell me exactly what you would like me to do."

She hesitated for just one fraction of a moment and then she spoke softly, confidently. "I'd like you to kiss me."

Her eyes closed as he leaned forward, his mouth just inches away and then not away, but on hers, warm, soft, sensual. The feel of his hand touching the back of her head, moving her closer to him. Their lips harder against one another. She leaned forward, feeling her breasts against his chest . . .

She started as she felt the car drifting to the side of the road. "Jesus, Mary and Joseph," she said under her breath. Had she taken complete leave of her senses? She could imagine the headlines: WOMAN DIES IN CAR CRASH, FOUND WITH DREAMY SMILE ON FACE. For the rest of the way she concentrated firmly on the road.

The rain was pelting down when she pulled up outside what she thought was Rohan's house. She peered through the windscreen, trying to see the number. Yes, that was definitely it, but there were no lights on outside. She clambered out, putting her folder over her head and running up the path, cursing her long skirt as she nearly tripped.

She knocked on the porch door and was relieved when the light came on. Rohan answered it. "Lainey, you found your way all right, then? Sorry, I forgot to leave the light on. Come in. Let me introduce you to my mother and my niece, Nell. They've just called in too."

As she walked into the brightly lit, centrally heated living room, she pasted a smile on her face. A family reunion. For a moment she wasn't sure if she was relieved or disappointed.

·   ·   ·

Two hours later, she gathered up her notes and prepared to leave. It had been an extremely useful evening, if not quite as stimulating as her imaginings. Mrs. Hartigan had been pleasant, apologizing for being in the way. They'd just happened to drop by to see Rohan on their way home from visiting a friend. The niece was the young woman

Lainey had seen with Rohan in town several weeks earlier. She was staying in Ireland for a few months while her mother, a doctor, was in America on a study exchange, Mrs. Hartigan explained. Nell was dressed tonight in a cross between Britney Spears teenwear and London street fashion—low-slung jeans, tight T-shirt—but despite the confident clothing there'd hardly been a peep out of her all night. Mrs. Hartigan made up for her silence, joining in on the discussions about the Hill of Tara, inquiring after Lainey's parents, asking about Australia and passing on bits of news about people she thought Lainey might know from her childhood. Lainey gave a bright report about the B&B, mentioning the mice problem in passing. Mrs. Hartigan tutted in sympathy. Apparently there were a lot of them about at the moment.

"Still, it's good to have May's house in operation again, mice or no mice. I'll tell you one thing, Lainey, we'll really miss your aunt around this area."

"Miss her? I thought no one"—she was about to say no one liked her, when she stopped herself—"no one really knew her that well."

"Well, you wouldn't want to be in her firing line, sure enough, but she was an entertainment in herself, wasn't she, Rohan? What was that story you heard about her, when you first got back from Germany?"

He shook his head, smiling at the memory. "She put an ad in one of the local papers, looking for people interested in forming a local branch of the Insomniacs Society. The ad said the first meeting would take place in a local hotel at four a.m."

"And the ad appeared?" Lainey said, laughing.

"It did. It slipped through somehow. She could be very funny. It was really just loneliness, I think. She needed people to take notice of her, to have to ring her or talk to her in some way. I don't think she minded if they were cross with her. It was just the human contact she needed."

"You were very good to spend so much time with her, Rohan," Mrs. Hartigan said.

"I liked her," he said simply.

Lainey felt that rush of guilt again that her family had lost contact with May. She was glad when the subject moved on to other local news. Throughout the conversation Nell sat in the corner, reading a glossy magazine, answering only if she was spoken to. She perked up briefly when Lainey mentioned she wanted to get some unusual photographs taken of Tara, to make her own cards and postcards to sell.

"I'm a photographer," Nell said.

"Well, not quite, pet," Mrs. Hartigan stepped in. "You're studying to be a photographer, you mean." Lainey saw a glance pass between Rohan and his mother.

"Have you photos here with you, Nell?" Lainey asked.

"At home. At Nana's, I mean."

"Could I see them? If they're what I'm after, perhaps we could talk about you taking some for me." They arranged for Nell to call out to the B&B some time.

Lainey buttoned her coat as she moved to the door.

"Well, good night then, Nell. Nice to meet you. I'll look forward to seeing your photos. And nice to see you again, Mrs. Hartigan."

"You too, Lainey. And good to see there's no hard feelings between you and Rohan."

"Hard feelings?" The double meaning of the words leaped out at Lainey.

"About that dare, and the scar on his arm."

"Oh, we sorted that all out, didn't we, Lainey?" Rohan said as he guided her to the door.

"Oh, yes." She gave a silly laugh, wincing inside at the tone of it. She turned as they reached the door. "Well, thanks for your time, Rohan, and your ideas. They're terrific." Close up, in the bright hall light, she noticed that he had gold flecks in his eyes.

"Any time, Lainey. And thanks for being so nice to Nell. She's been through the wars a bit lately. You do mean that about the photography, do you?"

"Oh, I do. I'd love to see her work."

"I'll drop her out to see you soon, then."

He leaned forward, his hand nearly brushing her face, and for a moment she thought he was going to stroke her cheek, kiss her even. Oh holy God, she thought. Had he guessed what she'd been thinking?

Instead, he drew his hand back and she could see the glistening of a spider web and a small wriggling body in his fingers. "Sorry about that. When Sabine's not here I don't usually bother getting rid of the spiders."

So his girlfriend *had* been in Ireland, then? Why wasn't she here now? Lainey hurriedly said goodbye and ran back out through the rain to her car.

.   .   .

The next day brought another newsy email from her friend Christine, chatting about the Melbourne weather: "hot, hot, hot, am I rubbing it in enough yet?"; **work gossip**: "if I don't win the lottery soon so I can retire I am going to go mad, I swear"; and **news** of a disastrous dinner date she'd been on: "I tried to stay awake while he was talking, honestly I did."

There was no mention of Adam or his restaurant.

. . .

Three days before the launch party Lainey was in the library photocopying sample menus for her information packs when she heard a familiar voice. It was Rohan. Peering through the shelves, she saw he was talking to Ciara the librarian, who was flirting mightily with him again. He left Ciara and went over to another librarian, beside a group of people in rows of chairs. He must be giving another talk. She should be getting back home, but if it was about Tara, then she really should listen too, shouldn't she? In case any of her guests needed to know, or had any questions? Yes, what a good idea.

She walked over to the desk. "Ciara, is it all right if I sit in on Rohan's talk?"

"Of course it is. I've sat through heaps of them, but between you and me"—she lowered her voice—"more for the lust factor than the search-for-knowledge factor." She gave a surprisingly suggestive laugh before turning to her next customer.

Lainey didn't know if Rohan noticed her taking a seat at the back. She could just see him between a gray-haired woman and a middle-aged man in front of her. He was talking about his current project.

"It's through oral histories that many of the most fascinating stories come to us. Stories that have been passed down from generation to generation. But how do they change as they are passed down? That's what I've been trying to discover as I travel around speaking to the older people in our community, hearing what they have been told over the years. I'd like to share some of those with you all today, starting with the fascinating story of the origin of the Hill of Tara's name."

Lainey stifled a yawn. She'd been up until nearly two a.m. the night before, her head bursting with ideas for the relaunch of the B&B, researching similar places around the world, surfing the net. She'd found it hard to sleep, between eyestrain from staring at the computer and the thoughts buzzing in her head. She blinked again now, her lids heavy. The warmth in the library was soporific.

"I first met Lainey when I was fifteen. Since that time I have thought about her and waited for her and now she is back as a fully fledged woman. We haven't made love yet, but I'm certainly planning to, and I know it's something she wants to do as well. Isn't that right, Lainey?"

Lainey sat up. "I beg your pardon?"

Rohan was talking directly to her. Several of the audience members had turned around, looking over their shoulders at her.

"I was saying that you've recently taken over a B&B at the Hill of Tara and are interested in hearing stories that you might be able to pass on to your guests."

She nodded. "That's right."

"So if anyone has any stories, perhaps you could let me know here at the library. Thanks for your time."

Lainey was too embarrassed to wait to talk to him. She was out the door and in her car before the applause had even finished.

• • •

"What do you mean you haven't invited Rohan to the launch party? He's one of the speakers, isn't he? Anyway, I'm dying to meet him again."

How did Lainey explain why not? Tell the truth? Actually, Eva, I'm finding that whenever I'm in the same room as him I'm getting overwhelmed by erotic fantasies and it's getting a bit embarrassing.

"Lainey, are you there?"

"Of course I am. I just haven't got around to it yet." She realized how ridiculous she was being. Of course she had to invite Rohan, out of courtesy to him as a friend of May's, if nothing else. "I'll give him a call in a minute."

"Good, I need to run an eye over him, to see whether I think he's the right man for you or not."

"Eva . . ."

"Now be sure to put on your huskiest voice when you ring him. The fates are good but they need a helping hand every now and then."

"Eva, stop it!"

Eva was laughing as she hung up.

Lainey picked up the phone again and dialed Rohan's number. As she did so, a particularly saucy image came into her head. She put down the receiver. She couldn't talk to him now, with her head filled with R-rated visions like that. It was as though she was recalling all the best times with Adam, but had transplanted Rohan's head onto his body. What on earth was happening to her? She went into the kitchen. Was there a cupboard she could clean, a floor to sweep? Where were Aunt May's handy household hints when she really needed them? "To banish troublesome and inappropriate erotic thoughts about a practically married man when in fact you're confused about the way you finished it with another man, use one part bicarbonate of soda and one pint of freshly squeezed lemon juice applied in a circular motion to the head." Alternatively, calm down and stop being so ridiculous. She tried his number again.

"Rohan, hello, this is Lainey."

"Lainey, hello. Was that you ringing before? Someone was trying to get through but I just heard some breathing."

"Oh, yes, sorry, it was me. I'm having problems with my phone here."

"How can I help you?"

"I'm having a party here at the house next Saturday night, to show off the new look and my plans for it. I wondered if you'd like to come along."

"I'd love to come. Thanks, Lainey. Will you be home tomorrow, by the way?"

"I will, yes."

She could hear a smile in his voice. "I have something for you, if it's okay if I drop around."

"What is it?"

"It's a surprise. But you'll like it, I promise."

A surprise. The mind-films started whirring into action, a tiny imp operating the projector. "Oh, good. Great, even. See you then." Was this really her, being so polite? So tentative? She hung up and was embarrassed to feel her pulse running quicker than normal. The room was obviously too hot, she decided, going across to open a window.

CHAPTER 22

Rohan arrived just after lunch the next day, a basket under one arm. Whatever was in it would not be able to compete with what her imagination had come up with, Lainey knew, as she watched him walk up the path. In the space of twenty-four hours, Rohan's surprise present had changed enticingly from a bottle of champagne, to airline tickets to Barbados, to a Tiffany brooch, to an interesting lace and leather combination that she couldn't recall ever having seen in real life.

He saw her and waved. The basket was tilting from the movement of whatever was inside. He looked delighted with himself. "I've got the answer to all your mice problems. Forget traps, forget poisons. What you need to get rid of those mice is right in here," he announced as he reached the front door.

She eyed the basket dubiously. "You've brought a shotgun?"

"No, think of four paws. A tail. A well-documented passion for mice."

"You've got a *cat* in there?"

He nodded, smiling broadly, then noticed her low-key reaction. "Don't you like cats?"

She could hardly tell him she'd been thinking more along the lines of sexy lingerie and champagne, could she? "Oh yes, I love cats actually. I own the finest cat in the world back in Melbourne. I just hadn't thought about getting a pet while I was here."

"Oh, it's not like a pet cat. This is more like a worker around the place. He's from a family of ratters. It's in his genes." Rohan opened the basket a little way, put his hand in and just as quickly pulled it out, to a sound of fierce hissing. There was a red scratch on the back of his hand. "I think it's still a bit wild."

"Shall I have a go?" She reached in and lifted out the animal. It was really hissing and spitting now, its fur puffed around its body. It wasn't as pretty as Rex, she thought, as it tried to bite her.

"So will you give it a name?" Rohan asked.

She studied the cat, its ginger fur all spiky around its head, the skinny legs, the wide-open mouth. It really reminded her of someone. "Yes, I think I will," she said.

. . .

"Here, Rod Stewart. Here, kitty," she called at the top of her voice that afternoon, as she roamed around the house. "Where are you, Rod Stewart? Here, kitty-kitty-kitty."

She finally found Rod Stewart in one of the back rooms, asleep on the single bed. She picked him up, holding him at arm's length as he hissed again, trying to scratch her with his paw, the spiky orange fur a halo around his head. "Come on now, Roddie. Come and show the mice in this house who's boss."

He just scratched at her face in reply.

• • •

Twenty-four hours before her launch party she was in the Dunshaughlin shopping center. She hated supermarkets at the best of times, and this was not the best of times. She'd thought she had all she needed for the launch party and had started decorating when she realized she needed lightbulbs and would have to go into town again, for the fifth time in two days.

They were the last things on her list though. Everything else was ordered and in place. She was loving the feeling of being back in charge of an event, running through all the details in her mind, like a director planning a film shoot. Eva and Joe would be bringing the food tomorrow, all prepared at Ambrosia—a clever combination of traditional Irish ingredients served in new ways. There would be smoked salmon blinis, little potato fritters, baked fish skewers and vintage cheese. They'd volunteered to be the food and drink waiters as well, leaving her to be hostess. A local wine shop had delivered the rented wineglasses and the wine that morning—a rich, fruity South Australian shiraz from a small Clare Valley winery called Lorikeet Hill, and a crisp French sauvignon blanc. She'd decided on open fires and warm lamps in every room, with soft music playing, the curtains drawn against the cold night, and the newly painted walls making the rooms plush and cozy. She'd prepared information packs for the guests to take home, outlining all her plans for the Feast of Ireland series of theme weekends at the Tara Lodge.

It was while she was checking that the lamps she'd placed in each of the rooms looked just as beautiful in real life as they had in her imagination that she'd discovered she'd run out of lightbulbs. Something so simple yet so important. She was cross that she hadn't thought of it on her last shopping trip.

It wasn't helping that she had a raging dose of PMS. Women should come equipped with a pair of red plastic horns that they could just slip on once every month, she thought. A sort of public-warning device that said: "I have temporarily turned into a she-devil and it might be best if you keep your distance until normal transmission has been resumed." She stalked around the aisles, trying to find what she needed.

She finally found the lightbulbs, ridiculously stored in the household items section. She bought six packs and then added several other items—notepads, pens, tea towels, cat food, hand cream—in a sudden shopping fever. She grabbed two more packets of mousetraps and some more poison too—Rod Stewart had lost complete interest in the mice, it seemed. The ratter gene had obviously skipped a generation.

The queue to the checkout was long, of course. And of course the register ran out of paper just as she was getting closer. As her temper rose, Lainey felt as though she had grown a long thick tail like a lioness, and was flicking it, slowly, angrily, waiting for the moment to sink her fangs into the spotty neck of the boy behind the register.

After finally paying, she badly needed a cup of tea. Dragging the bulging shopping bags like bad-tempered toddlers behind her, she found a seat in the café in the middle of the shopping center, ordered tea and then, with a long, deep sigh, willed herself to relax. She obviously wasn't used to the stress of organizing an event, even though she'd organized hundreds in her time. This party felt different, though, more real. It actually mattered to her. She wanted the B&B to work, her theme weekends to be a success, the guests to flock to her. Perhaps she hadn't really cared before if the new chocolate bar fulfilled expectations or if the new motor mower really did mow all the opposition out of the way. She'd cared about the launch events going well, but beyond that, they really had been products. As she sipped the tea, one part of her mind checked down the long to-do list for the launch. She was on top of things; it was all organized. She was in the nice calm before the storm time, when it was just a matter of waiting for it all to unfold. She knew the feeling well from all her years at Complete Event Management.

Gazing off into the middle distance, her eyes were drawn to the newsagent directly opposite the café. Standing between the magazine racks and the counter was Rohan Hartigan. As she looked at him, taking in his height, the width of his shoulders, the dark curly hair, her mind returned to her dream of the other night.

She could feel the strength of his body, feel the muscles in his back as she ran her hands down his shirt, the cotton cool, his skin hot beneath it. There was no mistaking how aroused he was. She could feel the hardness pressing against her and all she wanted to do was press hard against him, to feel the sensation without clothes, just hot skin against hot skin . . .

"Lainey, hello."

She nearly spat out her tea. "Rohan. Hi."

He was standing beside her, a car magazine in one hand. "So, all set for the big night tomorrow?"

"Just about." Was she blushing? Was it obvious that she had just been imagining him standing in the middle of the shopping center with an erection?

"Are you okay? You look a little . . . ?"

The words embarrassed and aroused came to Lainey's mind.

"Hot," he said.

"Oh, just a touch of the flu, I think. Or the heating in here."

"Well, I hope you feel better soon."

"Are you still coming tomorrow night?" Her voice sounded a little strangled.

"Oh, of course. Actually, I was going to call you about the party."

She waited, her heart beating faster.

"Sabine is over from Munich at the moment. You don't mind if she comes too, do you?"

"Oh no, not at all," she said in a voice higher than normal. "And please, bring your mother and your niece if you want to as well." And any livestock you have, she thought. They're all welcome. The more the merrier.

"Really? Thanks, I'm sure they'd love to come. See you then."

"Yes, see you all then. And Sabine, too, of course."

．　．　．

There was a parcel waiting on the doorstep when she arrived home. Another tape from Hugh. She cheered up, again delaying the moment of watching it, making herself a coffee, getting herself settled just so. Once she was organized, she put it into the video recorder and pressed play.

Within seconds she was laughing out loud. To a sound-track of snippets from "What's New, Pussycat" by Tom Jones, "Love Cats" by the Cure and "Kool 4 Cats" by Squeeze, Hugh had filmed lots of footage of her cat Rex. There was Rex lounging around her parents' house, lying fully stretched in the sun, his tail batting, playing with balls of paper, jumping up to catch at toys on the ends of pieces of string. There was even Rex dressed up in a ridiculous bow, with a fake moustache and a party hat. The final frame was Rex waving, a male hand obviously in shot making it happen, a speech bubble coming out of his little cat mouth—"Hurry home. They're tormenting me here!"

She watched it again, laughing just as much the second time. Then she played it frame by frame, puzzled about something. If Hugh was behind the camera, who was making Rex do all those things? Not her father, and her mother didn't really like touching him. She found her answer in one of the outside shots. There, reflected in the French doors leading out into the garden, was a tall, lanky man in a sombrero. She recognized the hat at the same time she recognized the body. It was Adam.

She played it through again. It was Adam's hand flicking a bit of paper on a piece of string and making Rex wave his paw. It was Adam's hand holding the party hat on Rex's head. Adam holding Rex in such a way that he appeared to be reading a book. She freeze-framed to see the book's title. *Of Mice and Men* by John Steinbeck.

She'd seen the book in his bookcase at home. They'd both studied it at school, discussed it over dinner one night. She guessed then the Rex tape had been as much his idea as Hugh's. As Lainey stopped the tape she realized she was laughing and crying at the same time.

CHAPTER 23

It was like some weird dream, Lainey decided as she looked around the house. There were about forty people in the two main rooms. Others were moving up and down the staircase, having a look at the rooms, leafing through the information kits packed with her plans for the theme weekends. She'd invited all the people she thought might be interested or might be able to recommend the guesthouse to friends or colleagues. She was pleased to see Mr. Fogarty and his wife, who to Lainey's disappointment was not in the least bit mouselike—more mooselike if anything. She felt a tap on her shoulder and turned. A man a few inches shorter than her, stocky in build, was smiling at her.

"Elaine, is it? It must be you. I saw you from across the room and knew you immediately."

He was sixty at least, she guessed, with an affected English accent. Hair a little too long, clothes a little too flamboyant. "Yes, I'm Lainey," she said cautiously. "I'm sorry, I don't think we've met . . ."

He held out a hand, with a theatrical bow. "My name is Leo Ramsay. You probably don't remember me, but I used to live here in Meath many years ago myself. I knew your mother very well. Tell me, how is she keeping?"

"She's grand, just grand," she said. "I'm sorry, Mr. Ramsay. I'm afraid I don't remember you at all."

He nodded as if, yes, he thought that would probably have been the case. "You were very young. I moved back to England just before you moved to Australia, in fact. What is it now, seventeen years ago next spring? Is that right?"

"You've a good memory."

"For the things that matter, yes, Lainey, I do." He was staring at her, appraising her, far more intently than felt comfortable. "You're very like your mother physically, aren't you? That same striking face, the same tall, lean body."

What was he, a doctor? A creepy doctor, at that. Just then Eva came up beside her. "Lainey, I'm sorry, we need you out in the kitchen . . ."

Lainey was glad of the interruption. Was he with one of the tourism groups? she wondered, a fake smile on her face. "A pleasure to meet you, Mr. Ramsay. Please enjoy the party."

"I will, Lainey, I will. And remember me to your mother, will you? Please tell her I still think of her."

The mini crisis in the kitchen dealt with—a lack of serving trays—Lainey returned to the room, looking around with pleasure.

"Congratulations, Lainey."

She looked down with a smile. "So what do you think of it, Mr. Fogarty?"

"It looks marvelous. I'm sure you'll have the guests flocking in for your program."

"And my wonderful dinners, too, I hope."

"Yes, I read the sample menus in the information package. You're certainly exploring all the modern aspects of Irish cuisine. I hadn't realized you were a talented chef as well."

"Me?" Lainey laughed at the idea. "I have to confess, Mr. Fogarty, I can't cook to save my life. I'm bringing in an expert, my friend Eva's cousin Meg, who's the real thing, thank God."

She felt a touch on her hand. It was Eva again. "Excuse me, Mr. Fogarty." Lainey smiled and moved away.

Eva whispered. "We're whipping through the wine. Just wondered, do you want to open some more bottles?"

Lainey glanced around, doing a quick head count. "Yes, try another six—three red, three white. And it's time for some more food, I think, too. I'll give you a hand with the trays."

"Is he here yet?" Eva hissed.

"Who?"

"You know who. Rohan. I'm dying to see him."

Lainey pulled a face. "Stop it, you." In fact, she'd noticed that Rohan had just arrived. He was in a corner of the living room talking to four women, including Mrs. Hartigan and Nell. Lainey glanced over, wondering which of the other two women was Sabine. One was dark-haired, pixie-faced, the other mid-height, groomed, smiley. He seemed to be paying them both equal attention.

"That's him over there, isn't it?" Eva whispered. "I recognize that curly hair of his. He's still lovely looking, isn't he? Come on now, Lainey. Over there and charm, charm, charm."

"Shhh, he'll hear you."

"Which one's the girlfriend? Not the teenager, I hope? Or that older lady?"

"No, that's his mother, you eejit. Remember her? And the other's the niece. It's one of the other two."

"Oh look, he's looking over at you. Quick, smile back at him."

"Eva, he's looking over here because you and I are standing here whispering behind our hands like school-girls."

"No, Lainey. It's because he's fatally attracted to you. I can feel it in my bones."

"That's early onset of osteoporosis, you mad woman." But Eva had moved away. Too late, though. The damage had been done. Another mind-film started playing in Lainey's head.

The loaded glances had been passing between them all night. She knew it was just a matter of waiting. Her patience paid off as she heard a soft voice behind her. It was Rohan. "Lainey, I need to be alone with you. Now."

"Lainey, can I introduce you to my girlfriend? Sorry, my special friend, Sabine?"

Lainey spun around, her smile more maniacal than friendly. Sabine was the dark-haired one. Lainey thrust out her hand. "Guten abend, wieviel kosten diese Brief-marken?"

Sabine smiled, puzzled. "I'm sorry?"

Oh, bloody hell, she'd just asked Sabine how much do these stamps cost, Lainey realized. She gave a giddy laugh and tried again. "I'm sorry, Sabine. I meant to say you are very welcome. Sie sind herzlich willkommen." Much better, Lainey. *Now try and behave like a normal human being, would you?*

Rohan's arm was around the German woman. "It all looks great, Lainey. Congratulations."

"And your program is terrific too," Sabine added, with a nod toward the information kit in her hand. "I just wish I could come to some of them."

Sabine's English was perfect, of course, the hint of an accent making it very attractive. "You'd be more than welcome." Lainey drank the rest of her champagne in one swallow and gave a big fake smile, feeling like she was auditioning for a toothpaste commercial. "Well, it's lovely to meet you, and please, make yourself at home. Excuse me, won't you?"

The rest of the night swept past in a blur of conversations, questions and two minor accidents with glasses. Lainey relaxed her guard, having a second glass of champagne—one more than she usually allowed herself at launches such as this. Then another glass. And then another—they seemed to be growing miraculously out of the palm of her hand. They were keeping the Rohan mind-films at bay quite nicely, too.

As it passed midnight, most of the guests started leaving, amid lots of congratulations, lots of good wishes. The music got louder, the talk and laughter more boisterous, as the younger ones stayed on. It wasn't until after one, about the same time that she remembered that she hadn't eaten, that Lainey realized she was spectacularly drunk.

• • •

She came into the kitchen after eleven the next morning, eyes half closed, hair in short black tufts, arms outstretched like a sleepwalking mummy. "I am evil. I am the evil slave-creature of the drink and I must be destroyed. My mind has been sucked out by a straw during the night, the zombies have taken over and left me with nothing, no memory at all." She opened one eye, expecting to hear her eyelid creak from the weight of the dried and smudged mascara. Rare white panda also spotted in Ireland.

"No memory at all? That's good," Eva said cheerily, looking up from the newspapers spread on the table around her.

"For the best probably," Joseph added, just as cheerily.

Lainey slumped into a chair. "Oh no, tell me. What did I do?"

"Nothing to be ashamed of, Lainey, really," Eva said. "You were great, actually. I had no idea you liked dancing on the table like that."

"And the way you lifted Mr. Fogarty up over your head and spun him around. It was brilliant, really," Joseph added. "Like that scene with Fay Wray in *King Kong*, didn't you think, Evie?"

Lainey laid her head on the table and howled. "Don't. I can't bear it."

Eva relented, smiling. "Lainey, relax. You weren't that bad. You got a bit drunk, started slurring a little and we had to put you to bed, but that was it. And it was only right at the end. Nearly everyone had gone."

"Who was still here?" She looked out blearily through one panda eye. Please don't say it. Please don't say his name.

"Only Rohan Hartigan. His girlfriend was here for a while, but then she left early, and he caught a taxi home."

So just Rohan was here. Splendid. An audience of one for her misbehavior. "What did we talk about?" Please don't tell me I started undressing him in the middle of the living room, please, please, please . . .

"We talked about school, then he talked about why he decided to start studying history, about going to Germany first, coming back here for this Tara project. You hadn't mentioned he'd done all of those oral histories, Lainey. It's fascinating, isn't it?"

Lainey made an odd, noncommittal noise, aching head still in her hands. No, Eva, I didn't mention those, because I've been far too busy mentally undressing him to worry about silly little niceties like actually getting to know him. But now at least they'd met Sabine, seen his girlfriend in the flesh. That would surely put a stop to any of Eva's fantasies, not to mention her own.

Eva poured her a coffee and handed it over with a sympathetic smile. "If you ask me, there's a few problems between him and his German girlfriend. I overheard them having a bit of a spat outside. You really might be in with a chance, Lainey." She lowered her voice. "He is quite sexy, isn't he?"

Lainey just shut her eyes and groaned again.

•   •   •

She'd finished a plate of bacon and eggs and was stroking Rod Stewart, wishing he'd keep his purring down to a soft roar, when the phone rang. The bell sounded like Big Ben to her fragile ears. Eva answered it.

"Meggie!" she said in delight at the sound of her

cousin's voice. "How are you? Oh no, are you serious? I didn't even know you liked horse riding." Eva laughed. "No, I guess you don't anymore. You poor thing. No, of course you can't. How could you manage it? Hold on, she's right here." She passed the phone to Lainey. "It's Meg."

Lainey hadn't liked the sound of anything Eva had just said to her cousin. She liked even less what Meg had to say to her. She had taken a fall while horse riding the day before and sprained her ankle and broken her left arm in two places. She was going to be in plaster for at least six weeks. "Oh, Meg, you poor thing. No, of course it's not the end of the world. I'll find another chef. Well, sure, it is short notice, but really, it's nothing to worry about. It's still a few weeks off. No, just rest up and take care and we'll see you soon. No, not at all, Meg. Don't worry about it for a moment."

Lainey hung up and looked blearily at her friends. "You'd better cover your ears. I'm about to do a lot of swearing."

CHAPTER 24

For three days after the party, Lainey lay low, Rod Stewart her only company. He made a halfhearted attempt to prove his hunting credentials, loudly meowing outside the front door one morning. She opened it to find him proudly displaying a dead bird and three bacon rinds.

She glared at him. "I fed you the bacon, you big eejit. You didn't catch it. And you're supposed to be catching mice, not birds."

She picked up the stiff little feathered body and took it down to the back of the garden. As she walked back up to the house she passed the chicken run. It was all right for them, clucking away happily in there. They were certainly never told that they were going to have to learn in record time how to cook gourmet meals for eight people. Eva had offered to take Meg's place until Joseph reminded her she had singing gigs with her band in Dublin over those weekends. They'd rung several people Eva knew, without success. Either it was too short notice or they

were otherwise booked. They'd rung Mrs. Gillespie down
the road, but she'd said no as well. She was a good baker,
but not a gourmet chef, she'd explained. Lainey had finally accepted that she would have to do it herself. "I can
give you lessons, Lainey," Eva had said. "You'll pick it up
really quickly, you wait and see." They'd both suspected
she was lying.

. . .

She was dragged back into the human race the next
morning by a phone call from home. She filled her father in on recent weather patterns and was brought up-
to-date by her mother on the latest instant food products.
"And everything's fine there, Lainey, I suppose? I bet the
local tourist industry don't know quite what's hit it, you
arriving like that."

I don't know quite what's hit me, more to the point.
"Oh, I think they're coping."

"I've been telling everybody here about that great idea
of yours to run those theme weekends. Perhaps I could
run one here, with all these new dishes I've been demonstrating. Mind you, mine are supposed to be time-savers,
not quite the thing for a weekend away. Perhaps I could
call mine Gourmet Quick Lunches." Lainey was trying to
keep up when her mother changed the subject. "Here's
Hugh to talk to. Hugh, come and say hello to your sister
in Ireland."

"Hello, sister in Ireland."

"Hello, my little pet. Anything I need to know about?
Been busted yet? Kicked out of college? Caught running
a counterfeit money ring?"

"No, all calm on the Melbourne front. What about

you, Lain? You all set for those weekends Ma keeps stopping strangers in the street to talk about?"

She hadn't meant to tell him, but somehow the whole story about her having to do the cooking came spilling out. After he'd stopped laughing he tried to console her. "You're not that bad a cook, are you? You could serve something up to them?"

"Hughie, even Rex won't eat my leftovers. I can scratch up a few pasta dishes and the odd stir-fry, of course I can, but that's home-in-front-of-the-TV food, not we've-paid-a-fortune-to-eat-flash-meals-in-this-guesthouse-for-the-weekend food."

"So what are you going to do? Give up?"

She bridled. "Of course I'm not. Eva's offered to come down and teach me, give me a crash course, which is a start. Beyond that, God knows. I'm just going to have to practice and practice until I get it sorted out." She'd already looked up every How to Cook Web site on the Internet and watched every TV cooking show she could. Apparently if she grew her hair long like Nigella Lawson and rode around on a scooter like Jamie Oliver everything would be just fine.

"Well, it serves you right. If you hadn't broken up with Adam you could have asked him for help. He's a genius in the kitchen."

Did Hugh think she hadn't had the same thought? Over and over? Stay cool, Lainey, sound nonchalant. "Yes, Hugh, I know that. But it's hardly fair to ask Adam for help, is it?"

"Well, I'll ask him for some tips for you, then. We're going to meet for another beer. I invited him. Thought he might want to get to know one of your brothers a little better, explore the family's hidden depths, try and fathom how it went wrong with you, you know the sort of thing. I'll ask him about the meals. I bet he'll have great ideas."

Now that Hugh had brought up the subject, Lainey couldn't stop herself from pursuing it. "Hugh, how often exactly are you seeing him? It's just I saw someone who looked a bit familiar on the Rex video." She'd phoned and thanked him for the video the day she'd got it, but deliberately hadn't mentioned Adam.

"I've no idea what you're talking about."

"Really? You know someone else who is six foot two with a taste for hats? Who is good with animals? Who Rex knows and doesn't try to scratch?"

"I know loads of people just like that."

It was time to get stern with her little brother. "Hugh, I don't want you to say anything to Adam about the cooking, all right?"

"Are you forbidding me?"

"Yes, I am."

"Too bad. You're not the boss of me," he chanted, as he'd been doing since he was a child.

It had made her laugh back then and it made her laugh now. She feigned a casual voice for her next question. "So you've seen a bit of Adam, then?"

"No, I've seen all of him. Geddit?"

Lainey got it. "And how is he?" If her voice became any more casual, she'd be drawling.

Hugh paused. "You know, Lainey, I could give you two answers here."

"What do you mean, two?"

"I could give you the one I bet Adam would like me to

give, which is that he is perfectly fine, probably glad to be rid of you. In fact, had trouble remembering who you were."

"Or . . . ?"

"Or I could tell you that in my opinion you've broken the poor man's heart and you are a cruel heartless wretch."

Lainey's heart flipped. "What makes you think that?"

"I'm speaking of course from very limited romantic experience, based mostly on repeated viewings of eighties films like *The Breakfast Club* and *Pretty in Pink*—"

"Hugh . . ."

"Well, he asked loads about you again. And I could tell he wanted to ask more, but he kept kind of stopping himself. He would have made a perfect guinea pig for a project I had to do on body language last month, actually. You know, how people say one thing but the way they sit or stand shows how they really feel? So, he was asking about you really casually, but then when I told him he kept himself really still, the way someone does when they're really concentrating on your answer. And then I just as casually brought up the fact that you can be a terrible bossy boots, just in case he wanted to let off a bit of steam, and he actually defended you."

"Defended me?"

"Said that you weren't bossy, not really, that you were just organized. And I said, if that's just being organized, he should have tried growing up with you, it was like living in a boot camp. And then he laughed but he looked sad. And so I told him, you'll get over her, Adam. Soon she'll be just a distant memory, you wait and see."

"Hugh, you did not say that, did you?"

"Well, I thought it."

"So then what did he say?"

"I can't remember. I think we started talking about football. And then he had to go. He's started opening up for breakfasts on the weekends now."

"Breakfasts? But when's he going to get any time off? He works too hard as it is."

"What do you care if the poor man has to throw himself into work to try and mend his broken heart? Some role model you turned out to be, breaking hearts hither and thither."

"Hither and thither?"

"Don't try and change the subject. You know what I mean. All I hope is that I never treat anyone as meanly as you have treated Adam. And I hope you manage to sleep with that thought on your conscience. Not to mention the disgraceful example of human relations you've shown me, at such a vulnerable stage of my emotional development—"

Lainey started to laugh. She couldn't help herself. Hugh had cheered her up in a strange way, though she wasn't too sure why. "Oh, forget it, Hughie. Is Ma still there? I've just remembered I've got a message for her."

"I know what you're up to, you just don't want to face the truth. Hold on, I'll get her."

Mrs. Byrne didn't bother with hellos again. "That's very kind of you to spend so much time talking to Hugh, Lainey. Heaven knows none of us can get any sense out of him."

Lainey smiled as she heard Hugh's protests in the background. Served him right. "Ma, sorry, I meant to tell you before. I met a friend of yours the other night. A Leo Ramsay, an Englishman, kind of arty?"

"Leo? Good God, I haven't seen him in—"

"Nearly seventeen years. He practically knew the date you left."

"And what did he say?"

"He just asked me to remember him to you. Told me I reminded him of you." She didn't mention the anatomical way he'd studied her.

"When did he get back from England? Is he living in Meath again?"

"Ma, all these questions! Don't tell me, he's an old flame of yours?"

Mrs. Byrne ignored her. "Good heavens. Leo Ramsay, that really takes me back. Do give him my best if you see him again, won't you?"

Her mother sounded wistful. "Who is he?" Lainey said, her voice sharper than she meant it to be.

"He was a painter back then, as in artist, not house painter. He lived in Meath for a while, taught part-time at the college. That's where we met. He used to come into the library."

"And?"

"And what?"

And what's the rest of the story that you're not telling me? "Go on."

"That's all, Elaine. Now, I'd better go or this phone bill will send us into even deeper financial ruin than we're in already." And then her mother hung up.

· · ·

"Still no more bookings?"

Lainey paced around the house, phone to her ear. "No, Evie, nothing. I've had one lot of midweek guests, tourists from Spain, but I can't exactly lock them in the house until the weekends come around, can I? I was mad to waste all that money on the party. I think everyone just enjoyed a good feed and a drinkfest at my expense and then went home and forgot about the whole place. All I have is two couples booked in for the Irish art weekend and two for the literature, but they're friends of Mr. Fogarty, nothing to do with the party at all. I should have saved myself the bother."

"Could you get an article into one of the newspapers?" Eva suggested. "Get someone to write about it?"

"It's not exactly newsworthy, is it? Australian woman opens gourmet guesthouse. Australian woman who can't cook opens gourmet guesthouse. Australian woman who can't cook opens gourmet guesthouse, then throws herself off the nearest bridge."

"You've still got ten days till the first theme weekend, haven't you? And you just need to fill four rooms, eight people each weekend. Calm down. It'll work. Just wait and see. Let me have a think."

"When exactly did we swap positions here? How come you're the sane one with all the ideas suddenly?"

"You don't have a monopoly on good ideas, Lainey. Now, take a deep breath and then go for a run or something. You have to keep in shape, remember. You don't know when your big nudie moment with Rohan might arise and you want to be looking your best."

"Eva Kennedy!"

"Better go, Lainey. I'll see you on Saturday for your first cooking lesson." She was laughing as she hung up.

Lainey took Eva's advice and set out for a run. She'd given up listening to the language CDs while she exercised. She'd discovered it was much more pleasant to listen to the sounds around her, the peace broken just occasionally by the sounds of cars. Sometimes she didn't even feel like running, doing a fast walk instead, or on soft, warm days like this, a slow gentle walk.

She was spending a lot of time up on Tara, taking the long way up through the tree-lined lanes, no longer dark tunnels of bare branches. There was a green haze appearing on all the trees, as though they were slowly being colored in by an unseen hand. The air smelled different. There was movement all around her. She'd seen rabbits in the fields, even a fox one morning, which had reminded her to keep the chickens locked up each night. The wild birds were her favorites. She loved the constant whistling and the sound of the sudden flap of wings, the rush of air as she walked past their nests in the hedges, which were also becoming lusher by the day.

She walked further than usual today, past the Tara parking lot and coffee shop, through the gate and right across the hill, to the very edge. There were other people wandering about, but she kept to the far edge, wanting to be alone, gazing out at the fields for miles around. They were changing too, as the crops started growing, a hint of bright yellow in one, a deeper green in another. She took off her jacket and laid it on the grass, sitting on top of it. She breathed deeply. The sky was a beautiful pale spring blue. There were scatterings of wildflowers in the grass around her. She heard the bleating of spring lambs, the rustle and chirping of nest-building from the birds in the oak and chestnut woods in front of her.

She'd learned from all her reading that this area of Tara was called An Grianan, the Women's Sunny Place. There were two large trenches in the steep slope in front of her, reputed by legend to have slid down the hill centuries before, after two Kings of Tara had made bad judgments. Beside them was the grass-covered mound called Ráth Gráinne, Gráinne's fort. Lainey thought again of the Celtic legend of Diarmuid and Gráinne. She knew it from her schooldays and had read about it again in several of the books from the library. It was a tragic tale, the story of Gráinne, daughter of Cormac Mac Airt, one of the Kings of Tara, who ran away with her beloved Diarmuid rather than marry the legendary but ageing warrior Finn McCool. After fleeing Tara, the pair were pursued all over Ireland by Finn, the whole tragic affair finally ending with the death of Diarmuid.

Poor Gráinne, Lainey thought. And she thought she had relationship problems. She breathed in deeply, trying to remember tips from a meditation book. Breathe in, breathe out, make sure you are placed in the here and the now. Look around, be where you are, be who you are.

Who was she? Lainey Byrne. Where was she? Going bananas. She was genuinely losing it, she decided. She didn't feel at all like herself anymore, especially in regard to Rohan. It was like she'd been taken over by an alien being, someone who blushed easily, stammered, whose head was filling with mad thoughts. She thought of something Eva had said once. She had a theory that there were a number of different emotions or feelings that every human being had to experience in a lifetime. A Life List, if you like. Some people did them in normal order—first crush, first disappointment. Then came the big ones— death of a parent, falling in love, getting married or having children. Others did them in a different order.

Perhaps that explained what was happening now. She'd just fallen behind with her Life List and was catching up on the crush one now. She hadn't gone through it as a teenager. At her prime crush time she and the rest of her family had moved to Australia. She had been too busy trying to make friends, adjust to different schools, a different country, a different life, to be able to take time out for something as frivolous as a crush.

The thought pleased her. Yes, that's all this was. A simple, ordinary, run-of-the-mill crush. Delayed development. A midlife crisis. She was going back to her teenage self. It had nothing to do with Rohan Hartigan per se and nothing to do with blocking out any confused thoughts about Adam, or any worries that she had made the wrong decision about breaking up with him. It was just her mind's way of ticking off one more thing on that list. Good. Fine.

She had a chance to put her new maturity into practice immediately. Rohan's car was parked in front of Tara Lodge. She noticed that Sabine wasn't in the car with him. She took control, marching up to him as he got out of the car, talking quickly to get in first, to try and stop the mind-films from playing in her head, taking over. "Rohan, hello. And before you say anything, I'm sorry for my drunken behavior at the party and for whatever I said and if I was rude and for trying and failing so badly to speak German to Sabine."

He seemed taken aback, then he smiled. "Don't be sorry. You were absolutely grand. Sure, we were all having a few drinks. You were no orphan. And Sabine said it was very nice of you to try and speak German. And she really enjoyed singing 'O Tannenbaum' with you. Germans don't often get the chance to sing about Christmas trees this early in the year."

Lainey groaned. "I didn't, did I?" Eva and Joseph hadn't mentioned that little jewel of drunken behavior.

"Just the one verse."

Lainey knew then why he was there. "You've come to cancel the Hill of Tara tours, haven't you? You don't want to be associated with an old soak." It was a relief to talk to him like this, her embarrassment about the party canceling out any nerves she'd previously felt.

"No, I've come about Nell, actually."

"About her photography?" Nell still hadn't called around with her photographs, though Lainey had reminded her about it at the party.

"About that and something else. Can I come inside?"

They went into the kitchen, Lainey putting on coffee, making general conversation, still amazed at how normal she was being with him. There was a tiny imp in the corner of her mind making lewd suggestions, but she was successfully keeping it subdued. This was just a nice, normal conversation with someone she used to go to school with.

He accepted the coffee with thanks, then started talking about Nell. Lainey sat opposite him, taking some pleasure in the fact that his curly hair was looking a little bouffant today.

"Nell's not just here for a holiday or to spend time with

her grandmother while her mother's away working," he said. "The main reason is she got into a bit of trouble in London. She got involved with another student in her photography class who was unsuitable, for lots of reasons. I won't go into details, I hope you don't mind. She'd hate it if she knew I was talking about her like this. I didn't meet the fellow myself but my sister took a real dislike and she's not one to overreact."

"So that's why she's here? To keep her away from this boyfriend?"

"Just until my sister gets back from America. The trouble is, Nell is getting very bored. Which is why I'm here today. We wondered, well, I wondered, could Nell give you some help here at all? No need to pay her. She's got an allowance from her parents, but just to keep her busy, give her something to do with herself?"

Lainey didn't need to think about it. "Well, sure, once the theme weekends get under way. Or if I start getting any midweek guests. Send her along. We can have a chat. And of course I'd pay her, if she's working for me."

He finished his coffee, and stood up, looking relieved. "Thanks, Lainey. You're a lifesaver. See, you must have been meant to come back here."

Where did he get a phrase like that from? "Yes, I must have been."

"So is Sabine still here?" she asked casually as she saw him to his car a few minutes later.

"No, she had to go back to Munich. I'm back to being a bachelor again."

She looked at him, trying to hide a feeling of dismay. Don't tell me that, don't say that. It was too late. As he drove off, the imp in her mind came out waving flags and gyrating its hips. Eva's words came flying into her mind as well, in neon block letters. *You really might be in with a chance, Lainey. He is quite sexy, isn't he?* Oh shite, she thought, closing her eyes. Here we go again.

*   *   *

Lainey was out in the garden the next day pulling up weeds, Rod Stewart snoozing in a patch of sun near her, when she heard a car. It was Nell, driving what Lainey assumed was Mrs. Hartigan's car.

Watching as Nell climbed out, Lainey noticed again that she was really just a child, only sixteen or seventeen, despite the makeup and older clothes. She stood up, holding her creaking lower back, and smiled. "Come in, Nell. Welcome to Tara Lodge."

"Hi."

She wasn't just shy, she was very shy, Lainey guessed that much immediately. But that was okay. She had the occasional shy moment too.

"Come in. Have a cup of tea. Your uncle was saying you're looking for some work."

She nodded.

"You're here for about six months, is that right?"

Another nod.

Rod Stewart got your tongue? "Are you liking being in Ireland?"

"No."

"No?"

"It's not where I want to be."

"Where would you rather be?"

"Back home in London. At my photography class."

Lainey wanted to hear Nell's version. "Why are you here, then?"

"Boyfriend trouble." She said it in a singsong, mocking voice, but then became sullen again. "Mum had to go away for work and they didn't trust me to be at home on my own, so they sent me here."

Lainey couldn't mistake the note of hurt in Nell's voice. "What about your dad? Couldn't you stay with him?"

The eyes went down again. "It's a bit crowded in his house already."

"Crowded?"

"All his other kids. His new wife."

"Ah."

"So why are *you* here?"

Lainey decided to tell her the truth. "So I can sell this place in a year's time and my father can get the money he needs."

Nell nodded, but didn't ask anymore. Perhaps she knew it all from Rohan already. "We're prisoners, the pair of us," she said gloomily.

Lainey laughed. "Then we should stick together, shouldn't we?"

"Are you offering me the job?"

"Do you want the job?"

"Yes, please." A big smile.

Hurrah, there was life in there somewhere. "Can you start next week? And bring your camera?"

Another nod. She'd gone back to being shy.

CHAPTER 25

The next time Lainey picked up her emails there was one from Hugh.

TO: Lainey
RE: Hypothetical situation

Dear Sister,
A puzzle for you. If by some chance I happened to own a restaurant in Camberwell and needed ideas for a special Mother's Day promotion coming up, what would you suggest? This hypothetical restaurant has some competition nearby and early bookings would be a relief, so a hasty (non-hypothetical) reply at your earliest convenience would be appreciated. Please feel free to use this secure email address.
Your loving brother, Hugh
P.S. How is the cooking going? What are you planning on serving them, jam on toast? Thoughts of you in the kitchen has caused much hilarity among your family, thank you for cheering us up.

Lainey felt a glow start around about heart level. Hugh was channeling Adam's requests, like some spirit medium. This had obviously come up when they had met for a beer. Should she answer it? Of course. She had loved coming up with ideas for Adam's restaurant. She typed as fast as she could, suggesting half a dozen possible promotions for Mother's Day, and then added at the end of her email:

P.S. re: cooking, you'd be impressed actually—the full menu attached for your reading pleasure. It's amazing, did you know that you can do other things with vegetables than stir-fry them???

There was an answer back the next morning.

Thank you. You are an angel.

Lainey read the message twice. Angel. That was Adam's pet name for her, not Hugh's.

*   *   *

"This, Lainey, is a fish. Officially known as a salmon. And this is a potato."

Lainey stood back from the kitchen table and glared at her friend. "I really can't think why you don't have your own comedy show."

"You said you needed cooking lessons."

"I haven't just arrived from the planet Zorg, though. I do recognize basic food items."

"Okay, smartie, what do you do with the fish and the potato?"

"Cook them in lots of oil and wrap them in newspaper?"

"No."

"Hurl them in the bin and run outside screaming?"

"No, not that either. Watch."

Eva really knew her stuff. Lainey took notes as her friend demonstrated the dishes she would need to cook for the theme weekends. It was just a matter of being organized, Eva kept insisting. All Lainey had to do was make sure she had the best quality ingredients she could find and then bring them all together.

"Just like running an event, really," Eva said cheerily. "You'll pick it up, Lainey. You'll be a gourmet chef before you know it."

Lainey wasn't so sure, still wondering if it would be possible to pass off frozen meals from the Dunshaughlin supermarket as her own cooking.

"Have you had any more bookings?" Eva asked, as she showed Lainey how to prepare the Connemara lamb for roasting.

"Four more. The first weekend is nearly full now, but I'm still really worried about the others."

"Don't be, I'm sure they'll come in. We Irish are notorious for late bookings, remember." Eva returned to her role as chef instructor then, making Lainey copy her movements exactly. "Well done. Just make sure you don't use too much salt. The lamb gets a wonderful flavor from the heather it's fed on over in the west, so you have to enhance it, not overwhelm it. See, it's all in the preparation. You'll have Nell to help you too, won't you?"

Lainey was trying to banish a mental picture of a

snowy-white animal gamboling across heather-covered fields. "Hopefully, if she's in a good mood on cooking days. I reckon there are actually two of them, twins. One day the shy one comes, the next day the talkative one. But she's a good worker. She helped me do the windows this week, and we're going to do all the floorboards and banisters next week, get everything shiny and gleaming. And I'll tell you what else, she showed me some of her photos and they're really good. I've asked her to take some of Tara for me. Maybe I'll use them as postcards or guest souvenirs or something."

Eva gave a wicked grin. "This couldn't be happening better if I had planned it myself. Rohan's niece working with you, the perfect excuse for him to drop in. He won't be able to keep away now."

"Eva . . ." Lainey warned.

. . .

It was no good, the damage was done. That night, the mind-films starring Lainey as herself and Rohan Hartigan as the leading man played in glorious Technicolor and with a definite Adults Only rating.

. . .

"Time for tea, I think, Nell, before we collapse of exhaustion."

Nell got up from the staircase without a word and followed Lainey down into the kitchen. They'd been scrubbing at the banister rails for nearly two hours now, both of them amazed at the layers of dirt that had accumulated over the years. It was Shy Nell Day, Lainey noted.

Nell was silent, staring at the photos of friends and family that Lainey had stuck all over the fridge door.

"Is that you and your mother? This one here, where you're all dressed up?"

It was a photo taken at the twins' baptism. "That's right."

"And who's that man in the wheelchair beside you?"

"That's my dad."

"Is he a cripple?"

Lainey winced. "He had an accident at work and he was in a wheelchair for a while," she said in even tones. "But he uses a walker now. He can get around on his own a little way."

"And these three fellas? They're your brothers, right?"

"That's right. Brendan's the oldest, then Declan and the one with the blue hair is Hugh."

"Is Hugh adopted? He doesn't really look like the other three of you, does he? I mean, apart from the blue hair even." She was studying the photo.

Poor Hugh had been getting asked that all his life. Short and stocky where the rest of them were like their parents, tall and lean, he was always being called the cuckoo in the nest. Lainey cranked out the usual family response. "My parents had run out of all the good genes by the time they had him, unfortunately. He's made up of leftovers."

"Or else your mother had an affair with the milkman," Nell offered.

"Or there's that, yes," Lainey said wearily. "Tea or coffee, Nell?"

• • •

"Tara Lodge, good afternoon."

"Lainey Byrne please."

"This is Lainey."

"Lainey, this is Leo Ramsay. Do you remember we met at your party?"

The creepy Englishman who had asked after her mother. "Yes, Mr. Ramsay. I passed on your message to my mother."

"I'm glad. Seeing you was like seeing her again, like being spirited back in time. That same long body, the lift of the chin, that combination of strength and vulnerability—enchanting in your mother and now here it is in you as well."

Lainey held the phone away and pulled a face. What was this, dial-a-weirdo?

"Lainey, I'm calling to invite you to come and pose for me. I'd like to paint you as I did your mother. But I feel it's important to get to know you better first, so I can be sure it is you I am painting, not just an echo of your mother. There are differences, I could sense that, but it is only in intimate surroundings, after long, searching conversations, that I will be sure of those differences, that I will know I have the essence of you, and not some pale reflection of my memories of your mother."

He was drunk, she realized. "Mr. Ramsay, I think—"

"You haven't had children, have you? There is a certain fullness to a woman's hips after childbearing which I couldn't see with you. I loved that about your mother, the animal sexuality of her tempered with the Madonna, the woman who was truly all woman after the rigors of childbirth . . ."

Not just drunk, but repulsive, too. "Mr. Ramsay, I'm

afraid I won't be able to help you. Thank you all the same. Good afternoon." And with that she hung up.

. . .

Spring was no longer on its way—it had arrived, in an explosion of yellow flowers. Lainey walked around the garden, in awe of the difference the mild weather had made. It was as if all the flowers had burst out of the ground overnight. The previously bleak garden was revealing its true colors—bright-green buds on the line of shrubs near the front wall, a low hedge of crimson fuchsia lining the stone pathway to the front door. There was still plenty of blossom, too, and the beginnings of wild roses. Out the back what had been a scrappy piece of land was revealing itself as a wild vegetable and herb patch. Lainey couldn't be sure, but she thought she could smell basil and parsley and oregano among the tiny green leaves poking through the soil. The only black spot was a sighting of a mouse near the compost pile. Still, better outside than in. Not that Rod Stewart seemed to care either way. He'd clearly decided he was in the house purely for decoration.

She walked back into the house, a bunch of flowers in her hand, then ran as she heard the phone.

"Tara Lodge. Lainey speaking."

"Good morning, this is Jenna Reid. I'm a reporter with the *Sunday Echo* newspaper. Is it true you have Hilly Robson and Noah Geddes staying with you this weekend?"

The celebrity couple? Lainey laughed. "Oh sure, I wish. Of course not. Who told you that?"

"We got a tip-off."

"Well, your tip-off is wrong. But I'll let you know if they do arrive," Lainey joked. To her surprise, the woman left her phone number, saying she would appreciate a call, thank you.

She'd just put the flowers in a vase when the phone rang again. Another newspaper, the same query, her same answer, followed by a conversation in the background. "She says it's not true." "Well she would, wouldn't she?"

By the fifth call, this one from a London-based tabloid, she'd had enough. "Yes, they are staying with me this weekend actually. I went to school in Melbourne with Hilly, or Hillary as she was known then, of course, and when I heard she was in Ireland I got in contact and invited her and Noah here. But why don't you all just leave her alone, the poor thing? All she needs is a bit of rest and recreation, some of my lovely cooking and a few nights in one of my luxurious bedrooms. Yes, that's right, t-a-r-a l-o-d-g-e, two words. My pleasure, lovely to talk to you."

By the eighth call, Lainey was shouting, "No, they're not here!" and hanging up.

She let three calls go unanswered until she realized they might be inquiries about her gourmet weekends. Gingerly she picked up the next one. It was Nell in a phone box in Dunshaughlin, sounding breathless. "Lainey, a huge limousine just went through town, pulled in at the new shopping center and asked where your B&B was. And apparently it was that Australian actress, you know, the one going out with the pop star. Are they really staying with you tonight? Do you want me to drive over and help you?"

Lainey made Nell go over it all again, slowly. "I mean it, seriously. My gran's neighbor said somebody told her they'd seen this big car parked outside a pub in Dunshaughlin. They apparently ordered a pint of Guinness and a large Coke, then sat in the car drinking them, because it was too smoky for her in the pub. That sounds right, doesn't it? I mean, I read that in a magazine. She's got weak lungs or something."

Lainey was too embarrassed to admit that she'd read the same article and yes, apparently Hilly Robson did have weak lungs. Lainey also knew that Hilly Robson was thirty-four, from Melbourne, and had started her career as a singing telegram girl. She had hit the big time in a small arthouse film called *The Wait*, which had broken box-office records around the world. She was a vegetarian. She went to the hairdressers twice a week to keep her long blonde curls in top condition. She had only learned to drive when she was twenty-eight, her favorite food was tofu and her favorite drink champagne. She'd been unlucky in love until recently when she had met English badboy white rap artist Noah Geddes with whom she had apparently been having a clandestine affair for the past eight months, conducted in luxury hotels all around the world. Lainey knew more about Hilly Robson than she did about some of her closest friends, all of it learned from reading magazine articles at supermarket checkouts. "And you said they were asking for directions for here? For Tara Lodge?"

"The Tara Lodge, definitely."

Lainey hurriedly said goodbye and stood by the phone, her heart beating. There had been rumors in the paper that the pair were planning a holiday in Ireland. And was she right in remembering an interview with Hilly in which the actress had confessed a fascination for ancient Celtic mysticism? Where better to come than the Hill of Tara then? And where better to stay than the Tara Lodge? Oh Jesus, Mary and Joseph. Lainey ran upstairs to check that all the rooms were ready, in case this piece of madness had just the tiniest link to reality. The doorbell rang. She nearly tumbled down the stairs in her rush to answer it.

A man and a woman were standing there, the man with a camera round his neck. The woman was English. "We've heard Hilly Robson and Noah Geddes are staying here. Is that right?"

"No," Lainey said, flustered.

"But our news desk in London said you confirmed it this morning."

"Nonsense," Lainey said, her heart thumping.

"Why are you in such a panic then?"

"I'm not in a panic—it's asthma." She shut the door in their faces.

Within the hour, waiting outside were three photographers, one freelance TV cameraman who said he was there for Sky news, and the local reporter who usually wrote about sport and looked annoyed to be covering celebrity gossip instead. Then the kids from the farm down the road wandered up. Then a tourist bus slowed down, went past, came back.

Inside, Lainey ignored the ringing phone, waiting for something to happen and not having a clue what it might be. She peered through the windows again and her heart gave a leap. A long black limousine with tinted windows had come into view and was now edging its way through the crowd. Driving toward her. Just as Nell had said.

She ran back into the kitchen, turned in a circle, wondering what she should do. I mean, it wasn't as if she had anyone else staying. There was definitely room, but bloody hell, Hilly Robson and Noah Geddes? Staying here? What would they eat? Would they need her to get some drugs for them? Some other famous people for them to talk to? Would the beds be comfortable enough?

Her mobile phone started ringing. Oh God, what terrible timing. She glanced at the display. It was Eva's number. She couldn't ignore her. She spoke quickly, moving up the stairs. "Evie, hi, sweetheart. This is a bad time, sorry. I can't really talk."

"I know. Just shut all the curtains, lock the back door, then open the front door and we'll come tearing up the path. And then make sure you shut the door right behind us, okay?"

"What?"

"You heard me. You've got about a minute, Lainey. Quick, just do it."

With no idea why, Lainey did as she was told, running to the back of the house and bolting the back door, pulling the curtains in the two front rooms, then opening the front door, just as the limousine door opened at the front gate. Two figures, heads covered in scarves and hats, one with long blonde curly hair, both wearing dark sunglasses, ran up the path hand-in-hand, ignoring calls for them to turn around. They rushed past Lainey, who took a step back, then slammed the door as instructed.

She watched, astonished, as the arrivals peeled off their scarves, hats, glasses and wig.

It was Eva and Joseph, in fits of laughter.

"G'day, mate," Eva said.

"Respec'," Joseph said in a very bad rap voice and with a peculiar hand gesture, which set Eva laughing even harder.

Lainey just stared at them in complete astonishment. "What on earth are you doing?"

Eva was beaming. "Getting you publicity. Look, it's worked, hasn't it? I read it in an old magazine at the hairdresser's last week. Apparently Princess Diana used to do it the whole time."

Lainey couldn't even pretend she knew what was going on. "Dress up as an Australian actress and hire limos?"

"No, call the media and let them know where she was going to be, tip them off. So that gave me the idea. I rang all the papers in Dublin and in London and told them I'd heard on the grapevine that Hilly Robson and Noah Geddes were coming to stay here. And then Joe decided we should take it one step further and actually pretend to be them."

"So we hired this limousine for the day—"

"Went to that costume shop in the city and hired this wig and Joe's rap gear and da da! Here we are. The driver thought we were the real thing, I'm sure of it." Eva was laughing so hard she could hardly speak. "Especially when Joe started singing this ridiculous rap song, 'Hilly you're the dilly and my number one babe.' And I just kept repeating all the Australian expressions I could remember you and I laughing about last year in Melbourne, you know, 'Strewth, look at that gorgeous cottage,' and 'Bloody oath, it really is forty shades of green.' Then as we were getting out, Joe said to the driver . . ." Eva looked over at her husband, giving him his cue.

Joseph put on the fake rap accent again. "Pal, let me tell you, I'm a fair man. Sell this story, make what you can."

They were nearly weeping laughing now. Lainey peered through the curtains. Sure enough, the limousine driver was down the lane, surrounded by photographers and a TV camera. Lainey jumped as someone peered in at her as she was peering out. She dropped the curtain as the ringing of the doorbell started again.

She turned back to her friends and started laughing too. "We're stuck here for the night, you mad eejits. Maybe even the weekend. You realize that, don't you?"

Joseph held up a case. "We've brought supplies with us. Champagne, wine, food. We can stay holed up for weeks if we need to."

"So go on, Lainey, get out there and give them a statement," Eva said, thoroughly enjoying seeing Lainey lost for words. "And don't forget to say the words Tara Lodge as often as you can. We'll nip upstairs out of the way. Come on, Noah. Time for a love tryst."

Lainey waited until they were upstairs, then opened the door, blinking as several of the photographers set off their flashes. Trying to keep a straight face, she stood her ground. "Could I ask you all to leave, please? My guests need their privacy."

The questions came flying at her. "So you can confirm that is Hilly Robson and Noah Geddes?" "Is that Hilly Robson and Noah Geddes?" "Is it true you went to school with Hilly Robson in Melbourne?"

Lainey smiled serenely, moving slightly to one side so the brass Tara Lodge nameplate was clearly visible. "I couldn't possibly say. But I have heard they both have very good taste and as you can see Tara Lodge is a wonderful place to stay. So who knows?" With that, she shut the door.

CHAPTER 26

Lainey put down the phone. Eva was a genius. Joseph was a genius. It had worked. Pictures of the alleged Hilly and Noah running into Tara Lodge had appeared in five newspapers. The place had been staked out all weekend, while the three of them had lived it up inside, drinking all the wine, eating the food, watching television, occasionally peering through the curtains. Come Monday morning, Lainey, Joseph and Eva had just walked out as themselves, disappointing the remaining reporters, climbed into Lainey's car and driven away.

Eva had insisted Lainey drop them off in town so they could catch the bus back to Dublin: "We need to get back in touch with our roots after the glamour of the limousine. Besides, you need to be home to answer the phone calls."

And there had been plenty of them, sparked either directly by the newspaper coverage or by people who had already heard about the Feast of Ireland weekends and realized they had better get in quickly if the place was in such demand. That morning she'd had a call from one of the social magazines too. Lainey just kept denying they'd been here, but it didn't seem to matter.

It hadn't been a matter of lying either. To any question about Hilly and Noah she'd simply answered, "I couldn't possibly comment." Perhaps there was a job as a media adviser to a politician ahead of her when she went back to Australia.

*   *   *

The next day another videotape arrived from Hugh. They were like little jewels arriving in brown paper, Lainey thought, going through her usual routine—getting a coffee, settling herself in front of the video player, looking forward to another update on her family. She was surprised when quite a different title came up on screen.

The Hatted Chef Bites

Then a subtitle

Cooking Tips for Guesthouse Owners

There was no pretense that it wasn't Adam this time. Lainey laughed as a scooter came into view down her own street in Richmond, ridden by Adam, who was at least two feet too tall for it. "Wotcha," he shouted, leaping off, letting the bike fall to the ground. It was Adam pretending to be Jamie Oliver, scampering up the stairs in their apartment building, speaking in an appalling Cockney accent. "Roight then, luvverly jubbley. We've bin to the markets,

roight, so wot I'm going to show you now is a roight delicious Irish meal."

The delicious Irish meal he started to cook came
straight from Lainey's Feast of Ireland menu, the one she
had emailed Hugh. Adam kept up the Jamie Oliver voice
and behavior, but it was his own sureness of hand and skills
as a chef on display. It was filmed in stages, with lots of
close-ups of him selecting oysters and crab claws, telling
her what to look for at the market, and how to prepare and
serve them both. A fast-forwarded segment came next,
showing him eating both dishes and drinking a pint of
Guinness, with a soundtrack of tiddley-aye Irish music playing underneath. Then he demonstrated the main courses
of oven-roasted lamb and baked fillet of wild salmon, taking her through every stage of the preparation. The final
shot showed the two dishes beautifully presented on serving platters.

There was an uneven edit, a flash of static and then a
new setting. The kitchen at Adam's restaurant. Lainey recognized it immediately. Then, into shot came Adam, but it
was Adam wearing a long black wig and a sexy dress, clearly
stuffed with a pair of football socks. One of the sock's heels
was poking out of his cleavage. He was speaking in a husky,
upper-class British accent, looking coquettishly at the camera. "Dessert should be sexy, indulgent, fulfilling," he/she
said slowly, batting his eyelashes (false, Lainey noticed in
astonishment). "First take plenty of cream." The camera
lingered lovingly on the thick cream, the melted chocolate, the soft butter, as Adam—or Adamma, as he was refer-
ring to himself—showed how to make a rich chocolate
pudding. At first every shot had a lock of hair draped
across the food, generally covered in cream. As the prepa-

ration went on, though, it became serious, as Adam showed Lainey step by step how to mix the ingredients, fold the mixture, grease the small ramekins, sprinkle the icing sugar—even where exactly to place them in the oven ("or Aga," he said, pronouncing it "Agaah"). He did the same with the golden syrup dumplings and fig and walnut pudding.

Then the credits rolled—a shot of a computer screen with hundreds of names scrolling upward so quickly there wasn't a chance of reading any of them. Lainey pressed pause and managed to read a few. There was every mad job title under the sun—Best Boy, Key Grip, Script Editor, Properties Manager, Caterer, Masseur, Driver, Runner, Walker, Crawler. In each case the name beside the title was Hugh Byrne. Until the end, when she saw the line Suggested, Devised and Produced by Adam Blake. And then the final line: An Angel Production.

* * *

The next day she was watching it again, taking notes on how Adam filleted the salmon, when Nell came in behind her.

She watched it silently for a moment. "Is that a home-made video? Not a real cooking show?"

"Yes, it's my brother and my—" She stopped. "My brother and a friend of mine did it in Melbourne for me."

Nell watched a bit longer. "Your friend's very tall, isn't he?"

"Mmm."

"Was he your boyfriend?"

"Mmm," she said after a pause.

"I thought you fancied Rohan."

Lainey spun around. "I'm sorry?"

"I thought you fancied Rohan. You go funny when he's around."

"No, I don't."

"You do. Your voice changes. You watch him all the time."

Lainey realized right then that she hated teenagers. They were ridiculous and should all be banished to a far-off island until they had grown up. "You're imagining it."

"No, I'm not."

Lainey made a point of staring at the screen for a moment, then she couldn't help herself. "He's practically married, though, isn't he? He and Sabine?"

"But she's not here, is she? She had to stay in Munich," Nell said matter-of-factly.

"Why was that?" Lainey asked in as casual a voice as she could muster.

"She teaches in a school for special children. Rohan said she thought it would be too disruptive for them if she left for the year."

"Oh, I see."

Nell had a mischievous smile on her face. "Maybe Rohan fancies you as well? Do you want me to ask him?"

Lainey leaned across and turned off the video. That was quite enough watching TV and talking to Nell for one day. "Don't be silly, Nell. Now come on, we've got floors to scrub."

•   •   •

A phone call from her mother that night put thoughts of Adam and Rohan right out of her head. The insurance company had sent someone to try and video her father. Lainey was livid. "Those stinking creeping bastards, that pack of—"

"Elaine Byrne, watch your tongue, please."

"I'm sorry, Ma. But how dare they try and film Dad like that? That's an invasion of privacy, isn't it? You're sure, are you? Sure they were from the insurance company? It wasn't some documentary film company? A news crew?"

"No, we're sure. Hugh picked them first. He was coming home and saw the car cruising, looking for an address. And then he saw them go past our house and stop and set up something. So he stood at the lounge-room window and started filming them. And that's how he saw it. He used the zoom lens and saw them filming him."

"Did they know he was filming them filming him?"

"They weren't filming him—they were trying to film your father."

"You know what I mean, Ma. Did they know?"

"No, Hugh was very careful. He was great, actually, just took control of the whole situation."

Lainey felt a pang of jealousy. She should have been the one there taking control, not Hugh. "So what were they waiting for? Dad to come out on a pogo stick? Isn't this against the law?"

"No, it's not, apparently. It's their job to satisfy themselves that the claim is completely valid, so they have to gather evidence."

"Why aren't you raging, Ma? Ringing up the police?"

"I was when it first happened, but Hugh said it didn't matter at all. It meant the case was progressing. He seemed pleased, to be honest."

"That's just because there was a video camera involved. And what about Dad?"

"We didn't tell him. We thought it would only make him more depressed."

"More?"

"He's had a bad week. Again. I spoke to his physio. She was asking if he'd been doing any of his exercises at all. He should have been up and about by now, she said."

"Well, give her a medal for that startling diagnosis."

"You getting cranky isn't going to get us anywhere."

Lainey forced herself to change the subject. "How are the boys? And Rosie and the twins?"

"Everyone's absolutely grand. Brendan's been working back late a lot these past weeks, some big project on, apparently."

"Give them all my love, won't you? I'd better go, in case anyone's trying to ring and book."

"Bye, love. And thanks again. For being there."

"For being there? For being me? Have you been watching too many Hollywood films?"

"You know what I mean."

"I know. And it's no problem, really. Bye now."

After she'd hung up she realized that she hadn't mentioned the call from Leo Ramsay. Her hand hovered over the phone for a moment, as she thought about calling back. Then she decided she didn't want to tell her mother. Something about the whole Leo situation had made her feel quite uncomfortable.

CHAPTER 27

Lainey stood back several nights later and gazed around the dining room. She'd decided to do a trial run of the two dinners, serving all the dishes just as she would when the theme weekends were up and running. She'd invited Rohan and Mrs. Hartigan over this evening to try Friday night's menu. Eva and Joseph were coming the following night to try Saturday night's dishes.

Rohan and Mrs. Hartigan were due to arrive any moment. The table was polished and set with real linen, for three places rather than the ten it would have during the weekends, but the effect was still charming. The fire was lit, there were fresh flowers, and candles flickered here and there around the room. She just had to hope that having Mrs. Hartigan there would stop the mind-film imp. Since Nell had planted the idea in her head that Rohan might in fact fancy her, she'd been cursed with lurid images at all hours of the day. She'd begun to wish she'd invited Mr. and Mrs. Fogarty for dinner rather than Rohan and his mother.

The ring of the doorbell brought her to her senses. She had to count to ten before she answered. It would be bad enough blushing in front of Rohan, but in front of Mrs. Hartigan as well?

Mrs. Hartigan wasn't there. It was just Rohan.

He smiled apologetically. "Lainey, I'm sorry for the late notice, but my mother isn't well tonight. I know how important it is that you try out the meal, so I thought you wouldn't mind if I brought a friend along instead. I met him coming out of one of the pubs in town."

His friend stepped into the light, having clearly just been relieving himself in the garden. It was Bill, the ginger-haired man from the pub.

Three hours later Lainey knew more about the Bayern Munich football team than she would have thought it possible to know. As for anything happening between her and Rohan—there hadn't been the slightest possibility of it. Bill had completely monopolized the conversation all evening, treating Lainey as though she was a rather annoying waitress who for some reason insisted on sitting down and eating with them. She and Rohan had barely exchanged any words, let alone anything else.

As for their opinion of the food—she could have served gnats on toast for all the two men would have noticed.

．　．　．

Second time lucky, Lainey thought the next night. Once again, the dining room looked beautiful. The fire was lit and the lamps were low. She watched, fingers crossed, as Joseph and Eva dipped their spoons into the chocolate puddings in front of them. They had already declared the crab claws delicious. They'd raved about her fresh salmon. She tensed now as their spoons broke the crispy chocolate crust of the dessert, releasing the molten chocolate inside. She leaned forward, waiting, holding her breath. They took three more mouthfuls each before they delivered their verdict. Joseph spoke for them both.

"Lainey, it's superb."

She opened a new bottle of wine in celebration. "Thanks so much, you two, really. I can't tell you how many practice runs I've had. There'll be a salmon shortage in Ireland by the time I'm finished here."

"You can relax, Lainey, really. It was all just fantastic," Eva said. "And not just the food, the whole room looks beautiful. We should have booked in for a couple of these weekends ourselves."

"I want you to come down as my guests when this is all over, anyway—let me spoil you rotten for a weekend after all you've both done for me," she said, trying to pour wine through the hand Joe had spread over the top of his glass. "Ah, go on, Joe, have one more. To mark the fact I didn't blow up the kitchen."

"No, thanks, Lainey. I'm driving."

"Come on, half a glass then. It'll drown out any bad memories of the meal."

"All right, just a half. And I don't have any bad memories of the meal to drown out. It was delicious, really."

Lainey didn't confess that she had watched Adam make it all on the video at least a dozen times before she tried it herself. She hadn't even told Eva about Adam's video. She didn't know why.

Eva and Joseph left soon after, running out to the car through the rain. They were barely visible through the mist as Lainey stood in her porch waving.

She went inside to the warmth of the kitchen and had just finished clearing the dining room and drying the dishes, about to go to bed, when the phone rang. Nearly midnight, it would be Australia calling.

She wiped her hands on the tea towel. "Good morning, Australia," she said.

It wasn't Australia. It was Eva, her voice barely recognizable. "Lainey?"

"Evie, what is it? What's happened?"

"We've been in a crash."

"Oh my God. Where are you?"

"In Blanchardstown hospital. It happened just after we'd driven through Dunshaughlin. The ambulance brought us here."

"The ambulance? Evie, what is it? Is Joe all right?" She felt like her legs were going to give way.

Eva just started crying. "Lainey, can you please come?"

. . .

She was at the hospital within twenty minutes. As she ran through the foyer, she saw Eva in the distance, sitting in a chair near the nurses' station.

Lainey sat beside her, took her hand. Her friend wasn't crying now. She was glassy-eyed with shock, strangely calm. "Evie? Is he . . . ?"

"He's going to be all right, Lainey, isn't he?"

Lainey shut her eyes in quick relief. So he was alive. She squeezed her hand. "Of course he'll be all right. And are you all right, Evie? You weren't hurt at all?"

Eva just shook her head. Lainey tried to find out exactly what had happened, what injuries Joe had suffered, but Eva could barely speak. Lainey took off her jacket and wrapped it around her friend. "Evie, will you drink a cup of tea?"

Eva nodded, her teeth chattering.

"I'll be back in just a moment, I promise." She hurried to the nurses' station to find out what she could. "He's in X-ray at the moment. We're checking for any internal injuries, broken bones," the woman behind the desk said. "As far as we know he hit his head against the steering wheel, which knocked him out for a time."

"But he's all right?"

"We'll know more in an hour or so."

Lainey got directions to the canteen, made two cups of hot, sweet tea and came back to Eva. She was calmer again, staring ahead. Lainey took her hand, put her other arm around her, feeling her trembling deep inside. "Evie, what happened? Can you tell me?"

Eva's teeth started chattering again, though she wasn't cold. "We were driving along the main road, just before Dunshaughlin, driving really slowly because of the mist. And we came to the crossroads and we could see these car headlights waiting to the right, but we had right of way so we didn't slow. But then they just came, Lainey, and they just kept on coming and Joe was saying what the hell are they doing and then they just hit into his side of the car. And I could see Joe fall forward and hit the wheel and then he made this noise, this terrible sort of shout, and I can't get it out of my head. Then he wouldn't answer me and I thought he was dead." The shaking became more violent. "And then the other driver appeared and he was just a kid and he kept saying sorry over and over again and I started screaming at him, that he'd killed my husband. Then another driver stopped and she had a mobile and called the ambulance and they took forever to come and then they brought him here. And I didn't know if Joe was alive or dead. He was warm but he wouldn't talk and I couldn't get him to open his eyes." Eva had to stop, her teeth chattering so hard she couldn't form words.

Lainey had a memory flash of forcing that last glass of wine on Joe. If he hadn't had that, would he have been able to avoid the crash? Would he have seen the other car coming, been able to stop in time? Oh, God, was she to blame for this? She looked at Eva, stricken. "It was my fault. I'm the one who made him have that last glass of wine. Evie, I'm so sorry, I'm so sorry . . ."

To her astonishment, Eva stopped shaking, threw off her arm and turned on her. "Shut up, Lainey. Bloody well shut up. It's not about you. You had nothing to do with it. We've been in a crash, I don't know if Joe will even live and what are you saying? 'Oh, it's about me. It's all my fault.' Me, bloody me."

"Eva, please, calm down. You're in shock. I didn't say it was about me."

Eva's eyes were blazing. "Yes, you did. You are not in charge of the whole world, Lainey. A whole lot more goes on than what you've made happen." She moved backward, as if being that close to Lainey disgusted her. "Just leave me alone, would you? Go and think of yourself somewhere else."

"Eva—"

"Lainey, I mean it. Please, just leave me alone. Go away."

Lainey stood up, staring at Eva, who had now covered her face with her hands. She went to talk to her, but didn't know what to say. Instead she turned and somehow stumbled her way outside. The air was freezing, the mist still heavy. She knew Eva was in terrible shock, but had she really meant all that? Was that really what she was like, thinking about herself all the time? Was she really that self-obsessed? Wanting everything to suit her and her alone?

She felt someone come and stand beside her, and for a hopeful moment thought it was Eva. But it was a middle-aged man, looking as distressed as she was feeling. She wondered why he was there at this time of the night but didn't want to ask, too confused, too shocked herself. She hugged herself, shivering but not really feeling the cold. She wanted to be sick, wanted to run, wanted to go back in and be with Eva, wanted to help Joe, wanted to do everything and nothing, all at once, confused, hurt and scared.

"Cigarette?"

She didn't smoke but she accepted it anyway, took the light, inhaled once and gagged at the taste. It brought her to her senses. What the hell was she doing out here? She needed to be with Eva. "Thanks anyway," she said, putting out the cigarette.

She went back inside. Eva hadn't moved. Lainey sat next to her, didn't speak, but slowly reached and took her friend's hand, expecting her to push it away, to recoil from her. She didn't. They sat in silence for a moment, then Eva spoke first, without looking at her. "You stink. Have you been smoking?"

"Yes."

"But you don't smoke."

"No." She took a breath. "Eva, I'm so sorry—"

Eva turned to her. "Lainey, I'm so sorry—"

They both stopped.

Lainey went to talk, then bit back the words. She waited, then Eva spoke again. "I'm sorry for shouting at you, for saying those things."

"If you meant them, you were right to say them."

"You're not like that, not all the time."

Not all the time. But some of the time she obviously was. This wasn't the time to gather dates and examples. She took her friend's hand. "Evie, let's forget about that for the moment. It's Joe that's important."

Her friend started to shake again and buried her face in Lainey's shoulder. "I just couldn't bear it, Lainey. I just couldn't bear it if he died. I love him too much. We've got years ahead of us, I know we have. All these things we have to do. It's not going to end, is it?"

"Of course it's not, of course it's not. He'll be fine. You wait and see."

"But what if he's hurt, if he's got brain damage? He would hate that so much. You know what he's like. He's so smart and funny. I want him back, Lainey. I want my Joe back." She was crying now, the tears streaming from her.

"You will, you will." Lainey held her tighter. "Just wait, just wait and see what they tell you. He's here in hospital. They know what they're doing."

• • •

They waited three hours until the doctor came over toward them. Holding Eva tight, Lainey could feel the tension in her friend. She hugged her tighter, pulled the jacket closer around her.

It was good news. Joseph had a concussion, but the CAT scan hadn't shown any skull fractures or serious head injuries. He'd broken his wrist, they presumed from when he had thrown up his arm to protect himself as the other car crashed into his door. This had cushioned the impact. He had lacerations on his chest, caused by the seat belt, and they expected some soft tissue damage, heavy bruising probably, but there were no broken bones, and no internal injuries. They'd keep him in hospital under observation for a couple of days, but things looked fine. "He was very lucky. That mist slowed both cars down, probably saved lives."

Lainey had to hold Eva up, as the relief ran through her, her legs starting to give way. The doctor noticed. "We'll admit you for the night as well, I think, Eva."

CHAPTER 28

Four days later, Lainey drove back down the main road toward Tara, after dropping Eva and Joseph back to their apartment in Camden Street. She had offered to have them at Tara Lodge for as long as they liked. She could look after them both, she'd said, cook for them, let them sleep all day, help them get their strength up. She'd cancel the Feast of Ireland weekends if needs be.

Eva had turned her down, gently. They both just wanted to be home, in their own place. Joe was much better, nauseous the first day, dazed and suffering bad headaches, but in remarkably good spirits. The cuts and bruises were sore, but they would heal. He just needed to sleep, he said. Eva just wanted to be with him. She had hardly left his side since the night of the crash.

Before saying goodbye, while she and Eva were alone, Lainey had brought up the topic of Eva's outburst at the hospital. Eva had tried to dismiss it. "Lainey, I can hardly remember it. I was in bits with worry. I'd just had a car crash and wasn't thinking straight. You are my gorgeous, kind friend and I love you and it isn't worth worrying about. Please, let's just drop it."

If Eva wanted to drop it, fine, but Lainey couldn't. It was as though Eva's words had unlocked a secret door into all the unsavory parts of herself. She had been plagued with memories of bossing people, organizing things, demanding that things be done in a particular way, to suit her. Yes, she did have a flair for organization, but did it matter as much as she insisted if things weren't done exactly the way she wanted? At work? At home?

"You are not in charge of the whole world, Lainey. A whole lot more goes on than what you've made happen."

As she drove, she tried to get her thoughts clear in her head. Was Eva right? Did she have very fixed ideas about the way things should be, what she wanted to happen? How and when she wanted them to happen, even?

In an uncomfortable moment of self-revelation, she realized she did.

And not just with Eva and Joseph, but with her parents, her brothers, her friends. Even with Celia, her rival at work. She realized she'd been really hoping that Celia would get in trouble at Complete Event Management, that she would have to call Lainey in Ireland for help. She had been subconsciously scripting the whole scene in her mind . . . Celia calling in tears, admitting that she wasn't coping and that she badly needed Lainey's help. Lainey had pictured herself, speaking kindly and patiently to the other woman, giving her advice, feeling a glow of post-kindness satisfaction.

Except Celia hadn't rung. Because it seemed Celia was getting on fine and didn't need Lainey's help. Or if she did, she wasn't going to ask for it.

And there was someone else she had treated much worse. Someone else she'd expected to behave in a particular way. Someone she'd pigeonholed, made ill-informed decisions about.

Adam.

As she turned down the Tara road, Lainey realized something had to change. Eva was absolutely right about her. She had to stop charging in, trying to fix things, trying to make people do what she wanted them to do. She had to learn to take a step back, let things unfold, let people live their own lives, and see things as they really were, not how she wanted them to be. Not be the one in charge of the world.

Then she realized something else.

It was going to be very, very hard.

* * *

On the phone several days later, Lainey knew from the sound of Eva's voice that things were much better. There was a lightness back to it again. "I'm so relieved, Evie. You must have been worried sick."

"I really was, Lainey. I don't think I've slept properly since it happened. I'm sure Joe's sick of me watching his every move as well."

"Would you like me to come up and whisk you away, just for an hour or two? I could bring a picnic lunch. We could go for a walk in the Phoenix Park, if you like." She had her fingers crossed that Eva would accept. Since their fight the night of the accident, Lainey had felt a subtle shift in their relationship, a wariness on her own side, a distance on Eva's side. She needed to see her, talk about it, if she felt that Eva was ready to talk about it, too.

"That would be great, actually. Are you sure you can spare the time?"

"Of course I can. And I'll organize lunch and everything. All you have to do is tell me your favorite food and I'll get it for you."

. . .

The weather was warm enough to sit on one of the benches in the Phoenix Park. Lainey took a final sip of her coffee, folded the paper that had contained the smoked salmon and fresh brown bread sandwiches she had brought for their lunch. She had been right, the old Eva was back. She had been relaxed, happy even, when Lainey had called up to their flat to say hello to Joe and collect her earlier that day. They had driven around the whole park, past Áras an Uachtaráin, the Irish president's house, and past the American ambassador's residence. They'd finally chosen a sunny spot not far from the zoo in the corner of the park near the North Circular Road. Their conversation was punctuated now and again by animal sounds, squawks and grunts, mingling with snatches of the commentary floating over from the tourist buses driving up and down the main road. "The Phoenix Park is the largest enclosed park in Europe . . . home to a herd of deer whose ancestry dates back to the 1600s . . ."

Eva finished her coffee and gave a contented sigh. "That was gorgeous, Lainey, thanks."

"Have you had enough? Can I get you anything else?"

"No, that was perfect."

"You're sure?"

Eva smiled at her. "I feel like I have a nursemaid all of a sudden."

"I'm just worried about you. You have to look after yourself as well as Joe, you know."

"I am, I promise. And it's just lovely to be out in the air like this."

"Do you fancy a walk, then?"

"I'd love it."

They put the basket in the car and set off down the tree-lined path, toward the polo ground beside the zoo. They both ducked under the white railing and started walking around the edge of the neat grass oval.

Lainey felt a flutter in her stomach and realized it was nerves. She was nervous about the conversation she needed to have with Eva. In all their friendship, she had never felt that way. It was unsettling.

"Evie?"

"Mmm."

"Are you up to a serious talk about something? If you're not, it's fine. I know you've had a lot on your mind recently. It's just I feel I need to talk to you about something."

"Is everything all right? Is it about your ma and da? About Adam?"

"No, it's about us. You and me. Can we keep walking?" She had a feeling it might make it easier in a way to be moving. At Eva's nod, she started feeling her way into the conversation. "I need to talk to you about what you said to me that night in the hospital."

Eva stopped walking. "Lainey, please. It's like I said, I was upset, I said it in the heat of the moment."

"Evie, we can't be proper friends if you think things like that about me, in the heat of the moment or not, and I don't know about it. And if that's what I'm really like, then it's awful and I need to change it." She rubbed her eyes. "Wouldn't you think I would know myself by this age, but it seems I don't. I need you to explain more about what you meant, how I've been with you."

Eva was silent for a moment as they kept walking around the edge of the grounds. She seemed about to speak when a jogger came up behind them. She waited until he passed, then looked over at Lainey. "Lainey, I don't know whether—"

"Please, Evie, I need to know. Be blunt with me."

Another long pause. "You can be a bit bossy."

"A bit?"

"Very bossy."

"I see."

Eva stopped, took Lainey's arm. "This is hard for me, Lain. You know I love you. That goes without saying, okay?"

Lainey nodded.

They started walking again, Eva's voice tentative at first, then gaining in confidence. "It's just that, well, you're a bit of a steamroller sometimes. A bit overwhelming. And I can see why. I mean, you're full of good ideas and you're so energetic and quick-thinking. It's just that sometimes other people find it hard to keep up."

"Other people? You, you mean?"

"Not just me. Maybe your friends, your family too, from what you've said. It's like you have an idea of how people are supposed to be, and what they're supposed to do, and you decide that's the only way. And perhaps sometimes they've got good ideas or would like to do things another way, but you don't often leave them, leave us, any room." A long silence.

"Can you give me some examples? Just a few will be okay. I don't need a long list."

Eva smiled, then became thoughtful. "I suppose things like me coming down to help you renovate. I would have offered—I really wanted to help—but somehow you had me organized to come down and do it before I'd had a chance to feel like I had any say in it."

Lainey shut her eyes briefly. She remembered that night. She'd done exactly that.

"You do it a bit with your parents, too, I think. You make it sound sometimes as though you are cross that they aren't behaving like proper parents should. That they're misbehaving, disobeying you. Your brothers too. And maybe Adam, from the little you've told me about him." Eva's voice was very soft. "Sometimes it's as though you've written the script for everyone's lives and you've decided that's how it has to be. And I suppose that's why I got so upset the night of the accident. It was almost as if you were put out, that the accident hadn't been in your plans. And I just got raging. It was Joe you were talking about, my Joe who might have been killed, and I felt very hurt."

Lainey couldn't look at her. She kept walking, while her mind filled with images of her family, of Adam, of the night in the hospital after Joseph's accident.

"Real life's just not like that, Lainey. Things go wrong or people do things you least expect or say things you don't want to hear. It can't all be scripted and managed."

Lainey suddenly wanted to start running. She wanted to run as fast as she could, far and away, from the mean way she'd treated Eva, from her selfishness, from the mess she'd made with Adam, from the mad imaginings about Rohan. Just run until she left it all far behind her and she could start a whole new life somewhere different—be a fresh, kinder, nicer version of herself.

She felt Eva's arm come around her shoulder. "But that doesn't change all the wonderful things about you, Lainey. You're a great person, you really are."

"Oh yes, I'm marvelous. Bossy. Controling. Selfish. Self-centered."

Eva squeezed her tighter. "Lainey, you're you and you're a great person," she repeated. "You might drive me mad sometimes and from now on, now this is all out in the open, if you try and boss me ever again I'm going to put my fingers in my ears and ignore you. But you'll always be my friend. My oldest, best friend."

"You do still want to be my friend?" Her voice was very quiet.

"I'll always want to be your friend. But you have to let me be, put down your barriers sometimes. I'm worried about you, Lainey. You were stressed to the hilt when you arrived, unable to cope if you weren't doing something twenty-four hours a day, going for runs even though there was hardly enough meat on your bones as it was, not eating properly. I meant it when I said I thought it would be good for you to slow down a little. Not that you've paid any attention to me, of course."

Lainey was going to pay attention now. "I am a bit stressed," she admitted. She was completely stressed. She felt like the world was spinning out of control, in fact.

"Then please, Lainey, slow down a little. Calm down, let things happen around you. Let us look after you for once. And I promise I'm not talking about the fates. I suppose I'm just saying there are gentle ways of living life as well. And please, tell me how you are feeling now and again, how you're *really* feeling. You don't have to be superwoman. You're allowed to have emotions, you know."

Lainey turned into the hug then. "Thanks, Evie."

"I mean it, Lainey. And I do love you, really."

"And I love you too." As she buried her face in her friend's shoulder and blinked away sudden tears, she felt like she was eight years old, not thirty-two.

CHAPTER 29

H er mother rang the next day. "Lainey, I'll go straight to the point. I've got bad news. Declan and Hugh have got themselves in trouble with the law."

In trouble with the law? What paperback Western had her mother been reading this week? "Ma, are you drunk?"

"I wish I was, Lainey. You'd think with three sons I had a fairly good chance that one of them would turn out normal, wouldn't you? But no, one of them's a worka-holic and the other two have turned out mad and, not only that, they've gone mad at exactly the same time."

"So what was it, the ecstasy or the dope?"

"What are you talking about?"

"They've been busted for drugs—that's what you mean, isn't it?"

"No, I don't mean that and frankly I don't want to hear any more. They've been trespassing." Mrs. Byrne told the story with some relish. It seemed Declan and Hugh had dressed up in suits and turned up with Hugh's video camera at the head office of the insurance company handling—or mishandling—their father's claim. They'd decided that if the insurance company could film their father, then they could film the insurance company. They managed to get past reception and were looking for the case officer, demanding to see if she really was on stress leave or just having a go-slow year, when the security guard stopped them.

"They got as far as that? Hugh and his blue hair?"

"It's black these days. Pitch-black, actually. He looks like Eddie Munster, if you ask me."

"So what were they planning on doing if they found this case officer? Standing by her desk filming her until she finished processing Dad's claim?"

"I don't think they'd thought it through that far. Declan was going to be the mouthpiece, which was Hugh's first mistake if you ask me. He said he had a fantastic speech all worked out. 'On what grounds have you taken so long to process this claim? Have you any idea what impact you have had on this family? One daughter forced overseas, the mother forced to take a part-time job to make ends meet. This poor family, little Aussie battlers, doing all they can to make a go of it in a new country. All their dreams dashed by the cruelty and incompetence of a huge corporation like yours.' You know the sort of nonsense Declan speaks. Though between you and me, I think he was embroidering the story after the fact. You know how he gets that twitch in his left eye when he's making something up? He's done it all his life, since he was a little fellow, and he's never known I know. But still, he gave us quite a repeat performance in the living room tonight."

"Tonight? So they're not in prison?"

"For walking into an insurance office with a camera? Lainey, this is Australia, not communist Russia."

"I thought you said they were in trouble with the law."

"Did I? Well, they were given a warning that if they did anything so stupid again they might have charges pressed against them—trespassing or something."

"Ma, that's hardly being arrested. You made it sound like they were being executed at dawn. Did they actually go into the insurance office at all or have you made that up as well?"

"Oh no, they did, with the camera and all. It's a great story, don't you think? Your father loved it. It gave him quite a lift, actually, the idea of Declan and Hugh going to these lengths on his behalf. It's the most I've heard him laugh in weeks."

Lainey tried to ignore a twinge of jealousy. She wanted to be the one who made her father feel better, the one who was doing the hard work on his behalf. That's the way it usually was. But she wasn't in charge of the world anymore, was she? She had to learn to stop interfering in other people's lives. "Well, tell them well done from me, too, won't you? And give them all my love."

Her mother sounded surprised. "That's it? You haven't any advice about what we should do next? Don't want to tell Declan and Hugh off?"

"No, they're both grown men. I can't tell them what to do."

"You've been managing fairly well for the last thirty or so years."

"Very funny. No, this is the new me. The new relaxed Elaine Byrne. You won't know me when I get home again."

"I don't know you now. You're sure you're not running a fever or anything? There's not the tiniest bit of advice you want to give them? Give any of us?"

"No, not a scrap," Lainey said breezily, fighting back a whole chorus of advice that was trying to make itself heard.

Her mother changed the subject in any case. "Tell me, Lainey, have you seen Leo Ramsay again by any chance?"

She hadn't seen him again. She had only received the creepy phone call and didn't want to mention that. "No, I haven't actually. Why?"

"I just wondered."

After she'd said goodbye and hung up, Lainey's fingers itched for a little while afterward, wanting to call back and offer some advice about the insurance company. She went into the kitchen and cleaned the stove instead.

.   .   .

After all the preparation and worry about the theme weekends, it was almost an anticlimax when the first one finally came around. She had a full house—an Irish-American couple, a husband and wife from Dublin, an intense Austrian woman and her mother, and an Australian woman and her female Irish cousin—all keen to learn about Irish art and enjoy good food and wine. She'd also had a late call from an American man, who had just heard about the program and was in Ireland for a month's work. Was there any way at all he could join in? he'd asked. A small cupboard he could sleep in? He wasn't fussy—it was just that the whole culture and cultural package had sounded right up his street. Oh, why not, she'd thought, if he really wasn't fussy. She'd warned him that the only available room was indeed small.

Over the weekend Lainey found herself needing to blink hard a couple of times, unaccustomed as she was to walking into rooms in the B&B and finding people there. The living room was the most popular with this first group, the roaring fire drawing them in each day. She had struck it lucky with Orla, her guest lecturer, who had been not only knowledgeable about Irish art but gregarious with it, happy to sit and tell stories during the day as well as give her more formal talk on the Saturday evening. Lainey had been asked twice about Hilly Robson and Noah Geddes and just said sorry, but she really couldn't comment. The questioners nodded and smiled back knowingly. "Of course you can't."

Lainey hadn't intended to go with Rohan when he arrived to take the group on their tour of the Hill of Tara. She'd been worried in case her mind went into action and she found herself blushing and imagining rude thoughts midtour. But then she'd changed her mind, urged by her guests to come along too.

Rohan was a far better guide than her father had ever been. He took them from site to site, explaining the history and all the different interpretations historians had placed on each mound and stone. He painted an engrossing picture of what life would have been like on Tara thousands of years before, describing dwellings made from wood, a whole settlement laid out with a huge banqueting hall at the center. He described day-to-day life—the cooking, the animals, the clothes. He spoke of rituals, including a particularly gruesome one involving the king of Tara performing a sexual act with a horse, which was then killed, cut up and cooked in a cauldron of hot water, from which the king had to drink.

"Oh, Rohan, you've spoiled Lainey's surprise for dinner tonight," Nell said from the back of the group, bringing laughter.

Lainey's dinners had been a success, to her astonishment. She'd had a back-up school of fish ready if she ruined the first lot of salmon. She had even been prepared to drive into Dunshaughlin to buy Ye Olde Authentic Irish Fish and Chips if necessary. But she hadn't needed to. The food had been delicious, the conversation lively, both dinners feeling like her casual dinner parties at home in Melbourne. The pre-dinner glasses of champagne and the amount of wine she'd served during the meals may have helped a little, she admitted to herself.

On Sunday morning she walked around the rooms, gently knocking on each door. "Breakfast in twenty minutes," she called. "Thank you." "Thanks." The replies differed from room to room. As she knocked on the American man's room she heard giggling. Female giggling. Well, well. He was interested in something other than Irish art. Which of the women was it? she wondered later as she moved around the dining room, delivering extra toast and brown bread to each of the tables. The Austrian? The Australian or her cousin? Or Orla, the Irish art expert herself? He was sharing her table—was that the clue? She watched them engage in a lively conversation, as Nell stood between them refilling their coffee. Orla was flushed, as she debated a point, passionate in her arguments. Lainey smiled a secret smile. It must have been her.

Nell had been a great help, electing to be Outgoing Nell all weekend. To Lainey's surprise she had been there early each morning, already in the kitchen and setting the fires when Lainey got up. And she had stayed late each night too. The work was doing her good. She was lively, eyes sparkling, happy. The poor kid—it must have been hard for her being dragged from home, treated like a child.

•   •   •

The day after the third gourmet weekend was over, Lainey went for a long run around the Hill of Tara to clear her head. She'd thought of nothing but food and wine and guest speakers and guest requirements for days. They'd all gone well, though, a full house each time. There had been a late cancellation for the second weekend but she'd simply moved the American man into that room. He'd had such a good time at the first weekend he'd booked for the whole series. Then she'd had a flurry of worry when her third guest speaker had phoned, voice croaky. He'd come down with a cold and wasn't sure if he'd be able to do it after all. She'd thought of her aunt May's handy herbal hints and called him back, reeling off a list of possibilities—could he try inhaling eucalyptus oil mixed with boiling water? Or take hedge mustard drops, or even slice an onion, simmer it in milk and cayenne pepper and take it as a soup? He'd phoned the next day, voice at full strength, delighted with himself. May's tips had worked wonders.

There was a minor hiccup when the Aga seemed to be cooking unevenly, and only half the main courses had been ready on time. But her savior and friend the Great Bottle of Wine had come to the rescue again. She'd staged an impromptu wine-tasting session, based entirely on what she'd learned when organizing the launch of a new chain of wine stores in Melbourne the year before, about riesling from the different wine regions of Australia. The Clare Valley had won hands down.

One night she'd had an awful feeling that the mice had come back to haunt her again, after waking suddenly and hearing a noise in the hallway. Her mind had filled with horrible visions of her guests waking up to find little rodents snoring on the pillows beside them. She'd got up there and then and checked the hallway, pausing outside each bedroom, hoping to God no one would catch her and ask what she was doing. All had been quiet, though she'd thought she heard some noise, laughter or conversation, coming from the American man's room. She'd hurried away from his doorway in case he caught her snooping outside. He was certainly a smooth operator, she thought. Perhaps he could lure the mice outside for her, Pied Piper of Hamelin style.

That morning she'd consulted Aunt May's collection of tips and found what looked like a good anti-mice solution. While her guests were being led around the Hill of Tara by Rohan she had driven into town, bought all the steel wool available, hurried home and shoved it into every nook and cranny in the skirting boards that she could get at, idly watched by Rod Stewart. It had worked. There hadn't been a squeak out of the mice since.

But now, with the fourth and final weekend just days away and her preparation all under control, there was nothing to distract her. Her confused thoughts about

Adam and this strange attraction to Rohan had come back with a vengeance and were now chasing themselves around her mind. She needed to talk to someone.

Back at the house, she rang Eva for the second time that day—she'd already called that morning for her regular update on Joseph's health. He was well on the mend. His left wrist would be in plaster for a few weeks yet, but he was back at college.

"Evie, it's me. Can you talk? You're not in the middle of something?"

"No, the shop's empty at the moment. Are you okay? You sound a bit funny."

Lainey took a breath. "I think I need some advice."

"Did I hear that right? Don't you mean you're ringing to give me some advice?"

"Evie, please don't tease me. I'm trying so hard to be nicer."

Eva softened. "I know you are and you're doing a very good job. I'm sitting down now. The shock has passed. Go on, how can I help?"

"It's a hypothetical situation, okay?"

"So it's not actually about you? It's not you needing this advice?"

A pause. "No. Completely hypothetical."

"Go ahead."

"Say you'd been going out with someone for nearly a year and he was a really lovely man and you had really enjoyed it but the problem was you hadn't really been concentrating properly on it."

"Why would that have been?"

"Um, let's just say that maybe there was a lot going on in your family life at the time."

"And you were busy at work as well, perhaps?"

"Yes, that too."

"Right."

"So then you find out you have to go away for a year and you decide the best thing to do is break up with this person before you leave. So you make the decision and then once you've made it, you have to stick to it."

"Even if you have some doubts?"

"I didn't say anything about doubts."

"No, sorry, of course you didn't. Right, you've made this brilliant decision. So you go away and then what happens?"

"You arrive in a new place and meet this other person."

"That you used to go to school with?"

"This is hypothetical, Evie."

"Sorry."

"And out of your control you start to imagine things happening with him."

"What sort of things?"

"Sexy things."

"Anything beyond sexy things?"

"No, pretty much staying with sexy things."

"So what's the problem? It all sounds good so far."

"But can you actually feel things for two people at once? I mean, either I'm in love with someone or I'm not, surely?"

"Did you say 'I'?"

"I mean 'she.' The hypothetical woman. The very confused hypothetical woman."

"What do you mean by confused? As to which man you like more? Which one you wish you were with? That sort of confused?"

"Exactly."

"It seems to me they're two completely different situations, Lainey. You're not comparing apples with apples. One was real and the other isn't."

"But why would you think it's happening at all?"

"Well, don't people generally have fantasies to either fill a gap in their life or to block something out that they don't want to think about?"

There was a long pause before Lainey spoke again. "Let's forget the whys of it. Not that we're talking about me, but what would you suggest someone should do if she found herself in a situation like this?"

"I think she would have a few choices. Hypothetically speaking, of course. She could simply forget about both of them. Put both of them out of her mind."

"No, I don't think she can do that."

"Could she put the two of them in a room together? Play Spin the Bottle, and let that be the decider? Whoever the bottle points to is the person she has to be with?"

Lainey shook her head. "No, they can't be in the same place."

"Could she put them on an even footing another way? Turn the fantasy into reality so she really was comparing apples with apples? See if that helped her decide how she felt. Or turn them both into fantasies, even? That would make them easier to control, at least."

A pause.

"Lainey? Are you there?"

"I am. Thanks, Evie. I really appreciate your advice. I mean, she'll really appreciate your advice."

"But do you think it will be any help to her at all?"

Lainey had no idea. "Can she let you know?"

CHAPTER 30

The next day, Lainey returned to the Hill of Tara, this time taking a rug with her. She walked to her favorite spot, right on the perimeter, out of sight of any other visitors but with a wonderful view of the fields all around. The sun was mild, the breeze soft. She could hear the bleating of lambs, a tractor in a far-off field, the occasional squeak of the gate as another visitor arrived. Now and again a murmur of voices floated over from one of the guided tours.

She thought of her conversation with Eva. She had made it sound so simple. If only it was. If only it was a matter of turning her entire life into a fantasy, letting the whole confusing situation with Adam and Rohan sort itself out that way. She lay back and shut her eyes.

The Hill of Tara had never looked so beautiful. All the wooden dwellings had been hung with brightly colored lengths of cloth, vivid against the blue summer sky. The women had been up all night sewing the final banners.

In her chambers, Elaine, the Queen of Tara, sat at the win-

dow. Her servant Eva stood behind her, brushing Elaine's long dark locks. At her feet, her manservant Mr. Fogarty was busying himself, his nimble fingers fastening the hundreds of buttons on her handmade kid leather boots. Her faithful cat Roderick Stewart purred on her lap.

"Are you nervous, Your Highness?" Eva asked.

"A little," Elaine confessed.

Outside, musicians marched around, congregating in the vast assembly area in the center of the Tara settlement. There was a sudden noise of drumming and a clamor from the crowd below. Eva looked from the window.

"Adam of Melbourne has arrived," she breathed.

Elaine's heart leaped, her hand going to her throat. She went to the window, waiting for her first glimpse of Adam in several months, since she had left him to travel over the seas. He hadn't changed. He was as tall, noble and handsome as she remembered. He was dressed in glittering golden robes, embroidered with his insignia of a knife and fork. On his head was a remarkable hat, at least two feet tall, made of black and yellow wool. Behind him, his faithful retainer Hugh of Box Hill followed, leading Adam's mount.

A second thunder of drumming heralded the arrival of Rohan of Dunshaughlin. His curly hair shone in the sunlight, as he strode across the Hill, stopping here and there to collect oral histories from the older members of the gathering. His own mount also stood ready for him, polished to perfection by his lady-in-waiting Mrs. Hartigan of Meath.

Eva touched Elaine's shoulder. "Your Highness, I think it is time."

Elaine took a deep breath, calming her nerves. She stepped regally down the wooden staircase and after a dramatic, well-timed pause emerged into the clearing. A hush went around the crowd *at the sight of their queen. Every member of the crowd was aware of the importance of today's events. In their hearts they had shared her pain, as she tussled with her feelings for both Adam and Rohan. Today would be a bitter competition, possibly to the death.*

Joseph of London stepped forward, raising his hands, his heavy jewelry evidence of his high standing in the community. "Bring your mounts forward," he called.

Hugh of Box Hill and Mrs. Hartigan of Meath moved forward, concentrating fiercely on their tasks.

"We want a fair duel, for the prize is surely one worthy of only a clean and noble fight." Joseph of London turned and gestured toward Elaine, her long hair a halo around her face. The crowd gazed in wonder.

Elaine studied both noble men in turn. Her mind was no clearer. There was Adam, kind, funny, sexy and good-hearted, a man of skill in the kitchen and the bedroom. And there on the opposite side of the clearing, was Rohan, clever, curly-haired, a mystery man in many ways, but one for whom she felt a strange attraction.

There was no turning back now. The decision had to be made. "Let the dare begin!" she called, her voice ringing true across the crowd.

Hugh of Box Hill and Mrs. Hartigan of Meath jumped out of the way as Rohan and Adam leaped upon their scooters. Everyone knew the conditions—both men had to ride the perimeter of the Hill of Tara. The one who finished first would win the love of Elaine, queen of Tara, as well as a rather smart gold brooch.

The crowd gasped as the dust cleared. In the distance Adam of Melbourne could easily be seen bypassing the Mound of the

Hostages, his scooter like a gazelle, leaping effortlessly from rise to rise across the green fields.

Back at the starting line, Rohan of Dunshaughlin was still struggling to get his engine started.

Lainey sat upright, eyes wide open.

. . .

The phone was ringing as she let herself back into the house. It was her brother Hugh, not bothering with pleasantries like introducing himself. "Just calling to remind you it's reward-calendar day, in case you'd forgotten. Four months down, only eight to go."

Lainey had forgotten. Her mind had been on many other things than the reward-calendar. "Hugh, why are you the only kind person in this family?"

"Because I was made up of leftover genes," he chanted in the singsong voice they all used when they trotted out that old family story. "No, I've been thinking about it recently and I've decided it's because I had more time at home with Ma and Dad, quality parenting time. It's just made me much more well-rounded as a human being, I suppose, able to respond to my fellow humans' instincts and longings."

"You don't have to lay it on too thick, Hughie."

He laughed. "I have to go anyway. Don't want Ma to catch me on the phone again. Enjoy the chocolate." He was gone before she had a chance to ask any more.

To ask if he'd seen Adam again, more to the point.

She went into the kitchen to open the latest door on the reward-calendar and pry out the little foil-wrapped sweet, glad of the distraction. It surprised her that it had in fact been a chocolate behind each door so far. Hugh had a tendency to get a little carried away with his projects sometimes. She could have found anything wrapped up there. She looked at the drawings of beds and egg cups again and smiled. He really was a sweetheart. Definitely the most softhearted of all of them. Lainey remembered finding him in tears once as a little boy after they'd been to a fun fair for the day. "Parents shouldn't ever give their children balloons," he'd managed to explain. "Why not, Hughie?" Lainey had asked, confused. "Because the balloons might fly away and the children will be sad."

She knew Hugh would be glad if she and Adam got back together again. Adam treated him like a regular little brother, not as a slave or an insect. While the kettle boiled, Lainey stood looking at the photos of her family on the fridge. There was a nice one of Hugh, taken just after he'd begun the mad-hair stage. He did look different to the rest of them, as Nell had noticed. Shorter, stockier. Arty, too, these days, with that hair and the nose ring, in a way that neither she, Brendan nor Declan were. They'd never have thought of something as creative as the videos, or the reward-calendar either. He was definitely the artistic one of the family.

She looked at the photo again. Hugh. Short, stocky, arty.

Like Leo Ramsay was short, stocky, arty.

At that moment everything fell into place.

How could she have been so stupid about this as well? What had happened to her recently? This made complete sense, the timing, the circumstances, even her mother's voice on the phone the other night, pretending to be casual. "Have you seen Leo Ramsay again?"

Her mother had had an affair with Leo Ramsay, the artist. Hugh was Leo Ramsay's child. That was why her mother had gone to England that time. But it hadn't worked out, so she'd come back. Or perhaps her father had begged her to come back. And then the whole family had gone to Australia, to make a fresh start, to get away from Leo Ramsay.

Lainey stood still, her heart beating fast. Her aunt May must have known all along, but she had sided with her mother. *Don't blame Peg. This is all YOUR fault,* she had written in that letter to her father. Perhaps it had been her father's fault. He wouldn't have been the best husband in the world, not always easy to get along with. Her mother must have looked elsewhere, met Leo, had an affair, become pregnant with Hugh.

She could picture it all as clearly as if she had been there watching.

Her mother, Hugh in her arms, confessing all to her father. "I have to be with Leo. I want Hugh to grow up knowing his own father."

Her father letting her go, struggling at home with the three other children, making them write letters to their mother once a week. What must it have been like for him, knowing that the letters were going to the house of the man who had destroyed his marriage, torn the family apart?

Lainey thought of her mother living in England with Hugh and her lover. When had she realized it wasn't going to work? she wondered. Was it one of their letters that had sparked it, made her see she was destroying the family, and made her realize she had to come back?

Lainey could remember the day her mother returned.

Her father had been excited for days before, making them clean the house, write welcome-home cards. Then he had gone to Dun Laoghaire to meet the boat and had brought her mother and Hugh home as though they were pieces of fine china.

How had her father been able to do it, to accept Hugh as though he was his own? Was that what real love was? No wonder they had gone to Australia so suddenly, to the other side of the world, as far from this man as possible.

One by one the pieces fell into place. She remembered her conversation with her mother at the shopping center before she left. Her mother had been teasing her, asking if Lainey would ever have an affair. Had she been trying to tell her something, wanting to confess? In case Lainey ran into Leo in Meath, exactly as she had done? She thought of her mother's wistful tone when Lainey first mentioned running into Leo at the launch party. Was that why Leo Ramsay had really wanted to see her? To find out about his son after all these years?

She couldn't condemn her mother. She was in the same boat herself—making a mess of relationships, having sexual fantasies about near strangers. Was there some sort of gene in the Byrne family that self-activated in the early thirties? First their mother, now her. She hated to think what her brothers would get up to in the years ahead.

But for now, she needed to talk to her mother. As soon as she could.

C H A P T E R *31*

The opportunity came the following day, a Tuesday, the night she knew her father's friend Ken usually called over. With her father occupied, it would be the perfect time to call.

She counted down the hours, waiting for the right time in Melbourne, then dialed the number. Her mother answered.

"Ma, it's me. I'm sorry to launch straight into it but I need to talk to you about something serious."

"Oh, Lainey. I have missed these dramatic pronouncements of yours."

"It really is something serious. Please, can you go into your room, so we won't be interrupted?"

"Yes, *sir*." A moment later her voice again. "Right then, I'm ready."

"I don't really know where to start or how to put this . . ." Lainey slowly found the words, telling her mother she had guessed the real reason the family had emigrated. She found confidence in her mother's silence, not knowing what to expect. Would her mother be angry with her for guessing or would she burst into tears and beg her not to tell Hugh because it would be better he didn't know anything?

"Is that the lot, Lainey?"

Her mother sounded choked up, Lainey thought. "Yes."

"Thank God for that," Mrs. Byrne said. She burst into peals of laughter.

"I don't really think this is a laughing matter," Lainey said, cross.

"Oh yes it is. Let me see if I have this right. We came to Australia because I'd been having an affair, and Hugh isn't your father's son?" She cackled away.

"Ma, it isn't funny."

"No, you're right. Of course it's not. It's better than funny—it's hilarious. And tell me, have you managed to deduce who Hugh's real father is in these remarkable investigations of yours?"

"I think it was Leo Ramsay."

Mrs. Byrne's laugh was now even more high-pitched. "Oh yes, of course it was."

"Stop it, stop laughing. It's not true?"

"Of course it's not true. Have you lost your mind over there? I've never heard anything so ridiculous in my whole life. It's bad enough to have your father moaning away over here without you losing the plot as well. I can't mind you both, you know."

"Stop talking about Dad like that."

"Like what?"

"About him moaning. You're supposed to be his wife, be nice to him."

"Lainey, it's because I am his wife, and his loving wife, that I can tell the truth about him. He has done nothing but moan for the past year and frankly I have had it up to here. He knows that now and he also knows I'm not going to put up with it forever."

Lainey needed to take back control of this conversation. "Is he Hugh's father?"

"No, Lainey, he's not," Mrs. Byrne said solemnly. "Hugh's father is in fact a well-known Irish bishop."

"Ma . . ."

"Of course he's Hugh's father. Lainey, calm down. Would you mind telling me in as clear and sane a manner as you can where on earth you got this load of nonsense from? Have you had a blow to the head recently or something?"

"No. I put two and two together."

"And came up with five million. Go on."

"I found one of May's letters to Dad, one she'd written when we first moved to Australia. It had been sent back, return to sender, no longer at this address."

"You should know it's bad to read other people's mail. Nothing good ever comes of it. Never mind, go on."

"She said in the letter that Dad couldn't blame you, it was his fault. And then I met Leo Ramsay and he was weird about you, as if something had happened between you both. And he reminded me of Hugh."

"What, short and mad?"

"Ma, stop it."

"He's my son, I can say what I like about him. Lainey, much as I'd like to spend all day listening to your extraordinary detective work, I think it might be better if I stopped you there."

"But I have more."

"Yes, I'm afraid you might have and I am afraid you are going to be even further off the mark than you already are. Are you sitting down yourself?"

Lainey sat down. "Yes."

"Then let me tell you the truth." She paused for a long moment. "What happened twenty years ago, when Hugh was born, was this. I got worn out. I had a breakdown, pure and simple. Nowadays it would be called postnatal depression. Back then it was called a nervous breakdown. You try looking after four kids. It would wear anyone out. I went to England to get better, to have a break. There was no man involved. I took Hugh with me because he was a baby and he needed minding, not because I wanted him to meet his real father." She started laughing again. "I'm not laughing at you, Lainey, I promise. Just at the idea of it. I could hardly brush my own hair at that time, let alone set up a love nest."

"So this Leo Ramsay? Who was he? Why was he all funny about you?" And why did you sound all wistful when I spoke to you about him? She didn't say that bit aloud.

There was a pause. "He flattered me, Lainey. Back then, I needed all the flattery I could get. Your father had been a great man for flowery words when he was courting me, but things had got stale. I didn't feel like me any more. I felt like Mrs. Boring Byrne, mother of four, housewife, cleaner, librarian. Then Leo came to teach art at the college."

Lainey kept quiet, realizing her mother was feeling her way carefully through these memories.

"He asked me to pose for him. He showered me with

compliments, told me I was beautiful, that I was something special, that my body was a temple to womanhood." She gave an embarrassed laugh. "See, all these years later I still haven't forgotten what he said. It was everything I needed to hear. It made me feel good in the middle of the night when I was trying to get Hugh to sleep or in the middle of the day when I just felt like weeping, with all the mess around me. So I said, yes, I'd be happy to pose for him. And I did."

"Naked, you mean?"

"No, Lainey, in a suit of armor. Yes, naked. That's what he painted, nudes. Oh, no one knew. It would have been far too shocking. And no one would ever have recognized me from the painting, if he had ever shown it in Ireland, which he had no intention of doing. He favored the abstract approach, whatever that was. All I knew was it felt good, peaceful in a funny way, to lie in a warm studio, be showered with compliments, to not have to worry about housework or crying children for two hours a week. To just be me, have myself back."

"Did Dad know about all of this?"

"No, he didn't and there was no need for him to know it, either. There still isn't. He thought I was having painting lessons, and I suppose I was in a way."

There was another question Lainey had to ask. "Were you lovers? You and Leo?"

A long pause down the phone line. "No."

"No?"

"I was tempted. Very tempted, in fact. It just felt so good to have someone saying I was beautiful, admiring me, when all I felt like was some kind of milking machine or housewife. Your father was having problems at work, so he wasn't interested in me, or I wasn't interested in him—I'm not sure what came first."

"But you and Leo? Why didn't you?"

"Let me just say I learned he wasn't particularly selective with his compliments or favors. I don't know if I ever would have, mind you. It was probably better just to fantasize about it. I don't know if you understand that, you modern things with no morals."

Lainey let that one pass. "So what happened? You caught him with someone else?"

"No. Someone else's husband caught him with someone else. He scurried off back to England fairly swiftly after that. Well, was pushed off back to England, in fact. That's why I was so surprised to hear he was back in Meath. Though all of this was a long time ago, of course."

Lainey could hardly believe all this intrigue had been going on in Dunshaughlin all those years ago. Los Angeles, perhaps. Dublin, even, at a pinch. But *Dunshaughlin?* "And is that when you went to England?"

"No, that's when I really had a breakdown. I don't really know if Leo's leaving triggered it or not, but I started crying one day and I just couldn't stop. For days."

Lainey remembered it. Remembered coming home from school and finding her mother in bed, and her father making the tea, asking the three older children to be as quiet as they could.

"The doctor said I was exhausted, that I needed a long break, to be spoiled, not to worry about anything. So that's when I went to England, to stay with Kay for those two months. Do you remember? You called her aunty Kay. My school friend."

Yes, Lainey remembered Kay. And she remembered

coming home from school the day her mother and Hugh came back from England and seeing her father fussing around them, so pleased to see them again. Not because he had lured her mother from another man, but because he was just happy to have his wife and son home. To have the family together again. Lainey still had more questions. "And what about Australia, then? Why did we really go there?"

Mrs. Byrne laughed. "Why? What extraordinary fact have you uncovered about that? Don't tell me—you've learned your father was a murderer and we were fleeing the law?"

"Please don't laugh at me."

She softened. "Lainey, I'm sorry. We went to Australia for exactly the same reason thousands of other Irish people went to Australia. Because we couldn't make a living in Ireland. Because we'd heard that there was more work there, because we'd heard there were good schools for you kids, that we'd have a better life."

"So why was May so mad at Dad? He had every right to go to Australia, didn't he?"

"She wasn't mad about him going. She was mad about him not coming back, as he'd promised. And she was mad about the money."

Lainey waited, holding her breath. Her questions didn't need to be asked.

"May always had lots of money. She was a better saver, more canny, and of course the house and land had been left to her, as the oldest child. Your father wasn't financially minded, never has been, you may have noticed. She knew we were having problems, not just with me and the breakdown, but making ends meet. It was her idea that we go to Australia, just for a few years, make some money, then come back to Ireland. She paid for everything—the fares, the set-up costs—on the agreement that once we could afford it, we'd come back to Ireland with a nest egg behind us to set us up properly."

"But we didn't."

"No, we didn't. When it came down to it, once things started going well in Australia, we just didn't want to go back. I was happy in the library, your father's business was going well, you and the boys had started to make friends. We didn't think you'd want to come back and we didn't want to split up the family, not when the boys were still so young."

"So she was cross?"

"She was furious. She said he had cheated her, that he had let down the family, that he was a traitor to the Byrne name."

All the insults Lainey remembered, but she'd thought they were for a different reason. She remembered what Rohan had said, that May had been lonely, had missed them all. "And what did you want to do?"

"I know Gerry told May we stayed because of me, that it was better for me there—the warmer weather, more library work. But the truth was I was happy to do whatever your father decided. Be where he wanted to be. I really didn't mind either way."

"So you did love him?" The question, the plea, had come from somewhere deep inside her.

"Lainey, I love him now. Oh, he's a lazy, feckless old lump sometimes, and I think he has done himself no favors since the accident, lying in bed feeling sorry for himself, but if he thinks that's it for the rest of his life, he's wrong. Once that insurance money is through, I am going to have such an army of physiotherapists and psychiatrists coming through this house he will get up and get better just to get away from them. I want my old Gerry back and I know he's still in there somewhere."

"It really is as simple as all that?"

"It is, Lainey. Sometimes that's all it needs to be."

CHAPTER 32

Lainey wasn't worried at first when Nell was late arriving to help with the last-minute preparations for the final weekend. She had enough on her mind as it was, between her mother and Leo Ramsay, Adam and Rohan . . . She went into town and bought the fresh flowers she liked to put in all the rooms. As she walked past a newsagent, a magazine headline caught her eye. "Hilly and Noah split! See inside for details." Lainey couldn't resist it. She went inside and flicked through the pages until she found the article. Apparently the pair had been on holiday in Iceland, not Ireland, and had been overheard having a ferocious row. HILLY GIVES NOAH THE BIG FREEZE, the subheading read. There were doctored pictures of the two of them throwing snowballs at each other. Eva and Joseph had done their impersonations just in the nick of time, Lainey thought with a grin as she read through the article. It seemed that Hilly had decided she just couldn't put up with Noah's bad-boy behavior anymore, a close friend had told the magazine.

Back home, Lainey made a start on the housework, vacuuming the bedrooms, dusting, polishing, making the rooms as attractive as possible. By lunchtime Nell still hadn't arrived. She phoned Mrs. Hartigan, concerned that Nell wasn't well, or had car troubles.

"No, Lainey, Nell's not here. You've got another one of those gourmet things on this weekend, haven't you?"

"Yes, I was expecting her here to help me."

"But she left here this morning with her bag, said she was staying with you for the weekend again."

"Again?"

"She said you'd told her to stay at the guesthouse each weekend, that it made more sense than driving back and forth every day."

"No, I didn't, Mrs. Hartigan. And she hasn't been staying here, I promise you that."

"But she hasn't been staying here, either. Not for the past three weekends. Lainey, hold on. Let me check her room." She was back moments later. "All her things are gone."

Lainey phoned the bus station while Mrs. Hartigan contacted the police. She called Lainey straight back. "They said there's nothing they can do yet. She has to be missing for longer than a morning before they can call her a missing person."

"This boyfriend of hers," Lainey said. "He wouldn't have come over to Ireland to see her, would he? Would you have noticed a young fellow hanging around?"

"Oh, he's not young. That was half the problem."

"What was half the problem?"

"That's why Caroline, Nell's mother, objected to him so much. He's over forty."

"Oh, well then. Would you have noticed a forty-year-old Londoner hanging around?"

"He's not English, either. He's American."

Lainey's stomach gave a flip. "American? What does he look like, Mrs. Hartigan, do you know?"

"No, I don't. We never met him, and Nell wasn't the type to be showing us photos of him either. She was far too cross with us."

"I think I've met him."

"Pardon?"

"I think I've met him. I think he's been staying here. And I think Nell was staying with him, in his room." It explained everything. Nell's change in mood. This American man appearing out of nowhere. The giggling behind the closed doors of his bedroom. It hadn't been Orla the lecturer in there that morning, or one of his fellow guests the other weekend—it had been Nell all the time. After she'd said goodbye each night, she must have waited outside, in the car probably, until everyone had gone to bed and then crept back in, using the spare key Lainey had given her. It was probably Nell she had heard creeping around, not the mice that time. And then Lainey realized something else. The American man had called himself Len. Which was almost Nell backward. Their little joke.

. . .

Rohan phoned later that afternoon. "I haven't any news about Nell, but I'm just ringing to say my mother wants to come over and help you this weekend. Nell should have been there and she isn't, and you can't do it on your own. And to be honest, my mother needs something to do. She's up the walls worrying."

Lainey was about to turn him down but realized she would need the help. "Are you sure?"

"We're sure."

"Then thanks. I accept."

The two of them worked perfectly together, even better than Lainey had with Nell. The guests—two American couples, one Canadian-Irish pair, and an elderly Australian pair of sisters—were delighted with Mrs. Hartigan.

"I'll have to hire you instead," Lainey joked. To her surprise, Mrs. Hartigan didn't dismiss the idea. "I wouldn't mind the occasional outing like this, to be honest. And not just because it's keeping my mind off Nell."

. . .

Late on Saturday night, Lainey was in the kitchen alone, washing up. Mrs. Hartigan was in the dining room talking to the guests, telling stories from her own childhood that were as interesting as the guest speaker had told earlier.

There was a knock at the kitchen door. Rohan appeared, smiling. "Nell's called. She's safe. She's back in London, at her house. You were right. That was her boyfriend staying here and she's feeling very guilty for deceiving you like that."

Lainey felt a rush of relief. As she turned from the sink, she was astonished to find Rohan right beside her, his hand on her shoulder. She went rigid. He was touching her. Rohan was standing beside her, touching her. Before she had a chance to think, he leaned over and kissed her on the cheek. "Thanks for all you've done, Lainey. I'm so sorry you got caught up in this."

She opened her eyes wide. His arm was still around her. Was this her chance to finally prove that the whole crush had been in her imagination? Should she test it properly? Without thinking, she thrust her arms forward, grasped him around the waist and pulled him close against her.

He seemed surprised but gave her another awkward hug back, still with his hand on her shoulder. They shuffled around one another for a moment, as if they were trying to waltz without music or had accidentally bumped into each other in the street. She was just summoning up the courage to try and kiss him again when he stepped back from her and took a mobile phone from his jacket pocket.

"I'll have to ring Sabine too. She's been worried sick," he said. "She's known Nell since she was a kid and is really fond of her. But I'd better tell Ma first. Do you mind if I go out and find her?"

"No, please, go right ahead. She's in the dining room."

As he left she stood, stock-still. That touch had done it, turned fantasy into reality. And the reality was she had felt nothing. Absolutely nothing. Except for relief. She thought about it again, rewound the scene quickly in her mind. It was as clear as day. There had been no spark between them at all.

Eva's words about why people had fantasies appeared in block letters in her head. At that moment, Lainey knew they were true. She had been having fantasies about Rohan for exactly the reason Eva had said— because she wanted to fill the gap that being away from Adam had left in her life. And why was that?

Because she loved Adam and she wanted to spend the rest of her life with him.

Her heart started thumping. She wasn't sure if she had felt that way about him before she left Melbourne. But somehow the feeling had come on since. She wouldn't have thought it possible to fall properly in love with someone if they weren't actually there. Or to fall in love retrospectively. But it had happened. That was exactly what she'd done.

It felt like a curtain had been flung open in her mind. All the fantasies about Rohan, the thoughts of him being Mr. Cholera, had been just that—fantasies. Distractions. She'd been trying to stop herself from thinking about the truth, seeing things as they really were. Which was that she'd made a terrible mistake breaking up with Adam.

Why hadn't she realized before now? Why hadn't she guessed? Why hadn't she realized that was the reason she liked being with Adam so much, why being in bed with him felt more exciting yet more comfortable, relaxed, than it had ever felt with anyone else before? She had thought that the lack of complication, the lack of drama between them, meant it wasn't real. In fact it had been the opposite—it had been without drama because it had been right between them.

She rubbed her eyes. How could she have even imagined anything happening between her and Rohan? She had always known he was head over heels about Sabine. Just as she had always known that the times he'd called around to Tara Lodge, invited her for dinner, met her for a drink or offered his help, had never had anything to do with her, Lainey. They'd had everything to do with him being a kind and helpful person—wanting to be friendly to someone he'd gone to school with years before, who had also happened to be May's niece. It had been as simple as that.

She jumped as he came back into the kitchen, putting his mobile phone away, having obviously just spoken to Sabine. "She's as relieved as we are," he said with a big smile.

Lainey gazed at him. Even his looks had changed. He wasn't a sex god, exuding passion and mystery. He was just nice, normal Rohan, the boy she'd gone to school with who had now grown up, still with his big mass of curly hair and a lovely pair of blue eyes. Who had come back to Ireland for a year but was clearly dying to get back home to Germany to be with his Sabine.

"Lainey? Are you all right?"

She blinked again, trying for the last time to imagine him naked, the two of them passionately kissing. She couldn't do it. She didn't want to do it.

"I'm absolutely fine," she said.

⁘ ∘ •

That night in bed she felt happier than she had in weeks. She allowed herself to think about Adam, let all the lovely memories rush into her mind, didn't block them with thoughts of Rohan. It felt as though she was holding a glowing ball of something, as though she had a secret deep inside her, something that made her feel warm and good and happy. A part of her wanted to get in touch with Adam immediately, to phone him, tell him how sorry she was, how she now knew she really wanted to be with him. Another part of her told her to be patient, not to rush things, to take it slowly. She lay in bed, touching the bracelet he had given her. She had been wearing it every day. *Come live with me and be my love.* Her answer to his question had been a long time coming. She just hoped he still wanted to hear it.

. . .

Lainey came in from feeding the chickens the next morning to see a light flashing on the answering machine. She hadn't heard the phone ring. She pressed the button and Hugh's voice filled the room.

He was in tears. "Lainey, can you call me? As soon as you get this message?"

Her fingers were shaking as she dialed. He answered after the first ring. "Hugh, are you all right? What is it?"

His voice was all choked up. "It's about Dad."

"What's wrong with him? What's happened?"

"Not that Dad. My real dad. Leo Ramsay. Lainey, I have to meet him, get to know him. Will you fly me over?"

Lainey experienced the odd sensation of relief flooding through her and hackles rising, all at once. "You brat. Ma told you about that? I'll kill her. It was supposed to be between us."

Hugh started laughing. "She couldn't help herself. She thought it was hilarious. Thanks for caring so much about my parentage, Lain."

"I'll kill you, too."

"Don't, I'm just teasing you. She didn't want to tell us, but Dad and I got it out of her. We knew she had a funny secret. She was all strange after she'd been talking to you on the phone that night." He lowered his voice. "To be honest, I think it did Dad the world of good, too. The two of them were up talking for hours, remembering all those times, when she was sick and then when she came back home, how he looked after her. Most I've heard them talk in ages, actually."

"And they're okay? They're not fighting all the time?"

"No more than normal."

"Are you sure?"

"Sure I'm sure. Well, as much as I ever know. I'm just the little kid, remember."

Not that again. "So any other news, then, or have you only rung to taunt me for my marvelous ability to jump to conclusions?" She was dying to ask him if he'd seen Adam again, but also trying to calm herself, be grown-up about it. There was no rush, she'd realized. She didn't have to go charging in to tell him how she felt. She'd finally learned that.

Hugh paused. "I actually have got some news—the real reason I rang. It's just it's a bit awkward."

"Come on, out with it. You've made a girl pregnant, is that it? Or you've caught some sexually transmitted disease?"

"You've got a filthy mind. No, it's not that." He paused. "It's just that, well, I sent you another tape. It's probably about to arrive. And the thing is, I was wrong. What I put on it. I was trying to be smart, trying to fix things up, and I made a mistake."

"I don't understand."

"I made the tape in good faith, believing something to be true, and then I saw something the other day—I don't know if you want to know about it—and well, I think it might cancel out what I was trying to say with the tape. So

I just wanted to tell you not to watch it when it arrives. Just put it in the bin or send it right back."

"Hughie, what are you talking about?"

He blurted it out. "I'm talking about Adam. I made you a tape about him and sent it off and then a few days ago I saw him having lunch with your friend. Kim. That one with the big—"

"I know the one you mean. Where?"

"In Camberwell. Near the restaurant."

"And what were they doing when you saw them? Just having lunch?"

"Well, they had food in front of them."

"What's that supposed to mean?"

"They weren't eating much. She was being all sort of, you know, flirty. Leaning forward a lot. Playing with her hair. We studied that in class last month and apparently it signifies a readiness to engage in sexual activity."

Lainey felt physically sick. Nauseous. "Are you sure? It was definitely Adam? Definitely Kim?"

"I'm sure. I said hello to them both."

"And was he embarrassed? Was she embarrassed?" Why was her voice so high-pitched all of a sudden?

"I don't know. I was too embarrassed myself to see whether they were embarrassed. I'm so sorry, Lain. I just thought you should know. And I had to warn you about the tape. I'd got it all wrong. Please don't watch it."

She felt deflated, as if she'd been punched. Flat. "It's fine, Hugh. I did need to know. I'm glad you told me."

"I'm sorry. I didn't mean to upset you."

She didn't deny it. She was more than upset. "That will teach me, won't it?"

"What?"

"I finally realized how wrong I was about him, that I should never have broken up with him, and now I'm too late. I was going to call him."

"Oh, Lainey, maybe I was wrong. Maybe it was all just innocent."

"No, Hughie, it's all right. You can't help what you saw. And it's not as if she didn't warn me. She told me she fancied him."

"But you could always ring him anyway, talk to him, couldn't you? I bet he'd still like to hear from you."

Oh, sure. Lainey could just imagine it. Knowing her present luck, she'd call him just as he and Kim were about to fall into bed. The thought of it produced another wave of nausea. "It's a bit late for that, Hugh."

"I'm sorry, Lainey. And you won't watch the tape, will you?"

She wanted to joke with him, say, "You're not the boss of me," but nothing seemed funny at that moment. "I'd better go, Hughie."

. . .

Hugh's tape arrived the next day. Don't watch it, he'd told her. Of course she would watch it. How could she not? She went through the familiar ritual, getting a coffee, settling herself in front of the TV, all the while a feeling of foreboding building within her.

The video began with just a black screen, with music playing underneath, simple notes on a piano. She frowned, trying to recognize the song. A few more notes. It sounded familiar. Then she got it. It was a cover version of Burt Bacharach's "This Guy's in Love with You."

Then the vision began. There was just one subject.

Adam. It was scene after scene of him in different locations, doing different things, all obviously outtakes from the videos of Rex and the fake chefs. There was one scene of Adam in his kitchen at the restaurant, laughing as he tried to get the Nigella Lawson wig to stay in place. Lainey started laughing too. There were outtakes of him trying to ride the scooter into shot for the Jamie Oliver segment, some in slow motion, some in fast motion. Hugh had even run one backward so it looked as though Adam was walking backward, leaping onto the scooter and then driving back to front along the street. There were slow-motion shots of Adam smiling, looking up from his cooking bench; another of him concentrating completely on the cooking, his face serious; a funny one of him holding Rex and then yelping as Rex scratched him on the cheek.

Hugh had been trying to matchmake, she realized. Or be a relationship counselor, at least. Trying to sort things out between her and Adam, get them back together again. Except he'd been too late. As Lainey had been too late in realizing how she felt about Adam.

She watched the video three times in a row, sitting there gazing at the screen, her knees pulled up under her chin. She hardly noticed the tears streaming down her face.

. . .

There was an email from her friend Christine in Melbourne when she picked up her messages the next day.

Lainey, what on earth is going on with you and Adam? Do you know that he and Kim have been out a couple of times? He might think it's innocent but I have to tell you SHE doesn't. You know she's keen on him, don't you??? I feel like I'm playing one of those "do you tell or don't you tell" party games but I really thought you should know. Would have rung but can't get a fix on the time difference at all. I'm up in Queensland for a fortnight's holiday, will call you or email with all the facts as soon as I get back. And you tell Adam you're on to him!!

CHAPTER 33

Tea, Evie?" Lainey called out from the kitchen.

"Yes, please," a voice called back.

Eva and Joseph had come to stay for the weekend, now that the first series of theme weekends was over. Lainey was trying to summon up the energy to organize the next series. The months left in the house stretched long and lonely at the moment. She'd tried to tell herself it was just that she was tired. She'd even tried to tell herself it was the discovery that Rohan was not Mr. Cholera, that she was sad that the days of the sexy mind-films were over.

But she knew that wasn't true. The truth was she was in bits about Adam.

Eva was lying on the couch in front of the fire, flicking through a photo album, when Lainey came into the room carrying the tray. She was on her own.

"Where's Joe?" Lainey asked.

Eva sat up and took the cup Lainey was offering. "He'll be back in a little while. He's just gone for a walk around

Tara." She put down the album she'd been looking at. "That's a shame Nell didn't do any more for you. These are very good."

"They are, aren't they? I'll have to buy more from a gallery one day, I suppose. Some New York one, when she and her elderly boyfriend run off and set up their love nest together." Lainey poured herself a cup of tea and sat beside Eva, looking into the fire.

"What's up, Lainey?" Eva's voice was soft.

"Nothing."

"Lainey . . ."

"Everything," she admitted.

"Is it Rohan? Mr. Cholera? Did he turn into Mr. Bubonic Plague?"

Lainey tried to smile. "None of that was true, you know. I'd imagined it all. The whole thing. He's actually really happy with his German girlfriend."

"Then it's Adam, isn't it?"

Lainey still wasn't looking at her. "It is, yes."

"Oh, Lainey. Have you realized you've made a mistake? That he's really the one for you?"

She spun around. "Was it that obvious?"

"No, not at first. You're a great woman for hiding how you really feel, you know."

"I didn't know myself. Not for a while."

"But you do now? Can you ring him? Write to him? Tell him you're sorry, you made a big mistake?"

"No, not now."

"But if he loves you and you love him—"

"It's not as simple as that anymore."

"Why not?"

Lainey told Eva why not. She told her all Hugh had told her on the phone and about Christine's email.

Eva gazed up at her, frowning. "And they wouldn't have made a mistake? They're both sure?"

Lainey nodded.

Eva rubbed her friend's arm sympathetically. "So what are you going to do?"

"I don't know yet. I don't know what I can do, to be honest."

"You're not going to just give up like that, without a fight, are you? The Lainey I know and love wouldn't do that."

"What can I do? I can't leave here for months and months. And even if I could, what are my options? March up to the two of them and tell Kim to go away, that I've realized I made a terrible mistake about Adam?"

"You could try that. It's the truth, isn't it?"

"Yes, but they could be living together by the time I see them. In my apartment block. That will be nice, won't it, seeing them together every day?"

Eva put her arm around her. "Lainey, something will come up. I'm sure of it. Just wait and see."

"You've got great faith in the world, Evie, haven't you? In things working out for the best?"

Joseph came in then, his black hair in tufts from the wind. Eva smiled at the sight of him, then looked back at Lainey. "Yes, I have, actually."

* * *

The next day, Lainey did what she had started to do every time she needed to think. She went for a walk on the Hill of Tara. It was starting to feel like her special place now. The furrows and mounds in the green grass were becoming familiar. She knew which times she would have it to herself and which times it would be crowded with tour groups. The view surprised her each time, never staying static—the changing light, the movement of clouds across the pale-blue sky, the crops growing in the fields all around, adding splashes of green and bright yellow here and there to the landscape.

She walked briskly, waiting for her head to clear, trying to recall tips from her self-help business books. But her mind was blank. A wind whipped up and she pulled her jacket closer around her body, pushing her hair out of her eyes as well. Concentrate, Lainey, she urged herself. Think of it as a business problem. But that's what had got her into trouble in the first place—thinking of Adam as a business problem, making a decision about him with her head instead of her heart. That would teach her, wouldn't it?

She came to her favorite spot, took off her jacket and sat down on it, pulling her knees up under her chin, gazing out over the trees. If she could just sit down with Adam, see him face-to-face, explain how she felt, tell him she was sorry to have made such a terrible mistake, ask him if it was too late. That is, if things hadn't gone too far with Kim . . .

A shaft of jealousy surprised her, as a fast-moving series of images of Kim and Adam flashed through her mind, like a rapid slide show—the two of them out together, holding hands, having dinner, in bed together. They galvanized her. Eva was right. She couldn't just sit back and let this happen. Of course there had to be something she could do about it. She could be back in Melbourne in a day if she needed to be. She could call him, tell him she was coming. Or she could surprise him, arrive unexpectedly.

Propose to him.

She blinked. Where on earth had that idea come from? She blinked again but the idea stayed. She could propose to him. Turn up unexpectedly at the restaurant, jump out of a cake, arrive bearing armfuls of flowers or balloons, hire a skywriter, take out a full-page ad in the newspaper asking him to marry her. She was an event manager, after all—she could do any of those things. Do them all.

She got the tingling feeling in her fingertips. That would prove to him that she really meant it, wouldn't it? That she was truly sorry for hurting him. Another woman might have phoned or written a letter, but he wouldn't expect her to do something so ordinary, would he? And she didn't want to do something so ordinary. Now she had realized how she truly felt about him, she wanted to shout it from the rooftops. Tell him. Tell everyone. And hope she wasn't too late.

She stood up, wanting to get cracking on her ideas, get everything under way, when a dart of reality hit her. She sat down again with a bump. She couldn't leave. She had to stay here for the year, to fulfill the conditions of the will. There had certainly been no coda to the endless documents outlining that the said member of the Byrne family could have a little jaunt back home for a week or two to sort out his or her personal life. But perhaps there was another way. She stood up again and nearly ran back across the hill toward Tara Lodge. There was one man who would know.

* * *

"I'm sorry, Lainey," Mr. Fogarty said, his tiny eyes looking kindly across his desk at her. "But it is quite clear. A member of the Byrne family has to be in residence for the entire year. That is really the crux of the whole will."

Lainey leaned back in her chair, still in her exercise clothes and runners. She had decided not to phone Mr. Fogarty, but had simply got in the car and driven into Dunshaughlin, needing to hear the good or bad news face-to-face. Mr. Fogarty had seemed a little surprised to see her looking so flushed and windswept, but had led her into his little office nevertheless. He looked at his watch now. "I do need to see another client but we can talk again later today."

She stood up. "Thanks anyway, Mr. Fogarty. I'm sorry to come barging in like this."

She had just turned when she heard a little squeak of excitement. She turned back. He was flicking through the pages. "Just one moment, Lainey. You've got three brothers, haven't you?"

She nodded.

He flicked the pages again, making them blur. "Your aunt specified that a member of the Byrne family had to be in residence for the entire year for you to inherit, but it doesn't specify that it has to be the *same* member of the family for the entirety of the twelve months. Could one of your brothers come over, just for a week or two, while you sort out your business in Melbourne?"

Hope rose in Lainey suddenly. "That would be all right? Really?"

"It would," he said, giving her his widest mouse smile.

It was all she could do to stop herself from picking him up off his chair and spinning him around. She'd have liked to have seen his little legs twirling, then watched him dizzily try to walk when she put him back on the ground. "Mr. Fogarty, you're a saint. I'll let you know as soon as I can which brother it will be." She surprised him with a kiss on the top of his head.

He blushed bright red. "Oh, Lainey. If Mrs. Fogarty had seen that."

• • •

Back home, she looked at her list. Just three names. Brendan. Declan. Hugh. Which one of them could she ask? Who was in the best position to take time off from work—or university, in Hugh's case—and come over and take up residence here at the B&B for a few weeks, perhaps longer? She got on best with Hugh. He was the one she would have most liked to ask, but she knew in her heart that he just wouldn't be able to do it. He was a worse cook than she was. She was getting quite a few midweek guests at the B&B now, and she really wouldn't like to leave Hugh in charge. He'd forget to cook, or forget to put sheets on the beds, probably. He'd be perfectly nice about it, of course, but she had taken too much pride in the renovations to let it all go to seed in a few weeks.

Declan? She checked her bulging diary, turning pages until she reached the table showing all the school holidays in Australia. The timing was very bad. Declan was just at the start of a new term, at least three months before he had holidays again.

Brendan. Mr. Environment himself. She rubbed at her temples. In some ways he was the best positioned. He had been manager of his department for the past four years, had worked with the company since he'd left school. He was surely due long-service leave, or was in a senior enough position to take some time off. Even just a week or two. Long enough for her to fly home, sort everything out with Adam and then come back. And Rosie had family in Wicklow, after all—a whole tribe of aunts and cousins, just an hour or two away. Lainey scribbled down her arguments on the notepad in front of her. Her credit card would have to bear all these airfares, she realized. She'd been living so frugally here, surely it was time she had a big splash out. She checked the time difference. As soon as it was morning in Australia, she would ring and ask him. Beg him, if she needed to.

·   ·   ·

"Jeez, Lainey, you've got some hide."

She nearly dropped the phone. She'd expected him to laugh at her, dismiss her with a joke. But she hadn't expected him to be angry. She felt her own temper rise in response. "What do you mean by that? I've got some hide to ask a favor? When I'm the one who gave up my whole life for a year for all of us? I don't think that's some hide. I actually think it's fairly reasonable to ask for some help."

"When it suits you. Sure, you're prepared to admit that someone else in the family might be interested in going to Ireland now. But only now, when it suits you."

"What are you talking about? No one else was interested. I was the one who had to do it. I don't recall you jumping up at that meeting at Ma and Dad's that night."

"You don't? And why would that be, do you think?"

She had never heard this tone of voice from Brendan before. "Why?"

"When do you ever give anyone else a chance, Lainey? Did it occur to you that Rosie and I might very much have liked to come back for a year? That in fact we've been thinking about doing just that? But no, Peg made it clear you're the number one choice and you had your bags packed and your savior-of-the-family costume on before I'd even had a chance to talk to Rosie about it."

"Hold on a moment here, Bren. You're saying you would have liked to come?"

"I'd like to have had the chance to think about it, yes. Maybe it wouldn't have been practical, but Rosie and I have been talking about taking a year out, maybe even opening our own B&B. You think I want to keep working in this job for the rest of my life?"

"Then why didn't you say something? Speak up that night?"

"Who would have listened? Not Ma and Dad. Of course they knew you'd do it. It's always been like that in our family."

"That is really unfair, Brendan. You can't just spring something like this on me. I think *you've* got a hide!"

His tone of voice changed. "I'm sorry, Lainey. I sounded harsher than I mean to. It's just I've had a terrible few days at work this week. Every day is a terrible day at work at the moment. I didn't mean to blurt it out quite like that. It's just I was awake half the night thinking about it, wishing we were somewhere else. That we were in Ireland, not you."

Lainey felt as though she was in a fast-moving car that

had suddenly taken an unexpected and dangerous turnoff. She had imagined this conversation taking a number of paths, but this had not been one of them. Eva's words leaped into her head. "You're not in charge of the world, Lainey." She bit back a sharp answer, the answer the old Lainey would have given. A snap at him, telling him not to be so silly, that of course she had to be the one who came to Ireland. Because in the back of her mind she had a memory of that night at her parents' house. Brendan had sat forward, looked a little bit interested. He had outlined all the negatives, saying that he was so busy at work, and of course they had the twins. But then that had always been Brendan's way—to be cautious, to look at all the options, before making his decision. Not like her, who thought quickly, made snap decisions, generally involving her taking a leading, organizational role . . .

"Lainey, are you there?" Brendan sounded puzzled by her silence.

She sat down. "Do you mean all this? Has it really been that bad?"

Now he paused. "It's not that it's always been bad. It's just that . . ." He paused again while he seemed to struggle for the right words. "I don't know, it's like I ended up with the role of the boring, sensible one in the family, the one who couldn't do anything surprising or interesting. You know what it's like, you and Dec and Hugh, always making digs at us, the perfect family—oh, look at Brendan and his boring wife and the first grandchildren."

Lainey felt sick suddenly, remembering all the times she and Declan and Hugh had poked fun at him and Rosie.

"Bren—"

"And all the cracks you'd make if we were ever late. 'It's just a matter of being organized, Brendan.' It's all right for you, sitting there all glamorous, not a hair out of place, going on about how many kilometers you'd jogged that day when the most exercise we'd done in months was get out of bed. *You* have kids and try and stay organized, Lainey. It was all we could do to get out of the house at all with the twins sometimes. We didn't have a clue what we were doing once they arrived. Nothing happens the way you expect it to anymore once you've got kids."

She was filled with guilt, able to picture every scene as he described it. He was right—she'd been exactly like that. When she spoke, her voice was soft. "I'm sorry, Bren. I didn't notice."

"It's not your fault. You were busy too. And that's what it's like with our family, I know that. We tease each other all the time. But it just wasn't feeling like teasing anymore. It felt like attacks."

"Why didn't you ever speak up about it? Say something to us?"

"Oh, sure, Lain. What, call a family conference and say, Could you all stop picking on me and Rosie? Stop picking on me? Let me do things in my time, in my way, sometimes? It's impossible, especially with you and Ma always the ones in charge, running the show. After a while I just gave up. I was never going to be able to do it properly enough, so it was like, why bother?"

Flashes came into Lainey's head again, against her will. Interrupting Brendan while he was doing the dishes. "Bren, you're not doing them properly. Here, let me take over. You go and watch TV." Her mother did it with her father too. "Oh, Gerry, that's not the way to carve the roast. Let me do it."

"So what's it like with you and Rosie? At home?"

"We worked out what I do well and what she does well. I like being in the garden, doing the handyman stuff, so I do that. And she likes the cooking and cleaning. It wasn't a matter of us being Mr. and Mrs. Traditional. It's just the way it worked out best for us." He changed the subject suddenly. "So why do you really want to come back? It's not a holiday, is it? Not work?"

Yesterday she wouldn't have told him. She wouldn't have wanted to admit she was feeling vulnerable, that she had made a mistake about Adam. Now it seemed different. "I've made a big mistake with Adam and I think if I don't go back and sort it out face-to-face then I'll have lost him."

"You broke up with him? Why did you do that? He's the best man you've ever gone out with."

Why were her brothers choosing to tell her how much they liked Adam now? she wondered once again. She kept her voice calm. "Yes, I've realized that myself."

"So how long would you need? A week? Two weeks?"

"You'll do it? You'll come over?"

"I'll talk it over with Rosie, see what she thinks. Work might be a problem. We're all having to do overtime as it is."

Lainey had to stop herself from leaping in, telling him what to say to his boss, spelling out that he just had to say it was a family situation. Let Brendan do it his own way. She dug her nails into her hands to quell the impatience. "So will you let me know?" She kept her voice measured too.

"I'll call you back as soon as I can."

* * *

What could she do while she was waiting for his call? It was too dark to go back up to Tara, much as she'd have liked to walk until she had no energy in her at all. And she didn't want to be away from the phone in case Brendan made a snap decision and called her right back. But she needed to do something, to go somewhere to think these new thoughts through. Because clearly she had been making a complete and utter mess of her life for *years* and hadn't noticed. She had obviously done nothing but bully and boss people from her childhood on. And now all the chickens were coming home to roost.

The chickens. She'd go outside and talk to them. At least they couldn't answer back. She grabbed a handful of grain and the bucket of scraps from the kitchen. As she came out, she heard a rustle in the bushes. She half expected to see Rod Stewart pulling a little cart, with a mouse comfy in the back, a rug over its little knees. She might be bossy with humans, but she certainly had no control over the animal kingdom.

The sky was bright with stars. She could just see the glow from the lights of Navan and Dunshaughlin some miles away, but here in the countryside there was little to spoil the view of the night sky. She threw in the food to the chickens and was rewarded with a kind of halfhearted clucking, the four birds too sleepy to be bothered with late-night snacks.

She sat down on the garden seat and looked up at the stars. What were you supposed to do with the personality you were given? she wondered. In her job, it was good that she was quick-thinking, organized, able to make decisions on the run, react quickly to situations, take control, see where problems lay and sort them out. But that same personality seemed to be doing nothing but cause problems in her private life. Was she supposed to get a work personality that she put on and took off like a jacket, left hanging in the hallway when she got home?

The phone rang and she nearly rolled off the bench in her hurry to get into the kitchen. It wasn't Brendan, but Barry, her guest speaker from the Irish music weekend a month or so back. He had a group of friends coming over from London in a fortnight's time and wondered if they could book out the whole guesthouse on the Saturday night. "Could you do it as a sort of one-off for us, Lainey, those beautiful meals and all? I've been raving about that weekend we had there." She thought quickly. She was only midway through organizing the next series of theme weekends. It would be good to have something like that to keep her occupied, either before she went to Australia or when she got back, depending on what happened with Brendan. "No worries," she said in her best Australian accent. "It'll be great to have you back."

It was nearly one o'clock before she went to bed. Brendan still hadn't called back.

CHAPTER 34

He rang the next day. It was clear within seconds what his answer was. No.

"Lainey, I'm really sorry. And it's not because we don't want to. To be honest, we were up all night talking about it. Thinking about whether I could just throw the job in and come over. Rosie said she'd love to live in Ireland for a while. But I just can't take the time off work at the moment. Can't you ask one of the others?" Then he paused. "No, I guess you can't."

If she could have gone out and adopted a brother or sister right then, she would have. "Thanks anyway, Bren. And I'm sorry again, for not giving you the chance back in February."

"It's fine." A pause. "I actually feel better just having told you what it felt like. Rosie said I should have told you years ago."

Lainey imagined a little whirring sound as her hackles stood up on the back of her neck. She mentally flattened them again, counted to ten in rapid time. "It's good we talked about it, Bren. We'll have to decide on a code phrase that you can shout at me if I ever start bossing you again."

"What about 'Cease and desist, bossy boots'?"

She laughed, despite her mood. "Yes, that'd do it."

So now what could she do? Her dramatic arrival and face-to-face proposal was out of the question. Could she ring Adam? She could—but he wouldn't be able to talk if he was at the restaurant, would he? She suspected that would be the only place she could get hold of him at the moment, the hours he was apparently working. She could write to him, but writing had never been her strongest skill. Business letters, perhaps, but how could she put something so personal down on paper? She could email him, but that was far too impersonal, worse than a letter. And her message could arrive jammed in between junk mail, be deleted accidentally . . . She needed to get some advice, talk about it with someone. She needed to talk to her mother. She sat on the stairs and dialed the number. She and her mother didn't have a lot of heart-to-hearts, but right now she needed the kind of blunt honesty that her mother specialized in.

The phone rang for some time. Lainey was about to hang up when it clicked. She could tell from her father's voice that he must have been sleeping. "Dad, it's me. Sorry, did I wake you?"

"Just having a bit of a nap, Lain. You're looking for your mother, I suppose? She's out at the moment, at the supermarket, doing those demonstrations."

"Oh, of course. Is she still enjoying it?"

"Well enough, I think. How's the weather been over there?"

Her heart sank a little further. Right now she needed to talk about more than the weather. "It's fine, Dad. Summer's on the way."

"And how are you, Lainey?"

"Fine. How about you?"

He sighed. "Up and down, I suppose. Still waiting for the insurance money. Everything is really on hold until that comes through or until we can sell the B&B."

A rush of anger surprised her. She was doing her best, wasn't she? "Isn't there anything you can do while you're waiting? Those exercises the physiotherapist suggested to build up your muscles again?"

"You're sounding like your mother."

The anger went up a notch. She wanted to shout at him suddenly. *You have to try, Dad. You have to stop feeling sorry for yourself. You have to do those exercises, not lie around in bed all day. Don't you realize the effect you're having on all of us, on Ma? Can't you think of someone other than yourself sometimes?* She only just stopped the words from coming out. It wasn't up to her to say those things to him, was it? She wasn't in charge of her father, either.

Her father continued. "In fact, your mother's been very forthright of late."

Lainey's temper returned to simmer levels. "Of late?"

"Well, let me just say she's been reaching new levels of forthrightness. She also said she's going to push me and my walker off St. Kilda Pier if I don't start at least trying to do some of the exercises soon. And she also mentioned something about setting my bed on fire if I keep spending so many hours a day in it."

"She said all that?"

"She did."

Lainey started to laugh. She couldn't help herself. "She's never really been one to mince her words, has she? I'm sorry, I'm as bad. I shouldn't have spoken to you like that, either."

"Don't apologize, Lainey. I probably need to hear it now and again. And I know I haven't said it as much as I should have, but I'm really grateful to you for going home to run the B&B. Doing all that for me and your family. You're a good girl."

His words made a direct hit on her heart. She felt a warm, light feeling inside. "It's been fine, Dad, really. Great even. And I'm sorry for trying to boss you before."

"It runs in the family, love. You didn't have a hope of missing out on the bossy gene."

"Maybe I just need to dilute it down a little."

"No, don't you change a thing. Do you want me to get your ma to call you back?"

"No, I'll call another time. Thanks, Dad."

"Thank you, love. For everything."

She felt better after talking to her father. Not just because it had made her feel good about being in Ireland for him, reminding her she was doing what she could. But she also felt glad she'd been able to stop herself from snapping at him. Well, even if it had only been because her mother had got in first. She gave a guilty smile. She and her mother really were some pair. Please welcome the all-singing, all-dancing, mother-and-daughter team— yes, it's The Bossy Byrnes.

She wandered about the living room, restless now, straightening cushions, checking the tops of cupboards for dust, so used to housework these days it was second nature. She picked up the Adam video lying on the TV and fought a temptation to put it on again, before realizing it wouldn't do her any good. If only she could talk to him honestly, face-to-face, tell him exactly how she felt, explain how sorry she was, that she hoped it wasn't too late. But how could she do it? Send a hologram of herself? Do a *Star Trek* and beam herself over? Then she stopped short, staring at the TV screen.

Could she send a video of herself?

She'd given plenty of video presentations at work, done video conferencing and knew how to operate a camera. Surely she could hire one in Dunshaughlin or Dublin? Was that the next best thing to being there? Would that show Adam how she felt, if he could see her face, read her expressions, rather than just read a letter or an email? Was it worth a try?

• • •

Twenty-four hours later she threw down a pen in despair. In the living room the video camera was all set up. In the kitchen, she was on her tenth version of the script. She couldn't get the words right, couldn't get her ideas straight.

She rubbed her eyes. She'd been working on it all day, had made several attempts at it already. The first version had looked more like a breezy holiday program, showing shots of the B&B, scenery around the Hill of Tara, even the kitchen. Watching it back she'd realized she had told him everything about the place and nothing about how she felt. She'd erased it.

"Come on, Lainey," she said aloud. "Focus." If she was advising a client, what would she say? The answer came quickly. Forget the tricks. Forget the razz and the glamour and the smoke and mirrors. Sometimes the most effective message is the simple message. Just say what you want to say—nothing more, nothing less.

She'd try it. She spent a few minutes in the bathroom upstairs, looking at herself in the mirror, wishing for the zillionth time that her nose was smaller, that her eyes were bigger, that her lips were fuller. That she looked completely different, in fact. She carefully wiped away the latest bit of smudged mascara, applied a little bit of lipstick, a touch of blush. She was very pale these days. She ran her fingers through her hair—still all it needed to style it. She straightened her dress, a deep maroon color. A good color for television, she remembered someone telling her once.

Down in the living room again, she moved the camera around, finding the right setting. She arranged the shot so it had her in a sofa chair, with the empty fireplace in the background, but it looked too much like a party political broadcast, the Prime Minister's wife relaxing at home. She tried it against the window, but the glare turned her into a silhouette. On the staircase? Too odd. In the end she settled for the kitchen, her at the kitchen table, where she had spent so much time. And apt, in a way, for a message to Adam.

She started writing a few notes, cleared her throat, then realized she was planning too much again. She'd do it, just say it, from the heart. And that's what she would send. Well, perhaps.

She pressed the "record" button on the camera and then moved quickly to her seat. She felt like an eejit, but then a mental picture of Adam came into her mind, and she realized what she was fighting for, what she wanted to say.

"Adam, this is Lainey." She groaned inwardly. She was as bad as her mother on Hugh's first video. Clearly she was Lainey. She kept going. "But you've probably guessed that. I've got a lot of things I want to say to you, and I didn't want to do it in a letter or on the phone or in an email. I wanted to come home, even just for a day, and surprise you, at home or in the restaurant. But that isn't possible. So I thought this might be the next best thing."

She looked into the camera again, silent for a second. "Ad, I'm sorry. I'm really, really sorry, for hurting you so much the morning I left. For making you feel that what we had meant nothing to me. That you were just a business colleague. It's gone round and round my head since that morning, the memory of the look in your eyes, your voice, what I must have made you feel.

"I wasn't thinking properly. I mean, I was thinking, but I was thinking in a different way. I was thinking on practical levels, and sensible levels and all of those non-feeling levels. And I've realized that was wrong. Because the way I think about you is completely on a feeling level. I feel good when I'm with you. I feel happy when you ring me. I realized I feel wonderful when I kiss you, when I sleep with you, when we"—she kept looking at the camera—"you know how I feel when we're in bed together.

"Ad, I made a big mistake. And now I have a terrible feeling I have left this too late. That it's taken me too long to tell you this. When I got the videos you made with Hugh, I was really surprised, I think. That even though I had hurt you, you were still prepared to go to those lengths for me. That maybe you still cared for me. And that's when I should have really thought things through. But I was too stubborn. And now I've heard from Hugh that you are seeing Kim." Her speed of voice quickened. "And that's entirely up to you. You've every right to see Kim—you've every right to see whoever you want. I dumped you, as Hugh so bluntly put it once. And it's my own fault if I have realized only now what a stupid thing that was to do."

She tried to find some more polite words about Adam seeing Kim, but suddenly there weren't any in her brain. So she told the absolute truth. "To be completely honest, Ad, the thought of you and Kim together makes me feel sick. The thought of you with anyone else makes me feel sick. The thought of me with anyone else but you doesn't feel right, either." She paused. "There's a man here in Ireland. I used to go to school with him, and I started imagining there was something happening between me and him, hoping there would be, because that way I wouldn't have to face up to being wrong about you. But I was wrong about him too. I was just using him to try and block out how I felt about you.

"I know I've been unfair to you. I should have realized long ago all the things that are so good about you, should have dared to ask for more time from you, given you more of my time, treated you properly. I did take you for granted. I wish we could start again. My problem was I thought real love had to be filled with drama and spectacle, loud cymbals. But I've realized now that it can speak in soft voices, sneak up behind you, play gently as a soundtrack, not overwhelm everything and everybody."

She gazed right into the camera lens, focused completely on the idea of Adam now, feeling as though she was talking directly to him. "Why has it taken me this long to realize that, Ad? Is it because I was scared? In case it all went wrong? I used to spend all my days at work planning in case something went wrong, putting in place hundreds of contingency plans, safety net after safety net. And I couldn't do that in real life, could I? If I'd told you I was in love with you too, if I'd relaxed and let it happen and then it had all gone wrong between us, then what? I'd have fallen in a heap and been hurt. And I think I didn't want to feel that. I hate feeling vulnerable or scared or unhappy and I've been feeling that way enough since Dad's accident as it is. But I didn't recognize that at the time and it wasn't fair on you. I should have known I could trust you.

"Ad, I don't know if I have any right to ask this any-more, but I just want you and I to be together again when I come back in February, with all the letters and emails and phone calls we can manage before I do. Which was just what you suggested that morning, wasn't it? What you expected we would do, to keep our relationship going while I was away. Except I was too busy organizing every-body to see that there might be another way than mine."

She rubbed her eyes. The little red "record" light on the video was still blinking at her. She looked into the lens for a moment or two. "I feel like this is one of those dating agency videos, that I'm sending it out into the wide world, hoping someone will happen to see it and think about taking me on. But it's only you I want to see it, because it's only you I want to be with. And I hope it's not too late and I hope that you will forgive me for hurt-ing you and that you will give me a second chance." She rubbed the bracelet on her wrist, then slipped it off, held it up to the camera. "I've kept wearing this, every day. So I must have known deep down what I wanted. It just took my brain a long time to catch up with my heart. So what I want to say, Adam Blake, is this, in a nutshell. I, Lainey Byrne, am in love with you and I would love to spend the rest of my life with you. And I hope you still feel the same way." She paused. "But I know this can't be about what I want. Or what I think. It has to be what you really want. So it's over to you now, to tell me how you feel. If you want to, that is."

She had a vivid mental image in her mind of his lean, clever face, those dark-brown eyes, the warmth and humor, and she longed with all of herself that it wasn't too late. She looked in the camera, knowing there should be a big finish, a summary even. But she had run out of words. So she sat there for a moment longer and then she got up and switched off the camera.

One hour later, she walked out of the Dunshaughlin post office. The video was on its way, sent by express post in the old-fashioned way. She could have emailed the footage but it didn't feel right. She wanted him to receive it as something solid, something he could hold in his hands. It would be in Melbourne within three days. She had checked it once, just to see it had worked, but not letting herself listen too closely to what she was saying, in case Miss Bossy Byrne took over and decided it could be done again, more professionally, more slickly. It was done. She had said what she meant. And now it was up to him.

CHAPTER 35

Nothing. A week since she'd sent the video and nothing. She was up the walls. She felt like she had traveled every mile with the parcel, picturing where it was since she had posted it. She'd imagined it lying in a bag with the other post. Being loaded into a van, onto a plane, lying in the cargo hold, arriving in Australia, being sorted in Melbourne, into another bag, being carried by the postman, dropped into Adam's letterbox. Maybe it hadn't fit. That was it, of course. It hadn't fit, so the postman had to leave a card asking Adam to collect it instead. And Adam hadn't time to collect it. So he hadn't seen the video yet. Which explained the lack of response. Or did it? She couldn't bear it. She had to ring him.

Heart in her mouth, she worked out the time difference and dialed his home number. It rang, her pulse rate increasing with each ring. Then a click. She thought at first it was the receiver being picked up, then realized it was his answering machine. "This is Adam Blake. Please leave a message after the tone." She hung up, paced the room for a moment, then dialed another number in Melbourne.

"Hi, Hugh."

"Hi, Lainey."

A long pause.

"So how are things?"

"Great. What about you?"

"Good, thanks. How's Dad?"

"He's pretty good actually."

"Ma?"

"She's good too."

Another pause.

"Declan and Brendan are good too," Hugh said.

"Oh. Good."

"You want me to run next door and see how the neighbors are?"

He'd seen right through her, she knew it. Lainey blurted out what was on her mind. "Hughie, please tell me the truth about something. You didn't make that up about seeing Adam and Kim together, did you?"

A pause. "No, Lainey, I didn't. I did see them."

That hope evaporated. She bit her lip. "Well, I'd better go, then. I've got to get organized for the weekend."

"Get organized? What for? All those theme weekends are over for the moment, aren't they? You're not going away somewhere, are you?"

His words got her back up. "No, Hugh. I'm not allowed to go away anywhere, remember? I've got a group of musicians here on Saturday night, as it happens. One of the guest speakers is coming back with a group of his friends."

"Oh, good. That'll be fun."

"Sure will," she said, trying to put some enthusiasm into her voice. "Well, I'd better go. See you."

"See you, Lainey. And have a great weekend."

She couldn't stop herself. She rang the number of the restaurant. Even if he didn't want to know her anymore, she had to hear it from him, have it confirmed, not just communicated by a lack of reply, a silence like this.

"Blake's, David speaking."

"Dave, it's Lainey calling from Ireland."

"Lainey, hi! Long time no hear. How's it going over there?"

"Good, good. How are things with you?"

"Flat-out. You can probably hear it, can you?"

She could. There was a lot of noise in the background, conversation, music, even though it was early evening. "Sorry, I was hoping I'd get you at a quiet time."

"We don't seem to have many quiet times just now. We're doing two or more sittings a night at the moment."

"I won't keep you, then. Um, I just wondered, could I have a word with Adam?"

"Of course you can. Hold on, Lainey. I'll go and get him."

Her heart started thumping. She pressed the receiver close against her ear.

"Lainey?"

"Adam." Her voice was as high as a bat squeak.

"No, sorry. Dave again. He's got a bit of a kitchen emergency happening. Can I give him a message?"

"Um, no. No message. Could you just tell him I called?"

"No worries, Lainey. He's got your number, I suppose."

No, he probably didn't, she realized. She quickly called it out.

Dave read it back. "I'll pass it on. Better run, Lainey. See you. Have a Guinness for me, won't you?"

"Sure will, Dave." She hung up, her hands shaking.

The phone didn't ring again that day. Or that night. By Friday morning she couldn't bear the waiting anymore. She'd gone over all the possible scenarios in her head. Perhaps Dave had got so busy he had forgotten to give Adam the message that she'd rung. Perhaps something had happened, an accident or something, and it had slipped his mind. Or perhaps Dave had given Adam the message and he had chosen to ignore it . . .

She swallowed her pride once more and rang the number again.

"Blake's, good evening."

She realized her hands were shaking. "Dave, hi, it's Lainey again."

"Lainey, hi."

She knew immediately he hadn't forgotten to pass on the message. She could hear it in his tone of voice, instantly wary. "I won't keep you, I was just wondering . . . um, I hadn't heard back and just wondered if you had a chance to give Adam my message."

"I did, Lainey, yes. I told him you rang. And I did give him your number."

He was feeling as uncomfortable as she was, she knew it. This was excruciating. Dave was clearly trying to cover for Adam. Because Adam clearly didn't want to talk to her. "Thanks, Dave. And there's no need to tell him I rang again."

"You sure?"

"I'm sure." She was. Whether the video had arrived or not, it seemed Adam didn't want to talk to her.

．　．　．　．

Mrs. Hartigan rang that afternoon, full of apologies. "Lainey, I'm so sorry. I double booked myself when I said I could help you out on Saturday night. I forgot Sabine's over from Munich and Rohan's taking us all out for a surprise birthday dinner for her."

Damn, damn, damn. "It doesn't matter at all, Mrs. Hartigan. Have a great time," Lainey assured her.

She rang Eva straightaway. "Oh, Lainey, I'm sorry. I can't. I've got a gig this weekend. And Joe's finishing a project for work, otherwise he could help."

She was on her own.

．　．　．

The next morning she turned on her computer and picked up her emails. There was just one new message.

SENDER: Adam Blake
SUBJECT: [no subject]

She clicked on it, her heart racing.

Lainey, I'm sorry I couldn't talk when you rang. I need to think about the things you've said. I'll be in touch again soon, I promise.
Adam

She read it again. Then again. And again, even more slowly. It was perfectly reasonable. Polite. To the point. She couldn't fault him on that. But was that it?

During the day she read it another ten times, but she still couldn't wring any extra meaning out of his words.

* * *

By eight o'clock Saturday night Lainey was in a mild state of panic. She was wearing one of her favorite outfits, an elegant skirt and top cut so well and made from such a beautiful deep-red material that it had cheered her up just to put it on. She'd done her hair, applied a little more makeup than normal, a touch of blush, lipstick, telling herself that if she looked in control perhaps they would all think she was in control.

"Forget the food, Lainey. We'll be happy just to look at you all night," Barry had said admiringly as she greeted them that afternoon. The group was in such high spirits she suspected she could have served toasted sandwiches and cans of beer and they would have been happy. There were six of them so far, though Barry said he was half expecting a couple of late arrivals. "You don't mind, Lainey, do you? They said they'd try and get down if they could, but they're not the most reliable of fellows, I have to say. Don't hold dinner for them, though. If they're late, they'll be happy to eat separately from us."

No problem at all, Lainey had said with a smile, cursing them inside. She still wasn't confident with her quantities and serving times and she only just felt on top of serving one lot of them on her own, let alone any extra groups.

In the safety of the kitchen, she was cursing them out loud now. Things were only just running to plan. They'd eaten the oysters and brown bread far more quickly than she'd expected and now her timing was out with the lamb, roasted potatoes and green beans. She decided to deliver another few bottles of wine to their table, hoping that would distract them while she got organized again.

She had just opened one of the bottles when the front doorbell rang. Damn it. Why couldn't the late arrivals have been really late, and given her enough time to at least serve the others their meals? Now there'd be a delay while they all started chatting and getting their drinks, while her lamb and vegetables shriveled up in the oven . . . She hurriedly took off her apron and went to the front door, mentally calculating how to add more place settings without disturbing the others too much and working out which of the back bedrooms she could make up. Bottle of wine still in hand, she opened the door and plastered a fake smile on her face to greet the new arrival.

It was Adam.

She nearly shut the door again in shock. She blinked. He was still there, smiling at her.

"Hello, Lainey."

"Adam? What on earth are you doing here?"

"I've come to see you."

"But how did you get here?"

"How do you think?"

"But I had an email from you this morning. From Melbourne."

"It wasn't from Melbourne, actually. I sent it from Singapore last night, during the stopover." He grinned. "Dave sent me an urgent text message to say you'd rung the restaurant again and he was worried you'd start getting suspicious that I wasn't there. So I sent you the email, hoping it would buy me enough time to get here. I wanted to surprise you."

"Oh." She stared at him. She didn't seem able to move or ask any sensible questions. There was a sudden burst of laughter from the dining room.

He looked over her shoulder. "You've got company? I thought your theme weekends were over until next month."

How did he know that? "They are. This is a one-off."

"And what are you serving?"

He'd flown from Australia to ask about her menu? "They've just had the oysters. I'm about to take the lamb in to them. Then the chocolate pudding for dessert."

"Are you doing the cooking and the waitressing?"

She nodded.

"Can I help at all? Would you like me to take over in the kitchen?"

"I beg your pardon?"

"Do you want me to do the cooking?"

She stared at him. "I would love you to do the cooking."

"Well, then." That smile. "Lead me to your kitchen."

This was all wrong, Lainey thought as he followed her into the kitchen. It shouldn't be like this, should it? Shouldn't they have run into each other's arms? Shouldn't she have burst into tears of joy and happiness? The truth was she was too shocked to know what to do. Adam, on the other hand, seemed perfectly relaxed. He took in the kitchen in a glance, checking inside the Aga, lifting the saucepan lids, starting to clear space on the bench to organize the plates. He glanced over at her, a very amused look in his eyes. "Are your guests waiting on that bottle of wine?"

She nodded, mute again.

"You might want to take it in to them."

"Oh. Yes, of course." She was on her way out when he called her back.

"Lainey?"

She turned.

"You look very beautiful, by the way."

Lainey wondered if her guests noticed she was suddenly beaming from ear to ear.

CHAPTER 36

Two hours later she was cursing herself and not smiling anymore either. Why had she accepted this group booking? And why, especially, had she accepted a booking from a group of musicians? The late arrivals had turned up, fifteen minutes after Adam, two of them already half-filled with wine and far more interested in getting started on a singsong than eating her carefully prepared gourmet meal. All the desserts had been put on hold, the group too busy talking and taking out their instruments. Lainey had counted two violins, a bodhrán, a guitar and a tin whistle when she'd delivered their new supplies of wine. Outwardly she was being the best hostess she could, while inside her heart was thumping, her pulse racing, her nerves on edge at the thought that Adam—*Adam*—was out in the kitchen.

They hadn't had a moment to talk yet. She was in a state of high tension. He, however, was completely relaxed, behaving as if he'd been brought up in this kitchen. He hadn't commented on any of her unorthodox cooking preparations. He'd diplomatically done some rearranging of the oven shelves, checked a few ingredients with her, raised an eyebrow once or twice at her answers. Anyone watching would have assumed he was the usual chef and she was the usual front-of-house. A perfect team, no less.

She finally delivered the desserts and the cheese, arranging them on the sideboard. "Come on over and join us, Lainey," Barry called from the head of the table, his guitar across his lap. "Sit down here and sing us a song from Australia."

"I'd love to, really, but I need to get your breakfast things organized."

"Oh, don't worry about that. Sure, we won't want breakfast till lunchtime tomorrow anyway."

"No, thanks all the same. I've some things to sort out in the kitchen." That was the understatement of the year, she thought.

Adam was wiping down the stove top as she came in. The kitchen was spotless, the dishes done, the floor washed. She shut the door behind her. Too bad if all the guests came down with food poisoning or the roof caved in. Adam was here and they needed to talk.

"All done?" he asked.

"All done," she said. She swallowed. "Hello again."

"Hello, Lainey."

The crease appeared in his cheek, the first sign of a smile. She gazed at him, taken aback by how good it felt to be able to look at his face. Not in her mind, for real. He was here.

"Adam, I need to say lots of things to you." She needed to hear lots of things too. The idea of Kim was looming very large in her mind. "I need to ask you lots of things too."

"I need to ask you a few things too."

The mood had turned wary. "Ad, I want to—"

"Hello? Anyone here?" They were interrupted by a knock at the kitchen door. It was one of the musicians. "Sorry, Lainey. We've had a bit of an accident with a bottle of red wine."

A good hostess would have cared about the carpet, hurried to mop up. To her own surprise as much as the surprise of the guest, she thrust a bottle of soda water and a packet of salt at the man. "Here—try that." Then she put a chair under the door handle so it couldn't be opened.

Adam raised an eyebrow. "That's an interesting approach to hospitality."

She was too keyed-up to joke. They were standing just a short distance apart, but it didn't feel right to be any closer yet. "Ad, please. I know we've lots to talk about but there's something important I need to say again first." There was nothing to do but blurt it out. "I'm so sorry. For breaking up with you. For saying those things that morning I left."

He was very still, his expression serious now, too. "That was a bad morning, Lainey. I couldn't believe it, just couldn't believe I had got it all so wrong." He paused, looked at her for a long moment. "I just couldn't understand how someone I loved and I thought loved me could say those things. I knew then—I still know—that we could have survived on emails and letters. I loved the idea of it actually, being able to write to you, getting letters from you, amassing a little collection of love letters that we could read to each other when we were old and gray."

Lainey kept quiet, much as she wanted to interrupt, to say sorry again. She knew she had to hear all of this.

He slowly shook his head. "It was a very strange time. I was angry with you at first, then I was confused about us, and then I just got sad. Really sad. Then I met Hugh and I realized that you hadn't told him you'd broken up with me. And I realized you hadn't told Christine or the others that you'd finished it either. And that gave me some hope that maybe you weren't too sure about it yourself."

"That's why you did the videos?" she asked softly.

He nodded. "Hugh was very determined about it. He made us a bit of a project of his, I think."

She remembered her last phone call with Hugh, how bothered he'd sounded at the thought she might not be here this weekend. Now she understood why. "He knew you were coming over here, didn't he?"

He nodded again. "He drove me to the airport. In your car, actually. His is broken again. Your parents are in on it as well. We had to get the directions for this place and Hugh couldn't remember where it was."

"You've gone to a lot of trouble."

"You're worth a lot of trouble."

She felt a shimmer of hope, before she remembered something else. "Ad, I need to ask you about something else, about—"

"Is it about Kim?"

She nodded.

"There's not a lot to say about Kim. Not really."

She felt like there was something stuck in her throat. Not a lot was too much, as far as she was concerned. "I know it's not really my business, but . . ."

He seemed to want to tell her. "She called me, about six weeks after you had gone. She suggested we meet for lunch. She had some good ideas about a joint promotion with that wine company she works for."

Lainey vowed then and there never to drink their wine again.

"Then we met again, a few times."

"And?"

They looked at each other.

"Did anything else happen?" She hated asking the question but she had to know.

"Anything?"

"Anything . . . physical?"

Adam paused. "I kissed her. She kissed me. We kissed each other, I suppose."

Lainey knew she had gone pale and then turned red. But what right did she have to be upset about it? None at all. "And then?" Did she actually want to know what happened next?

"And then nothing. That was it. We met for lunch once more, but it just wasn't working. I had a feeling she felt differently, but it was no good. She wasn't you."

Lainey was watching him very carefully. "And is that when you decided to come here?"

"I've been wanting to come here for a long while. Then your video arrived and I got the first flight I could." It was his turn to ask the questions. "Tell me about the man you mentioned on the video, Lainey. What happened with him?"

She swallowed. "There's not a lot to tell."

A pause. "Did you sleep with him?"

"No."

"Did you kiss him?"

"No. Well, he kissed me once, just a peck on the cheek, after his niece was found safe. After she'd gone missing." She took a deep breath. "Adam, I don't know what happened. I was so confused about everything. I think I just needed the distraction, talked myself into getting some strange sort of crush on him."

"A crush?"

She nodded.

A smile had started in his eyes. "And this would have been about the same time you started listening to the Osmonds and trying on makeup for the first time?"

She frowned. "What?"

The smile reached his lips. "It's just that a crush sounds so teenage."

"It felt a bit teenage. And I'm too old for crushes, aren't I?"

"Too old, but still lovely." He moved closer to her, tucked the hair behind her ears. "How are you, Lainey?"

The feel of his hand was doing extraordinary things to her body. She told the truth. "I feel better now you're here."

"I feel better now I'm here too." He moved even closer, gently touched her cheek. "I've missed you, Lainey. Things were very dull without you around the place. You have this way of walking into a room that lifts the colors for me somehow. Things seem brighter for me when you're here." He gave a soft laugh. "And you surprise me. I never know what you're going to do or say next. And that's why I thought it would be a wonderful thing to live with you, to spend the rest of my life with you. Because whatever else it would be, it would never be dull."

"You thought it would be?" He was talking in past tense?

"I still think it. I'm thinking about it now." He touched her chin, lifting it slightly. Then he leaned down and kissed her, a soft, sure, beautiful kiss. "What do you think, Lainey? Did you mean everything you said on the video?"

"Every word of it." She was momentarily thrown by the big smile he gave her, but she needed to explain further. "It just took me a long time to realize it. I got scared, Ad. I still am a little. How do I know it's all going to work out between us? How do I know I won't do something that hurts you again?"

"I know exactly how you feel."

"You do? You've had those doubts too?"

He nodded solemnly. "I've been worried sick. How do I know you won't wake up tomorrow morning covered in boils and be so hideous I can't even look at you?"

"Adam . . ."

"How do I know I won't develop some ailment that makes my laugh sound like a donkey braying?"

"Be serious. That's not what I mean. I know those sorts of things won't happen."

"They might. And if they did, we'd just deal with them. I promise I'd learn to love your boils." He gazed down at her, held her gently against him. "Lainey, my angel, you'll never be able to control everyone and everything. But if you just let things happen sometimes, put down your barriers now and then, let things take their own course, good things can happen as well as bad things, you know."

"Like what good things?"

"This." He kissed her. "And this." He kissed her again. "Lainey, I don't know for sure what will happen with us either. But can't we try? Take a risk? See how it goes day by day? We can have a business review meeting once a year if you like, see how things are, set an agenda, record the minutes, set some objectives. Or we can just think, what the hell—let's give it a whirl and have some fun along the way."

"Just some fun?"

He pulled her in close against him and kissed her once more. "No. Let's try for plenty of fun."

The kiss lasted for a long time, weeks of longing and hurt and misunderstandings dissolving in the feel of their bodies close against one another. She slipped her hands up under his T-shirt, feeling his warm skin, her eyes closing in pleasure as his hand moved up under her top, cupped her breast. They were pressed hard against the kitchen bench. Only the thought of the others in the room beyond stopped them from taking the next step.

She broke away first, slowly, reluctantly. This was real. This wasn't in her mind, and it was even better than she had remembered. She noticed his eyes had darkened, the way they always did when they were about to make love.

"Adam, I want to give you something."

"Yes please, whatever it is."

She took off the bracelet she'd been wearing and offered it to him. He took it, turned it around in his hand. "You really have been wearing it all this time?"

She nodded.

He was puzzled. "But you don't want it now?"

"Yes, I do. But I'm also asking you a question."

It dawned on him then as he looked at the words on the bracelet. *Come live with me and be my love.* She watched as a smile slowly appeared on his face. "Do you mean that? You're sure?"

She nodded. "If you still want it."

"I want it very much."

"But we're still going to be apart for months." A hope rose. "Unless you're here to stay?"

He shook his head. "I wish I was, but no, the most I could manage is a week. But we'll cope, Lainey. We can talk as much as we can while I'm here, stay up all night, look at each other all day long, lock ourselves away. And after I've gone we can still phone and email and write to each other. In fact, I can write some letters for you while I'm here and all you'll have to do is post them. I could pre-write some emails too, I know exactly what I'd like you to say. We could even pre-record some phone conversations."

He meant it, she realized. He was completely sure that everything would be fine. She gazed up at him. "You're quite mad, aren't you?"

•   •   •

The next morning she woke early. She looked at the clock—six a.m. She'd have to get up soon and get the breakfasts started for her guests. Mind you, they hadn't finished up till very late, from what she'd heard. It would probably be some time before she saw them. She and Adam had joined them for a little while, then gone up to her bedroom. She stretched luxuriously, remembering all that had happened after that. There was a lot of communicating that could be done without words, she'd realized.

It was quiet outside, the only noise in the room the soft sound of Adam's breathing. She rolled over and looked at him asleep beside her. She could look at him all morning and stay in bed with him all day. "I missed you so much," he'd whispered during the night, as they lay arms wrapped around each other, bodies tangled. "We're going to have to do this six times a day, you realize, until we catch up on that lost time."

"Let's try for seven. Get our averages up," she'd whispered back. With a fingertip, she traced his face now. She moved the sheet, touching him on his chest, moving lower and lower. He stirred.

"Ad, are you awake?"

"Mmm." He stretched out an arm, wrapping it around her, pulling her naked body close against his. She lay beside him, their bodies stretched against each other. She kissed one closed eye, then another, then his nose, his lips, the kiss quickly deepening into something passionate. His hands moved down her back in slow, stroking circles, moving farther down. Eyes shut, he rolled slowly until he was on top of her. He lifted his lips from hers and began tracing a slow, gorgeous path down her body to her breasts and beyond. . . .

•   •   •

It was nine o'clock the next time she looked at the clock. She stretched again, aware of every inch of her body, feeling completely kissed and loved and sated. A noise downstairs stopped her movement and she lay there, listening for a moment. It sounded like someone was in the kitchen. She lay still a moment longer, hearing laughter, voices in conversation. Her guests were already up. Oh hell, what sort of hostess was she? She rolled back the sheet, about to get up, moving slowly so she didn't wake Adam.

A brown arm shot out of the bed covers and held her around the waist. "Oh, no you don't. I didn't fly halfway across the world for you to abandon me on our first morning back together."

"Ad, I have to," she laughed. "I need to cook their breakfasts."

"No, you don't."

"I do. That's part of the deal."

"No. I explained to Barry last night that breakfast would be a little late this morning on account of some special circumstances. And when I explained what the special circumstances were he said he couldn't possibly trouble you and they would be perfectly happy to make their own breakfast."

She remembered him talking to the musician the previous night, the two of them having quite a conversation. "And what did you say those special circumstances were?"

"I just told him the truth. I said that I loved you and that I hadn't seen you for many months and that I planned to keep you in bed all day long until you said yes."

"Yes? To what?"

"To marrying me."

Her heart flipped. "And if I don't say yes during the day?"

He pulled her body close against his and kissed her gently. "Then we're staying here all night long as well."

Three months later

So what do you think, little Liam? What about you, Sinéad? Do you love your new home?"

Lainey roamed through the house with her niece on one hip, her nephew on the other. Behind her Brendan and Rosie were still unloading the large rental car. There were suitcases and boxes all around them—they seemed to have brought everything they owned in Melbourne with them.

Rosie was all smiles, yet less rabbitlike than Lainey had ever noticed before. "Lainey, you didn't tell us it was this beautiful."

"It wasn't this beautiful when I first got here, to be honest. But it looks good, doesn't it?"

Rosie was entranced by it. Not just the B&B, but the countryside all around. It was a beautiful October day, midautumn, the sky a bright crisp blue, the orange and red of the leaves in the lane nearby almost glowing. Inside, the warm walls and open fires were cozy and welcoming.

To Lainey's dismay, Liam suddenly burst into a high-pitched wailing, Sinéad joining in moments later. She hurriedly handed them both over to Brendan, picking up the suitcases he'd been carrying. "Have you left anything in Melbourne at all?" she asked.

"Not a lot," Brendan said with a grin. "Once we decided we just got cracking."

He had rung her six weeks previously, sounding brighter than he had in a long time. He'd launched straight into the reason for his call. "You know how Dad's insurance money's finally come through. Well, Rosie and I started to wonder if there might not be the same urgency about selling the B&B. So we went around to Ma and Dad a few nights ago and they've said I should discuss it with you and if you think it's workable and you still want to come home, then I'm going to resign. We'll come over as soon as we can and take over the B&B. Just for a while, to see if we're cut out for that kind of life. What do you think?"

They'd talked for nearly an hour, Brendan in Melbourne in his living room, Lainey in the B&B in Ireland, sitting on the stairs, looking out of the hall window. Outside, Rod Stewart had crossed her line of vision, stepping gingerly through the flowers in the garden. She'd guiltily noticed he was carrying a bird in his mouth, and turned away to concentrate again on Brendan's voice. By the end of the call, it was agreed. She would continue with her current series of theme weekends, but not make plans for any more until Brendan, Rosie and the twins arrived. Brendan had hesitated when she'd asked if he wanted her to keep taking bookings for them. "I'm not sure if we'll keep doing the weekends the way you have been,

Lainey. Would you mind about that?" he'd asked. She'd realized she didn't mind. She'd already proved she could make a success of them. And it sounded like Brendan and Rosie had plenty of ideas of their own, in any case.

That night over dinner, after the children had finally settled, Lainey heard some of them.

"We thought we'd call them parents' weekend getaways, directed at local people rather than just tourists," Rosie explained, her cheeks flushed. "You know, they can come and stay for the weekend, with their kids and all. And then at night, we mind the kids for them and they can go out for the night, into Navan or Dublin. Or I could cook for them here. There's plenty of room, isn't there, and it would be much more friendly than a hotel, and the fact we've got kids ourselves will help too. I mean, we know ourselves how hard it is to go out sometimes."

"We might even call them 'Save your marriage' weekends," Brendan added. "What do you think, Lainey? You're the ideas woman of the family."

Lainey lifted her glass of wine in a toast to them both. "I think it's a fantastic idea."

Rosie blushed a bright red.

Lainey spent her final afternoon up on the Hill of Tara on her own, her cheeks red from the cold, her sheepskin coat just managing to keep out the icy wind. The blue skies had disappeared the past few days, the days getting shorter, the first preview of winter. She stood near her favorite spot, looking out over the fields. Mist lay in the distance, while closer by the scenery was soft-edged and shadowy, the colors muted, the sounds low.

She'd come up to say goodbye, but now the moment

had come, she realized there was no need for goodbyes. Not just because she'd be back as soon as she could. She wanted Adam to see it again, at a slower pace this time. In their emails and letters and phone calls over the past few months, they had talked a lot about him returning to Ireland for a proper visit. They had talked about lots of things in the past few months. It had been like a brand-new courtship, a second chance at getting to know one another. It had been even better than the first time.

Lainey gazed around. She had spent so much time up here over the past months that each mound, each tree, the view from Newgrange to the ruins of Skryne church and all the fields in between, were imprinted in her mind. She had a store of memories to draw on until the next time she was here.

The day before, she'd gone for a drive to say two particular farewells. First she called in to an office in Dunshaughlin to say goodbye to Mr. Fogarty. "Thank you for everything, Mr. Fogarty. You've been lovely to me."

"It's been a pleasure, Lainey. A great pleasure." Had she really noticed a tear in his little mousy eye?

Then she called in to say goodbye to Rohan. He was outside painting the porch. "Sabine's coming over this weekend. I thought I'd brighten it up a little for her."

"It looks great," Lainey said.

"Not a patch on what you did at the B&B, of course. May would have been very proud of all you've done there, I think."

Lainey was moved by the idea. "Really?"

Rohan grinned. "Well, she would have told you all the things you'd done wrong. And she would have told lots of other people all the things she thought you'd done wrong as well. But I think deep down she would have been happy."

"Thanks. I think."

"And will you tell Brendan to give me a call if he needs any help or wants to have a pint? I'm here for a few more months yet. And I know my mother is still keen to give a hand with any cooking, if Brendan and his wife decide to do any more of those theme weekends. I'd be happy to do more of those tours of Tara, as well."

"I'll pass all that on, Rohan. And thanks for all the help you've given me, too. And please tell your mother thanks and goodbye again." Mrs. Hartigan was in London staying with her daughter and Nell for several weeks.

"It's no problem at all. It's been good to see you again. Good luck back home if I don't see you before you go." He kissed her on the cheek and she felt absolutely nothing.

"And good luck back in Germany."

He smiled. "I can't wait to get back home, between you and me."

"I know the feeling," she said.

•   •   •

She stayed with Eva and Joseph the night before she flew to Melbourne. They had news for her as well. Joseph's mother and father, now living in the Clare Valley in South Australia, had invited them out to spend Christmas with them.

"That is brilliant," Lainey said. "You can come and spend two weeks with me afterward. Or beforehand.

Or . . ." She tailed off, smiling sheepishly. "Or you can organize yourselves and I'll be happy to see you whenever it suits you."

"Thank you, Lainey. We'll let you know what we decide to do." Eva's voice was solemn but there was a sparkle in her eye.

There was just time to make a quick call from Dublin airport before she boarded the plane to Melbourne. "I'm on my way," she said.

"Hurry," Adam replied.

Six months after that . . .

"You see, Adam, it's really very simple." Lainey turned from the kitchen bench and tipped the garlic and onions she had just finished chopping into a frying pan. She breathed deeply as they started sizzling on the stove. "It's just a matter of choosing the best ingredients and being well prepared. So watch carefully, won't you, because quite frankly it's not often you get to see such a marvelous cook as me in full flight like this."

Adam leaned against the kitchen wall, watching her, amused. "It's a privilege, believe me." He watched as she added freshly chopped tomatoes, capers and anchovies. "It's a puttanesca sauce, did you say?"

"That's right. Known for its heat. Puttanesca is Italian for whore. Did you know that? So in fact it's whore's pasta."

"Good heavens. And so will you be adding chili as well, to give it that heat?"

"Oh, I might and I might not," she said airily. "Should I?" she said in a stage whisper.

He nodded.

"And now, of course, it's time for my secret ingredient, some chilies."

"Some? How many exactly?"

"Oh, just a handful," she said vaguely.

"A handful? Of whole chilies? Are you sure?"

He was laughing at her, she realized. She handed the knife over to him. "Right, Mr. Expert, I hereby hand over all cooking duties to you. I'd hate you to feel I was moving in on your turf, after all."

As she moved past, he leaned down and kissed her on the lips. "Go and relax, you mad woman."

She wandered into the living room looking out through the French windows on to the river. It was a wet Melbourne night, the rain battering down on their small balcony. She could see the lights in the houses across the river. The view was just as good from this second-floor apartment, they'd discovered. When she'd first come back from Ireland she had stayed with Adam in his ground-floor apartment. There'd been several lively discussions about whose apartment they would live in once the tenants had moved out of hers. Then the solution had presented itself. The tenants on the floor between their two apartments had announced they were moving out and Lainey and Adam decided to take over their lease instead. Sometimes she forgot they had moved floors at all—the layout in this apartment was exactly the same as their old ones and their combined furniture had made it instantly homely.

The phone rang. On the couch, her cat Rex lifted his head at the sound, then shut his eyes again, going back to sleep.

"Lainey, love, how are you? Are you in the middle of anything?" It was her mother.

"No, we're just about to have dinner. Are you all right, Ma? Your voice sounds a bit funny. Is Dad okay?"

"Oh, we're grand. I just wanted to run something past you. You know how Hugh's graduation ceremony is coming up?"

Lainey realized then it was laughter that was making her mother's voice sound strange. "Yes, Ma . . ."

"We've had a great idea. Wouldn't it be funny if we rented some different-colored wigs, and all turned up to his graduation ceremony wearing them? Your father thinks it would be hilarious. Declan said he'll only do it if you will. I thought I could call Brendan and Rosie in Ireland, see if they could do the same over there, send Hugh a video message. Can't you just see the twins in funny wigs? What do you think, Lainey? Will we do it?"

How sad. Her mother had finally gone over the edge. "I might just sleep on that one, Ma, if you don't mind. Good night. Love to Dad."

She wandered back to the kitchen, where Adam was now stirring the sauce. The rich tomato smell filled the kitchen. Beside him, the pot of water was bubbling, the fresh pasta on the counter beside him ready to be cooked. The radio was playing a pop song, Adam singing along with it. He glanced over at her, winked and kept working.

Why on earth had she resisted this? she thought for the hundredth time since she'd come back from Ireland. Living with Adam hadn't been hard, it hadn't been scary, it had been like falling into a big warm bath. They'd talked more about getting married, even talked about children, agreed they would like to try it all. Not just yet, but sometime very soon.

She was trying hard not to be bossy, not to feel she had to be in charge all the time. She'd slowly discovered it was a matter of making choices. She could choose to be in control, worrying about every detail, wanting to run everything, or she could choose to relax, to take a backseat occasionally. The ideas were still tearing around her mind all the time. It was just that she didn't have to act on every one of them.

The new approach was working at Complete Event Management, too. She had made a promise to Adam, and to herself, not to bring work home and not to go into the office on weekends. In return, he had taken on another chef and had two nights off a week. There was another option on the horizon, too. A way to spend more time together. Adam had asked if she wanted to come and work as his manager. Dave had announced he wanted to head off overseas in a few months. She was tempted, and not only because it would mean she might never have to clap eyes on Celia King again. Celia was now second-in-charge at Complete Event Management and taking great pleasure in letting Lainey know it most days. Twenty-four-seven, in fact. So far, in her new tranquil approach to life, it hadn't bothered Lainey as much as it might have once. But she couldn't stay tranquil forever. And perhaps it would be better to leave than be caught locking Celia in the stationery cupboard one night. Much more civilized.

Eva had been amazed when they had all met up over Christmas. "Lainey, I can't believe you're being so relaxed about this, Adam, work and everything. I don't think I've ever heard you say you were just going to see how things went."

"I'm a new woman, Evie. Well, not new, but a trying-hard woman."

She watched Adam again. He was chopping fresh herbs now, the movement swift, skilled. He really did have beautiful hands. Lovely, long fingers. As he turned, she looked at his long legs, the way his jeans fitted him so well. He reached up for wineglasses and his T-shirt lifted, showing an inch or two of brown skin. Her breath caught. A warm glow had started somewhere in her body and it had nothing to do with the thought of a puttanesca sauce.

"Adam . . ."

"Mmm."

"You know how we agreed to discuss things whenever either of us gets a good idea?"

"Mmm."

"I've had an idea."

"Have you? What is it?"

"You know how it's your night off?"

"Mmm."

"And we've got that lovely new bedroom with that nice view of the river?"

"Mmm."

"I just wondered if you'd be interested in going in there with me instead of eating dinner."

He stopped and turned to her. "Oh, I might. What did you have in mind once we got in there?"

She walked over to him, took the wineglasses from his hand and slowly took off his T-shirt. Then she drew him to her and gave him a long, very slow, sexy kiss. "That kind of thing. Only if you're interested, of course. You know I don't want to force you into doing anything you don't want to do."

He looked down at her, his expression thoughtful. She could see that his eyes had darkened, were almost black. "It's a very interesting idea, Lainey, thank you for that. It definitely has some merit."

"So you could be interested?"

"Let me think for a moment." He reached behind him and turned off the pasta sauce.

"So is that a yes?" she asked in a very polite voice.

"It's a yes."

She smiled up at him. She'd hoped it would be.

A C K N O W L E D G M E N T S

Thanks to all at Penguin Books Australia, especially Clare Forster, Ali Watts, Anne Rogan, Sally Bateman, Cathy Larsen, and Andrew Mazzer, and to Laura Ford, Lisa Barnes, and the great Ballantine team at Random House in the United States.

For research help, my thanks to Maeve O'Meara, Sabine Brasseler, Michael Boyny, Neil Oram, Chris Craven, Deanna Williams, Aoife Sheehy, Kristin Gill, Karen O'Connor, Dymphna and all the Dolans of Donaghpatrick, Michael Maguire and Annette Peard of Maguire's at the Hill of Tara, and a very helpful publication—*The Tara Walk* by Michael Slavin.

Big thanks to my friend and mentor Max Fatchen in Adelaide and to my agents: Fiona Inglis and all at Curtis Brown in Australia, Jonathan Lloyd at Curtis Brown UK and Christy Fletcher and Gráinne Fox of Fletcher and Co. in the United States. My special thanks and love to my mum, Mary, my sisters Lea, Marie, and Maura, and most of all, to my husband, John.

GREETINGS FROM SOMEWHERE ELSE

Monica McInerney

A READER'S GUIDE

Random House Reader's Circle: You feature families who have migrated from Ireland to Australia (or vice versa) in several of your novels. Can you talk a bit about the large migration of Irish to Australia?

Monica McInerney: Australia and Ireland have a long and rich shared history, with something like one in five Australians claiming Irish heritage. Thousands of the first white settlers in the nineteenth century were Irish convicts; Irish people emigrated to escape the famine and poverty in the 1840s, and to seek their fortune in the gold rush of the 1850s. More recently, it's been a combination of economic reasons and the call of the wild—there's something exotic and romantic about Australia for Irish people, as there is something romantic and mystical about Ireland for most Australians. My own great-grandparents on my mother's and my father's side emigrated to South Australia in the 1840s, both from

County Clare. Looking back through our family tree it's obvious from the surnames how the Irish community stuck together—my ancestors all have names such as Hogan, Canny, Fitzgerald and O'Brien. I laughed to myself when I first moved to Ireland with my Irish husband nearly twenty years ago, all the trouble my ancestors took to go to Australia, two months on a ship, and there I was turning it around with a flight lasting less than a day.

RHRC: Nuggets of Irish history are sprinkled throughout *Greetings from Somewhere Else,* as Lainey does research for her plans for the B&B. Did you do much research for this novel, or did you grow up knowing a lot about Ireland's past?

MM: I grew up with a basic knowledge of Irish history, key dates and names, for example, but it's living in Ireland that has expanded my knowledge. History is such a part of everyday life here, the political situation constantly evolving in regard to Northern Ireland, the streets full of statues of greats from Irish history and literature such as Daniel O'Connell, James Joyce, Oscar Wilde.

When I first moved here with my Irish husband in 1991, we lived in County Meath, very close to the Hill of Tara and it became—and still is—one of my favorite places in Ireland. We spent many hours there, roaming across the fields, imagining how it might have looked, talking to local people about it, reading books of legends. Lainey's reaction to Tara in *Greetings from Somewhere Else* is very close to mine. At first glance, Tara seems quite ordinary, but then your imagination takes over and you can feel and almost hear its history.

RHRC: There are so many delicious meals described in *Greetings from Somewhere Else*, and food is often a vivid presence in your books. What importance does it have in your non-writing life?

MM: Food and books are two of the great loves of my life, so it is such a treat to bring them together in my writing. I love to cook, to eat out, to eat in, to shop, to visit markets, to read recipe books. I'm the world's messiest cook, which I suspect stems from the fact that when I was growing up in a big rowdy family of nine there was a rule that whoever cooked didn't have to do the dishes. So I volunteered, got hooked, began to cook elaborate meals for my family, three-course meals sometimes, all in the safe knowledge that I didn't have to clear up afterward. My poor in-laws found it out to their cost too—I offered to cook a big Asian banquet the first year I moved to Ireland. I used every single dish, pot and pan in the kitchen. It took my brother-in-law and sister-in-law three hours—seriously—to clean up from a meal that took us all less than twenty minutes to eat.

RHRC: Which contemporary writers do you enjoy reading? What's the last great book you read, and why did you love it?

MM: I've a long list of favorite contemporary writers, including Garrison Keillor, Laurie Graham, Tim Winton, Helen Garner, Neil Gaiman, Adriana Trigiani, John le Carré, Kristan Higgins, Meg Rosoff, Stephenie Meyer . . .
My current favorite book is *The Guernsey Literary and Potato Peel Pie Society* by Mary Ann Shaffer and Annie

Barrows. I've recommended it to many friends and sent it as presents to my mother and sisters too. It's the story of the islanders of Guernsey and their relationship with a sparky, funny, and wonderful writer who corresponds with them in the years following World War II. On the surface it is a funny, cozy, heartwarming tale of a complicated group of people, but there is so much else to it: hard and stark tales of life during wartime and beautiful depictions of resilience in the face of difficult choices.

RHRC: Your novels provide such a wonderful escape for many readers—is this one of the reasons why you like writing fiction? Have you ever written nonfiction or wanted to?

MM: Everything I love about writing comes from what I love about reading. When I pick up a book, I love that feeling of losing myself in other worlds, and when I am writing my novels, I love that same feeling. It's wonderful for me to hear that readers of my books get swept up in the same way I do when I'm writing the story. I love the feeling that anything is possible when I am writing fiction. I can send my characters to the moon if I want to (though some of them might be alarmed to find themselves there). Through my characters, I've managed to live so many different lives, experience different emotions, explore my own feelings toward many different situations. It's akin to being on a psychologist's couch sometimes—I write how I think a character will react and then I need to take a step back, and realize, no, that's how *I* would react, not this fictional person. Fiction writing means a constant exploration of personality and cause and effect and I find that fascinating.

Lately I've written quite a lot of nonfiction, articles about my real-life experiences with aunts and how that led to *The Faraday Girls*, stories about my childhood as part of a big family of railway children. I'm finding that a great experience too, a different way of delving into my own memories and emotions.

RHRC: How much interaction do you have with book clubs, and how have your experiences with them been? Are you part of one yourself?

MM: I love talking to book clubs and have done several great chats with clubs in the United States through the Random House Author Chat program, me here in Dublin, sometimes in the middle of the night, the book club gathered around a table in places like California or Long Island. It's fascinating and also nerve-racking to listen to your own book being discussed, because of course not every word is going to be positive. So far I've been very fortunate. Perhaps they were more frank after I'd hung up.

I'm in a book club here in Dublin, with male and female members, and it has added so much to my reading and writing life. I've been introduced to books I would not otherwise have read, revisited classics like *Wuthering Heights* and Rudyard Kipling's *Captains Courageous* and also participated in many lively discussions. We're all quite serious about it. Yes, we meet over wine and food, but the chat is always quickly directed to the book in question. It's also been helpful for me as a writer to hear a book being discussed in such detail, to realize that there isn't a book in the world that is universally loved and also to hear all the different reasons people read, what they look for in plot, character, setting, how your mood at the time you are reading can affect your experience of a book.

RHRC: You were a book publicist in your past life. How has that experience influenced your career as a writer?

MM: It was an invaluable experience to me, in some ways like doing a writing course by osmosis. I met and talked to many different writers, from different countries and all genres, and heard them speak about their methods. When I started writing fiction myself, I was able to draw on those memories, to remind myself that the ups and downs I was going through were normal. I also know from experience that publicity tours and reviews and speaking engagements are all a great help to spread the word about the book. I'm lucky in that I love that side of being a writer. I'm social by nature, so after a year locked away in my office with my fictional characters, I'm always very eager to get out and about and meet real people.

RHRC: You've been on book tours all over the world. How do you think readers in different countries vary? Do you find audiences generally want the same thing in a novel, or is there a range across cultures?

MM: What surprises me is how little they vary. I love to see how curious readers in each country are about people in other countries. My books are usually set in several different countries, and I've been lucky enough to meet readers in most of those countries. The great thing is when an Irish reader tells me they love reading about Australia and feel they've been there through the pages of my book, or an Australian says that about Ireland, or an American reader about both Ireland and Australia. I think most readers are seeking the same experience in books—a chance to step into another life, to experience a wide range of emotions, to be challenged and entertained, and that is international.

RHRC: You've now written two novels featuring the delightful heroines Eva and Lainey. Do you think they'll ever appear in any of your future novels? And what are you working on now?

MM: They may well. I'd like to come back and see how they are all getting on in ten years' time.

In terms of my new book, I'm in the early chapters, planning research trips, reading many books on subjects that I'll be covering and also doing lots of walking and daydreaming. It's one of my favorite parts of the writing process, when everything is possible. My head is full of characters and ideas and it's a matter of choosing which ones I want to live with for the next year or so.

1. Lainey assumes the position as caretaker in her family—with three distracted brothers, a hapless father, and a mother at her wit's end, she thinks of herself as the one who holds them all together. Have you found that in large families there is always someone in this role? Do you think she should feel as accountable as she does for her family's ability to function?

2. How do you feel about Lainey's decision regarding Adam when she moves to Ireland? Do you think she made the right choice? In your opinion, do long-distance relationships ever work?

3. Why do you suppose Lainey has such a type A personality and needs to control everything? How does she change in terms of her rigidity over the course of the novel, and what accounts for her transformation?

4. Lainey and Eva are best friends, yet have such different personalities. What are the defining dynamics of their relationship, and how does their friendship work so well? In your own experience, are you more drawn to people who are similar to or different from you?

5. What is your perception of Aunt May and the decision she makes in her will? Is she selfish or eccentric, or does she have the best intentions at heart?

6. Lainey trades her office job for a vastly different one when she runs the B&B . . . and comes to enjoy the experience. When have you been pleasantly surprised after entering an experience you dreaded?

7. Lainey has the unsettling experience of questioning her mother's loyalty to her father, making a discovery that changes her childhood perceptions about her parents. Can you remember the first time you realized your parents were complicated adults with lives of their own?

8. Discuss the theme of risk in this novel. Does it generally pay off for McInerney's characters? How do you think Lainey's life would have turned out if one of her brothers had gone to Ireland instead?

9. Eva is very candid about Lainey's faults, providing a wake-up call for her friend. Have you ever had anyone do the same for you? How did your reaction compare to Lainey's?

10. There is a rich sense of setting and Irish history in this novel, and as a result the reader is immersed in a different culture. What other books have you read that have had a similar "armchair travel" effect?

11. On page 188, Lainey states, "Evie, things happen as a result of your actions, by putting your mind to it, not through fate or some preordained life plan." Do you agree with her or Evie, who earnestly asks, "But don't you ever think things happen for a reason?"

12. There are many thematic messages—about family, friends, romance, and living life in general—to come away with after reading *Greetings from Somewhere Else*. Which resonates with you most?

MONICA MCINERNEY grew up in a family of seven children in the Clare Valley of South Australia, where her father was the railway stationmaster. She is the author of the internationally bestselling novels, *The Faraday Girls, Family Baggage, The Alphabet Sisters,* and *Upside Down Inside Out.* She now lives in Dublin with her husband. Visit her website at www.monicamcinerney.com.